Praise for *The Dog Master*

"Cameron's latest canine-themed novel will appeal to fans of Jean Auel's classic *The Clan of the Cave Bear* as well as those of more contemporary dog and man tales." —*Library Journal*

"A five-star page-turner . . . Storytelling at its best."
—*HuffPost*

"This story is filled with all the emotions you might expect from a book about primitive man. The characters and the scenes are raw and emotion filled. . . . The way of life of primitive man (as [Cameron] envisions it) is fascinating." —*Examiner.com*

"There's much imagination here. . . . Interesting speculative history with a satisfying conclusion, one opening the door for a sequel or series." —*Kirkus Reviews*

Praise for *A Dog's Purpose*

"I loved this book." —Temple Grandin,
New York Times bestselling author

"*Marley & Me* combined with *Tuesdays with Morrie*."
—*Kirkus Reviews*

"An amazing book. I laughed and smiled and cried. Wise . . . and sure to open the hearts of all who read it."
—Alice Walker,
Pulitzer Prize–winning author of *The Color Purple*

"This book gives you a glimpse into the heart and mind of a dog—and will change your view of our furry friends forever." —*Guideposts*

BY W. BRUCE CAMERON

A Dog's Purpose
A Dog's Journey
The Dogs of Christmas
Emory's Gift
The Dog Master
A Dog's Way Home

REPO MADNESS SERIES

The Midnight Plan of the Repo Man
Repo Madness

8 Simple Rules for Dating My Teenage Daughter
How to Remodel a Man
8 Simple Rules for Marrying My Daughter

FOR YOUNGER READERS

Ellie's Story: A Dog's Purpose Puppy Tale
Bailey's Story: A Dog's Purpose Puppy Tale
Molly's Story: A Dog's Purpose Puppy Tale
Max's Story: A Dog's Purpose Puppy Tale
Shelby's Story: A Dog's Purpose Puppy Tale
(forthcoming)

THE
DOG
MASTER

<<<< >>>> <<<< >>>> <<<< >>>> <<<< >>>>

W. BRUCE
CAMERON

A TOM DOHERTY ASSOCIATES BOOK
NEW YORK

THE DOG MASTER

Map by Jennifer Hanover

A Forge Book
Published by Tom Doherty Associates
175 Fifth Avenue
New York, NY 10010

www.tor-forge.com

Forge® is a registered trademark of Macmillan Publishing Group, LLC.

ISBN 978-0-7653-7468-4

Our books may be purchased in bulk for promotional, educational, or business use. Please contact your local bookseller or the Macmillan Corporate and Premium Sales Department at 1-800-221-7945, extension 5442, or by email at MacmillanSpecialMarkets@macmillan.com.

First Edition: August 2015
First Mass Market Edition: September 2018

Printed in the United States of America

0 9 8 7 6 5 4 3 2 1

For my mother, Monsie Cameron,
who has been on my side every step of the way

TERRITORY OF THE NORTHERN CREEDS

THE
DOG
MASTER

PRESENT DAY

A t exactly 9:00 A.M. the uniformed guards at the back of the room pulled every door shut in muscular coordination, a metallic clang echoing throughout the college lecture hall. The security men were grinning: maintaining the peace on a liberal arts campus mostly consisted of tolerating unruly students while keeping them approximately in line, so this exercise, an annual ritual, gave them a fleeting sense of order triumphing over chaos.

The loud crash of the doors had startled the conversations into silence, and now the students arrayed in the stadium-style seats sat with their necks twisted toward the back of the room to see what was going on. Immediately a loud and urgent pounding of fists on metal proclaimed the desperate despair of those who hadn't made it inside in time for class. Then, after just a moment, the pummeling abruptly halted, as the guards on the other side of the double doors told the late arrivals they were tardy and therefore had to exit the building.

It was the first class of the first day of the first semester for these freshmen. Prompt attendance was strictly required.

Welcome to college.

Dr. James K. Morby—"Morby the Mortician," as he wasn't supposed to know he was called—broke from the shadows at the back of the stage and strode briskly to the podium. He wore a crisp blue suit, a white shirt, and a tight necktie, an outfit he'd don for just this first week before slipping into his more habitual plaid shirt and baseball cap. There was a purpose to his clothing, for the careful way his sparse brown hair was combed back, for the clean shave he'd applied to his baby-faced cheeks, for the stern glare in his normally folksy hazel eyes. It was all costumed and choreographed to turn these kids from high school students into college students. Morby had just three classes over the next week to get it done.

"The reason," he intoned into his microphone, "that you have been assigned seats is so that I may call on you by name."

Morby waited, watching the students glance at each other before they uneasily rearranged themselves—who knew the seating chart was serious? Morby spotted a bank of empty chairs and then glanced at the screen in front of him. "Thus when I call on Mr. Brosh—are you here, Mr. Brosh? Kevin Brosh? No, you are not here. But had you been here, I would have been looking directly at you."

Morby paused and savored his mental image of Brosh's friends telling him that Morby had been *looking for him in class*. Mr. Brosh would not be absent again.

Morby let them mull that one over. He knew that the freshmen who had by plan or chance arrived early enough to clear security and make it to the lecture were feeling a bit smug about themselves at the moment, and he knew their smugness wouldn't last much longer.

Freshman orientation had taken most of the weekend. Then Sunday afternoon, yesterday, parents had tearfully departed and the students had seized their new independence and ridden it hard into the night. Most of the eyes regarding him now were blurry and unfocused, shimmering with fatigue and hangovers. They'd caroused, they'd pursued fornication, they'd approached ceramic bowls on humble hands and knees—they thought they had college figured out.

It was up to Morby to slap that notion out of their heads. This was the only 101-level class required for all incoming freshmen, and the only one that accelerated to full speed from the first moment—the other professors mostly ran through their syllabi and passed out materials the initial few days, waiting for Morby the Mortician to work his magic.

"Your reading assignment is the first five chapters of your textbook on the Upper Paleolithic." It was 120 pages, probably more than any of them had been required to read in any two-day period in high school. "We'll have a test on the material and today's lecture on Wednesday. Friday your papers are due at the start of class."

They were bright kids or they wouldn't be here, but Morby's class, Early Humans, was the scholastic equivalent of being tossed into the deep end of the pool. Wednesday morning they would be dismayed at the depth and complexity of the exam; Wednesday afternoon they'd be panicked over their grades. A scientist at heart, Morby had been tracking Wednesday test performance in a database for a decade, and was proud of the defibrillating effect of his scoring: 75 percent would fail, 20 percent would barely get a D, and a handful of students would freakishly pass.

There had never been an A given on the first test in the history of the class. Morby doubted he, himself, would ace the thing—those questions were *hard*.

In a cold sweat—how were they going to tell their parents they were *flunking out of college*?—most of them would dig into their essay assignments with the fervor of the newly converted. Wednesday and Thursday nights the security guards would have far fewer intoxicated students on their hands.

"So: about your essay assignment. For many years, it has been thought that early man lived in peaceful, communal harmony within his family, tribe, and at large with other *Homo sapiens*. Of late, however, a new school of thought has argued that there's no reason to think that prehistoric man was any less brutal or warlike than we are today." Morby surveyed his audience, most of whom had sunk into a swamp of complete lethargy. "Your papers will be twenty-five hundred words. Please address this issue, arguing for one point of view or the other. Warlike, or peaceable? I don't care which side you take, just make sure your logic is sound, your resources reliable, and that your words are your own."

Despite this last admonition and the prominent warnings about plagiarism on the first page of the student manual, Morby knew that by Monday morning, when the essays, bloody with red ink, were handed back to their authors, nearly two in ten freshmen would find themselves facing academic probation. Raised in the cut-and-paste generation, they literally didn't understand what constituted intellectual property theft.

Being called out publically as a plagiarist was humiliating, but it gave enough shock and awe to the rest of the freshmen that the problem was far less prevalent on this campus than at other, gentler schools.

The probations would be erased from their records by the end of the semester, and the grades—few of them would get better than a D on the essay—would also be mitigated by more papers and more tests that were designed to the academic purpose of learning and not the enculturating purpose of boot camp.

"All right. The last great glaciation, commencing approximately thirty thousand years ago." The slide on the screen behind Morby flashed a map of the eastern hemisphere. "This was, beyond a doubt, the most dramatic time in the history of our species. You think we have climate change issues today? We're talking about temperature fluctuations in the *extreme,* up to seven degrees Celsius year to year. You could bounce from a fairly normal period to years in which the ice never melted, not even in summer. Trees were bull-dozed by the advancing glaciers, uprooting us from our arboreal environment and driving us out onto the steppes, where we served as hunters and hunted, predator and prey."

A new slide went up behind him: a drawing of an enormous cave lion, almost the size of a bear, rendered by the artist to appear ready to pounce. The animal had a face something like an African lion, but was covered with a shaggy, light grey coat.

"Look at the size of this thing! When we examine bones from that era, we see that many of the most dreadful creatures were *monsters* compared to today. So when we went hunting, we not only had to compete with lions, bears, wolves, and other tooth-and-claw animals, we had to run from them. No wonder life expectancy was so short—most early humans didn't manage to make it to your age, and the average life expectancy was around thirty-three—though someone clever enough to make it to fifteen probably survived to be fifty or so."

Grudgingly, they were giving Morby their full attention.

"We also had to compete with this fellow." A slide went up of a Neanderthal standing next to a modern human. "Look at him. Not taller, but certainly bigger, hugely strong, and with a *larger brain.* Yet here we are today, running the planet, when by all indications this guy's descendants should be in the literal driver's seat. Why us, then? To paraphrase Faulkner, how did we not only endure, but prevail?"

Morby put up his favorite slide of the lecture and glanced with a knowing smile over to where his TA, Tommy, normally sat. His smile wavered—Tommy's seat was empty.

Very odd, to miss this delicious day. The professor shrugged it off and turned back to the slide. It was a wonderful photograph of some recently discovered cave art dating back to the Aurignacian era. There was a jumble of shapes; more than one artist had plied his skills over the years, painting reindeer and elk and lions over one another in a crazy two-dimensional prehistoric stampede, but for Professor Morby there was really only one image: the young man in the middle, holding the end of what was unmistakably a leash, leading to what was unmistakably a red collar, around the neck of what was unmistakably an enormous canine. A domesticated wolf.

"As you will discover," Morby continued almost reverently, "I have my own theories."

He and Tommy would have exchanged another glance at this juncture—the point at which some of the students, looking at their textbooks, would suddenly make the connection and look up in surprise: *Hey, Morby* wrote *this thing.*

There would be no faking their way through their reading assignments in this class, not with the author evaluating their comprehension. So they'd focus, many of them detesting the subject so much that when, about halfway through the textbook, they did stumble across Morby's theory, the one on which his entire career had been built, they'd largely miss the significance.

"We have no written record of this, the most dangerous time for mankind, we have only our conjectures, based on the fossil record. Have we unearthed every skeleton of every species that walked the land and swam the waters? Probably not. Can we describe the topography of the landscape before the ice sculpted it into its current shape? No, no more than we can say precisely what hills and valleys existed under what the glaciers eventually turned into Lake Michigan. But we can say this: They were *us,* these humans. They had our brains. They weren't as tall and they didn't live as long, but there's no reason to suppose they didn't have language. They just didn't have symbols—or at least, symbols that have survived the eons. So remember that, when you read of the harsh challenges facing prehistoric man. They were *us*."

And then something unprecedented: A single set of doors in the back banged open and, like a deputy set on serving a warrant, Tommy the TA marched in. Ignoring the freshmen necks craned to see him and the freshmen mouths gaping open at the bold interruption, Tommy came straight down the aisle, his eyes shining.

Morby pulled in a breath and held it, his heart suddenly pounding. Tommy read the question on his face and nodded with delight, bounding up the short set of stairs to join the professor on the stage. He reached out and placed his hand on the microphone to shield their conversation, while a low murmur began to build in the crowd.

"I just hung up with Beauchamp," Tommy said, something like triumph threading tension into his voice.

"They found her," Morby whispered, a shiver traveling up his spine.

Tommy nodded exultantly. "They found her," he affirmed.

The two men, teacher and pupil, mentor and student, stared at each other in amazement over what they'd just dared to say. Then, slowly returning to his role as professor, Morby turned to face his class. Tommy's hand dropped away from the microphone.

"Gentlemen and ladies, this is Mr. Rooker, my assistant. He will complete today's lecture and will be leading the class for the next week or two. I have something I need to tend to. I need to catch a plane."

* * *

Seventy-two hours later, Morby was crouched over a dig site, the earth peeled back to reveal the treasures underneath. Standing above him were a French graduate student named Jean Claude and Morby's longtime friend and collaborator, Bernard Beauchamp. Before him, the dirt brushed away with strokes as careful as an artist applying paint to canvas, lay the skeleton of a *Homo sapiens*—a male. The body was nearly intact, a beautiful find—someone long ago had taken care to inter this corpse with respect and even love.

But it was what lay next to the human that was so remarkable: an enormous canine, larger than any modern wolf Morby had ever seen. Carbon dating would confirm what the professor already knew to be true: The man and the wolf had been buried together.

Beauchamp was grinning because Morby was weeping. He put a hand out and gripped Morby's arm.

"Tu avais raison, mon ami." You were right, my friend.

Jean Claude, looking barely older than the freshmen from the lecture hall, had driven Morby the four hours it had taken to get to the dig site and knew only that the American was good friends with his boss. He was a little bewildered, now, watching the two men wrestling with such profound emotion.

"Regardez le cou. Tu vois?" Morby whispered. *Look at the neck. See?*

"Red," Beauchamp nodded, answering in heavily accented English.

All soft organic matter had been leached away by the greedy demands of the soils and their denizens, though in return the bones had been gifted minerals that had helped preserve them. Whatever might have been looped across the wolf's neck had been lost forever, but the ferrous oxide that had decorated that loop still remained, a thread of dusky red. Just as it appeared in the cave painting.

"What is it? A wolf? Or a dog?" Jean Claude asked, mimicking the quiet tones of the other men.

"A wolf, but also a dog," Beauchamp murmured.

"No," Morby corrected after a moment. "Not a dog. *The* dog." He turned to Jean Claude. "You've found the very first dog."

Jean Claude contemplated this. Morby wondered if the young man saw what Morby saw, what Beauchamp saw: fossil evidence of a turning point in human history. No: To mimic the sentence structure he'd just used, not a turning point, *the* turning point. When we went from enduring to prevailing.

"But then, who is the man? There must be a reason why he is buried with the dog."

Morby stood, his knees snapping back into position. He slapped his palms on his sides, raising dust in the afternoon sun.

"Well yes, you raise a very interesting point," Morby agreed. "I have spent so much of my career pondering how it is possible that wolves evolved into our friends and companions—evolution being the glacial process that it is. But suppose we look at it a different way: How did we humans go from being preyed upon by wolves to *living with them*? From wolf food to dog masters, if you will? Now you're talking adaptation, instead of evolution. Now you're not talking centuries, you're talking a single generation, the life of one person. Twenty years, let's call it. So, Jean Claude, you ask an important question, a very important question, indeed.

"Who is the man?"

BOOK

ONE

ONE

Year Nineteen

The big mother-wolf and her mate had made a den in a small cave along the stream. She was heavy with her pups, and she and the father had left the pack to give birth. She had done this before—left to bear her young, tended to by her mate, only to return to the howling site when her pups were able to travel and eat solid meals. Memory and instinct were both guiding her now.

The male-wolf was out searching for food. It was still cool, this spring, and the air carried elements of ice and water, buds and new leaves, stale grass and lush shoots. She took a deep whiff of it, noting that though he had been gone some time, she could still smell her mate on the breeze. He was not far away.

A shift inside of her told her the time had arrived. The birthing would start momentarily. Suddenly extremely thirsty, she left the den and eased down to the stream and lapped at the clear water. This would be her last drink on her own for several days. Her mate would regurgitate all of her sustenance while she lay nursing. But right now she drank and drank, some primitive part of her calculating the need to take on liquid.

Her senses alerted her to a shift in the breeze. She heard it in the trees and smelled it before it stirred her fur, but by that time her head had already whipped around, her pupils dilating and her nostrils flaring.

Lion.

The wind was now flowing straight from the direction of the den and it carried with it the scent of a killer. The mother-wolf could tell that the lion was approaching, whether by chance, or because it was tracking the tantalizing odor of the fluids that had started to leak from her.

She hesitated. Her instinct was to flee, but it battled with the urge to return to the den to give birth. She padded a few feet toward the den, then halted. No. The lion was coming from that direction, coming *fast.*

She turned and ran for the stream, which even deep with meltwater could be forded without swimming. She lunged across, her pregnant belly slowing her down, scrabbling up the opposite bank and hearing the lion hit the water behind her. She turned and the lion was upon her.

The attack was swift and brutal. The mother-wolf ignored the pain as lion claws raked her flanks and she twisted, snapping her teeth, trying to get the lion's throat.

Then a massive impact tumbled them both. Male-wolf had arrived and had thrown himself into the fray, slamming into the lion and seizing the feline behind its head. Yowling and growling and screaming, the two did battle.

The mother-wolf turned away and fled toward the den. She could not rejoin the fight; her only concern could be for the pups.

Her rear legs gave out when she was still two dozen yards from the mouth of the den. She crawled ahead, panting, while behind her she could hear the yelps and screams of her mate's final moments. The lion was nearly twice the size of the male-wolf—the outcome of this bloody engagement had been foretold the moment the feline found them.

She was still struggling toward the mouth of the den when

the sudden silence behind her pronounced the end of the fight. She kept her eyes on the opening where a gap between rock and ground made for the entrance, dragging her useless legs, focused on getting to safety and not looking back even when her senses told her the lion was coming after her.

The man had never been alone. Not like this, not with no prospect of seeing another human as he made his way along the rocky bluffs bordering the slender stream. No prospect of *ever* seeing another human, not ever again, though that seemed impossible, even ludicrous. Of course he would return to his tribe, would be *allowed* to return. He could not imagine anything else.

But on this day, with winter still lurking in pools of crystalline snow in deep shadows and buds barely making their long overdue appearance on the trees, he was turning his back on his people, both literally and figuratively.

Just as they had turned their backs on him.

He had tracked along the stream for most of the day, trekking into unfamiliar territory. This was land that belonged to no clan—he was safe here.

He carried a pouch sewn from reindeer hide looped over his shoulder, and carefully extracted some dried meat to chew on while he walked. His mind was on rationing, stretching his supplies as long as he could, but his stomach was focused on hunger and the easy availability of food. As a sort of compromise, he did not use the smoldering horn dangling from his neck to make fire to heat his snack, as if depriving himself of that luxury was a relevant sacrifice. The horn was packed with coals and moss and, with a few sticks and leaves added every so often, would still be potent enough to allow him to make camp before dark.

He carried both club and spear and was watching the

ground for animal tracks when he heard a strange, almost ghastly, grunting and hissing. Several creatures of some kind were just ahead. He stopped, tense—hyenas? His heart was pounding—though he had never seen one, he knew he could neither successfully flee nor fight a pack of hyenas.

A shadow crossed the path and he jerked his head upward as a huge bird ghosted out of the sky and landed to a chorus of loud hisses and furious wings beating the air. Less afraid—no one had ever, to his knowledge, been killed by birds—he eased forward.

There was blood on the trail, here. Something had happened on this path, something savage and brutal, with lion tracks and wolf tracks jumbled together.

He tightened his grip on his club and, drawn by the noise, went down to the stream and stopped. A flock of immense, hideously ugly birds, with deadly beaks and featherless faces, were pecking at what he determined was a dead wolf on the opposite bank. He had never seen them before, but he supposed these were vultures. He watched their greedy plunder of the corpse for a moment, his lips twisted in repugnance.

"Yah!" the man yelled. "Away!"

The birds all but ignored him, so he stooped and picked up a rock. He hit one and the entire flock took flight, beating the air as they strained to take off.

The wolf was completely torn apart—the tracks suggested the fatal injuries had come from a cave lion, whose immense paw prints sank into the mud, but the vultures had stripped the flesh to the bone.

The man knelt, puzzling it out. It appeared that there was a vicious fight on the other side of the stream, the lion taking on the wolf. The male-wolf was eventually killed in the battle right there where he lay. Yet the blood trail was on *this* side of the stream. What had happened over here, away from where the vultures had been feeding?

He studied the tracks. They told a contradictory story, both lion and wolf prints seeming to go back and forth to the stream. But the blood only went in the direction away from the banks, away from the dead wolf. How was that possible?

What if he had it wrong? What if there were two wolves? Both fought the lion. The shredded carcass of one canine lay where it died, on that side of the stream, while the other one fled to this side.

But a lion probably would not attack a pair of wolves unless they were pups, and, judging by the tracks, the surviving wolf was even larger than the dead one. But *something* brutal had occurred here. Also, where did the wolf go when it escaped? By all appearances, it had crawled off to die.

The corpse of the wolf on the other side of the stream was too picked apart to be of any use, but if he could find the other one and it was more intact, the man decided to harvest its fur. There was great honor in wearing a wolf pelt.

He cautiously followed the blood trail, his club at the ready. A wounded wolf would attack instinctively, though judging by the blood loss he felt fairly certain the other wolf would be dead.

The track led directly to a small hole in the rock wall—a dark semicircle where the rock pulled back from the soil like an upper lip curling to reveal an open mouth. Blood was smeared on the earth in front of the hole.

The wolf was in there.

He drew in a breath, considering. If he went in with a torch held out in front of him, the wolf could not attack without getting a mouth full of flame. He could at least assess the situation, and retreat if the wolf was aggressive.

Or, if he went in with the torch, the wolf might rip it from his hand and then tear out his throat.

This was, he reminded himself sternly, why he was a man, not a boy. A man needed to meet challenges such as these. He, *he* needed to meet the challenge. There were those who said he would not survive the year—he would not allow himself to prove them right by failing on the very first day.

He made a torch by winding dead grasses around the end of a branch. His heart was beating strongly in his chest, and when he lit the torch from coals in his fire horn, his hands trembled.

The wolf, he reminded himself repeatedly, was probably dead.

He shoved the torch into the hole in the rock, listening for any sort of reaction, but heard nothing. He could not see much past the flames, not from outside, so he squirmed in, hating how vulnerable he was as he pushed past the lip of the cave.

Inside, it was a narrow squeeze, and he was only able to advance if he remained on hands and knees. His palms picked up a sticky liquid as he crawled: more blood.

At a very tight turn, he had to climb over some rocks, and then a shaft of light fell on his shoulders. He glanced up and saw that a crack in the rock extended all the way up to the sky, many times a man's height and large enough in radius that had he known about it, he could have climbed down it instead of wriggling through the hole.

Starting with the crack, the cave was larger, tall enough for him to stand if he stooped, wide enough that he could not quite touch both sides with his fingers if he spread his arms.

His torch seemed weakened by the light from the shaft, but just past it and the flames licked back the darkness with authority.

He saw the wolf, a female. She was lying on her side, her eyes closed. He stopped, holding his breath. Pressed up against her were three tiny pups: newborns. The mother-wolf's side had been raked by lion claws and glistened with blood.

She was breathing, though he could not tell if the pups were also alive.

Now he understood. It had been a fight to the death by a male-wolf defending a mother-wolf ready to whelp.

He stared at the scene, his vision becoming more clear in the dancing flames from the torch head. The mother had a white spill of fur on her dark grey face, looking a little like a man's hand. She was still motionless. If she were almost dead, the pups would never survive.

He needed meat—while he had never heard of anyone eating an adult wolf, the very young of nearly all animals could usually be made into palatable meals. He decided to take the pups and harvest the adult's fur. There were plenty of rocks he could use to finish off the mother, though judging by the way she looked—her eyes closed, her chest barely moving—she was very near to death.

Should he wait, or pick up a rock and get it done?

Tired of stooping, he knelt in the gritty sand. It was an awkward motion for him, and he made some noise as his knees hit the ground.

The mother-wolf opened her eyes.

TWO

A larm coursed through the mother-wolf and she growled, struggling to her feet. A human was inside her den, a human and a fire. Instincts as old as her species told her to attack this threat to her pups.

Her back legs were not cooperating so she lunged with just her forelegs, dragging herself at him, her throat full of enraged snarling.

The man smelled frightened and made a lot of noise as he scrambled backward. The fire followed him. She registered the burning thing in his hand even as he tossed it wildly away, and then the human was in the part of the den where outside air and light flowed down from the roof. She went for his legs, her teeth ready to tear into his flesh, but he was able to climb up out of reach in a shower of small stones and dust.

She looked up at him, still growling deep in her chest. He was panting, but less fear was pouring off him. He was wedged up in the rocks like a leopard in a tree. She wanted to return to her newborns, but could not as long as this menace remained.

The tiniest squeal behind her told the mother-wolf that her pups were missing her, and her teats ached at the sound. She stared at the man, wanting him to leave the den so she could take care of her young.

"Hey," the human called softly. "Want some meat?"

The mother-wolf heard the man's sounds and they were

reminiscent of the calls from the humans who often fed her. She growled again. The smell of the still-burning fire from the front of the den was upsetting, and this human reeked of smoke as well.

When something small and light fell from the man's hand, the mother-wolf backed away from it, then eased forward and sniffed suspiciously.

"It is reindeer. Eat it."

The flesh was familiar, if dry and tasting strongly of smoke, but it was edible. She crunched it.

"See? It is good."

So. This human was one of the kind who fed her. She looked him full in the face and saw the same raised eyebrows she had long ago learned meant no threat.

Nothing in her instincts would allow any animal, even a friendly one, into her den. But the lion's attack had altered everything. She could smell the faint odor of her mate's blood and knew intuitively that he would not be coming back. Her life's focus now needed to be her puppies. Nothing else mattered.

Another piece of odd meat fell. She ate this one without hesitation—something beyond hunger told her to take in all the food she possibly could. Then she turned away to drag herself back to her litter.

Later, the mother-wolf registered the grunts and scrambling sounds as the man moved around. She did not know it was the sound of him climbing up the shaft, that the cascade of small stones bouncing off the rock face was from his near fall as he groped for handholds. The scent of fire remained even as the man's smell abruptly faded from fresh to stale as the man succeeded in his ascent.

She closed her eyes, pushed away her pain, and let her young suckle at her side.

She awoke a short time later: The man was coming back, making noise as he squeezed through the entrance at ground level. She stiffened, her hackles rising, but her growl never made it past her throat. Her tolerance was learned behavior, overriding her instincts. She needed food and the man was providing. Now she smelled wet wood and, deliciously, water.

She was unhappy when the flames, which had died away, started flickering higher, shadows jumping up the walls again, but she did not move, watching the man in the steadily building light, as he crept forward with a log.

"You need water. I am going to pour it in the hollow here, in the stones. See?"

The mother-wolf registered the man sounds and then the enticing spill of water from the branch he was holding as he pointed it down. A small pool of water formed, close to her head, and her young made tiny peeps as she pulled herself forward with her two front legs, leaving them behind.

The man backed away abruptly, then cautiously returned when the mother-wolf lapped at the water.

"I will take the hollow log back to the stream for more."

The mother-wolf returned to her young, lying down with a groan. The pain in her flanks bit hard when she moved, though it dulled if she lay still. She licked her pups carefully before falling back to sleep.

The light building and waning as it filtered down the shaft, and the noises and smells coming in on the air currents, gave the mother-wolf the sense of days passing. During the daytime, the man was often absent for long stretches, but as night fell he would build a fire at the bottom of the crevice and remain until sunrise. She could not directly see him: a large pile of loose rock separated the den from the rest of the cave, but he was detectable by his scent. In the morning he would climb over the mound of rocks and toss her small pieces of the odd dry meat. He came very close to her, and she could eat without having to rise fully off the cave floor.

Then one morning he broke the pattern. He left and did not return. The mother-wolf had grown accustomed to regular, small feedings, and though her food cravings increased daily, these consistent meals staved off the worst of her hollow, empty pains. This day, though, her hunger and anxiety rose within her mercilessly. She had to have food or her pups would perish. Normally, her mate would bring her food, regurgitating for her and, when they were old enough, her young. Now, though, the man had taken on that role.

And he was gone.

The fear was a motivator even stronger than starvation, and the mother-wolf whined. She would have to leave her young and go hunt.

She did not contemplate the impracticality of her decision. Even as she moved, dropping her pups from her teats and dragging her useless rear legs, there was no understanding that there was nothing she could possibly pursue in her wounded condition. She was driven by maternal imperative.

She had made it no farther than the base of the shaft, which stank from the pile of burned wood marking the now cold fire of the man, when a sudden riot of smells came to her nose. It was him, the man, and something else—a fresh kill.

When the man appeared, crawling, and saw her standing in the dwindling light from the shaft, he made a loud, frightened noise, startling her. She growled reflexively, feeling vulnerable, and the two of them froze, facing each other, tense.

"I have brought you fresh meat. Reindeer."

There was a tremor in the man's sounds and he still smelled strongly of fear, but the mother-wolf felt herself relaxing. This was familiar to her: a man, afraid but determined, bringing food.

She associated being fed with the den, so she turned and, as quickly as she could manage, pulled herself back over the pile of rocks. It felt good to be by her young, who registered her return with small squeaks. She waited expectantly.

Before he came, the man lit a fire. And then he crawled over the rocks and came to her, extending a bone with a knot of meat clinging to it. Mouth watering, the mother-wolf took the food from his hand.

"I wish I could tell you I took down the reindeer myself, but I have thus far not been successful hunting on my own," the man said.

The wolf crunched down on the bone with her powerful jaws.

"Where is your pack? I do not understand why you are here by yourself, though I do not know very much about what happens when a wolf gives birth. I have never seen any animal with newborn young. Perhaps it is your way, that the mating pair goes off by themselves. I would be very unhappy if a pack of wolves was here to greet me when I came back. I think from this point forward I will come down the shaft, just to avoid such an encounter."

This, too, was familiar to the mother-wolf. The humans who fed her often made their low, monotonous sounds while she ate.

"And I do not understand why you just accepted food from my hand." The man's sounds were softer now. "No wolf has ever done such a thing, to my knowledge—I would have been told of it. Is it because of the wounds you have suffered?

"And do you wonder about me? Who I am, and why I am sharing a cave with you, a wolf, instead of with my own people? How this came to be?"

The man drew in a great breath, exhaling it in a loud, mournful sigh.

"For now, we both are alive. But no lone person can survive the winter, though that is what will eventually be upon me: a winter on my own, in this place. Until I starve."

He sighed again.

"I do not even know what I am to do about you. You may die soon—your wounds do not appear to be festering, but clearly something inside you is broken and your rear legs cannot function. I have never eaten wolf meat. And your young—what will happen if I let them live?"

When the mother-wolf had consumed the bone, she felt sated. She put her head down.

"I have heard of how a pack of wolves kill a man. How he will scream while they tear the flesh from his body."

There was a silence. The wolf licked her lips, tasting reindeer on them.

"I cannot let that happen to me. And I know if I tried to take your pups from you now, you would fight me with all your remaining strength.

"I do not understand why you are here. I cannot really even comprehend why *I* am here. And I do not know what I am going to do."

THREE

Year One

His name was Silex. He was of the Wolf People, the Wolfen, and had been chosen to pay tribute to the wolves. He was seeking the pack that his tribe had been giving offerings to for as long as anyone could remember, but he did not find those wolves—instead, he was tracking three young wolves who were new to him, juveniles he had only been able to glimpse at a great distance. He was following them because they were younger and, he hoped, less dangerous than full-grown adults. The friendly wolf pack allowed itself to be approached and given meat, but that did not mean they would not kill a man if they had the chance.

He was afraid. He was only sixteen years old and had never been asked to do this before. The duty of providing food to the wolves normally fell to Silex's father. Silex's father led the Wolfen, but he had stumbled in some rocks and broken his ankle so severely a bone had pierced the skin. Now the wound festered and was hot to the touch, so Silex had been pressed into service.

The young wolves' trail was not difficult to follow, though he still had a sense of being far away from them. There was a path along the stream, here, the ground moist and imprinted with both claw and hoof. To the south, downstream, a settlement of humans who called themselves the Kindred spent their summers among some small caves. Between the stream and the wide cold river to the east was Kindred territory. The other side of the river was where the Wolfen roamed. The land this far north, though, belonged to no tribe. These were the northern wilds.

He carried a spear in case he encountered any threat, human or otherwise, and he also carried the front quarter of a reindeer, awkwardly tied in a sling fashioned from strips of hide. The food was the tribute. It was heavy and the excitement Silex had felt when his people solemnly bade him farewell with it had evolved into something like resentment. He was Wolfen, so he ran wherever he went, but his gait was awkward with the tribute bouncing on his hip.

The stream turned away from the path after a time, clinging to a jumble of large rocks to the right. On the left a sunny, grassy area shimmered in the summer sun. Silex felt uneasy as he passed the pleasant, safe-looking area, a defensible space where, had he been hunting, he might have stopped to camp for the night. Where were the wolves taking him?

It was the first time the three juveniles had left the main pack to hunt on their own. Their enthusiasm felt as if it were bursting from the earth into the pads of their feet, their gait gloriously unrestrained as they followed their noses toward the succulent presence of a herd gathered somewhere up ahead.

The scent had grown no stronger for some time and the female suddenly slowed, her instincts telling her that their jubilance had cost them too much energy on this hunt.

The summer had been good to them thus far. The juveniles had known hunger but not starvation, which was why they had the reserves to keep this pace over the miles. Yet the older wolves would never pursue such a faint trace at such speed for so long. They knew better.

The other two wolves faltered when the female fell back. Though they were both males, she was taller than either of them by a head, as well as stockier through the chest and extraordinarily powerful in her haunches. They looked to her for leadership when they played together, and had torn off away from the pack on this great adventure only because she had done so. Their tongues lolling, they circled her, sniffing, unsure.

The big female lifted her nose to the wind. Now that she was no longer racing headlong through the grasses, new smells came to her, clean and cruel, unknown yet imprinted into her instincts, her species' memory. She would some-day experience all of these sensations and know them as winter, but for now, with the summer flowers waving in the slight breeze, they were abrupt and unfamiliar.

She set out in the direction of the cool flowing air, with its promise of something new, because she was a large wolf, accustomed to being unafraid. The males fell in behind her in submissive single file, finding their places in line according to the pack order they had decided amongst themselves for the purpose of the day's hunt.

After a time, the soil changed. The few trees vanished and the grass gave way to sparse, coarse ground cover. The earth squished beneath their pads, and where the landscape dipped into depressions here and there, soupy, dark water lay stagnant, the air above boiling with black insects. Then there was a clear, cold brook, and then another. The wolves drank from these slender streams, invigorated.

This was land unlike any the large she-wolf had ever seen before, and she found herself lured irresistibly forward. When a scent traveled past like a wave of heat the wolves stiffened in unison. Elk, up ahead.

She couldn't help herself: she ran, joy coursing through her veins. Her male companions caught her enthusiasm. They came over a rise and hit the elk herd in a straight line but immediately were disarrayed, made ineffective by their inexperience. There were far too many animals to have a sense of the herd as anything but large. Confused by the elks' sudden, chaotic scramble and wary of the enormous antlers of the bulls, the wolves found themselves with no clear target. Frustrated, they milled in confusion, snapping at haunches and dancing back from one bull who was charging them with deadly determination, his rack lowered and slashing.

And then the large she-wolf heard the plaintive bleat of a calf that had been separated from the others, and she turned and sprinted in the direction of the sound. The calf bolted and the chase was on, but the wolves were fatigued and ineffectual in their initial charge and thus were forced to pursue fruitlessly, unable to organize a way to cut off the elk calf as she fled.

Nothing in the short lives of the young wolves prepared them for this pursuit, because without warning the earth beneath their feet turned white and slick. Though it was summer, a huge tongue of ice was imperceptibly grinding its way over ground, and the wolves were unsure what to make of it.

The young elk, in flight for its life, was heedless of the abrupt change in footing. She smelled water ahead and her instincts told her swimming would keep her safe. She rushed on blindly, registering but not caring that the ice was sloping forward, that up ahead the world seemed to impossibly end on a near horizon. By the time she realized she'd been betrayed by geography and that the glacier on which she was running was plunging off a rock shelf high above the ground, she was too far down the slick slope to do anything but fall, her legs splayed out and useless.

The wolves watched her vanish over the glacier's edge without comprehension. None of them, though, wanted to venture down the steep ice to find out what had happened. They stopped, panting, nuzzling each other for reassurance.

Eventually they raised their snouts, picking up a new scent. Meat, plus a living animal of some kind. They turned to follow their noses.

As for their prey: the elk landed with cruel impact on some rocks midway toward the base of the cliff, breaking her spine, but the spray of intensely cold water from the glacier numbed her, and the pain didn't register as fully as it would have otherwise. If anything, she felt relief—she had evaded the wolves. Now she was in landscape more alien than anything she'd ever encountered, slippery white ice coating everything, a constant rain of meltwater pelting her. Immobilized, peering without grasp at the frozen sheet, she was surprised to see, staring blankly back, another elk, an older female, shallowly buried beneath a layer of ice. Other animals had come this way before, perhaps for the same reason, and had fallen the same way.

A herd animal, the elk drew comfort from the presence of another. The pain had faded, the wolves were gone, and she felt sleepy and warm. In a way, she had never known such peace.

Silex gasped. After so many days of tracking them, the three wolves were suddenly on the trail in front of him, less than fifty paces away.

Breathing raggedly, his mouth dry, he began fumbling with the sling tying the deer meat around his shoulders. The wolves trotted forward, their advance casual, their looks sly. This animal did not look dangerous, and it was alone. And the juveniles detected something else—the tantalizing odor of blood and meat—this, and their inexperience, led them to be incautious.

They weren't experienced enough to encircle, to outflank. Instead they bunched together on the path, as if they were meeting other wolves instead of prey. When they were less than a dozen paces away, they stopped, their boldness evaporating as they warily eyed the spear pointing at them.

"It has been a good year. You have led us to good hunting," Silex greeted, his voice quavering. "Soon the summer will withdraw and you will lead us through the snows to where the herds winter. We thank you."

The males had no reaction to his voice—they sniffed and paced and drew ever closer, working up their nerve to attack. They were both wary and eager, enticed by the smell of the blood hammering through the human's veins. Silex wanted to drop the meat and run, but it was important, now, to stand his ground. It was not a tribute if he fled.

"Please," he whispered. He pictured the wolves setting upon him, tearing him open with their teeth, and he nearly could not breathe.

When Silex glanced at the enormous female he was shocked to see her staring him full in the face. No wolf ever did that—their glances were always furtive and clever, never telegraphing their interest.

She was by far the biggest wolf he had ever seen. She was mostly grey, black, and white, but on her forehead was a white mark that looked remarkably like a handprint of a man.

Still staring, the she-wolf took several steps forward, her nose twitching. Silex realized it was to this wolf that he should offer tribute. Could he kneel down and present the gift with humility? No, he was not that brave, so he gripped the foreleg and swung it, tossing it half the distance to the female.

The males shied back at the sudden movement, but the female simply regarded the offering calmly as it dropped to earth in front of her, as if she had been expecting it. She bent to feed, but not before giving Silex one last, contemplative look.

Silex backed away slowly, but the wolves were ignoring him now, content to tear into the reindeer meat. He kept his eyes on them until he was far enough away that they were mere brown specks on the trail, then he turned and headed back down the path in a near run, elated.

He would tell his father about the gigantic female, and the way she had received the tribute. Surely it was a sign that the wolves intended an even closer pact with the Wolfen! The she-wolf had peered into his eyes, *knowing* him, somehow.

There were those who insisted that the Wolfen were descended from the pack, and many argued that upon death, those who followed the wolves *became* wolves, while cowards became prey. Silex had not been a coward.

An instinct that told him to look back, a whisper of something alerting him to danger. He turned and his legs went weak.

The wolves were coming.

They were fifty paces behind him and were trotting, not running, adopting the easy lope that would sustain them for miles. The female was in front and the males were filed behind her. Their approach was all the more frightening for its utter silence.

The worst thing he could do was run but he couldn't help himself. A sob broke from his lips as he pictured how he would now die. *No.*

When he glanced behind him, of course the wolves were closer. No humans could run as far and fast as the Wolfen, but the Wolfen were not wolves, and the predators behind him would catch him and kill him.

Silex came to the flat grassy turf that lay between the stream bank and the crumbling, boulder-strewn outcropping. He was nearly falling down with terror, so faint with it he wanted to cry for his mother like a child.

He had just been here a short time ago, and the grasses had looked so inviting, the waters so sparkling. Now everything was hazy, his panic nearly blinding him.

Silex stopped running. What did he think he was doing? There was no way to outrun this threat. Gasping for breath, he considered throwing himself in the river, but it was shallow and afforded no escape. He looked upstream and saw that the wolves were closing fast.

All right. It would happen here.

Silex went over to the outcropping, a face of rock thirty feet high. There were no caves, but the soil was strewn with huge rocks and two round boulders shoulder high were close enough together that he had to squeeze between them. Now he had the rocky wall behind him and the two boulders in front of him. The wolves would not be able to surround him—they would have to come through the narrow gap one at a time.

He had his spear, but it was forbidden to use it. Wolves were sacred, never hunted, never killed. If the wolves decided to rush him, he would have to die today.

Perhaps he had been a wolf once before, out of the reach of human memory. Or perhaps now he would join the pack for the first time in his existence. Silex was not sure what he believed about death. His only hope was that the wolves would kill him quickly and that if he did come back, it would be with honor, and not as an elk.

The wolves arrived, tracking him to his hiding place.

They milled around, smelling him, whining with their eagerness to feed. The males came right up to the slot between the boulders, emboldened by the chase they'd just won.

Silex set his spear down.

"I offer myself," he said, his voice almost unrecognizable as it tremored. "I am ready to die."

FOUR

The wolves could see their prey hiding among the rocks, and they lusted to take it in their jaws. Some blood from the reindeer remained on the human's skin, and this tantalized them further.

Yet they were unsure how to attack a creature who was barricaded behind boulders. Instinctively, they knew rushing a cornered animal was almost never something they should attempt, though it was a rare animal that was so large and yet so passive as it awaited its fate. Why wasn't it fleeing, or bleating, or attacking? The male wolves whimpered with frustration.

The large she-wolf stood farther back. She wasn't as sure as the other juveniles that this was a meal they wanted—there was something very different about this creature. And the reindeer meat had come from him, somehow.

Then her head whipped around, her ears twitching. Downstream, a sound.

"Urs, *come on*," a woman's voice cried, laughing.

The call meant nothing to the wolves, but they all heard it, and now they could smell more humans approaching. They hesitated for a moment, but by the time a young man and woman came around the bend, the wolves were silently gone.

This is the place," the woman announced, coming into Silex's view. She appeared to be around his age, perhaps sixteen. She had large, pretty eyes, Silex saw, but it was her hair that caught his attention—it was tied in intricate knots, braided the way a leather string was braided to make rope. No Wolfen woman ever wore her hair like that.

The man with her was older by a few years. He was taller than the woman—indeed, he was taller than nearly anyone Silex had ever seen, tall and slender. His beard was black and full, unlike Silex's, which was tendril-thin.

Silex's skirt was short to allow him to run and was made of fox fur—like the wolf, his tribe viciously hunted the fox, though unlike wolves they did not tear the creatures apart and leave the carcasses strewn across the ground, but harvested the fur and what little of the tough meat they could get. These two people wore no fur at all—they were both dressed in animal hides tied around their waists, though the tall man's skirt was longer, descending to midthigh and slit on each side. Where the woman's upper garment was a simple tunic with slits for her arms and long enough to be tucked into the same belt, the man's similarly cut top was short enough for some of his taut belly to show.

All this Silex took in with a single glance, and then he was crouched down behind the rocks, scarcely breathing. They could not be Kindred; that tribe never ventured this far upstream. But who, then? The Cohort? Silex swallowed. If they were Cohort he was in great danger, but, though they were known to arrogantly wander where they wanted, the Cohort had never been seen in such a small group as two people, and their women never left the river valley.

Silex reached for his spear. If they were Cohort, he would have to kill them.

"And how did you find such a place?" the man, Urs, asked, mock-stern.

"I did not find it, it was already here," the woman, Calli, teased lightly. She held her face to the sun and beamed.

"Calli Umbra," Urs chided, addressing her with her formal name. One of the reasons the Kindred knew themselves to be superior to the other creeds was their naming convention. During the third summer of a young one's life, the oldest woman in the family told a story about the child— the narrative that would guide the children into adulthood. The narrative ended with a legend name, which was a full sentence long, plus a formal appellation suggesting the legend. Thus Calli's formal name—Calli Umbra— reflected her legend: "Her Thoughts Come from Mists and Shadows." By giving her this legend, Calli's grandmother had shrewdly put voice to what everyone suspected, which was that Calli's brain was complex and calculating.

"You should not have come here. *We* should not have come here," Urs scolded. "This is wild territory."

Urs's legend told the story of how Urs grew so much more quickly than all the children his age, so that he was as tall as boys several years older, and how he would someday be as large as the great bear. And he was, indeed, tall, with the gangly look of a young man who needed to hang more flesh on his bones. His formal name was Ursus Collosus, but it was of course shortened to Urs, just as Calli was the diminutive of her own formal name.

"I violated a rule," Calli admitted cheerfully. "Now you do the same."

"I already have broken the rules by coming here," Urs growled at her. But he was grinning, the sort of smile a man cannot help giving to a woman when they are courting all but openly.

"Not that. Another." Calli's eyes were dancing. She took a step forward, closer to Urs.

"What do you mean?" Urs asked after a moment, his voice hoarse, no longer playful.

Moving silently, Silex eased himself into a more comfortable crouch. If he broke from these rocks he might have enough surprise on his side to get on the path up-stream, but the tall man looked like a hunter and Silex doubted he would get far before a spear pierced his back. He would just have to wait here until they left.

Unless they found him first. Then the position that had been so defensible against wolves would be wildly vulner-able to a weapon thrust. Silex would be effectively trapped. The fight would be bloody.

That made him stop and consider. What if he lunged with spear and took down the big man first? The woman might well run rather than fight, and Silex had no intent to pursue her. He looked at the point below Urs's shoulders where a wound from behind would be fatal.

"Is there something you wish to say to me that you know you should not?" Calli asked, her voice a whisper.

Urs was staring at her. His hands twitched as if prepar-ing to take her in his arms.

"No?" Calli asked lightly. "Then I am mistaken."

She danced back and Urs stepped forward.

"Oh, are you stalking me, great bear?" she mocked.

"Calli, I . . ."

Silex had the feeling that what he was about to hear had been spoken many times inside the cave of Urs's head, but had never been given the freedom of an utterance.

"I do, I am intending to say, I love you."

Calli clapped her hands together joyously. "Urs! And I love you, why has it taken so long for you to say it?"

Urs didn't answer and Calli reached for him and then they were kissing in the sunlight.

They were not, Silex decided, Cohort. This was not how Cohort were said to act. They must be Kindred, and that was what was meant by "breaking the rules"—they were out-side of their territory.

The Wolfen always ran from the Kindred, avoiding altercation. Should he make his move and stab the tall man now, while the Kindred's arms were wrapped around the woman?

A wolf would watch and wait, Silex decided. That was what he would do, too.

"What will happen to us, Urs?" Calli asked after they had broken off their kiss. She still clutched him.

Urs shook his head. "I do not know."

"No, that is not the answer!" Calli responded sharply.

"The women's council . . ."

"No!" Calli said again.

Urs drew in a breath, frustrated. "People cannot decide who they are going to marry without the approval of the women's council," he finally declared in a heavy voice.

"Of course," Calli agreed impatiently. "But mothers often negotiate between themselves, and bring an arrangement to council. My mother will speak for me. What would you like my mother to say?"

"My own mother is long dead, so the council speaks for me," Urs noted. "Who I marry is up to the women."

Calli regarded him. "You are brave. You are not afraid of the women," she said after a bit.

"Of course I am not afraid," Urs snapped.

Calli smiled at this. "Then say we will never be apart. Not ever."

Some of the tension went out of Urs's shoulders, the way men relax after a spear has been thrown and there is nothing more to do but see if it strikes the intended target. "We will never be apart, not ever," he repeated dutifully.

"We will marry," Calli said.

"Oh Calli."

"Urs, I have been waiting my *whole life* to have this conversation," Calli pleaded. "Just give me your pledge."

"If Albi found out we had made a pledge to each other, she would do everything in her power to stop it."

Calli paused. "Albi is the council mother, but that does not imply she gets to decide everything. She is supposed to reflect the will of the council, not the other way around."

"That is not what I have observed," Urs reflected drily.

Calli clenched her fists. "Why does it matter anyway? If two people wish to marry, that is all that is important!"

"Now you are just being silly."

"I hate how the women interfere in our lives! When I am council mother, women will be able to marry whomever they choose."

"Ho!" Urs laughed. "*When* you are council mother?"

"I am serious," Calli fumed.

"I have no doubt of that."

"Then say it. Say we will be married," Calli commanded fiercely.

"Oh Calli."

"Please, Urs!"

He stared at her, warmth filling his eyes, love softening his smile. "Yes, we will be married, Calli. I love you."

More kissing. Silex was getting tired of hiding behind the rock.

"Urs?"

"Yes?"

"Do you know of this thing that a man and a woman do together?"

Urs froze for a moment, then pushed back so he could look into her mischievous eyes. "Of course I know," he replied.

"Oh? Have you perhaps been visiting one of the widows?" she asked, her voice lilting.

"What? *No.*"

"All right then. You just spoke with such authority."

"I am not a child, Calli. I am a member of the hunt. Spearman."

"Ah. And are you good with that spear?" she whispered.

Silex had never heard two people talk so much about nothing in his whole life. Compared to having to listen to this, being stabbed behind the rocks did not sound so bad.

"I am."

"I'll bet you are very good." Calli was groping for Urs's front cloth.

"Calli," he groaned.

"This thing that a man does with a woman, spearman. Would not this warm, soft grass be a wonderful place for such a thing?"

Silex was no longer bored. He watched as Urs and Calli untied their garments and tossed them aside, their breathing coming in short pants. He was soon surprised to see them mating face-to-face, with Calli lying on her back. Wolfen approached each other like wolves, with the man always behind the woman. It seemed perverse, somehow, to see two humans doing something so unfamiliar.

After staring at them for a long time it occurred to him that this was the perfect moment to get away: Urs was certainly preoccupied. Reluctantly he stood, flexing the stiffness out of his legs. The woman's face was turned away from him.

Now.

Silex broke from the rocks but did not get far before, with a shout, Urs had jumped to his feet. Now it was a pursuit, but Silex was of the Wolf People, fleet and agile, and he bobbed a little as he dashed up the path, his shoulders tense as he waited for the spear.

FIVE

Calli pulled her clothing together and waited for Urs, feeling sick at heart. Everything had happened the way she had imagined until, bafflingly, a man burst up out of the very earth, seemingly born of rock and soil, and fled, drawing Urs after him. Urs went from being her lover to something else, to man hunter, in less than one breath.

When Urs came trudging back down the path, carrying his spear loosely in his hand, she was relieved to see that he was uninjured. She read his disappointment when he saw she was no longer sprawled out in the warm grasses, waiting to receive him, and it made her smile. "Was it one of the Frightened?" Calli called. "I have never seen one before."

Urs shook his head. He came up to her, still naked, and a small shiver of pleasure ran through her at the sight of his lean, strong body.

"No, a human. Frightened Ones are bigger and they look different in ways for which I lack descriptive words."

She nodded. "No doubt he was very afraid, when he saw you coming at him with both of your weapons out," Calli noted, glancing down significantly. Urs blushed and bent to pick up his garments.

"Though I see you already put one of them away," she continued.

Urs simply had no idea what to say to that. He reached

out to her, holding her so that he could look into her eyes. "He was very fast, faster than any Kindred. I barely missed him, but I did miss."

"So. Just one person fell victim to your magnificent weapon today," Calli speculated.

"You are too smart for me, Calli Umbra," Urs said, laughing.

A man who thinks I am smart, Calli thought to herself. *Imagine such a thing.*

They began making their way on the path back toward the summer settlement. Urs fell silent and Callie hoped it was for the same reason she had run out of words herself: the memory of what they had just done together was too profound for any more banter.

They walked slowly, their hands entwined, but when the trail became strewn with loose rocks they released each other to better balance through the uneven footing. This fortunately meant there was no obvious intimacy between them when, at a bend in the path, they encountered Palloc, at nineteen summers a full year older than Urs. Where Urs towered and was thin, Palloc was stocky and short—Calli's height, in fact.

"Any luck?" Palloc demanded. He was standing with his spear near a den of rabbits that had been completely exploited the summer before. This year, though the Kindred kept returning to the same spot, there were no rabbits.

"Yes!" Calli replied gaily. "We had much luck!"

Urs turned and gaped at her audacity.

"What did you get?" Palloc asked, eyeing them suspiciously.

"Nothing," Urs admitted, giving Calli a stern look to stay quiet.

Palloc snorted, looking between the two of them. "You two are such children."

This bothered Urs. "I am no child. I am spearman," he challenged softly.

Palloc was one of the oddest-looking members of the Kindred. While nearly everyone else shared homogeneous dark brown eyes and complexions to match, Palloc's coloring was fair, his brown eyes so light the facets seemed to glow in the sun. It made the mood in them easy to read, somehow, so that Calli knew he was angry before he spoke. "And I am spear *master*," Palloc icily reminded Urs. "Your attitude does not please me, spearman." He glanced at Calli and his face flushed because he knew she was examining the hairs on his arms, which always turned nearly invisible in the summer. "Someday I will be hunt master and I will remember those who caused me disapproval."

Calli did not want to spend any more time with Palloc. "I need to help prepare dinner," she declared.

"Then go," Palloc ordered dismissively. "The hunt master has instructed the men to look for prey close to camp. Urs will help me hunt rabbits."

"But I should not be unescorted, not this far up the trail," Calli smoothly pointed out.

Impatience flitted across Palloc's pale features.

"She is right, Spear Master," Urs observed.

"Then both of you go. There is real work to be done; you would be of no help to me anyway."

Though the stiff set to Urs's jaw told Calli how furious this made him, he responded to the slight bump of her body against his and moved off without a word. Soon Palloc was out of hearing range.

"Thank you," Calli said softly.

"You were right, a woman should not be alone, not this far away."

"No, I mean thank you for leaving him. Leaving the . . . discussion."

"Discussion," Urs repeatedly moodily. Then his wonderful smile flickered back on his face. "Yes, it was very much a *discussion*. With Palloc, he talks, and you listen, and that is the discussion."

"Do you think it is true? That he will be hunt master someday?" Calli asked.

"We do not need a hunt master. Hardy is the best we have ever had."

"But someday," Calli argued. "Is it not a natural progression, from spear master to hunt master?"

"Well maybe."

"You should be hunt master," Calli declared glowingly.

Urs allowed himself a small smile, and Calli felt her affections for him soar. A thought he had apparently entertained only in his mind was revealing itself to her in that smile.

"What would you do, as hunt master?" Calli probed.

Urs looked at her eagerly. "We need to send the stalkers back out. That is what they are for. They split from the hunt and search for prey and then return to tell the spearmen. It is how the Kindred have always hunted."

"I do not understand what you are saying. 'Back out'?"

Urs's expression turned grim. "We know that the stalkers who vanished two summers ago were taken by the Valley Cohort. Hardy is afraid to send anyone out, now. We stay together as a group. When we do manage to spear prey, Hardy releases the stalkers to pursue and club the animal, but only as a full body of men."

"That makes sense to me." Calli nodded. "If the Cohort is out there, we should not risk another encounter."

"You are telling me how to hunt?" Urs's eyebrows were arched.

Calli regarded him, reading his defensive reaction perfectly. "I am not telling you, Urs. Of course you know better," she placated. "I am just saying I am afraid of the Cohort."

"Hunting is not going well. We need to send the men out to stalk."

"Do the men of the hunt agree with you?"

"Some do. Most do. But Hardy says it is not worth the risk."

"The women's council has its own disagreements," Calli said after a pause. "Everyone despises Albi as council mother. We all wish we had an excuse to vote her out."

"Really?" Urs stopped and stared at her. "Because that would solve everything."

"I am not sure I understand," Calli replied slowly.

"You must come up with a way to get the council to get rid of Albi as council mother. Elect someone reasonable, someone who will endorse our marriage."

Urs's expression was so optimistic that Calli wanted to hug him. "Oh Urs, for men it is all so simple: if it is hunt business, any member of the hunt can raise an issue."

"Well, the hunt master is the decider," Urs corrected.

"Yes, but anyone can pronounce their opinion without fear of retribution. The women's council, though, is . . . hushed. Albi's job is to put to voice our consensus, but often she suppresses discussion. You think that if a majority of women want Albi out, she would be out. I understand that is how it might work for the hunt, but for us that is so, so far from the case. You just do not understand about Albi," Calli said sadly.

"Understand what?" came a loud voice from behind them. They turned, startled, and there, of course, her hands on her hips and a suspicious scowl on her face, was Albi.

Year Nineteen

The big mother-wolf opened her eyes and suspiciously regarded the man who had been feeding her. He was approaching her at a crawl. There was fear on his breath and an earthen smell, wet and pungent, coming from his hands. The animal skin he carried, into which he often reached for food to give her, lent a delicious aroma of freshly killed meat to the mixture.

He halted near to her, so near that with a single lunge she could close her jaws on his throat. And, for a moment, her instincts told her to do this, to protect her pups from this human's encroachment. She drew her lips back from her teeth and the man inhaled audibly, frozen in place.

After a time, though, the mother-wolf's alarm receded. When he resumed his motion, she did not react, but just regarded him drowsily as he made his sounds.

"This is the mud mixture we use to prevent fester in our wounds. If we put it on the cuts from the lion, you will heal. So I must touch you to apply it. It will not hurt you. It is for your good and the good of your young."

The mother-wolf put her head down with a sigh. The battle within her, instincts warring with her willingness to trust this human who brought her food, wearied her. She was conscious of him moving slowly behind her, approaching her tail end.

She came alert when he lifted the flap of animal skin and the scent of food flooded the air. "All is good. I am doing this now." A piece of meat landed by her head and she greedily snatched it up.

When she felt his hands touch her, a low growl rumbled in her chest. Her pups stirred nervously. A wet and cool sensation caressed her wounds, and another piece of meat landed nearby.

She growled again, putting more warning into it, staring at the man in the gloom.

"Just a little bit more."

She snarled, snapping at the air, twisting toward him. He scrambled back. "All is good, all is good."

She regarded him for a moment, her pups squalling for their mother, the smell of meat dancing on the air. Her muscles tensed, she could feel her attack building, ready to be released.

When he threw another piece of meat to her, she connected the feeding to the man and his presence in the den and it altered her reaction. She turned from him and ate the offering.

Year One

The Wolfen were a nomadic people, living like the wandering wolves who led them to prey. But just as the wolves had a gathering site where they went to howl and play, the Wolfen returned from hunting to the same spot along the riverbanks, a defensible space where their young were safe.

Silex ran most of the way home, his back muscles knotted in tension, as if the Kindred spearman were still taking aim at him. Only when he smelled his tribe's fires did he manage to relax.

The mood was gloomy when he arrived in camp, people nodding solemnly in greeting—it was a somber time for the Wolfen. "Your father wishes to speak to you," his childhood friend, Brach, informed Silex in quiet tones.

"Any better?"

Brach shook his head grimly. As was true of all the northern creeds, the eyes of the People of the Wolf were dark, their hair black and kept shiny with the tree sap they used to keep it out of their way. But the Wolfen were differentiated by their slight builds and sinewy legs—because they ran everywhere, they tended toward lithe bodies.

Silex's father lay by the fire. He was stripped of all but a single fox fur tossed across his lap. His right leg was black at the ankle where he had snapped it in the rocks, and scarlet streaks tracked up the leg toward his groin. He was panting, his face dotted with perspiration.

"Father?"

For a moment Silex saw nothing but a wildness in his father's eyes, and then the look focused. "Silex. You are back," the older man greeted, his voice strained.

"I paid tribute. A she-wolf looked me right in the face, stared in my eyes. She was enormous, and had what appeared to be a human handprint on her forehead."

The older man grunted. "Perhaps there is a message for me in that. I am afraid my fever will take me soon. I am cold and then hot."

"You are sitting close to the fire. That might be why you are sweating."

Silex had to glance away from his father's angry glare. "It does not provide me any comfort to be lied to," his father chided. "We both know what is happening."

"Yes, Father."

"I am glad you are back. I have asked Duro to gather everyone by the center fire. I will speak my wishes for the Wolfen, and my wishes will be obeyed."

Silex briefly closed his eyes. "Of course," he murmured, but he dreaded what was coming.

"Listen to me now. When I am gone, you will be the dominant male of the Wolfen. You will marry Ovi, the dominant female, and have my grandchildren. This is how it is done among the wolves—the superior mating pair produces the best offspring, whatever the families they come from. This means one of your sons, my grandson, will go on to lead from there."

Silex drew in a breath. "Father. About Ovi. I . . . I love

someone else, Father. Fia. I love Fia, and would marry her instead."

His father struggled to a sitting position. "No, you will do what I say," he said dismissively. "You are lucky to even have a wife. Though recent births have given us daughters, the long period where only boys survived childhood means we now have far more single men than women." He gave Silex a contemplative look. "I should have anticipated the problem, but for so long I was only thinking how good it was to have so many hunters. Now this is something *you* will have to solve. You might want to consider raiding another clan and taking some females."

Silex was shocked. "The Wolfen are not like the Cohort. We do not steal *people*."

"Well. You may find your ideals do not suit the demands of leadership." He motioned to Silex to help him walk, and Silex took his father's weight on his shoulder as they limped down to where all the Wolfen adults were gathered by the fire. Silex glanced around for Fia, hoping to spot her, but he did not find her eyes. Instead, he saw Ovi, who stood gazing sadly into the flames.

"We are Wolfen," Silex's father began when he had everyone's respectful attention. "We follow the ways of the wolf. We run when other creeds walk, so that no man can keep up with us. And we are led by a dominant male because that is what is best." He coughed, looking dizzy, and Silex almost staggered with the change in weight. "My leg is turning to poison and I have a fever that will not pass. I will not live for many more days," he continued. "When I am gone, my son Silex will be your leader." He glared, waiting for an objection, but there was none. "And he will marry Ovi."

Silex glanced over and met Ovi's eyes. She was three years older, her body rounded and her face pretty, though it was grave now as she stared back at Silex.

"They will have strong children." This last pronouncement seemed to take everything out of the old man, and he sagged against his son. If anyone was going to challenge these pronouncements, now would be the time, when their leader was faltering and weak.

No one said anything. No one defied him. Not any of the Wolfen men who might resent being led by a sixteen-year-old boy. Not Ovi, who probably had not known of the marriage plan until this moment. Not even Silex, who loved a girl named Fia but now, instead, was fated to marry Ovi.

Ovi, his sister.

SIX

Most little children of the Kindred were frightened of Albi. She was big boned for a woman and had the same odd pale-eyed coloring as her son Palloc, though Albi had lived for more than three tens' worth of summers and had a weathered, blotchy face to show for it. She had stopped tying her hair back when her husband was killed by a mammoth, so it was a long, tangled mess. Once a lighter shade of brown, it was increasingly wispy with grey. It gave her a wild, nearly savage look.

Albi had recently taken to walking with a straight, stout tree branch, thumping it on the ground for emphasis when she was speaking. She had it with her now and was leaning on it, glaring at Calli and Urs with her strange eyes narrowed.

"You said 'understand about Albi.' Understand what?" Albi demanded to know.

Calli kept her feelings hidden but when she glanced at Urs everything was revealed on his face: their secret afternoon, their forbidden vows, their heretical ideas of marriage. "Urs feels your son is too bossy as spear master," Calli blurted. Nothing less than a shameful admission would explain Urs's guilty expression. "He wanted me to ask you to talk to Palloc about it, but I was saying you would never interfere with the hunt."

Albi sneered. "That is right. Why do you run to me? Perhaps Palloc deals with you sternly because though you are offensively tall, inside you are a small, cowardly child."

Urs's lips twitched with his anger. Calli turned so that she faced him full on, her back to Albi. Her eyes pleaded with Urs even as she said, "So there is your answer. You should speak to Hardy the hunt master if you have issues with Palloc."

Calli bit her lip, watching Urs struggle with the insult. Then he locked his eyes on hers and her heart filled with affection. He understood what she was doing. "I must go now and help prepare for the hunt," he said stiffly.

"I suppose you should," Albi responded mockingly. Calli sighed in silent relief when Urs turned away.

"Calli Umbra. That is not what you were talking about. You cannot fool me."

"I do not know what you mean, Council Mother," Calli responded lightly.

"You do not want to defy me, girl of mists and shadows."

"I'm sorry, old woman whose colors are the palest shades of white," Calli answered gravely, mocking Albi's formal name. The two of them locked eyes, and it was Albi who looked away first.

F ood was scarce for the Kindred that summer. In the days after Urs and Calli encountered the fleeing Wolfen, hunt master Hardy took the hunt out often, frustrating the couple's plans to be together in their special place. Every moment he was gone, Calli felt as if her arms ached with a special, empty lack.

On this day, the hunt was back at camp, but were assembled on the men's side of the settlement. Calli could see Urs's back as he crouched in the circle with other men, and she stared at him, willing him to glance up at her and give her that shiver when their eyes met. But he did not.

Cook fires smoldered around the settlement, but nothing was cooking. When there was so little to eat, the Kindred pooled their meager resources, and it was up to Calli and Coco, Calli's mother, to stretch their meals so that all might feed.

Coco had gone to dig for some tender roots to add to their meal. Into the hollow of an enormous log, Calli had poured water, added grass, and was now carefully shredding a small bird that had been roasted over the coals. Other than the bird, they had two recently skinned rabbits, and that was it—scarce protein for the entire Kindred, which at more than forty members was the largest of the northern creeds. Calli would strip the rabbit meat and then pound the bones to fragments and add them to the soup. The men of the hunt would feed first, of course, which meant the children and women would lie hungry in their sleep.

Renne came to the cooking fire, trailing four children who were all just a little over three years old. Calli noted that recently Renne had taken to wearing her hair braided like Calli's, which was uncharacteristically bold for her. Renne was a nineteen-year-old orphan and therefore answered to the women's council, and many of the older members disapproved of the fancy braids. "What is Calli doing for the Kindred?" Renne asked.

"Cooking!" the children shouted in unison.

Renne and Calli exchanged a smile. Teaching the children was a task most of the women enjoyed, something they all shared. Renne, who was shorter than Calli despite being three years older, seemed especially to enjoy it.

"Now, who can show me their man's side hand?" Renne asked the children.

There was some confusion, but Calli, standing behind

Renne, raised her right hand and eventually all of the children were waving their right hands in the air. "All is good, that is correct," Renne beamed. She pointed off to her right, where the single men slept beneath their tents of skin, and the hunters gathered around their fire to discuss important matters. "And that is the men's side. Do children go to the men's side?"

"No!" the children chorused without guile. They all knew they were not supposed to visit their fathers over there, but they would all do so until they were old enough to understand.

"Now show me the woman's hand," Renne instructed. Kidding, Calli held up her man's hand and the children laughed at her as they wildly thrust their left hands into the air. "That is correct." The women's side was far more open—children ran in and out of the area. Only men were forbidden access.

Then Renne spread her arms to indicate the rest of the settlement. Behind her, a hill of rocks revealed some small caves, and in front of her, families had leaned skin-covered poles on boulders or had fashioned tents out of mammoth bones and animal hides. Unlike the relatively small men's and women's sides, the section in the middle, the communal area, spread from the hills to the stream. Anyone might wander in the communal area, though it was only polite to give family tents a buffer zone of privacy. "And this is for all the Kindred," Renne pronounced. "From here to the stream. But should children ever try to cross the stream, take the stream path up water, from where the stream flows, or down water, to where it goes?"

"No," the children ventured as one, but without the joyous enthusiasm. They knew why they should never enter those places: the Cohort was out there and would steal them away from their parents.

Renne and the children left just as Bellu joined Calli at the fire. "Is this it? Only two rabbits?" Bellu looked dubiously at the two small carcasses.

As fire maker for the Kindred, Bellu had probably the least arduous job of anyone—the communal fire burned perpetually, so that only when the tribe was on the move was there any actual "making." She even had children assigned to fetch her kindling.

But, at age sixteen, Bellu was beautiful. Her legend told of a face so charming that grown men sang to her, and her formal name, "Her Face Brings Happiness to All with Its Beauty" was an apt appellation for a woman who had straight teeth, a face free of scars, flashing dark eyes, and symmetrical features. Her hair was thick and black and long, and she wore it free and flowing like a child. Like Calli, Bellu was eligible for marriage now—it was a topic they discussed frequently.

"I hope the hunt is successful," Calli remarked. "Who is going?"

Bellu was an authority on the hunt because she had five brothers, but Calli already knew who was going; she just wanted Bellu to bring up Urs's name.

Bellu was frowning, her pink tongue in the corner of her mouth as she concentrated on scooping up a hot rock from the center of the fire using two sticks. She looked up at the question and the rock rolled back. "Here comes Albi," she hissed.

Calli bent over, concentrating on stirring dinner.

"So," Albi pronounced, her bulky shadow falling over the younger women as she dipped a dirty finger into the soup. She tasted it and made a face. "You cannot feed the hunt with this! You need more grass. Go fetch some."

Calli and Bellu looked at each other. "My mother went to get . . ."

"I do not care what your mother said, I am telling you this needs more grass." Albi thumped her thick stick on the ground. "Are you arguing? No. Then go."

They went. When Calli glanced back, Albi was standing with her arms folded, glaring at them.

"I am so sick of grass," Bellu muttered. "Where are the reindeer? Why is hunting so bad this year?"

"Why does Albi want us to leave the fire?" Calli wondered out loud.

The day after being fed by the man, the large she-wolf and her two lanky male companions followed their noses back to the pack and were instantly beset upon by the four pups who had been born that past spring. Clumsy and playful, the young pups tripped over themselves as they rushed to greet the returning hunters. When the pups sat and licked at the large she-wolf's mouth, she quietly regurgitated a meal for them, the taste reminding her of the human who had given her the meat. The males who had hunted and fed with her also obliged the wolf cubs. She watched approvingly as the little ones ate. She nosed the largest of the cubs, a male, and he responded with an uncoordinated lunge at her ears, pulling at her fur with his tiny teeth.

What she felt toward these pups, who were not hers, was not so much love, but a sense of prideful responsibility. The pack was strong, now. These new members added to that strength. They were healthy and were eating well. That was good.

She thought again of the source of the meat, the human. She had smelled the fear coming from him, but there had been something else underlying it, something oddly compelling. And his face: when it came to other species, wolves had no experience outside of prey and predator. Prey was always implacable—even a charging bull elk had cold, expressionless eyes behind his lowered antlers. Predators were more revealing, but wolves knew little from bear or lion other than aggression or fear. The human's face, however, throbbed with his strong emotions and the she-wolf actually *felt* them, even though she didn't understand them. When suddenly the meat came flying at them it carried, for the wolf, the same sense she had as when she just now brought up a meal for the pups. The human had been *providing*.

The mother of the pups, the pack's dominant bitch, her teats now dry but still slightly distended, was approaching. The big she-wolf watched her, sensing an odd tension rippling through the wolves of the pack.

This was this particular wolf's first litter. The large she-wolf thought of the dominant female as Smoke, an association not built of words but of smell and taste. When the she-wolf and her siblings, as puppies, had been fed a regurgitated meal a year ago by this dominant wolf, it carried with it a tinge of the smoke that sometimes floated on the air near where humans gathered. Smoke had obviously eaten something burned, because the smell lingered on her breath and oozed from the pads of her feet for many days.

Smoke's approach alerted the rest of the pack because it was direct, her unwavering eyes focused on the large she-wolf, who knew she should grovel before the dominant bitch, but something stopped her. She held herself rigidly, tail slightly aloft, as Smoke sniffed her. She was risking punishment, but something compelled her not to yield. The rest of the pack grew even more agitated when Smoke put her head on the large she-wolf's shoulder, an aggressive move just shy of an attack.

As if her youth and unreadiness suddenly occurred to her,

the she-wolf cringed instead of continuing her insolence. She dropped her tail until the tip of it brushed her own stomach, she whimpered and blinked her eyes rapidly, she licked Smoke's mouth.

Smoke's low growl and unwinking stare was all the punishment the dominant bitch chose to administer, this time. But the she-wolf's insulting lack of submission had been observed by all the wolves in the pack. Yes, she was young and inexperienced, but she was also huge, bigger than even the dominant male. She was healthy and strong.

A fight was coming, and the pack knew it.

SEVEN

Coco was waiting with her arms crossed for Calli and Bellu as the two young women returned with their arms full of new grass. "Where have you been?" she hissed furiously.

Coco was, in many ways, an older version of her daughter Calli. Both were slightly tall for women. Both had stocky legs and muscular buttocks, drawing men's eyes when they wore their shorter summer garments. Neither had Bellu's perfection, but they were still considered beautiful among the Kindred. Their eyes carried laughter more than fury, but not now: Bellu actually held back a few paces, cowed by the inexplicable rage on Coco's face.

"We . . ." Calli looked to Bellu for support, then down at the grass in her arms.

"Look!" Coco commanded. She thrust a finger at the flat rock by the fire on which the skinned rabbits lay. Calli stared, then exchanged horrified glances with Bellu. Only one carcass remained.

Bellu scanned the sky for the bird that might have done this, but Calli knew no bird would come in so close to a smoking fire. This had been a human, who had done this. One of the Kindred.

"You can never leave food unguarded during times of great hunger!" Coco scolded.

Bellu made a small whimpering noise. She was unaccustomed to anyone being angry at her. Coco ignored her—she remained focused on Calli, waiting for an explanation.

But Calli was looking over her mother's shoulder. Albi was approaching, leaning on her heavy stick.

"What is happening here?" Albi demanded.

Coco reluctantly explained that they were short a rabbit. Albi raised a furious finger and stabbed it at Calli. "You should have piled stones on the carcasses," she raged. "Now we have even less to eat!"

Bellu looked close to tears, but Calli said nothing. She was staring at Albi, whose chin was shiny with a new, slick coat of grease.

Silex was at the front of a party of five other Wolfen hunters. They ran easily, keeping the wolves to their left, far enough away on the rolling plains that only their fur-covered backs were visible above the grasses, rippling like water flowing over rocks. The Wolfen hunters did not know where the pack was going, but the wolves ran in the single-file lope they usually employed when they were tracking game.

The Wolfen, mimicking their canine benefactors in all ways possible, also ran in a single-file line, but now Duro—a large, muscular hunter several years older than Silex—increased his speed until the two men were side by side.

"So you are to marry Ovi," Duro grunted.

Silex glanced sideways at him. Duro's face seemed drawn into a permanent scowl, his dark eyes furrowed under a heavy brow. The ridge of bone at the base of his forehead was almost as thick and prominent as the facial features of Frightened Ones, the massively built but shy near-humans who always fled when they saw the Wolfen. Now, when

Duro met his gaze, Silex felt that the other man seemed even more dour than usual.

"It was my father's final wish," Silex reminded the other man neutrally. Several days had passed since they had buried the Wolfen leader, placing spearheads and some bear teeth in the hole with him. Since that time, Duro had been behaving petulantly, so Silex thought he knew where this conversation might be headed.

"Your father is dead."

Silex increased the pace slightly, and the larger man followed suit. Silex prided himself on the light touch of his feet on the ground, so similar to the running wolf. Duro's footfalls fell more heavily.

"Ovi is a rounded woman. She has good breasts. She will be a fertile mother," Duro panted.

Silex abruptly signaled a halt. The rest of the Wolfen reacted instantly, but Duro had been caught off guard and overran their position, returning sheepishly to rejoin the group.

"We have lost sight of the wolves," Silex told his fellow hunters, who circled around him. He directed his men to travel in two groups of two and locate where the wolves had gone. Duro he would keep with him.

"So," Silex said, looking up at Duro.

"Ovi is large boned. Like me. She is tall for a woman." Duro put his hands on his hips, straining to speak without sounding breathless.

"This is true."

"She has good breasts."

"That does seem important to you," Silex observed mildly. "You have said it before."

Duro's scowl deepened. "You are not large and are not as strong as me."

"Yet, my father chose me to lead the Wolfen, and it is I who have given tribute to the wolves."

"Your father is dead."

"You have said that before, too."

"You are a boy. That is what matters," Duro insisted. "In the wolf pack, the males will challenge to see which one mates with the largest female."

Silex sighed. "You are forgetting that my father taught us that there are times when we cannot be exactly the same as our wolf benefactors. Would you vomit up your food to feed our young?"

"Your father," Duro sneered.

"Is dead," Silex interrupted. "Yes, I know."

Simultaneously, both hunting parties returned. Silex could tell by their expressions that neither group had found the wolves, but the two young men on his right had found something else.

"Kindred," they reported, pointing over some low hills. "Hunters."

Silex considered this. The Kindred usually traveled in large parties, often with many times more men as the Wolfen.

"Well?" Duro taunted. "Do we run away? Or do we show the Kindred that the Wolfen fight when they trespass on our side of the river?"

The abrupt dare was so startling that, without context, the rest of the hunters could only gape at Duro. Silex, though, pretended the challenge was not at all obnoxious, giving his face a contemplative expression. "Of course we do neither," he finally said carefully. "We do as the wolf would do. We observe them unseen while continuing the hunt."

Silex did not wait for acknowledgment—he simply turned

and ran toward where he hoped they would regain the wolves' trail.

"When I am leader," Duro hissed at Silex, "I will attack the trespassers. I will kill them all!"

The wolves had killed, and the scent of blood sweetened the wind with a wild succulence. What little remained of the two elk calves stained the dirt. The wolves were wagging and playing near the stain, touching noses and tumbling with the pups. The large she-wolf lifted her snout and sniffed. It felt as if a howl was coming, a song of joy.

The dominant bitch, Smoke, was not nearby; her scent was barely detectable above the blood. Perhaps that was why the wolves were so insouciant—without Smoke making her increasingly hostile moves, the pack was relaxed.

Three times the large female had been abruptly and viciously challenged by Smoke, and in all three instances the younger she-wolf had opted for the good of the pack, accepting the punishment, submitting to it. Her anodyne behavior calmed the other wolves, but Smoke thus far was unmollified.

Disappointed that the pack came to the verge of a howl before the mood shifted and the wolves opted to curl up with full bellies and nap instead, the she-wolf trotted off in search of the two young males who, more and more, were her companions each day. The woods here were thick, fallen logs damp underneath from a recent rain. The she-wolf gracefully leaped over the trunk of a downed tree, and that's when the dominant bitch struck.

There was no warning, just a blindsiding attack. Smoke must have been lying patiently just on the other side of the log, the wind sweeping her scent away, watching as the younger wolf approached. Now Smoke lunged, growling, her chest slamming into the larger she-wolf, teeth slashing, drawing blood.

The younger she-wolf rose up on her rear legs and the two wolves engaged in a brief, vicious battle, their voices mingling in a shockingly ugly growl. This was it, a fight for dominance, for fate.

And then the younger wolf dropped to all fours, turned, and ran. She had felt, in one second, both her superior strength and her inexperience coming to the fore. This was not a fight she could win. She might be larger but she was unskilled, and she was too young to mate. She could not be the dominant female at her age. It would not be good for the pack.

Yet she knew she was fated to mate, eventually, that her size and strength meant the pack needed her pups. It was why Smoke had attacked, defending her rank, and it was why now, when the larger she-wolf wanted so much to circle back and rejoin her pack, she kept going, slowing but moving steadily. For the good of the pack, she needed to leave the very social order that had sustained and nurtured her for her whole life. It was her destiny.

She could not calculate risks, but her instincts did a good job of giving her a heightened sense of danger, of urgency. She needed to find food quickly, not because of hunger— she had just fed—but because she was callow and still clumsy and utterly alone.

After a time, the she-wolf stopped at a stream and drank. The pack was downwind and she could no longer detect its scent, or smell anything worth pursuing for a meal. Instinctively electing to conserve energy, she found a cool spot of shade and circled around in the grass, lying down for an afternoon nap.

Soon she raised her head, staring alertly. She smelled them long before she saw them.

Her two young male companions, coming toward her across a field of grass, throwing their fate in with hers.

EIGHT

The thin soup of two days ago had done little to ease the hollow hunger in their bellies, and now the Kindred hunt, twenty men in all, pressed a hard pace as they trotted out onto the plains in search of prey. They were breathing raggedly, especially those who fell out of line to squat and ease their cramps and then had to sprint to catch up.

Hardy, hunt master, was nearly the oldest man among them, having spent a full forty summers hunting game on these steppes. Never could he remember there being so little to eat—just a handful of years ago there was enough game that the hunt would return to the settlement after only a day, dragging reindeer and elk behind them. Now they had been forced to cross the great river into Wolfen territory, though he was hardly worried about a confrontation—the Wolfen were as cowardly as the Frighteneds, and would run from the Kindred spear.

There was an odd rocking motion to Hardy's gait, as the leg on his left side, the woman's side, turned awkwardly in its socket with every step. It was a pain that had bothered him his whole life, but he had never mentioned it, never told anyone that it was more than just a hitch in his step—it hurt, and at this pace felt as if he were being repeatedly stabbed, but he would not let up. He was hunt master and the Kindred were starving. His legend told of a man who was always strong and fit for the hunt, acknowledging his stocky build and broad chest—he would die before he would betray that legend.

Urs ran easily on Hardy's man's side, while Vent—Aventus, "He Runs as Fast and Strong as the Wind"—kept pace on the woman's side. Urs impressed Hardy; he could run for miles and then throw a spear on target without hesitation. Palloc was up front with them, trotting along a few steps back.

Palloc did not impress Hardy. The spear master's loud breathing was distracting—did the fool not understand that they all hurt, that they were all tired?

Hardy signaled he wanted to speak to Urs alone. "What is it, Urs?" Hardy asked softly. "You have sighed like a woman several times today."

Urs gave a guilty start. "I was just thinking perhaps we should send the stalkers out ahead to find prey," he finally responded respectfully.

"No," Hardy answered curtly.

"But if they fanned out, we would be able to search far more ground."

"No."

Urs bit back his frustration.

By late afternoon, the men were on the verge of collapse. The hunt master called for frequent stops, and had worked the hunt back to the river so they could drink and cool off. Urs felt light-headed, and his legs trembled whenever they halted. They were not running now; Hardy had taken them out wide and fast, as if casting a net, and was now traveling them more carefully, alert to the slightest movement. They were out of the trees and it kept them on edge—predators could see them. They strayed away from the river, then back to its banks, combing the grasses. They were on the east banks, the Wolfen side.

When the Kindred startled up a reindeer herd it rose from

where it had been lying in the dry grass, creating a cloud of dust. Shouting, breaking discipline, the men dashed forward in a ragged assault, hurling their spears.

Urs did what he was supposed to, keeping his eyes on Hardy. The hunt master watched the herd, waiting for the mad scramble to sort itself out, spotting a doe who was running to the man's side. It was behavior that served the ungulates well when their hunters were four-legged: a straight line retreat gave the predators organization, and it was easy to pull down the slowest. When the first frantic milling produced no direction, the lions and wolves could not pick the young or weak out from the rest of the herd, and often wound up facing deadly antlers as a result.

Not true for humans. They tracked chaos without confusion, and the doe breaking to the man's side presented a fat target for the hunt master's spear. Urs's toss was the better of the two: while Hardy's weapon nicked the animal's back, Urs's spear sank home in the front leg on the reindeer's right side.

Another reindeer had taken a hit as well, and most of the hunt broke after this one. Hardy reached a hand out to stay Urs's impulse to follow. "Wait," he instructed.

Urs did as he was told, though he was obviously itching to join the hunger-fueled melee that had broken out among the men. The speared prey was bounding out far ahead of her pursuers. Hardy stood still, studying the terrain.

Palloc had given chase, but when he glanced back and saw the hunt master and Urs standing still, he halted, confused. Why were they not running?

The spear master should be by Hardy's side, Palloc decided. He turned back. He was panting as he approached the two hunters. "What . . . ?" he started to ask.

Hardy cut him off with a curt chop of his hand. "There,"

Hardy declared, pointing to a flat area far distant. "We go there."

They stopped to pick up a couple of the spears that the hunt had abandoned in its reckless dash.

It was half a day's trot. Palloc exchanged glances with Urs and was mollified to see that the taller, younger man appeared as clueless as he was. Hardy signaled for them to slow as the grasses thinned. They crept silently, mimicking Hardy.

What they found was a young lion who had opportunistically seized the Kindred's prey and was feeding, oblivious to the approach of the three humans. The reindeer was lying on its side. Not yet dead, its eyes were dull with shock.

Hardy gestured them down, speaking in a murmur. "A lion will not allow itself to be encircled. I will charge up the center. You," he pointed to Urs, "attack from the man's side. You, Spear Master, you attack from the woman's side. Make no sound unless I do, and do not release your spears, but impale the lion if he does not flee our attack. If he flees, we stand back-to-back with spears out to guard against his return, and await the rest of the hunt." Hardy squinted at the sun. "Our fellow hunters may be here at any moment, but we cannot wait, that beast is making short work of our prey."

Hardy nodded at them, and Urs and Palloc nodded back. Palloc was glad to see the fear in Urs's eyes—he himself was terrified. *Charge a lion?*

The lion's jowls were bloody, its immense teeth ripping savagely at the deer's entrails. Though young, it was still longer from nose to tail than a human stretched to full length. If the predator cat chose to defend its meal, a single swipe of its claw could disembowel a man.

This was not something they should do. Palloc opened

his mouth, wanting to say something. *They needed to talk about this!*

"All right." Hardy turned. "We go."

The men stood up out of the sparse shrubbery, and the lion raised its huge head, staring at them.

The men of the Kindred often said Hardy's face was made of stone. A gouge under his left eye did appear as if it had been chipped out with hard flint, and his impassive demeanor steadied the hunt when conditions were less than ideal. But that did not mean the hunt master was incapable of fear.

He was afraid now, watching the enormous lion devour the reindeer they had speared. With only Palloc and Urs aiding him, he might very well die, this day. But the fear lent him a focus like none he had ever had; it made his legs strong, filled his lungs, firmed his grip so tightly on his spear the wood might snap. The Kindred needed food, needed that reindeer.

Hardy ran straight at the lion.

And Urs was afraid. He actually hesitated, hoping for more time, feeling sure that if they were going to do this thing, run straight at this killer, they needed to discuss it more. *Wait!* he almost shouted. Then he realized the hunt master was heedless and that Urs was being left behind. Urs began twenty paces back and veered to his right, his man's side, not sure how far out he should go before he curved back to close the circle on the lion, who was not even looking at Urs—just at Hardy, its animal gaze malevolent and intent.

They were more than a hundred paces out. Urs was the faster runner and began catching up, but when he turned to look for Palloc on his woman's side, it caused a stumble: Palloc was not where he should be. He was far behind the two men, moving, but at the speed of their dust, barely more than drifting.

The cat began lowering its head, raising its shoulders. Its lips drew back from its teeth. When Hardy could see its eyes, the irises were completely black. It was not retreating from the three-pronged attack. This would be a fight.

Hardy raised his spear and yelled, hating this beast, his heart filling with rage.

The cat sprang, coming up on its rear legs and clawing the hunt master across the chest just as his spear flew and went wide, burying itself in the felled reindeer. Hardy staggered. Urs was still twenty paces away, sprinting hard. He gasped as the lion took the hunt master's head in its mouth. Still running, Urs was close enough to hear the skin on Hardy's skull pop.

Urs yelled, too, gritting his teeth, and lowered his spear and drove it with all his weight behind it straight into the lion's neck. The impact nearly threw Urs to the ground. A thick spray of blood painted the air. The lion dropped Hardy and roared, twisting, yanking the spear from Urs's hands. Snarling, the cat bit at its wound, trying to dislodge the weapon, and Urs reached down and yanked Hardy's spear from the reindeer's flesh and when the lion pounced he hurled the spear and it went true, a solid hit that split the cat's ribs as the stone point rammed into its heart. The lion fell forward, dying at Urs's feet.

For a moment there was nothing but silence—Urs could only hear his own panting—and then a strange sound made him look up in surprise. There, at the top of the rise, were the members of the Kindred hunt, and the sound was them cheering. They came down the slope at a run, shouting, while Urs, awash in what felt like sickness, sank to his knees.

Palloc and the hunters of the Kindred reached the kill site simultaneously. They all wanted to grab Urs, to rap their knuckles on his back in congratulations, and none seemed to even want to talk to Palloc, the spear master. Palloc stood there as if invisible, panting, his mouth taut in a resentful grimace.

Two of Bellu's brothers were kneeling by Hardy, whose head wound bled bright red in the sunlight. Hardy was moaning, and his eyes were closed.

The she-wolf and her two male companions had gone for seven days without a meal. Their hunger had led them farther out onto the grassy plains than they had ever ventured, where they felt exposed and vulnerable, but they ultimately had found nothing.

Their snouts were dirty as they touched noses for reassurance, because the wolves had spent a fruitless day digging among a warren of holes perforating the earth and emitting the tantalizing scent of warm-blooded mammals. There was prey, down in those holes, but never visible, never audible. The wolves dug until their feet were raw, all for nothing. It was a worthless expense of energy while the strength in their muscles palpably ebbed. The large female could smell the weakness on the breath of her two male companions, taste it in their exhalations like an illness.

When the sun was directly overhead and the air dry and still, the large female went rigid, her nose twitching wildly. The two males bounded over to her, wagging, and they spent several moments sniffing each other. Elk. There were elk ahead.

Now the hunger gave strength instead of sapping it, pushing them into a reckless dash over a small hill and down toward an elk herd grazing under the summer sun.

It was bad strategy: normally lethargic in the heat, the bull elks were alarmed by the wolves' charge. While the cows and their calves milled in agitation, the bulls closed ranks, facing the wolves.

Frustrated, the large female whined. The barrier of lowered antlers looked impenetrable, deadly. The wolves probed, creeping forward with their teeth bared, but the elk didn't panic. When the bulls lunged the wolves scampered out of the way. Behind the males, the rest of the herd was back to feeding, seemingly confident and unconcerned.

The juvenile wolves had been on hunts, but not many, and were without any sense of how to separate calf from mother, or how to get past the phalanx of elk antlers scything the air just inches from their faces.

Over time the she-wolf had come to consider the largest of her male companions to be her mate, though he wasn't as large as she was. The other was her brother. Though wolves often mated with siblings, for her, Brother was too small. She knew that when the time came, she would have pups with the bigger one, Mate. Brother knew it, too, but hadn't yet peeled off to search for a female of his own—they were all too young for that.

Now, faced with the seductive scent of young elk on the other side of the barrier of antlers, the wolves instinctively split. The large she-wolf went right, and Mate stood in the center, lunging and snapping at the male elk, drawing their attention. Brother went left, slinking low in the grasses.

A huge bull, wise and old, tracked the she-wolf. He wasn't fooled, and his rack of antlers came at her with lethal intent as he charged. She tumbled out of the way, panting, growling her frustration.

And then a scream broke the air, a wolf's scream. The large she-wolf retreated, scampering away, looking toward Mate, who was also fleeing.

Mate was unhurt, but Brother was crying. A rack of horns had skewered the inexperienced wolf, and now he limped away in a straight line, ignoring his two companions.

The large female caught up to Brother and could see the blood leaking from his sides and sense the agony coming from his broken ribs. And she knew where he was going: the pain had shocked him back to needing the pack, the comfort of the other wolves.

Mate nuzzled the she-wolf as they stopped and watched the other wolf go. Brother never looked back at them.

When the large female looked at the elk herd, they had all smugly returned to grazing.

Exhausted by the failed assault, the she-wolf stretched out in the dirt. Mate, seeking reassurance, curled up next to her.

They fell asleep knowing they were starving.

NINE

Hardy's wife, Droi, knelt by her husband and examined the wound across his chest. She had ministered to it constantly since the injury, applying the special healing mud as directed by Sopho, the Kindred healer. Droi kept the gash clean, turning the hunt master so that the raw scrape from the lion's claws was always facing the sun.

His head injuries, too, she tended, but there was no denying something had happened to her husband. His eyes were wet and rheumy when they regarded her, and he seemed to prefer lying with them closed most of the time. A thin line of drool could often be seen weeping from the corner of his mouth, and when he spoke, his voice sounded strange, as if he were holding his tongue with his fingers. His old wound, the gouge beneath his woman's side eye, had always bothered her, but now seemed laughably trivial in comparison to the obscene sea of slashes in his face.

"Are you sleeping now, husband?" Droi asked. Her formal name called out her long, straight hair, which she wore pulled back from her face and tied with a leather cord like the rest of the Kindred women her age.

Hardy's left eye swam in his head. "Yes," he grunted.

"Do you hurt?" Droi pressed.

The hunt master sighed. That question, every day, often asked once for every finger on his wife's hands. What was he supposed to say? He hurt. He had been bitten in the head by a lion. What did she think, that he liked it?

"I will be fine," he said flatly. "Leave me alone."

Droi turned as a shadow fell across her. She turned and her expression turned unhappy when she saw who it was.

"Leave us," Albi ordered Droi curtly.

Droi inhaled sharply, then stood, raised her head defiantly, and walked away without giving Albi a glance.

Albi watched her departure, then squatted next to Hardy. "You will never return to the hunt," Albi stated matter-of-factly. "You cannot see at any distance, nor can you do good with a spear."

"My vision is improving," Hardy slurred.

"What did you say?"

"I said, my vision is improving."

"You talk like a man who has been eating snow. No one can understand you."

Hardy said nothing.

"So you see pretty well? Your vision is improving?" Albi flicked a hand at him as if to strike his face, and the older man flinched as the open palm suddenly appeared in his field of vision. "No," she said coldly, "it is not. You cannot see. We have not many more days until the cold season. If we depart to the winter settlement without a hunt master, we will starve along the way."

Hardy grunted. His eyes slid away.

"You must make my son hunt master," Albi continued. "He went out with the hunt and they brought back reindeer."

"Palloc." Hardy's gaze turned wetly upon Albi.

"He is the one," Albi told him. "You owe it to me."

Hardy did not respond, his ruined face infuriatingly blank.

"Who do you come to when the nights are cold and your wife's bed is colder? Who will have you now, with the mark of the lion stabbed into your chest, and your face squashed, your eyes bleary? You men think the widows are there for you to use at will, but you will be turned away now. Only I will take you into me."

Hardy inhaled slowly, then exhaled in a long, low sigh.

"Then it is settled," Albi declared. She reached for the wolf pelts that were thrown across Hardy's waist, pulling them away. His slack face regarded her, eyes unfocused. He was hideous, but Albi did not care. So much the better—she really was his only option, now. She seized him with one rough hand, smiling triumphantly. "I see that all of your injuries are above the waist," she noted.

Year Nineteen

The mother-wolf opened her eyes. Her three cubs were in a pile near her—they had just nursed not long ago, and had fallen asleep under the gentle ministrations of her tongue cleaning them after they'd made waste.

The man was coming. She could hear him grunting as he descended from the crack that ran up to the sky, and then there was a louder noise when his feet hit the dirt.

The mother-wolf sighed heavily. The pain in her hips had dulled, but was always present. When she moved, which was seldom, it caused her agony deep inside, but she ignored it because of the pups. She needed to care for her young.

The man brought food and water. She accepted this, and felt affection toward him when he was in her den. Her pups could feel his presence as well—she could sense their awareness—but they took their lead from their mother, and remained content. And, while she was unable to prevent herself from tensing at the fire he brought into the den, she had come to accept this, too. The man was feeding her, and she could not feed herself. These things she did understand.

The instinct-strong love she felt for her young as they nursed also flowed through to feelings for this man feeding her. Because of him, her puppies lived.

Fire licked a yellow light onto the walls, and the man's head appeared. She flapped her tail on the ground, already salivating over the meat she could smell.

"Hey wolf, want some food?" the man called quietly.

The sounds were meaningless to the wolf, but she heard no threat in them, and as the man approached, she wagged harder, then lifted her head. "Here," he offered. His hand was flat, a succulent piece of meat lying there. She licked it off his palm and chewed quickly, watching eagerly as he reached into the fragrant animal skin at his feet and pulled out more chunks. For several moments the only sound was her crunching and the tiny peeps of her cubs reacting to her movements. Finally his hand was empty, though she licked the residual oils from his fingers and then, when he gently touched her forehead, she thumped her tail and licked him again, the same way she groomed her young, feeling the same sort of affection.

From that day on, he stroked her head, and she licked his palm. The first time he reached to pick up one of her puppies she watched alertly, but his hand was coated with her scent and they felt no threat, not even when he lifted them to his face and touched them with his lips.

"You are all such wonderful little babies," he whispered. "I do not know how I am going to do what I need to do, when you get older." His eyes looked into those of the mother-wolf, and she felt no hostility in the gaze. "You will not let yourself die as long as your pups need you. It is the most courageous act I have ever witnessed. I will not kill them until you perish. I could not allow you to see that."

Later, when he set her young back down, they smelled like the man and she did not lick it off. The scent comforted her and, because of that, it comforted her puppies.

They were alive. Her young would grow up healthy and add to the strength of the pack.

All due to the man.

Year One

Calli sat with her feet in the Kindred stream. With the days growing ever more dry, the stream had lost its depth, but also its bracing cold.

Bellu joined her, slipping her own feet in the water and sighing with the pleasure of it. "Soon we leave for the winter settlement," she remarked.

Calli considered this, looking at the cloudless sky and taking a sniff of air, smelling summer smells of warmed grasses and flowers. "Maybe not soon, but before too much longer," she agreed.

"Winter quarters. Weddings," Bellu continued, naming the best part of the Kindred's home during the cold season. Calli raised her eyes speculatively, and Bellu nodded knowingly.

Calli blushed. She still had not told Bellu about Urs.

"Why do you suppose Albi has waited so long to have weddings? It has been several winters gone by. Is she jealous of us because we are young?" Bellu gave her pretty hair an unconscious flip with her hand as she said "jealous."

"No. Albi just holds it back, the way my mother sometimes keeps the fat out of the stew, only to add it when needed."

Bellu's face was completely blank. Calli sighed. "What

I am meaning to say is that Albi knows every woman of fifteen summers longs for a wedding, but she has delayed having one as a way to control our behavior. No single woman will do anything to earn her disfavor."

"So another winter might pass without me getting married?" Bellu demanded, distressed.

"No, I am sure that you and I and Renne, at least, will have the topic of our weddings discussed at council. Watch Albi closely and see if she has private conversations with your mother. Though, to be truthful, I am not sure there is a man I would want," Calli bluffed haughtily. Bellu laughed, seeing right through her. Every young woman their age wanted to get away from their mothers and start their own families.

"Bellu!"

The two young women turned, startled. Ador, Bellu's mother, whose legend said her heart was full of love, was striding toward them, her face tight. "Bellu. Come here right now. It is important!"

Silex glanced at his five companions, sharing a fierce grin with his friend Brach. The reindeer twenty paces away knew of the Wolfen hunters and were lifting their heads and closing ranks, some stamping their hooves.

Silex stood. *Now.* The hunters sprinted toward the herd, spears in each hand, taking aim on the run and letting loose with their throwing arms. One reindeer fell instantly, while two others fled in terror, dragging spears in their haunches.

Silex nodded and two groups of Wolfen split off to follow the wounded animals, one hunter from each group running hard and one moving much more slowly, tracking instead of chasing, conserving energy for when the prey circled back so that the fresh man could finish the kill with his remaining spear.

That left Silex alone with Duro, who had been frowning, even scowling, at Silex for several days, almost childish in his silent dissatisfaction. Silex kept his eyes on the dying reindeer at his feet, feeling Duro next to him. This close, Duro's superior size felt oppressive and threatening, his thick brow turning his whole face into an angry grimace. Silex used his spear against the prey's throat, dispatching the animal while he suppressed a sigh, feeling the other man's eyes burning him. "You wish to say something to me, Duro?" Silex asked quietly.

"We must finish this," Duro stated gruffly. "Ovi will be my mate and I will lead the Wolfen. Your father's authority ceased when his fever turned him into a babbling fool."

Silex turned and looked up at his brutish nemesis, whose face was twitching with strong emotions. The insult about Silex's father was deliberate provocation.

"You are challenging me, then, Duro, my friend?" Silex responded.

"Yes."

Silex, like Duro, was standing with his spear held loosely in his hand. Now Silex turned as if to fully face his adversary, and in doing so smoothly raised his spear tip up until it was just touching Duro's stomach. The taller man paled, turning rigid.

"I am sure you have seen that when the dominant wolf is challenged by other males, punishment is often swift and bloody."

Duro took in a shaky breath, staring at the spear.

"My father always said that among the wolves it is not always the strongest, but rather the most clever, who is the one who mates," Silex continued. "But you would rather fight me now, spear-to-flesh, and decide who is best to lead the Wolfen on that basis?"

Duro looked unhappy with the spear-to-flesh part. "I did not think . . . ," he began in a hoarse whisper, stopping when the point of Silex's spear pressed forward.

"I do agree that you did not *think,* Duro. Do we want the Wolfen led by a man who does not always think?"

Duro licked his lips. Silex lowered his spear, shrugging. "If you wish to challenge me, let us simply ask what the tribe wants. I will not stand in your way."

"But what of Ovi?" Duro asked when he found his voice. "It is not enough for me to lead. I still want to marry your sister, regardless of what your father said."

"I must honor my father's wishes."

"But I want her!" Duro protested.

Silex glanced at him. "Yes, well, that is a problem," he agreed.

TEN

Baffled by Ador's odd behavior, Calli sought out her own mother, Coco, and found her kneeling in the tall, thin reeds that grew in the marshy area upstream where the banks became less disciplined and allowed the water to seep through the soil. Her mother favored the hairstyle of the older women, a simple strap of leather holding her hair back from her face, and not the more elaborate braid preferred by the women of Calli's generation. Her knot, though, had loosened, so that Coco needed to keep pushing the hair out of her eyes. Combined with her bent back, the gesture gave her a weary, old look.

Calli was, she knew, about to embark on the next phase of life—marriage to Urs would change everything. Yet, at that moment, what Calli craved was to be a little girl again, running at her mother's feet while Coco dug for the tender roots she would use in her cooking.

When Coco looked up, Calli joined her—but her mother knew nothing of any significant developments. Worse, she ordered Calli to help gather roots, so that mother and daughter toiled the day away while apparently huge events were taking place back at camp. Calli had never felt so frustrated!

It was not long until dark by the time Calli and her mother, their arms laden with moist roots freshly cleaned in the stream, walked out of the gloom and into the flickering light of the campfires. Bellu had been pacing anxiously, waiting, and dashed forward when the two cooks finally approached.

Coco, of course, insisted that Calli carry the roots to the fire and help arrange them so they would cook in the smoky heat. Only after this final chore did she release Calli. Bellu grabbed her friend's arm. "Come with me."

They went to the women's side, finding privacy in the pooling shadows beyond the light of the fires. "What is it? Has something happened to Albi?" Calli hissed.

Bellu was nearly hopping up and down. "Albi? No, no, but she is very angry."

"Angry?"

"Oh, I hardly know where to start. Where have you been all day?"

From her perspective, Calli could see into the Kindred's camp, and it was a very unusual evening. The men of the hunt had retreated to the men's side and were keeping congress, talking in a circle. Calli could see a few faces, but mostly she saw their backs, while shadows began to form in the firelight as the sun gave up its dominion. Likewise, the women who might normally gather and help Coco were missing, as if they, like Calli and Bellu, had withdrawn into small groups. To discuss what?

"I had to help my mother," Calli replied, unable to keep the bitterness from her voice.

"Well everything has happened."

"Tell me, Bellu!"

Bellu clapped her hands together. "Hardy called the hunt together."

This was going to be a long story, Calli could tell. Bellu loved being the center of attention. Calli bit back her impatience and waited.

"He said he cannot see well enough to be hunt master.

Which everyone *knew*," Bellu announced. "So guess who is the new hunt master?"

Calli frowned. Why was Bellu so excited? Was it one of her brothers? Mentally Calli ticked through them. All were known as good, capable men, but none were said to have the leadership skills required to be hunt master—not even the eldest, Mors, who was stalk master. Her brother Lux, for example, whose legend described a man who was a fierce hunter in daylight, was known to be afraid of the dark. Five brothers in all, they were something of a voting bloc, but Calli doubted they would be able to elevate one of their own kin, or even that they would want to.

"Do you not know?" Bellu pressed.

Well of course she did not *know*. Calli regarded Bellu, who was hugging herself. It was difficult not to resent the way Bellu was doling out information. "Who?" Calli asked a bit flatly.

"It is Urs."

Calli inhaled sharply.

"My brothers came together and said he is the best hunter, and my father said so, and Hardy said so."

Calli's pulse was pounding. *What did it mean?* The hunt master was a man to be reckoned with, even a new one, even someone as young as Urs. If he declared his desire for Calli as his wife, would Albi attempt to block the move? The women's council held sway over marriages, of course, but there was no real *reason* to stop Urs and Calli, not really, not now. Now that Urs was hunt master, it would be a political risk for Albi with no possible gain.

"This," Calli breathed, "this is wonderful."

"Yes!" Bellu spun in a circle. Calli's heart warmed, watching her celebrate. She never thought of Bellu as being particularly perceptive, but perhaps Calli and Urs were more obvious than they had intended. Bellu must be making the same connection: Albi would have a tough time stopping Calli and Urs now.

They would be married.

"And now for the best!" Bellu sang.

"What?" Calli blinked, pulling herself out of her thoughts.

"The best news of all, Calli, the most wonderful, most beautiful, most happy news of the . . . of the sky, of the water, of all the Kindred," Bellu babbled.

"What is it?" Calli asked, baffled.

In the settling gloom, Bellu's dark eyes glinted with joy. "Urs. It is why my family supported him. It is all worked out."

"What is?" Calli asked, her heart suddenly fearful.

"Urs," Bellu repeated. "He and I are going to be married!"

The seductive odor of blood dancing on the air captivated the two wolves, consuming them. They had sustained themselves on mice and large insects but this was real prey. Though weak with the hunger carving at them from within, they drove themselves hard toward the scent, not slowing even when a threatening characteristic—the smell of man—lifted into their nostrils.

Then something else—fire—lent even more danger to their heedless pursuit of food. The large she-wolf felt the resolve of Mate, her male companion, fade. The closer they drew to the scent, the stronger the presence of man and flame tainted the air, and the more tentative Mate's pace. He whined anxiously.

When the mix of odors was substantial, when blood and fire and human were right *there,* the wolves finally halted. Though still out of sight, they could approach no farther without engaging the men—the canids' noses told them there were several of the humans. Mate touched his snout to the she-wolf for reassurance. They circled each other, sniffing, and finally curled up for the night. The empty pain in their stomachs wouldn't let them abandon the blood scent, but they were incapable of pressing any kind of raid.

As she fell asleep, the big female thought of the man who had given her meat once before. She could very definitely find his smell mingled with that of the other humans.

Calli was waiting for Urs at their secret spot, where the rocky boulders provided cover and the long grasses were so soft and inviting. Now yellowed and dry with the changing seasons, the grasses no longer appeared to be a lazy, warm blanket, but Calli could not help but think of Urs as she regarded them from the banks of the stream. She remembered so vividly lying with him on top of her, feeling him move within her, his back hot from the summer sun, his beard touching her face.

And then there he was, tall, slender, and handsome. Moving, to her eyes, with a newfound confidence. The hunt master.

"Urs," she called softly. There was more anguish in her voice than she had intended.

He looked startled, as if they had not arranged this encounter with whispers exchanged by the cooking fires. No, not startled: more guilty, or something.

Calli more than anything needed to feel his arms around her. She flew to him, burying her face in his shoulder.

"Oh Urs," she whispered. "What are we going to do?"

He took a deep breath, holding her back so that he could look into her eyes. He saw the tears in them, and bit his lip. "Calli. Do not cry. Please."

"How did this happen?"

He shook his head. "All I have ever thought about was being hunt master, but I had no idea it would happen so quickly," he murmured.

"Urs!"

He focused on Calli.

"I think that is wonderful," she told him. "I really do. And when I heard, I was sure that it meant we would be together always, because the women's council would never go against the wishes of the hunt master. He could pick his wife. You, Urs, you can do so, you can pick your wife."

His eyes searched hers.

"It is true," she pleaded desperately. "Can you not see? We were afraid that Albi would turn the council against us, but now you are hunt master. When we return to winter camp, we can have our wedding, you and I. Just as we promised."

"But," Urs responded slowly. "What about Bellu's brothers?"

"Listen to me now," Calli said urgently. "Everyone says this is the best choice. You are the one who killed the lion that attacked Hardy. You are the man everyone looks to. Who do you think they would pick? Palloc? *You lead the hunt.* If you say that your heart belongs to me, they will all listen to that. Even the brothers."

Her face was beaming and hopeful now.

"What of the women?" he asked after a moment.

Calli shook her head. "Albi is furious that she had no say in this matter! If you declare your choice now, today, I will go to Albi and suggest to her that this is how she might regain control over what has become a near rebellion. When the council does meet, there will be confusion, but with my mother, and Albi, and me all standing together, we will have no trouble with the women. Believe me, they love to meddle—for them to step in now will give a lot of them something to chatter about all winter long. This will work, Urs! We will be together!"

Urs stared at her. "You think everything through to the end."

It was far from an endorsement of her plan. "You do love me?" Her voice quavered, dreading his answer.

"Yes," he answered firmly. "I love you, Calli. I could never love anyone else."

She gasped her relief into his chest, taking in a shuddering breath, then raised her lips to his. Within seconds their breathing tightened, their hands stroked each other, and an urgency stormed into their blood. They had not managed to find their way together to this spot for many, many days.

When his hands worked their way under her tunic and touched her breasts, she moaned, feeling herself moisten, feeling the tingle start. Her need was wanton and certain and without caution. She tore at his skirt, yanking at it with shaking fingers. She gasped when she finally freed him and saw how ready he was to take her. She fell back, pulling him with her, unable to think, already throbbing. It was fast and hot and urgent. Calli felt the pleasure seize control and peak within her, and then clutched Urs and smiled when he called out and shuddered. This was how it should be. Urs, her love. Husband and wife.

She stroked his hard muscles, his long lean back, gloriously relaxed, now. It was, she decided, as if their passion was lightning and their mating was the thunder—the brighter the flash the more quick and loud the noise that came after, shaking bones, driving out the very breath of a person.

After several moments of just lying there panting, she kissed his face. He seemed dazed. "We will do this again and again," she promised him. "Just like that. As . . . powerful as that, as wonderful as that."

"Yes," he grunted.

"I have never felt this way, Urs."

"I felt weak and strong at the same time."

"Yes! That is it exactly. I love you, Urs. You are the only one for me. I love you and want nothing more than to be married to you."

"I love you and want to marry you, too."

"Then we will do as I have planned."

"All is good. I will tell the council I have changed my mind, that I want to marry you."

"You may be hunt master to the Kindred, but for me, you will always be my master spearman," she said.

They laughed together, pulling their clothing together as the wind licked the sweat from their skin and made them cold.

ELEVEN

Though it had been many days since the hunt had been successful, Palloc still retained some reindeer meat, which he held over his fire on a stick. As food ran low among the Kindred and the families turned to Coco's communal stews and soups, it was considered ill manners to create such succulent odors at one's own home fire, but he was in a foul mood and did not care what anyone thought. With his other hand he stroked his beard, which was a normal dark color and had not paled in the summer sun like the rest of his hair.

"Palloc?" A woman's voice.

His vision blurry from staring into the fire, Palloc frowned as he tried to make out who was calling him from the shadows. He grunted when Renne stepped closer.

"Are you well?" Renne whispered. Her slender build appeared so delicate in that moment, as if she and her shadow were one and the same. She politely squatted next to him by the fire.

"I am well," Palloc replied stonily.

"The hunt made an error. You are spear master. You are a wonderful hunter. It is you who should be hunt master."

Palloc did not react to the compliment. In his opinion, women knew less than nothing about the hunt.

"Urs and Bellu. Engaged," Renne continued. "This means you and Bellu will not be . . . well, I had always heard that the two of you were fated, you and her." Her hand reached out and softly touched his for just a moment. "With Bellu promised to Urs, the council will need to find someone else to be your wife," she whispered demurely.

Numbly, Palloc considered this. Did she really suppose Bellu would marry him? And then he considered Renne. She was being very frank and forward with him, but with her parents dead, she had no one to speak on her behalf but the council, which was notoriously scattered when it came to arranging marriages for the orphaned women of the Kindred. A man without parents might prove himself on the hunt, but a woman in a similar position was no asset as a wife.

She came into focus for him then. Her face flickering and her dark eyes glittering in the strengthening light from the fire. She looked very pretty. And she had picked a flowering vine and tied it around her neck, drawing his eyes to the tanned skin below her throat, where a hollow between her breasts showed above the deer hide vest she wore. Alone among the Kindred, she recognized the great injustice that had been done to Palloc. Calli and Bellu tittered at him with great disrespect, but Renne had never treated him with anything but affection.

Wordlessly, Palloc pulled his meat from the fire. The end of the stick was smoking, the fat spitting. He proffered it in Renne's direction: a man offering a woman food. A clear element of courtship.

Renne drew in her breath. Something—perhaps the thin tendril of smoke curling up from the stick—made her eyes bleary and wet. Blowing on the food, she snatched a morsel from the spear and tossed it from hand to hand to cool it before tearing off a tiny bit with her teeth.

Palloc watched her eat. He felt an inexplicable heaviness in his loins, then, something about Renne's wet lips stirring him. When he moved to bring the stick to his mouth, Renne reached out a hand to stop him. Instead, she leaned forward, passing him the rest of the chunk of reindeer she had ripped off for herself.

Palloc ate from her hand, the fat deliciously mingling with the charred flesh on his tongue. The two of them had their eyes fastened on each other, and it was as if neither dared to speak.

"What is this?" Albi demanded. She came into the circle of light from the fire like a charging bear. "What are you doing here?" she demanded of Renne.

Renne sprang to her feet. She swallowed. "I was only . . ."

"This is my home fire and I did not invite you here," Albi snapped. "Do not come here again."

Far from jumping to Renne's defense, Palloc lay on the ground helplessly, as if pinned beneath a boulder. He said nothing. Renne gave him a desperate look. "I am sorry," Renne apologized.

"Go!" Albi shrieked.

Nodding, Renne backed away three steps, then turned and fled. Albi spun on her son. "You," she hissed.

"We were only—" That was all Palloc managed to say before his mother's foot kicked sharply into his ribs.

"You idiot! *Urs* is hunt master? How does this happen?"

Palloc's lips moved. He massaged the point where his mother's toes had bruised his side. "Well," he finally managed to say.

"I told you after Hardy's injury to act as if the decision had already been made, to help organize the hunt, to direct the men, to lead. Instead you walked around like a pompous fool, telling Urs what, that you were 'pleased with him' and that 'someday he could be spear master'? Do you realize what you have done?"

"It was Bellu, the marriage," Palloc replied, letting his

resentment creep into his words. *Council matters.* The things his mother was supposed to take care of.

"Of course, do you think I do not know that?"

"Well, but can you not fix it?" Palloc reasoned. "Tell them Bellu can only marry me. Then her brothers will shift their allegiance, and I will be hunt master."

"'Her brothers will shift their allegiance,'" Albi repeated in a mocking voice. "Do you think I can defy the new hunt master now? The deal is done."

"But I was supposed to be hunt master," Palloc whined. It was still difficult to believe the prize was being denied him.

Albi looked as if she wanted to kick him again. "You are stupid," she pronounced.

Palloc moodily took a bite of food from the end of his now cool stick. Albi snatched it away from him. Staring at him defiantly, she gnawed at the meat. "All right," she finally pronounced through a mouth full of food. "I have an idea."

"You do?" Palloc replied hopefully.

"I think I know how to undo the mess you have made," Albi said, stripping the last of the reindeer from the cook stick.

Silex was aware that other creeds had become less nomadic in recent times. The River Fish Clan inhabited caves to the north and somehow survived the winter there. The Kindred did migrate, but occupied a speluncean area along a stream all summer before trekking south to parts unknown for the winter. The nonhuman Frightened Ones, elusive and timid, wandered the land in small groups, while the Cohort claimed the river valley as theirs and perhaps, during cold weather, followed the waters to the south end of the world—the Wolfen, like everyone else, did their best to avoid contact with the Cohort, so no one knew if they migrated.

Silex did not give much thought to how the other tribes lived. His people followed the wolf, usually at a run, and the wolf led them to food. Often this strategy meant the women and children were left behind, along with a few men to guard against danger, while Silex and his fleet contingent shadowed the hunting canines.

With several reindeer slain, the Wolfen hunting party was headed back to the families. They were a day or two away, so they stopped well before sunset and made a fire and fed on fresh meat, the men smiling their contentment with the feast. The night was deliciously warm for so late in the summer. As the gloom settled, Silex looked over to the other side of the fire and watched Duro's internal struggle, the larger man's face betraying his emotions.

Now would come the challenge.

Duro grunted and everyone turned to him expectantly, sensing something. "A very important decision is upon us," he announced, sounding nervous.

The men glanced at each other. "About . . . ?" Brach, probably Silex's best friend in the Wolfen, inquired politely.

Duro pursed his thick lips. "Among the wolves, the largest male mates with the largest female," he declared portentously.

Everyone looked baffled at this pronouncement. Duro was glaring at them, waiting for them to get it.

"That is not actually always true," Brach ventured. "We have seen times when it is neither the biggest male, nor the biggest female."

"Still, it is mostly the way," Duro argued.

"Perhaps mostly," Brach conceded. "But I do believe that wolves might sometime select the most clever, or use something else to guide them. Remember, Silex, when we saw that female with the white face?"

"We are talking about what wolves do *most of the time*!" Duro barked.

There was a long silence, the men staring at the fire, all of them fairly apathetic despite Duro's apparent passion for the topic. "Perhaps this is often true," Silex observed. "What Duro has said."

Everyone nodded, glad to have the issue settled.

"I am the largest man. I am older than Silex. Ovi is a well-rounded woman, very healthy, who will bear many strong children," Duro asserted.

The men stared at him in noncomprehension.

Silex cleared his throat. "Duro believes that since my father is dead, we need not follow his wishes any longer. There is perhaps some sense to this."

Everyone except Duro appeared alarmed. "I am the strongest," Duro stated. His scowl invited physical battle with anyone who disagreed.

The man sitting to Brach's left stirred. "Wolf," he said softly.

As one, they looked where he was pointing. Standing just at the boundary between the illumination cast from the fire and the remaining daylight, a large female wolf stood rigid, her amber eyes glowing as she stared at them.

Silex abruptly stood, gesturing for everyone else to remain seated. "Be silent," he urged. He stepped away from the fire. "You are starving," he called to the huge wolf. Time had not been good to her—he could see her ribs, and her skin hung loosely from them. There was no mistaking the handprint-shaped mark between her eyes, though: this was the same she-wolf who had taken tribute from him earlier that summer. "Where is your pack? You are too young to be on your own."

Silex looked back to his tribesmen, who were frozen in place, both awed and frightened. "She is not eating. She is too young and inexperienced to hunt successfully," he told his men. Moving decisively, he bent and picked up the haunch of one of the reindeer. When he glanced at Duro, he saw confusion, though the rest of the Wolfen were gazing at Silex in disbelief.

"Here," Silex offered. He advanced slowly and the large she-wolf tensed. He was unnerved by the way her eyes locked on his, her ears up inquisitively, but he had gone too far with this to turn around. "All is good. This is for you."

Her lips drew back from her teeth. *All right, far enough.* Silex halted, still holding eye contact. He swung his arm and the meat arced toward the large female and she recoiled, scrambling backward.

The men behind him all began speaking at once and Silex viciously chopped the air without looking at them, signaling for silence. He got it. Silex waited, now—he could see the female twenty paces away. She was yawning with tension, unsure.

When she started forward again, Silex nodded encouragement. "For you," he repeated.

The large female managed to close her jaws around the offering without ever breaking eye contact with Silex, appearing ready to flee if he so much as twitched. But when she had it, when she held the meat in her mouth, she gave the Wolfen leader a frank, almost appraising look before turning and dragging the haunch into the darkness.

Silex forced himself to inhale several times, willing his hands to stop trembling. He affected nonchalance as he turned back to the fireside, pretending not to notice the reverential stares from his men. This night would be legend.

"Now, Duro, what were we talking about?" Silex asked lightly.

Assessing Duro's scowl, Silex realized the next challenge would not be verbal.

TWELVE

Year Nineteen

The mother-wolf heard the man leaving through the hole that went to the sky. His scent carried with it some of the marmot meat he had recently eaten, and for a moment there was a slight increase in the smoky odors always present in the downdraft—she couldn't know that as he scaled upward, the man was dislodging soot left from his cave fires, sending a fine black powder wafting on the air.

Usually the man's scent faded entirely on days such as these, but she was drowsily aware that he was still up there, somewhere, close enough for his smell to come to her in a steady flow.

She was now so accustomed to his presence that she easily fell back to sleep, but her eyes jerked open when she heard him making noises. "Run! Wolves! *Run!*" There was an alarm in his sounds, and the fur on the back of her neck rose, her body stiffening. Though slumbering, her pups reacted, instinctively moving closer to her with soft peeps.

"No!"

The mother-wolf remained on uneasy alert, tense, wondering what was happening.

Year One

Albi determinedly strode toward Urs, her stick thumping audibly. His stomach felt as if he were digesting bad meat when he saw her. Now what? He had to brace himself against the impulse to flee to the protection of the men's side of camp.

"Hunt Master," she greeted evenly.

He nodded warily.

"The weather is turning dry and cold. Though it would be somewhat early, I believe it is time to prepare for our move to winter quarters. We do not want to be caught in the snows, and it would seem they want to descend upon the Kindred hastily this year. We should leave in just one handful of days."

He was surprised. In his opinion, it was really the women who decided when they were to move, as the men instinctively knew that if their wives were not ready to go, the husbands could not make them. The women did all the labor anyway, hauling children and the animal skins, as well as dried berries and roots. The men carried their weapons. But such an important decision was obviously best made with the hunt and the council working together. Hunt master was a job he needed to learn while simultaneously doing it.

"You are right," he grunted.

She eyed him. "So what are you going to do, Hunt Master?" she asked.

Calli and Bellu, walking together, strode by on the other side of the camp, both of them staring at him. Suddenly the question *What are you going to do?* carried more than one meaning. His whole *life* was teetering on that question. It was too much and he turned away from the two women even as Bellu raised her hand and smiled. "It is time to hunt," Urs said decisively. "We go tomorrow."

Out on the hunt, away from Kindred, he could contemplate, figure things out.

What are you going to do?

Year Nineteen

Gya's family stayed behind because his woman was set to give birth. None of his children were old enough to hunt with him on their own. So, though it was unusual for him to hunt without his mate and her brothers, Gya was by himself, tracking reindeer through a treed area near a small stream. He held a spear and was advancing steadily toward his prey—a young reindeer who had strayed just a few paces away from its mother, munching steadily on new spring grasses.

When Gya sensed he was being watched, he looked up and saw someone standing on the top of a small rock bluff, many paces distant. It was a member of what Gya's creed called the Horde—the tribes of smaller, odd-looking beings who moved in such large numbers, unlike Gya's people, who formed units based on family and rarely comingled with others of their kind. Gya had never seen a lone Horde before, and stared. The Horde-man stared back.

There was no threat, so, after a moment, Gya turned back to the task before him. He crept slowly forward, hiding in the grasses, until he was well within spear range. When he stood, it was in a smooth, unhurried motion that caught the herd's attention but did not scatter them.

He heaved his weapon and followed through on his throw by picking up a rock all in one movement, launching himself at his target, which had frozen in shock when the spear caught it in the neck. Now it turned away but Gya was on it, seizing the reindeer by the antler and clubbing at it with the rock. The reindeer bucked wildly, trying to shake the hunter off, but Gya's hold was fiercely strong. The wound bled hot and in profusion, and the blows to its head stunned the animal. After dragging Gya twenty paces its knees buckled and hunter and prey fell to the ground together.

Gya grunted but held on, evading the reindeer's kicking hooves. When the animal halted its struggle, he leaped to his feet, withdrew his spear, and finished the kill.

Gya rubbed his shoulder. A pain had flashed through him when the reindeer fell on him, and now his right arm moved stiffly, something grating inside. Still, he would feed his family.

When he had caught his breath, Gya seized the back legs of the dead reindeer and began dragging it away. He had not gone far at all when he heard a noise—a human shout.

He had forgotten about the Horde-man. Gya looked up. The small man was still on the rock, but was waving his arms now, waving them at Gya, his yelling barely audible across the distance. "Run! Wolves! *Run!*"

Gya stared. The Horde did not speak the Language, so there was no sense to what was being said, nor really anything Gya would call "words." Just sounds, but they nonetheless seemed to convey alarm, somehow. The Horde-man was still gesturing wildly.

Gya could make no sense of any of it. It was strange enough that a member of the Horde would be alone, but that he was trying to communicate with Gya was unprecedented. Was he angry that Gya had taken prey so close to where he stood? Did the Horde-man live in the rocks? The Hordes were hostile people who attacked without provocation.

Gya was still pondering this and the Horde-man was still

shouting when a ghost of movement caught his eye. He whirled, sucking in a breath.

Six grey wolves, coming straight at him, moving fast. Gya gripped his spear and shouted, baring his teeth, full of fear and rage. His first impulse, that he could not abandon his kill, that he needed the meat for his family, froze him in place, which gave the wolves time to close the distance. By the time he decided to run the wolves had committed to taking him.

The injury in his shoulder caused his throw to go wide and Gya was unable to spear a single wolf before they caught him, hitting him high and low. He fought them but they were savagely strong, their jaws crunching his bones, and Gya's screams were quickly extinguished.

Gya was still struggling when he lost consciousness. His last thought, oddly, was for the lone Horde-man still shouting up on the rocks—could he have been trying to warn Gya about the wolves?

Year One

The Kindred migrated by following their stream as it meandered south, but their path was never precisely the same from year to year because they also tracked migrating herds of ungulates. At about midpoint, they came to the place where their tribal stream joined the much larger river. The confluence held grave significance—their territory lay between their stream and this river, so now it was as if they had run out of land.

From here the waters turned and flowed into a wide, fertile valley. The herds of deer and elk might follow the river but the Kindred could not—that land belonged to the Co-hort. And now, at the rim of the river valley, the tribe moved silently, carefully placing their footsteps. Mothers held their babies to their breasts—older children who were too small to understand found a parent's hand clamped over their mouths. The hunt stayed close and alert, clutching their spears. The slightest sound from anyone drew angry glances.

No one knew what would happen if their trespass was detected by the Cohort.

Calli carried her burdens without complaint, her eyes on Urs's back as he led the Kindred. She was so proud to see him in front and in command. He had managed to avoid her during the entire trek, but he had not spoken to Bellu, either—Bellu was both vocal and bitter about that.

"Perhaps," Calli had suggested to her friend a few days before, "he does not want to spend time conversing because he has many important decisions to make."

"The most important decision has already been made," Bellu had pointed out loftily.

Bellu's brothers had the honor of guarding the rear, though it seemed something of a challenge to be walking backward. Vent, in particular, could not seem to master the technique. They were a full two days past the river junction when Vent tripped over a root and went sprawling. Nix, Bellu's youngest brother, was next to him, and began giggling, unable to stop even when he jammed his own fist into his mouth. Soon all of Bellu's brothers were snorting, trying to hold it in, and then laughter swept through the Kindred. No one had ever seen sign of the Valley Cohort this far south. They were safe.

Bellu ran to Urs and threw her arms around him, and he hugged her back. Calli approached, hands spread, and first hugged Bellu, and then Urs, and then nearly everyone in the tribe—but it was the feel of Urs's strong body pressed up against her that she remembered.

That night, Pex, Bellu's father, invited Urs to their family fire. The Kindred had fresh reindeer meat from a recent kill, and the good feeling of having eluded the Cohort made them merry.

Calli helped her mother prepare the communal meal for the widows and orphans who did not have a man involved in the hunt. When a roar of approving laughter rose behind her, she turned and saw Urs kissing Bellu—or at least, she was kissing *him,* leaning far forward on her hands and knees, thrusting her face at him. From Calli's position, Urs looked trapped. Yet the kiss went on, Bellu's brothers all yelling, long after Urs should have broken it off.

Calli gasped in a breath. She had not realized she was weeping.

"Let go of this," Coco murmured beside her. Calli turned and cried harder when she saw the sympathy in her mother's eyes.

"He is promised to marry Bellu. It is settled," Coco said.

"He is promised to *me,*" Calli corrected fiercely. But even as she said it, Urs pulled his lips away from Bellu and stared into his betrothed's beautiful face, his eyes shining, an expression Calli had seen many times, always directed at her. He reached for Bellu and they kissed again, to much hooting from her brothers. Finally, Ador, Bellu's mother, reached out and good-naturedly broke the couple apart, shaking a mock-warning finger at Urs, clearly telling him to wait until after the wedding.

Coco seized Calli's shoulders. "Calli, what did you think, that the two of you could do whatever you want? That is not the way."

"Why not?" Calli grated. "What would be the harm?"

"It just is not the way."

Calli looked back at Urs. He and Bellu were kissing again.

Year Nineteen

The mother-wolf's vision swam in a thick blur when she opened her eyes. She felt and smelled, rather than saw, her pups, who though blind were now able to move around in the den and did so with great enthusiasm, squeaking as they bumped into each other.

They drew back in alarm from unexpected noises, such as the man's feet landing on the floor of the crevice when he returned to the cave, but his touch and smell alleviated their fear—the mother-wolf could feel them take comfort when he held them.

He was there. She smelled him, and could make out his shadow as he crouched over her head. He had a tension about him, and she could smell a change in his sweat. She twitched her tail in greeting, her ears back.

"I saw something just now. A Frightened One—they are the strange clan who look like us but who are not human. They speak, but do not voice intelligible words." He audibly inhaled. "The Frightened was hunting alone and he charged a herd of reindeer and speared one and then jumped on it and clubbed it. One Frightened, on his own, took down a reindeer."

The mother-wolf, blinking, could see the man more clearly. He was not looking at her; he had picked up one of the pups—the largest one, the female—and was staring at the puppy intently. So comfortable was the little wolf that she fell asleep in his hands.

"I could never do that; I am not fast enough, not strong enough. And then . . . and then some wolves caught him. I saw them coming and tried to warn him, but I do not believe he understood. He died with courage: he was resolute. But it was horrible to watch."

He made a shuddering noise. "I cannot lose sight of

what you are. I must accept what is true. It is a human's way to kill animals, and it is the wolf's way to kill humans. Nothing can change that. I do not want to die like the Frightened."

THIRTEEN

Year One

The turning point in the Kindred migration was marked by their arrival at the Blanc Tribe settlement. These were people who never went north in the summer nor south in the winter, but seemed content to remain camped on the shore of an enormous lake. Like the River Fish Clan, they used nets to pull fish from the waters, but they also hunted whenever the beasts of the plains were nearby.

They were also very odd looking. Their eyes were pale, their hair and skin yellowish. They had been asked many times why they appeared so abnormal, but they did not know. They were like Palloc and his mother, Albi, in that way—no one could explain it. The Blanc did have a few children with normal dark eyes and brown skin, and no one could explain that, either.

Urs, as hunt master, offered some reindeer meat to the Blanc, and they, in turn, proffered fish—the only time the Kindred ever sampled such odd flesh was on these migrations. Some claimed to like it, but most of the Kindred thought the stuff tasted strange. The Blanc also ate the green plants from their lake, which as far as the Kindred were concerned were bitter tasting, and hunted birds that floated on the water.

Long ago, before Albi was born, her mother had broken her leg on the trek south. Albi's mother was tended to by the Blanc Tribe and ultimately had spent the winter with them, while her husband went on with the rest of the Kindred. When they returned the woman's leg had set, though she never walked without a limp after that. Soon after returning to the summer settlement, Albi was born. Perhaps, it was speculated, all the fish her mother had eaten that winter was what turned her baby's hair and skin so white. At age three, during her naming ceremony, Albi's mother-in-law, the oldest woman in the family, gave the child the formal name of Albine Pallus, "Her Colors Are the Palest Shade of White." The short form, Albi, was the only name of its kind.

No one knew why the Kindred always came to the Blanc, whose settlement was a little out of the direct path to the winter quarters—it was just done. And no one knew why the tribes were so friendly, or why they offered food to each other. Out on the plains, tribes did their best to avoid one another. But here with the Blanc, their children mingled and played, the men threw their spears at a tree and boasted over who could impale the wood from the farthest distance, and the women complimented each other on their babies. Of particular interest were the shiny shells the Blanc traded for food, bear teeth, and other Kindred wares. They were fragile and beautiful and highly prized by everyone in both tribes. Both the men and women of the Blanc tribe wore small shells in their hair, making them appear even more exotic.

Calli had spoken little to anyone since her mother confronted her, and now, instead of joining the social interactions, she withdrew to a place where she could watch moodily.

After a time, she concluded that the Blanc did not know

how strange they looked because no person ever really contemplated how they themselves appeared—they only saw other people in their tribe, catching a glimpse of their own faces when they bent over still water. In the Kindred, only Bellu thought it necessary to gaze at herself in reflecting pools every day. So, while the Blanc must think that the others in their tribe were odd looking, they probably thought of themselves personally as normal, forgetting that they did not have dark eyes.

This was, Calli reflected, the sort of thing that she was good at figuring out, and as wife of the hunt master, she might have provided wise counsel to her husband.

But now, she knew, that would never happen.

The Wolfen hunters had been jubilant to return to their tribe, camped along the east banks of the river. In theory, they were safe here—the River Fish Clan were well to the north, and the Kindred usually only ventured as far as the western banks—their recent trespass was both unusual, forced by hunger, and confined to a limited area far south of this encampment. The Wolfen did, however, have scouts out on the plains to watch for the Valley Cohort.

The men with mates were eager to spend time with their wives, and everyone wanted to talk about Silex's astounding commune with the female wolf. In the retelling, she was the size of a bear, and had understood every word Silex had spoken to her.

Silex watched as the person he most cared about—Fia, a beautiful woman a year younger than Silex—listened to Brach's version of the tale. When everyone turned astonished stares at their leader, Fia realized he was watching her, and her expression became almost haughty. She deliberately glanced away. "The big female has a mate, but they are far too young to be on their own. They have not yet learned to hunt. I worry they will not survive the winter," Silex told them, wishing Fia would look at him.

Harvesting had gone well, with many fat berries and pine nuts to supplant the hunt's take. The Wolfen ate in imitation of the wolves who were their benefactors, so Silex and his betrothed, Ovi, were solemnly presented with a meal first, as befitting their rank.

Alone with Ovi, Silex gazed at her, thinking all that Duro had said was true: she was ample of bosom and nicely hipped, rare attributes in the tribe. The fact that she was allowed to eat while lower-ranked women might be forced to skip a meal from time to time probably had something to do with her fecund figure. Ovi's face was pleasant, though a subtle, dour pull at the corners of her mouth undid much of what Silex might otherwise find attractive.

Fia's mouth was usually turned up, flashing her smile, and her skin glowed in the summer, as if it took in the sun's heat and then emitted it like a stone placed by the fire. She was muscular and thin and nothing like Ovi—yet it was Ovi he was to marry.

"Ovi. It has been very nice to spend time with you. We will go out hunting again tomorrow or the next," Silex told his sister.

Ovi sighed. "Winter. It will soon be cold again."

"That is true," Silex agreed. He watched her eyes, which were not meeting his. "Ovi," he finally said.

"Yes, Silex."

"While on the hunt, Duro challenged my leadership. He said he is bigger and that he should be leader."

"That is not how it is to be," Ovi replied simply.

"Yes. But with father dead, Duro feels I am open to challenge."

"He is wrong."

"He also said he wants you, Ovi. Duro. He wants to marry you."

Silex did not know what sort of reaction he expected, but Ovi only shrugged.

"How do you feel about that?" he pressed.

"Feel?" Ovi looked away, as if the answer lay out on the horizon somewhere. Her expression was maddeningly apathetic. "I am to marry you, Silex."

"The thought seems to make you feel sad," Silex stated pointedly, though in fact the thought seemed to make Ovi feel *nothing*.

"It is what is to be," she answered.

"Ovi, what would happen if I were killed on the hunt?" Silex continued, resisting the urge to shout at her. "Who would you marry then?"

For the first time Silex thought he saw a flicker of life in her eyes, but her answer was pure Ovi. "I suppose I would then marry whoever became leader of the Wolfen. It does not really matter."

"So that is how you see yourself? You would just mate with the next man?"

"It is what is to be," she sighed. "The dominant wolves mate."

Silex stood. "We are not wolves, Ovi. We are humans who follow the ways of the wolf, but we are not wolves. You do not have to marry me if you do not want to do so."

She gave him a bland look. "I never said I would not marry you, Silex. We were both there when our father died. We both heard what he said. I accepted it then and I accept it now."

Winter snapped at the Kindred on their migration, icy temperatures blowing in on stiff winds, unusually early. The Kindred pulled out their furs and wrapped themselves as best they could, their heads down as they plodded south. They bound their feet with elk hide for walking in snow, and at night used rabbit pelts, fur side in, to keep their toes warm.

After the fifth day of cold, there was relent, the sun gaining strength. The mood of the Kindred lifted, particularly when the hunt came across a large herd of reindeer and managed to bring down two of them after only half a day's chase.

Urs was a good hunt master, everyone said so. He accepted their congratulations with real gratitude, though in his stomach he felt a fraud. He had not known that the herd was there, moving slowly south. The hunt just stumbled upon it by accident. Urs had been about to steer everyone off in a different direction, just to have something to say to the men who looked to him for all the answers. If he had, they would be hungry, living on what little was left from a kill eight days ago.

Urs knew what no one else knew: he should not be hunt master. He remembered the passionate declarations he had made to Calli, stating so confidently that if he were in charge of the hunt he would send the stalkers out to find game, even though it meant risking contact with the Cohort, because that was how Kindred had always hunted before Hardy changed the rules. Yet now that he was the leader, Urs was unsure, questioning his own choices on everything, and was doing everything Hardy's way. But Hardy had always known how to find game. Urs did not.

Seeking advice was out of the question: Urs could not understand anything Hardy said, the former hunt master's words sliding out of his mouth in a mangled slur.

Urs stared out at the rolling grasslands, making a decision. "Mors," he called, gesturing.

The stalk master, Mors (Morsus, whose legend told of his

unfortunate habit of biting his siblings) hustled to Urs's side. Mors, like all stalkers, carried a club instead of a spear, and was known to be fast on his feet. Since Hardy had pulled the stalking men out of the role of scouting for prey, Mors and his men fulfilled one role, which was to chase down wounded animals. And even in that they were hardly special; the whole hunt joined the pursuit now, so that they would all be safe together. Yet Mors had never once complained, unlike Palloc, who as spear master was petulant about everything.

"We are far from the Cohort Valley. Safe from their raiding parties," Urs declared to the stalk master.

Mors nodded agreement, pulling thoughtfully on his beard, which was black and full. Like his sister Bellu, his four brothers, and his mother Ador, Mors had unusually thick hair, though it was scraggly as any man's; not at all as attractive as his sister's.

"So from this point forward, the stalkers will go out and search for game and report back to the hunt, as it used to be done," Urs told him.

Mors's face broke into a delighted grin.

"You have been wanting this, but have said nothing to me," Urs guessed.

Mors nodded happily.

Their conversation was interrupted by a cry from Palloc: "Go!" the spear master yelled.

Urs turned and watched, astounded, as nearly his entire contingent of spearmen took off running, weapons raised. Only Valid, Urs's good friend from childhood, remained behind. "What is happening?" Urs demanded as Valid trotted to where Mors and Urs were standing.

"Wolves," Valid said.

"What?" Urs snapped. "What do you mean, 'wolves'?"

Valid spread his hands. "There were a couple of young

wolves out there, pretty close. Palloc gathered his spearmen and went after them. He said he was going to keep one pelt and give the other to the man with the truest aim."

"We are not here to chase after fur," Urs grated. "We have no time for this." He turned to Mors. "Take two of your fastest men and go after them and tell them I want them to return *now*."

Mors nodded and left instantly.

"We need food. We do not lack for *garments*," Urs seethed.

Valid shrugged. "They probably have already killed the wolves and will be back soon."

"Then I will make Palloc and the spearmen eat the wolves," Urs vowed. "That will teach them." Urs turned and scanned the low hills around him, waiting for the spearmen to return with the wolf carcasses.

FOURTEEN

The large she-wolf and Mate were shadowing a herd of reindeer, watching, hoping to find an opening, when they smelled the humans and then the blood. It was all so similar to the encounters she'd had before; she felt drawn forward toward the men and their meat, though once again it broke the male's nerve and he hung back, afraid.

This time none of the scents was familiar. They were strangers, which was why the she-wolf was so wary even as she deliberately approached the humans. She stood rigid, waiting to see what would happen.

The humans gathered, much like reindeer coming together in a defensive bunch, but then with a loud noise they ran directly at her. For a brief moment she froze, staring at the face of the man at the front of the pack of charging humans, and then she bolted, running for the trees, Mate streaking out of the grasses to take to her side.

She registered the spears hitting the ground around them without understanding what they were. The wolves could hear the pursuit behind them and so they unquestioningly fled from it, easily getting away once the first volley of weapons missed their targets.

The face. She had sensed the humans' aggression, sensed it the way she and the pack could feel the pain in an aging elk or the weakness of a new, undernourished calf. Even before the chase began she knew something was radically different about these men, and it had something to do with their faces. The memory of the human who gave her meat now came strongly to her mind, and the contrast between the expressions, the set of the eyes and the brows and the tightening of the mouths, was real and significant.

Not all humans would feed them. Some would hunt them.

Though they referred to their winter habitat as a "settlement," in truth the Kindred were fairly peripatetic throughout the cold season, moving from one familiar area to another in search of food. None of these campsites was as comfortable as their summer quarters: fire pits lined with rocks licked black by generations of smoke, crude depressions where the earth had been scooped out to allow a family to sleep, thin branches and curved mammoth bones supporting animal hides arrayed over these hollows to protect from the worst of elements. Still, the Kindred always divided their camps into the men's side on the right, the women's side on the left, and the communal area in between.

By tradition, the winter camp was where the Kindred held their weddings, just as the summer settlement was where they named their children, and in the same ceremony performed the rite of passage, declaring boys of fourteen summers to be men, and girls who had started their cyclical bleeding to be women.

"Who else will be involved in the marriage celebration this winter?" Bellu pressed Calli eagerly. Calli deflected such obvious gambits by pointing out that the women's council had not yet met to discuss weddings. No one yet knew what Albi might say of Bellu and Urs's nuptials. It represented one last, dim hope for Calli—that Albi would challenge the wedding, slamming her stick down and thundering that the informal tradition of mothers discussing their children's fates had grown into a vulgar political power swap that the council must reverse.

"Urs told me that he spoke harshly to Palloc for chasing some wolves," Bellu confided to Calli in tones to indicate she was sharing a great secret.

"Everyone knows of that," Calli replied with a snap to her tone that Bellu blithely missed.

"Yes," she agreed cheerfully, "but Urs told *me*."

Calli announced she needed to find moss, and Bellu nodded with a sunny smile as Calli left. "Find moss" was a woman's way of saying she was beginning her regular menstruation—a roll of moss served to absorb the blood, though a small wad of rabbit fur was a fairly close substitute. Women who left to find moss were given their privacy, though younger males were usually mystified by the expression.

Her path took her near her mother's fire, where she saw Albi and Coco in deep discussion. The sight gave her pause—there was an odd intensity to the conversation. Calli wondered what the two of them could possibly be talking about.

That evening, the only food for the Kindred was a soup made from the meat clinging to the bones of the last reindeer they had taken, plus some roots Coco had carried from their summer quarters. There had not yet been any rain; it was the driest winter anyone could remember.

Palloc found his mother squatting by their home fire. Somehow, she had managed to procure a large handful of reindeer fat for herself, and was sucking it off a clean stick.

Palloc took a breath. "I need to speak to you, Mother," he said.

She fixed him with a baleful look. "Why do you say it like that? What foolish thing are you about to demand of me?"

Palloc glanced away. He despised that she always seemed to be ahead of him. "I need to speak to you about Renne."

"Her? I will not waste my words on her."

Palloc squatted next to his mother. He reached for some fat, cooking slowly on a rock by the fire, but she slapped his hand away. "As council mother, you can help me with my choice of who to marry," Palloc began.

"Yes. That is my choice to make," Albi responded.

He hesitated. That had not been what he meant. "I am saying that if I, your son, came to you and told you I favored a woman, you would be able to tell the council that she and I are to marry. Especially if she has no mother alive, so that the council negotiates her marriage for her."

Albi stared at the fire for a moment, as if she had not even heard him. Palloc fidgeted uncomfortably. "Mother . . ."

"I know what you have been doing with her," Albi said. "You think you are clever, the way you sneak off together. You have been fornicating with her outside of marriage. *That* is what I could tell the council."

Palloc swallowed. "Well, not outside of marriage if she becomes my wife."

"Your wife is to be Calli Umbra."

"What?"

"That is what has been decided. I told you I was working on a plan. Calli is smart, and the women have been thinking she would be a good council mother. I have promised her mother I will support such a move, but in five years. That neutralizes her as a threat for now. But it also keeps the power in our family."

"That is your plan? That, that is not any sort of plan! The plan was to make me hunt master," Palloc sputtered.

"You are a fool who copulates with a low-status girl, when you could have been married to Bellu and been hunt master. I need to protect myself. If you do not see how this also is good for you, you are as blind as old Hardy."

"I will not marry Calli," Palloc snapped back. "She of all women treats me with the least respect. I hate her."

"Would you please not say so many stupid words? You make my ears ache. Once she is your wife, she will be forced to treat you with respect. *You* will force her—do you think you can manage to do at least that, Spear Master? If you cannot, your mother will come into your marriage and do it for you."

"I am in love with Renne."

"Then keep fornicating with her, I do not care!" Albi roared back. "That is where you just were, is it not?"

Palloc could not meet her eyes and looked down.

"No one else will have her, she is an orphan who cannot even make a decent rope. So do what you want. But you will marry Calli. It is the only way I will stay council mother."

Palloc shook his head. "For five years," he pointed out scornfully. "And then you will depend on me for food and wish you had found a way to make me hunt master."

"I have no intention of stepping down in five years, you stupid hyena," Albi snarled. "But this assures I will not be challenged in that time. Now do you understand?"

Palloc sneered. "So this is a plan to benefit you, then. You marry me off for your good, not mine." He stood. "I was but one step behind Urs when he killed that lion. If not for that, he would never have been made hunt master. Even now, he is hesitant and unsure—everyone, not just me, can see that."

"Now is not the time for a direct challenge," Albi informed him. "The hunt hates change, and Bellu's family, as a voting bloc, is simply too powerful. How a woman as stupid as Ador can manage to be the only mother in the Kindred to have all of her boys survive to adulthood is a mystery, but there it is."

Later that night, lying under his elk hide and trying to stay warm as the cold winds shrieked and threatened to blow out the fires, Palloc reflected on his mother's words, black fury in his heart. Maybe he had his own plan. Maybe he did not need her help. It would be easy, as spear master, to find times out on the hunt to be alone with the hunt master. Palloc would watch for such an opportunity, and when it came, he would strike.

He would kill Urs the hunt master.

FIFTEEN

Renne was bent over her rope when she saw the stick.

To anyone watching casually, she was spending the final hours before nightfall practicing her craft, clearly intent, seriously focused, and not easily interrupted. No one bothered to examine her closely or long enough to see that she was less bowed over her materials than folded in a cramp, her eyes closed, her fingers moving on her strip of hide without accomplishing anything other than appearances.

Palloc had come to her, had mated with her, and then had stood up and abruptly told her it was to be the last time they could be together. When, in her shock, she begged him to explain, he became cross and turned away without a word.

She sat cross-legged and her legs were wet from her tears. She was still bent over when the thick end of a walking stick thumped the ground in front of her.

Renne looked up, blinking. Albi towered over her, her face unreadable but her voice kind. "Come with me, child," she said in low, sympathetic tones.

Nodding, Renne scrambled to her feet, wiping her eyes with a hasty hand. Albi's cane, a thick rod as big around as a man's arm, came down with every step as they walked out of camp, toward the low hills and shrubs that offered some privacy.

Renne found her heart pounding. Albi was silent, offering

no clue as to the purpose of their hike. Where were they going? It was late afternoon, not a prime time for predators like lions, but not the safest time to be out, either. To stray so far from camp made Renne nervous.

They were now in the low hills, completely out of sight of the camp.

Albi stopped and surveyed the area. Nothing growing here yet—the rains had been nonexistent. They stood on the remnants of last year's grasses, clipped short by the deer whose tracks still scored the earth. Albi nodded, satisfied about something. "I understand," she began, "that for women of your age, it is not enough that the council has graciously begun to listen to mothers in accommodation when a marriage is suggested. I even allowed Ador to approach Urs directly about him marrying Bellu, bypassing the council as if its blessing is a mere formality. And still, you want more. You want women and men to make decisions on their own, defying the Kindred way of life. Is that right?"

Renne found she was weeping. "Council Mother," she began helplessly.

"You want to marry my son, and he wishes the same," Albi continued tonelessly.

Renne nodded, wildly hopeful.

"You are in love."

"Yes."

Albi picked absently at a grey hair growing from her chin, looking deep in thought. Renne held her breath, waiting. The council mother shifted her grip on her pole and examined it, holding it as men held their spears.

"So," Albi finally said. She drove the walking stick straight into Renne's stomach. With a cry, Renne doubled over. Albi stepped forward. *Crack.* The rod clubbed Renne on the head and she pitched to the ground, her face slamming into the dirt. Albi raised her stick and viciously jabbed Renne in the ribs.

Renne screamed. She rolled onto her side and drew her knees to her chest, wrapping her arms around her head.

"Look at me," Albi said, eerily calm. Renne, sobbing, kept her eyes closed and her face hidden. "Renne. Look at me. Please."

Bewildered, Renne lifted her head. The club whistled and smashed into her bleeding face, a tooth dislodging with the impact. Renne screamed again, spitting blood.

After a moment, Renne managed to make it onto her hands and knees. Her head hung low, thick blood seeping from her mouth, and she wailed, terrified.

For several minutes nothing happened. Renne, shuddering, managed to stop sobbing. She probed the soft, broken area in her jaw where the tooth had been, she pressed a hand to the gash on her cheek.

When Albi knelt beside her, Renne flinched. "Renne," Albi said softly. "Look at me."

Renne was not going to look at her.

"I will not strike you again. That is over. Look at me now."

Raising her arm to protect her face, Renne risked peeking at the council mother with one eye. The stick lay on the ground next to them.

"You will have nothing further to do with my son. You will stop interfering with the will of the women's council. What is done is done. He would never marry someone like you, and for you to offer yourself to him outside of marriage is a trick that will never work. Instead of throwing yourself at him, you should get pretty and attract the affections of someone who is available. As council mother, I can help you to this end."

"I love Palloc," Renne grated.

Albi laughed—an ugly, insulting noise. "Oh child. *Love.* Look what love has gotten you." For emphasis, Albi reached out a thick finger and drove it into the split in the scalp at the back of Renne's head. Renne yelped with the pain. "No, true love is what the council decides, and I decide for the council." Albi stood up. "I am glad we were able to have this conversation, Renne. I would suggest you get back to camp as soon as you can stand—the scent of your blood will draw the wolves."

Few women walked right up to the invisible line that marked the men's side of the settlement. Some sort of buffer zone existed, unseen, but there by tradition. Only an angry wife, calling to her husband to return to the home fire, might approach so close that her voice could be heard by the hunt as the men congregated.

It was after the meager supper when Calli invaded the buffer zone and stood with her feet virtually resting on the border that marked the men's side. "Urs!" she cried urgently. "Please, I need to talk to you!"

The murmur of conversation around the men's fire ceased. Urs rose, every man's eyes upon him, and made his way stiffly toward where Calli waited.

"Calli," he whispered as he approached. "Please, you cannot come to our side and call for me. I do not know what they are thinking, now."

"It is urgent we speak!"

"Come with me," Urs ordered grimly, turning and marching away so quickly that Calli almost had to run.

They strode silently out of camp, not speaking until they were out of sight. Then Urs stopped and turned to her.

"Oh Urs," Calli sobbed, collapsing onto him. Tears ran down his chest as she wept brokenly, and after a time his bearing lost its stiffness, and his arms came up to awkwardly embrace her.

"Calli, I do not know what, why you are crying. But please stop. Tell me."

"Urs, I have been promised to Palloc."

His face opened wide with shock. *"What?"*

She nodded. "My mother just told me. It is to be arranged that I marry Palloc, and then, in five years' time, Albi announces for me as council mother."

"Council mother," Urs repeated. He nodded slowly. "This will be very good for you."

"Urs!" she shouted at him. "I have to *marry Palloc*."

His face became very serious. He held her by the shoulders, staring into her face. "Calli. Listen to me. We cannot fight this."

"What? What? Are you not hearing me? Is that what you want, for Palloc, of all men, to marry me? To take your place in my bed? To give me the children who should be yours?"

"Of course it is not what I want," Urs snapped. "Nothing is happening the way I *want*. But the council has decided, just as the hunt decided to make me hunt master. For the good of all, for the Kindred, it is not up to us to make our own decisions. This is the way it has always been."

Calli stared at him with hot eyes. "It is because she is beautiful," she finally said in a flat whisper.

Urs flinched as if she had slapped him.

"That is it, right? Bellu is so beautiful. You said you would always love me, but this was before you realized you could mate with *her*," Calli spat.

"No, how can you say such a thing? Do you not understand what has happened? I have been made hunt master. Hardy cannot tell me anything, his words are incomprehensible, so all the decisions I make are on my own. I have to focus on finding prey, on a successful hunt. Matters of marriage have always been left to the women and I cannot compromise my position by attempting to interfere!"

Calli took a deep, shuddering breath, feeling a sour apathy seep into her heart. Somehow, none of this surprised her.

"It is very ironic, is it not?" Calli murmured softly. "You hunt master and me council mother. With such power, no one could deny us if we were to announce that we were to be wed. It would be done with our simple statement, and at the winter weddings, my mother would hand me to you and the Kindred would watch in joy."

Urs frowned. "But you said five years," he began dubiously.

"Oh Urs, do you really think I am saying this is what we should do *now*? I was just . . ." He would not, she suddenly understood, ever get her point, here. She shook her head. "Do you love me, Urs?" she asked abruptly.

He looked uncomfortable. "Yes," he replied. "Of course. But Calli . . ."

"Oh no, Urs. Please." Calli pressed her fingers to his lips, her voice barely a murmur. "Do not tell me anything but that. You love me."

"I do, but now things . . ."

"Shhhh," she said. She pulled at the knot on her hip, dropping her skirt away. "You love me."

His eyes were large. "Yes," he replied automatically. "I love you."

It was not the same, lying there in the sparse, dead vegetation. Calli gripped her man fiercely, and when he put his lips to her breast a thrill went through her, but once he was inside her it occurred to her that soon it would be Palloc on top of her, staring at her with his strange eyes, taking her as a man takes a woman. She shoved such thoughts aside and watched Urs with wet eyes as he gave himself to his passion.

He is mine, Calli thought with each gentle thrust. *He is mine. He is mine.*

Year Nineteen

The little female pup was larger than her two brothers, something they were just beginning to sense as they wrestled and tumbled in the den. For the most part, this meant that the two males mounted largely uncoordinated attacks on her with their tiny teeth, combining forces when all three of them were upright but instantly pouncing on whichever wolf fell on his back. They played all day, ceaselessly, pausing only to feed or to nap.

For them, the man was just another animal to wrestle with. They felt no fear of him, nor really any sense that he did not belong as a member of their pack. He was in the den and he played with them; that was all that mattered.

When the man was gone they happily frolicked with each other. The mother-wolf, however, was not receptive to having the pups bite at her and they had earned enough snarls and snaps to stay clear of her during play.

The area of the cave that smoldered from the fire also brought down rich scents of the world on currents of air that swirled in the crevice. The pups did not understand what they were looking at when they raised their noses to the smells and peered at the sky, but the exotic odors were tantalizing.

Another part of the cave also lured them; the same world-scents pouring in through spaces between rocks and dirt. The pups yearned to smell more, to explore and learn.

One day, with the man gone and the mother-wolf asleep, the three pups took out their frustration on the barrier between them and the outside, digging with their tiny paws at the soft dirt and nosing aside the stones they found. It was the first day that the males deferred to their larger sibling—when she pressed forward to dig, they hung back to allow it. She would dig until she lost interest, but her brothers' continued efforts would eventually attract her attention again, and then they would once more step aside to allow her access.

The lush odors became stronger. Soon she could poke her nose out of the den, inhaling the yet-to-be-discovered in deep snorts. Panting and whimpering in excitement, her brothers danced around behind her, and eventually she allowed them to have a turn. It was something she understood, another new thing that day: she would make decisions and her brothers would follow her lead.

Yet it was one brother, and then the next, who first squeezed out of the den and into the sunshine. The big female pup held back, conflicted, smelling her mother behind her. Yes, she wanted to go out there, but something also told her to stick close. Normally, the wolf parents would guide their young when it came to exploring the world.

She thought of the man, and wished he were there with them. She whined, her instincts telling her this was dangerous. She should stay in the den.

In the end, though, she pushed through the hole and followed her brothers.

SIXTEEN

Year One

Shadows were long, the day nearly done, when Calli stepped into the communal area of the settlement. She felt sore from mating with Urs, but the sensation, which had once given her a secret joy, held no comfort for her today. She was simply tired, looking forward to night and to sleep.

Albi approached her and Calli stiffened, realizing the council mother wanted a conversation. As she drew closer, Albi held out her thick arms for an embrace Calli hardly expected.

"My daughter," Albi murmured.

Calli stood woodenly inside the hug. Albi's shoulders were ridiculously big, her bones solid and arms fleshy.

"I am happy for these developments," Albi gushed warmly. "I have always thought of you as the smartest woman of all the Kindred, even at your age. With my help over the next five years, you will be a great council mother."

"Plus," Calli could not resist pointing out, "I will be married to your son."

"Of course," Albi replied, almost as if this were an afterthought. "That is the reason for my great happiness."

"Why do you do this?" Calli asked. "Yes, there were birds squawking as they fluttered about, but none would dare to attack you in the nest. I know my name is often spoken as the next council mother, but I was not moving against you. You could have won without this marriage."

Albi regarded Calli with shrewd eyes. "Yes, you see? The smartest one. Birds squawking, indeed."

"Why?" Calli persisted.

"Well," Albi said with a sigh, "you will understand when you are council mother. All the women support you and vote for you and then they turn on you. They hate what they have created. They become jealous and petulant. Everything you do, they see as wrong, or inadequate. They need a council mother, but they resent that need. The only way to maintain power is to manipulate circumstances. To think, in other words, in mists and shadows."

"If they do not want you as council mother anymore, why cling to it?" Calli challenged.

Albi's look turned pitying. "You are, in so many ways, a child. You will understand someday. This is why it is a good thing we have five years, for me to teach you all you need to know."

Gasps and murmurs caught their attention. Albi and Calli looked over toward the edge of camp, where someone was limping out from the deepening shadows.

Renne.

Silex watched as the unmarried women paraded past the men, who sat mostly cross-legged, each with a piece of reindeer bone cracked open to expose the juicy marrow. It was a ritual intended to mimic when the female wolves saucily waved their asses in the males' faces when it was time to mate, though in this dance courtship was far from predetermined.

The men pretended boredom, or to be more interested in good-naturedly shoving each other, but they were watching hungrily as the women sauntered around. The women were laughing behind their hands, tossing wildly enticing glances at the men before darting their eyes away.

It was good, Silex reflected, to indulge in this familiar ritual, to pretend everything was as it had always been, but the fact was that there were so few single women and so many men, it lent a brittle tension to the proceedings, threatening the very stability of the tribe.

His sister Ovi was in the line—the Wolfen recognized no formal couples until marriage, which often occurred quickly after a man and a woman declared for each other. But she was promised to Silex and so it was eyes-off for every man except Duro, who Silex noticed was staring at Ovi with unconcealed desire.

Ovi was oblivious. She did not seem to know why she was even there, and she walked as if her feet hurt. She did not seek Silex's eyes. Silex, on the other hand, was focused as intently as any lion. His eyes could not leave the brown legs, the rippling hair, the female curves underneath the garments, which were decorated with feathers that bewitched him.

Fia. Silex could not imagine any man desiring a woman the way he craved Fia.

Fia caught Silex staring at her and laughed at him, taunting him, and his mouth went dry. Fia's parents both had the same curl to their hair, an exotic feature given to only a few of the Wolfen in any generation. Some found the difference unsightly, but Silex was bewitched by it.

A few men had stood, offering their marrow bones as enticement for a private conversation, but they were largely rejected. Too soon; the dance needed to play out more.

Silex could no longer wait. When he rose, all took notice— he was their leader. If he took Ovi aside now, it would be signal for the rest to pair off. Sometimes, after a dance such as this, there were weddings within mere days and children less than a year after that.

Ignoring Ovi, ignoring everyone, Silex walked up to Fia, who stared at him in shock, the laughter gone from her eyes.

"I wonder," Silex offered formally, "if you would like to share this with me?"

Calli ran over to her friend Renne, who had obviously been attacked. Her nose was bleeding, her eyes were blackened, and a gash in her cheek pointed in a straight line to a wrecked mouth. Soon Bellu and Coco and everyone was there, all the women, crowding around Renne, touching her.

"What happened? Was it the Cohort?" Bellu cried fearfully. This, of course, was ridiculous. An encounter with the Valley Cohort and Renne would not be here.

"A bear?" someone else guessed.

The light was fading so quickly now that the women needed to pull Renne over to a fire to get a closer look at her. She went without resistance, the women gasping when they got a better view of her wounds.

"What happened to you, Renne?" Coco asked solicitously.

Renne did not answer. Instead, she stared with dark, unreadable intensity at Albi, who had come up to join the group.

Calli, looking back and forth between Renne and Albi, understanding, and it made her sick. *Albi had done this.*

"We are all aware of how dangerous it is to go against the will of the women's council," Albi observed quietly. "We are the hands that hold the Kindred together. The men hunt, but we make all the important decisions, and our decisions cannot, not ever, be ignored."

Bellu turned a mystified look to Calli, clearly not understanding. Calli bit her lip. "You did this, Albi?"

"Night is falling. It is time to gather the children and call out to the men," Albi said decisively, ignoring Calli.

No one moved. The women were rendered immobile by the implication of Calli's question. They glanced among themselves, horror written on their faces. They began to murmur quiet, shocked protests.

"Night," Alibi insisted again, more forcefully. *"Now."*

Renne was not even looking at the council mother. Instead, her gaze was intent to her right, and Calli followed it.

Palloc had left the men's side and had wandered into the communal area. Drawn by the circle of women, he had approached them and their fire until he caught sight of the person standing in the middle. Renne, the blood still streaming down her chin, her one eye nearly swollen shut. Inhaling sharply, Palloc stood, stunned.

Renne lifted her hands to him, as if willing him to come another five paces and take her in his arms.

"Palloc," she pleaded, weeping openly. "Palloc."

Palloc turned away. Not meeting Renne's eyes, he began walking carefully over to the men's side of the settlement.

And then the rain came.

The first drop was followed instantly by thousands, a roar of it, the fires sizzling angrily under the assault. The drama of Renne's injuries was obliterated by the sudden storm.

Nearly as one, the Kindred cheered, because the rain would fill the water holes and the lumbering mammoths would come to drink and wallow, and there would be food for the winter. But all Palloc could think was that somehow, what he was doing was so wrong it had torn open the very sky, a shame bringing a downpour of celestial tears. In his mind he saw himself going to Renne, defying his mother, declaring his love for her. That was what he wanted to do.

But he did not.

For a wolf, a howl isn't just enticing—it's compelling, an imperative as strong as the urge to hunt, to feed. So when the she-wolf and Mate heard the ululating song of their old pack on the wind, the tantalizing cry stretched thin by the miles between them, they reacted by racing toward it, cutting fresh tracks in the shallow snow. They could hear in the howl the joy of a meal just eaten, but it wasn't the thought of food that drew them. It was the experience of mingling their voices with other wolves that they craved.

Enough time elapsed, as they ran, for the she-wolf to develop an unease. Smoke, the dominant bitch, would not welcome their trespass. For the first time since setting off on her own, the she-wolf was affected by the instinct-deep aversion to invading a larger pack's territory. They hadn't just gone for a day-hunt, they had voluntarily separated from the others. They would not be welcomed home—they would be attacked, perhaps even killed.

When the large female slowed, it had no effect on Mate. He was intoxicated, heedless, lusting for the pack. It was as if he had forgotten all that had transpired since the summer.

She slowed further, watching Mate's retreating back, waiting for him to sense that she was no longer right behind him. Though she could not calculate that her odds of surviving alone, at her age, were slim, her instincts told her she and Mate were a hunting pair and must remain together.

But Mate did not look back.

SEVENTEEN

Fia did not answer Silex when he proffered the glistening marrow, but she did not stay in the dance, either—she marched away, so that he was not at all sure what he should do. Follow her? Return and sit with the men and accept their good-natured jeers?

In the end he trotted after her like a little boy trying to catch up to his mother. Her eyes flashed angrily as he drew up alongside.

"Fia," he said, his words sounding as rehearsed as they were, "I have known you for a long time. I have always appreciated your spirit, the way you . . ."

She whirled on him. Her face was flushed, breathtakingly beautiful. Her amazingly smooth skin—he wanted to put his lips to it.

Silex had spent many hours fantasizing about what would happen when he finally unveiled the secret, told this woman of his affections. Some of the more vivid imaginings were clouding his mind as she glared at him now, so close to him he could feel her passions as a heat. "And what," she hissed, "did you suppose would happen *now*? That you would mount me? Because you are our leader, our dominant male?" Her contempt hardened her eyes.

"No, of course not." Silex inhaled, trying to get his thoughts in order.

"Then what do you want from me?"

"I thought . . . we have always laughed together and I believed you probably knew how I felt about you."

"But now you are promised to Ovi."

"Yes, I know that is what my father wished, but he did not care what was inside me."

"So? Why does that matter to me? It is decided."

"Fia," Silex pleaded. "Are you saying you have never felt anything for me?"

Her hot eyes lost some of their fury at his plaintive question. "You never said anything," she finally answered.

"My father forbade it."

"Forbade what?"

"For me to tell you how I felt, that I have loved only you since we were children. That I think of no one else, nothing else, but you, always you, eternally and forever you. That I cannot stand the thought of any other man with you, that I need you. I love you."

She stared at him. Moments went by, Silex in agony. "Fia?" he finally asked timidly.

She lunged for him and kissed him desperately, nearly knocking him down. Silex's legs went weak, his head dizzy. They were both panting, grasping at each other, and then she pushed him away. "No!"

"Fia . . ."

"I cannot be this person. You tell me you love me, but you marry her!"

"I will not."

She shook her head. "Oh no, you tell me that now because you want me to copulate with you, but you will marry Ovi, and you know it. It is what your father wanted, it is what the Wolfen want. Everyone agrees."

"I do not love Ovi."

"That does not seem to matter."

"What do you feel, Fia? Are you saying you do not feel the same way?"

"Why are you doing this?" she yelled at him.

"Kiss me again."

"No, Silex! I will never kiss you again!"

S ilex."

Duro's voice was a hoarse whisper. Silex had just relieved himself in the snow, well away from the others, and was standing and staring off in the distance, thinking of kissing Fia, when he heard his name.

He turned slowly, knowing what he would see: a spear, pointed at his stomach. Duro was grinning fiercely down at Silex.

"You see? I do *think*," Duro mocked.

Silex assessed the larger man, who was holding the spear out with his arms extended and locked, ready to absorb the shock of a lunge. It was, Silex reflected, the perfect position to ram someone through if you were running straight at him. Perhaps not so good if you were standing flat-footed.

"You should have submitted," Duro taunted, his eyes gleaming in triumph.

In a quick move, Silex reached up with his left hand and grabbed the shaft and yanked on it. Duro stumbled forward and Silex punched him hard in the face with his right hand, three quick jabs. Gasping, Duro let go of the spear and raised his arms to ward off more blows. Silex stepped back and turned the weapon around, raising it in a throwing position.

Duro's mouth was open. He seemed stunned at the turn of events. Now he had no move at all—at this range the spear would surely kill him. He stared at Silex, blood running from his nose. Silex was not even breathing hard.

For Silex the conundrum could not be more difficult. If he did not finish this now, Duro would come at him again and again, challenging him because he was obsessed with Ovi. Yet Silex could not just hand her over: Fia was right, Silex and Ovi had been commanded to marry by their father. Duro probably would not even accept Ovi if Silex gave her up—in his mind, he needed to lead the Wolfen, and only then could lay claim to the woman he desired. The irony made Silex ache: passionate, beautiful Fia wanted him. She would not admit it in so many words, but Silex knew it. Fia had *kissed* him, why were they fighting over Ovi?

Silex thought of the she-wolf with the hand-shaped marking above her eyes. So young, but she had left her pack. Driven off, Silex had concluded, by the dominant bitch. She stared Silex in the face. *A message in that for me,* Silex's father had suggested. But the old man was dead, and still the she-wolf met Silex's eyes. Perhaps the message was for *Silex.*

Duro was now lowering his head in submission, mimicking a defeated wolf, surrendering. For now. Next time his spear would be better positioned.

His spear.

"Duro."

The other man raised his eyes.

"No spear. The dominant wolf rarely kills the challenger. It would weaken the pack." Silex threw the spear with all his strength into the trees, then showed Duro his empty hands. "No weapons."

The other man's jaw was still slack, noncomprehension in his eyes. Silex sighed at the stupidity. Then he punched Duro's open mouth with his right hand, splitting the larger man's lip.

There. Now Duro understood.

Silex stepped in and swung again, catching Duro's eye. Then Duro hit back solidly, a rib shot, and the man's strength was breathtaking, knocking Silex back. No, the blows needed to be on Silex's face, they had to leave a visible mark for all to see and be convinced. Silex stepped closer, feinting, and Duro came through with a swinging punch that could have been ducked. Instead, Silex took a glancing hit on the cheek, feeling the skin tear. He raised his hand, smearing the blood. Good.

Energized now, Duro lunged. Silex dodged and then was caught full in the face. He staggered back, shocked by the pain. *Enough.*

Silex lowered his head. "The victory is yours."

Duro looked doubtful and suspicious. Silex held up his open hands—he did *not* want to be hit again. "You may marry my sister. I renounce my claim to her."

Duro dropped his fists, a delighted grin on his bloody lips. "I will mate with Ovi," he declared wonderingly.

"Yes. All is good."

Now that the fight was over, the pain was stinging Silex's face. He wanted to go splash cold water on himself.

"And the Wolfen. I am to lead the Wolfen," Duro reminded him. "We will no longer have to follow the orders of a boy."

Silex inhaled carefully. This one would not be as easy as giving up Ovi. "Often in the wolf pack, mating pairs will split off on their own to raise their own family," he ventured finally.

Duro shrugged. "Yes, but the subject is that I am to lead the Wolfen now that I have defeated you."

Silex wondered how well the Wolfen would manage with this idiot running things. "What I mean," Silex continued patiently, "is that if you are to lead the Wolfen, I would choose to leave. And perhaps others will come with me."

"I will allow that," Duro grunted. "And you can take others. But not Ovi."

"No, not Ovi," Silex agreed impatiently.

Duro grinned at him. "She will bear strong children. She is shapely and has fine breasts."

Year Nineteen

A sudden change in the airflow roused the mother-wolf from a deep sleep. For the first time in many, many days, the smell of outside was coming in from the front of the cave, the entrance she had used when she entered the den. She inhaled, locating the scent of the stream nearby, of summer grasses, wet soil, small animals. Things she had not smelled this sharply in a long time.

When her pups left the cave through the hole, she knew it. There was an increase in their smell as each individual pup stood directly in the incoming breeze, and then an abrupt lessening as they squeezed outside. She felt their absence.

It was the time of life when wolf puppies liked to romp and play. Normally, a mother and her mate would watch over them and keep them from straying, but even when her instincts dug at her, the mother-wolf did not try to move. She thought briefly of her mate, and then about the man.

She slept for some time and then awoke with a jolt. The air coming in from the front of the cave carried a new scent.

Lion.

EIGHTEEN

Year One

What saved the large she-wolf from being abandoned by Mate was a shift in the wind.

Mate was far enough away from her that his scent was beginning to dissipate, so that she understood he was never coming back. But then the breeze changed, the current's new direction bringing with it the electrifying scent of blood, particularly strong above the dead smell of snow. The tantalizing odor stirred her hunger and she turned her nose to it.

She felt Mate streaking toward her before she smelled him, her inner senses alert to the approach of a male wolf. They touched noses and circled each other when he arrived, wagging their tails, excitement rising inside them over this wonderful aroma. Reindeer blood.

They tracked it and knew they were stalking a living animal. They could also smell the herd, now, but could sense that it was farther away. An injured reindeer had been abandoned by the rest.

There was no fear, and very little consciousness, in the large female ungulate when they found her. They circled warily, because though she lay on her side, the stink of man was on her, and there was something unusual, smelling of wood and stone, sticking up at the sky from her rib cage, as if she had grown a tree branch out of her body.

The reindeer did not register their approach. Her eyes were milky and her breathing came in short pants. Her blood stained the snow as it leaked from the rent in her skin. Mate carefully sniffed at her, made afraid by the stick-thing, but the she-wolf was less timid, almost dizzy from the aromatic wound in the reindeer's side.

The two wolves fed ravenously and hurriedly—if they had so easily tracked the blood trail, there were other predators who might do the same. But they turned from the kill with full bellies, sated and replenished. They would not need to eat for several days, now.

The scent of man on the stick connected the she-wolf back to other memories of food and man, particularly the one man whose face fascinated her so. The next morning, when the wolves uncurled themselves from sleep and stretched, yawning contentedly, the she-wolf led Mate off in the direction from which that one man's scent had last drifted on the air. For reasons she did not fully grasp, she wanted to see him again.

There was always a thaw three-quarters into their sojourns at the Kindred's winter encampments, a break in the weather. Often a few reindeer might wander close from wherever they had been wintering, the females sometimes heavy with pregnancy, or sometimes the thick mud around the watering holes would encumber a mammoth, making the dangerous giant easier to take down.

With a good chance for fresh meat and the temperatures warm enough for the snows to retreat from the communal area, the Kindred held their annual wedding ceremony. This year was special: Urs the hunt master was getting married, as was Palloc the spear master. The women tried to be equally excited about the three other weddings to take place the same night, but Bellu, with her beauty, and Urs, the tall, handsome hunt master, was all they could talk about.

The night of the ceremony, Calli watched sourly as Bellu fussed with the laying of the fire in the center of the camp. As fire maker, it was always her job to prepare for the weddings, but because it was her own wedding, she was laying in each piece of wood with extreme care. *It is only a fire! Just throw the wood in and light it!* Calli wanted to shout. In the end, though, she said nothing at all.

That was her way, now. Say nothing. Endure.

Coco was excited for the wedding. She dragged her daughter down to a deep watering hole and bathed her until Calli's lips were blue and she was shaking violently, and then mother and daughter stood by their home fire and let the delicious warmth dry them off. Coco could not stop smiling—Calli tried smiling back, but her effort was tepid.

She did not know how she was going to get through this.

Night came. The fire was lit. The men settled down on their side of it, laughing and pushing at the grooms. Urs, as hunt master, might have been spared such frivolity, except that Bellu's brothers kept shoving him and chortling.

On the other side of the fire, the women sat primly, in a much more organized semicircle. Where the men were boisterous, the women were solemn, and more than one wife caught her husband's eye and gave him a firm, disapprobative frown. A lot of men's grins vanished over such a stern glance.

Darkness settled firmly over the Kindred—this was the one night of the year where they stayed up well past sunset.

Sopho stood, bringing a hush.

Sopho was the oldest living member of the Kindred, so ancient that a hand, open and clenched repeatedly ten times, would not flash enough fingers to account for all her summers. She was of the generation of Albi's mother, and bore the scars of long life: all but one of her daughters had died in childbirth. All of her children were dead. Her grandson, Valid, was married and had had one child stillborn and another lost to disease. Her granddaughter Tay was apprenticed to Sopho as healer to the Kindred—it was Tay who ministered to Hardy's wounds, at Sopho's direction.

Hardy was here tonight, his misshapen face making everyone uncomfortable.

Sopho's bearing was stiff with formality. "The Kindred were born on the same day as the first sun. She is our mother," Sopho pronounced in a surprisingly strong voice. She pointed toward the east. "As with the sun, our birth was red with blood. And then the sun went from weak to strong, from lying on the ground to standing tall." Sopho pointed dramatically straight overhead. "But, just as we have the lion and the bear, the hyena and the wolf, the sun, too, has enemies who lurk in shadow. Every day there is a bloody battle." Sopho pointed to the west. "The sun fights for us to live, and many times her life ends with her blood smeared across the horizon. Later, in the dark, we often see her blood scattered in tiny droplets, each gleaming with the light that was once hers. Many nights, her full skeleton is visible, or a fragment of it, as white and mottled as any elk bone in the grass. But she leaves us a daughter, who is born of the earth, rising up strong and hot in the morning." Sopho pointed to the east.

As many times as those assembled at the fire had heard this tale, it still transfixed, because it explained who they were, and why they were special and better than any of the other creeds. Calli risked a look at her tribe and saw faces rapt and attentive with the exception of two: Albi scowled, jealously awaiting her chance to speak, and Bellu looked impatient, as if none of this had anything to do with *her*.

"This is why we marry. The sun gives us life and we cannot squander, cannot waste, must avail, must requite. We marry to give birth, and we give birth to honor the sun who sacrifices her life, and those of her children and her children's children, every day."

A stir went through the Kindred, because with these words, Sopho's ritual pronouncement was at an end. She had barely taken her seat when Albi stood, thumping her stick into the ground. Now all the eyes were on her, and she savored the attention until everyone had begun to fidget impatiently. When it seemed no one could wait another moment, the council mother spoke. "It is a night when men and women come together."

With a whoop, the men jumped to their feet. The women rose much more soberly, and then the two groups came to where Albi stood, mingling with each other. Wives hugged their husbands, and single men shyly went to stand by the women they favored. Bellu's brother Nix, Calli noticed, made his way to Renne, who was no longer bruised but who would forever carry a white scar on her cheek. Yet he did not speak to Renne, or even really look at her, as if he had picked the spot out of mere chance.

Paired off, the Kindred arranged itself around the fire. The women who were to be wed that night sat with a tight knot of widows and young girls, while their grooms remained standing, as if lost and confused.

The men began singing, a low humming sound, and stomping their feet rhythmically. The women soon joined in, clapping, and weaving a higher note into the song.

Calli was sitting next to Bellu, who was bobbing up and down with excitement. She seized Calli's hand, giving her a broad smile. They both wore their hair in the traditional wedding fashion, tied in a complicated knot with identical bows of leather, up on their heads and adorned with colorful bird feathers that every woman collected and kept for just this occasion.

Now the grooms, shuffling as a pack, looking nervous and tentative, went over to their brides, but before they got there, the brides' mothers sprang up and formed a barrier, arms crossed like lowered antlers.

Everyone roared with laughter.

As hunt master, Urs was the elected spokesperson for the males. "We will provide for your daughters," he declared tremulously.

Calli hastily wiped at her eyes. He was so handsome. She had so many times pictured this moment, and it had always been exactly this way: her standing with the other brides, waiting for Urs to come over, Coco blocking him with her arms crossed, shaking her head.

She glanced at Palloc and saw that he had noticed that her gaze was on Urs. She blinked the wetness out of her eyes and lowered them.

The mothers did not accept the hunt master's claims at face value, so each groom retreated to his family. Urs, parentless, and without any surviving siblings, turned to Bellu's brothers. In staged whispers, the grooms asked for help, and in each case came back to the center of the circle with some food to offer as proof they would be good providers.

Coco accepted a tender cut of reindeer, killed just that day, and gazed at it as if it were infested with insects. She handed the meat to Calli's father Ignus with a shrug. Ignus was the most taciturn man in the Kindred and could go an entire winter without uttering a word to anyone. Ignus appeared bored with the whole procedure, as if his daughter's wedding was an inconvenience, dragging him away from the men's side, where he preferred to spend his time, silently sitting with the hunters. He accepted the meat and sniffed at it.

"Go," the mothers commanded, making shooing motions. "You are not worthy."

The Kindred laughed and cheered and applauded. Calli watched as Urs played the part of dejected petitioner, returning to Bellu's brothers for more help. Bellu was giggling uncontrollably, hugging herself with excitement.

The men returned with fur pelts. These the mothers examined, frowning, picking through them and shaking their heads over the poor quality. The men hung their heads.

"No no," said Ador, Bellu's mother. "My daughter's husband must do better than this!"

The final offering was traditionally something decorative. Palloc handed Coco a small, gleaming shell of the type that the Blanc Tribe traded for knives. Urs gave Ador a smooth stone that had been rubbed with a shiny powder made from dried lumps of red clay, a substance the Kindred referred to as "rouge." The other men had bones that had been carved with decorative designs.

These final gifts seemed to do the trick. One by one, the mothers turned to their daughters. Ador was first, reaching a hand out to Bellu, who stood eagerly. Ador grasped Urs's hand in the other. The three of them walked into the center of the ring.

"My daughter will be wife to Urs. She will take care of him and bear him children. I give my daughter."

The crowd cheered with approval as Urs and Bellu kissed.

Calli swallowed, tears streaming down her face. The next woman to be wed was Tay, to Bellu's brother Vent, whose first wife had died. Then Coco, smiling, grasped Calli's hand. It was time. Nodding bravely, Calli walked with her mother, Palloc on the other side.

"My daughter will be wife to Palloc. She will help him through good times and bad times. She will bear him children. I give my daughter to Palloc."

Calli closed her eyes as Palloc leaned down to kiss her in a prelude to what was coming next, when the two of them would lie together as husband and wife, and the roar from the crowd matched the sound of the blood pulsing in her ears.

NINETEEN

Year Nineteen

The mother wolf lay at the front of the cave, exhausted from her agonizing crawl from the den. A small hole told the story of the wolf pups digging at the dirt, curious about the air flowing in, widening the breach until they could each, in turn, wriggle outside.

The mother-wolf's nose was pressed to the hole. She had made it as far as she could go, her maternal imperative driving her to get out to save her pups, but her way had been blocked. Now she could smell what the lion had done, smell the blood of her offspring.

She heard the sound of the man landing on the floor of the chimney. "No!" he screamed. *"No!"*

He crawled to her. She did not resist when he picked her up, not even when the pain flashed through her at the rough movement. He carried her gently to the floor of the chasm, laying her down in the light.

He leaned over her, his face wet, smelling salty. "This is my fault. I did not adequately block the entrance. It is my fault they got out. I saw the blood. It is my fault they are all dead."

He made choking noises. The mother-wolf took raspy breaths. A long moment passed with no other sound.

"It is going wrong," he finally said. "There are dangers everywhere, and I cannot protect either one of us against them. And even if I manage to survive the summer, winter will come, and that will be the end."

His hand was on her fur. The mother-wolf took reassurance from the touch. She could feel how easy it would be, now, to close her eyes and follow the deepest sleep imaginable, but she could not.

Not yet.

There was a small noise, startling the man, who whipped his head up and gasped in disbelief at the reason why the mother-wolf could not yet let go.

The female pup stood at the top of the rock pile, gazing down at them, her little tail wriggling. She had retreated to the den when the lion appeared, and managed to escape the fate of her two brothers.

The mother-wolf still had a pup to raise.

The man stood, wiping his eyes, and reached for the little wolf, who bounded into his hands.

Year One

The news stunned the Wolfen: Silex had been deposed in battle with the much larger Duro. Evidence of the brawl was all over their battered faces—Silex had not given up without fighting back with all his strength.

As a tribe they prided themselves on their ability to move out quickly. Silex would leave in the morning.

Silex's friend Brach had already committed to accompanying him wherever he went, and Silex imagined he might attract a few other Wolfen males as well, the adventurous ones willing to take a chance on splitting from the pack—especially since there were so few unmarried females in the tribe. The parting would be free of enmity. As Silex had already announced, a mating pair might leave the main group but still remain friendly when they encountered one another out on the steppes.

"Fia." Silex caught up to her standing alone at the edge of the circle of illumination from the fire. She must have heard of the fight by now and known he would seek her out. She stared at him, eyes unreadable in the flickering light. He stopped a few paces away, not trusting himself to come any closer. He ached to grab her; it was like a hunger. "I have been challenged by Duro."

"I know this."

"I am leaving. In the morning. Going away."

Her face glowed in the firelight. "I will miss you," she finally whispered.

It was as awful as when Duro punched him in the chest. He swallowed, staring at her. "Will you not come with me, Fia?"

"You assume I will just leave the Wolfen, my friends and family, to run off with you," she accused.

"I did not assume," he protested.

"Then why did you not ask me first?"

"Ask you? This just happened."

"Oh, I *know* that is not true. You did not have the courage to tell Ovi of your bold declarations to me, so you arranged for Duro to take her from you."

Silex was speechless, astounded she had figured out so much. "That is not entirely true," he ventured.

"Not entirely?"

"I tried to speak to Ovi. She would not listen to me."

"So you are a man who cannot stand up to his own sister. Why should I go with you?"

"Because," Silex pleaded, "I love you, Fia. I think of nothing but you, I *want* nothing but you. Is it easy for me to leave this tribe, when I lead it and everyone listens to me, and set out with just a handful of others to hunt on our own?

It is not easy. I am giving up a lot but I give it up to be with you. Please, Fia, can you not hear me on this?"

He saw something on her face and seized the moment. Now it was him lunging for her, and when he pulled her into his arms it was with a force that surprised them both. His bruised face nearly flinched from the pain when they kissed, but he pressed it, clinging to her, and when he felt her respond he wanted to sing out loud. She did not say it, but her answer was yes. She would go with him.

It was morning before Silex approached Ovi. His sister squatted next to a fire, her mouth set in an unhappy line. Silex crouched next to her.

"I am leaving," he said simply. There was no way she could not already know.

Ovi stared at the fire as if she had not heard.

"Duro has bested me. He will lead the Wolfen. Brach and his wife are going with me, as well as a few others, men who have no prospects for wives. And Fia. I am taking Fia with me and we will marry."

Ovi regarded him with eyes that looked weary.

"This will be the best for all, Ovi," Silex said softly.

"You are the only family I have, Silex," she replied, surprising him.

"It is not as if I will never see you," Silex reasoned after a moment. "We will all be following the wolves. It is just now Duro needs the validation of the tribe's embrace. Once he is secure, I am sure he will greet us all without hostility. And *he* will be your family, Ovi. As you said, you will marry the leader."

"So it does not matter what I want. It is decided." She said this without bitterness, just a resigned acceptance.

"But what is it you want, Ovi?" Silex felt like clenching his teeth. "To marry me? Is that really what you desire? Duro will make you happy."

"Happy," Ovi repeated. She regarded him blandly, her eyes full of a dark irony.

Calli had no appetite. Her teeth tore only the tiniest shreds of meat from the bone when she held it to her lips. Yet everyone thought she was feasting—it was her wedding night! The big fire collapsed in on itself, sparks swirling upward, the light ebbing away. Couples began drifting toward their sleeping areas. When Urs and Bellu stood, holding hands, her brothers cheered and clapped, and Calli turned her face away and vomited cleanly onto the ground.

And then Palloc came to her, holding out his hands, and she nodded, steeling herself, and stood.

"Calli. My wife," he murmured.

The men of the hunt made their hoots, less boisterous than for their hunt master, but still laughing and stomping their feet.

Calli followed Palloc into the dark. He had spent a few days making a place for them, carefully building up a wall of dirt and rocks and laying thin branches up against them. Underneath this low roof, he had laid out elk hides and a piece of bear pelt that had once, Calli remembered, belonged to his father.

Palloc stirred his fire, adding wood to it, and the licking flames brought their faces out of the gloom. Then he turned to her.

"Are you tired?" he asked solicitously.

"Yes."

The answer seemed to bother him. He involuntarily glanced at the bed he had made for them.

"Not too tired for . . . that," Calli sighed.

He smiled. Gradually, his smile faded. "You have not spoken to me in recent days."

Calli, rather ironically, could think of nothing to say to that.

"I have . . . you sometimes make jokes at my expense. Your wit, for which you are well known, can bite."

This surprised her a little—she would have thought him too thick-headed to know when she was making fun of him. "Sorry," she said.

They stood regarding each other. "Well," he declared finally, "you will not be doing that anymore."

"No, I suppose not."

Wordlessly, Palloc knelt down, gesturing for Calli to follow him into the lean-to. She limply obeyed, and when he reached for her garments, she helped him remove everything she was wearing. The rough bear fur felt good against her skin.

Unbidden, thoughts of Urs came to her mind. He was with Bellu now. They were doing this very thing, by their fire.

Calli turned her head so that Palloc would not see the tears that sprang to her eyes. When he lay upon her, she reflexively wrapped her arms around him, and his broad chest felt wrong. Urs was much taller but not nearly so wide, nor were his bones as thick and heavy. Palloc's back was more muscled. Still, in other ways, this was very much like being with Urs. Palloc seemed to know what he was doing, lining himself up in the correct position. Eyes pressed shut, Calli realized how she was going to get through this, how she would be a wife.

By thinking of Urs.

When Palloc's hands stroked her, they were Urs's hands. When he fumbled his way into her, she received him as Urs, and even felt the fantasy stir a response. Yes, it was Urs she clung to in the dark.

Palloc's breathing became labored, his movements fast.

She was jolted by how strongly he was thrusting. She blinked her eyes open because she was not accustomed to such forceful mating. Movement caught her vision, and as Palloc groaned in her ear, she looked out by the fire and saw someone crouched there, watching.

Albi. Her mother-in-law.

TWENTY

Year Four

I t was her favorite thing to do on a beautiful day like this: sit with her ankles in the Kindred stream, her hands resting comfortably around her distended abdomen. While everyone else had been remarking on how cool it had been that summer, for Calli, the temperature was always annoyingly warm. Her baby was probably not coming for a little while yet.

She sighed. The elk hide she wore was uncomfortable, though it was nothing more than a simple drape, a hole cut in the center for her head and the front and back flaps tied loosely at the waist so that the side slits allowed ventilation. The garment stuck to her sweat, irritating her when she moved.

A sharp impact rang out from downstream, and Calli turned to see Hardy at work chipping a flake of stone that had been buried under the fire for several days, so focused he did not seem to know she was there.

Barely able to communicate, slow to walk, his eyesight worthless beyond a few paces, Hardy had reinvented himself as the best toolmaker of the Kindred. To see a stone he held it so close to his face that the children suspected he was smelling the correct way to strike it, and then with precision his strong hands would chip until a point or cutting edge emerged. Most of the men made weapons, of course, but Hardy was the best. At his urging, people had begun to call him "tool master."

As she watched, a pack of young children, all naked boys under the age of five summers, crept up on the tool master, wet mud in their hands. They were grinning and nudging each other, delighted with the mischief they were about to visit upon the old man, and there, in the center of them, was Calli's son.

This was his third summer. Calli had delighted Coco by swelling with child not long after her wedding—speculation was she may have gotten pregnant on her wedding night, which was considered a real blessing.

With a shout, the boys darted forward, slinging their mud. Hardy, though, had laid a trap, and with a roar he was on his feet, armed with his own dirt balls. His sight was poor but his range was long and by aiming at the middle of the crowd he was able to strike more than one. Calli winced when her own child took a hit smack in the back, but to his credit he only shrieked with pretend fear, fleeing and giggling with the rest of the boys.

Calli clapped her hands with delight, and Hardy turned and squinted in her direction. His expression was unreadable, but his shoulders were shaking, and Calli realized the old man was laughing.

"So," Albi said from behind her. Calli started, a jolt of something like guilt flashing through her. Albi sat next to Calli, raked her stringy hair back from her forehead, and thrust her own feet into the water. Calli saw odd discolored spots on the older woman's ankles and wondered what might have caused them. They reminded Calli of the spots on her elk hide. "You have not said what you think of his name," Albi chided her daughter-in-law.

Just two days ago, the Kindred had held its naming ceremony for the children who were in their third summer. The oldest woman in the family was afforded the right and responsibility to bestow the legend and name upon the child, so it had been Albi's honor.

What Albi said about Calli's son almost made her wonder if her mother-in-law had even *met* the child. Albi spoke of "A Boy Who Practiced Solemnity, Prudence, and Thoughtful Calculation." His formal name, Dognus Seria, was immediately shortened to "Dog," though the nickname sounded ugly to Calli.

More to the point, if there was ever a child who was *not* solemn, prudent, and thoughtful, it was her little boy. He was a constant source of mischief and laughter—it was as if Albi thought that by naming him something so inappropriate, she could alter his personality.

"Tell me, what led you to name him that?" Calli responded, dodging Albi's question.

Albi grunted. "I have always hated my name, given me by my grandmother, the same rodent-woman who named my son. A name should say something about character, about potential. My name says I have pale skin. My son's name says he has pale eyes. And that is it, as if this is all that is important about us. No, not for my grandson. Someday, he will be hunt master."

Calli knew some sort of response was expected of her. "He certainly has a way about him," she finally commented.

"Look at that fool," Albi said.

Calli looked up, catching Albi's stare and following it across the stream, where Bellu's brother Nix was strolling aimlessly. He soon vanished into the woods. "Now there is someone named incorrectly," Albi observed. "He is not 'He Who Has Mastered Hunting in the Snow,' he should be 'He Who Is as Dumb as His Brothers.'"

Calli suppressed a laugh. The two women looked at each other, and for at least a moment, they shared a relationship without strain or tension. "I have heard Nix favors Renne and would like her as his wife," Calli remarked after a moment.

Albi's eyes turned cold and vicious. "Do not *ever* do that," she hissed.

"Do what?" Calli responded, shocked.

"Marriage is up to the council. If we let the men pick us, we would become mere prey to them. And Renne. Do you know what happens within the Kindred when a man and woman are not happy as husband and wife? You have seen it, right? Anger runs high. The man goes to the widows for comfort, the woman cries to all her friends and stops doing her work . . . one of the reasons there even *is* a council mother is to prevent such a thing."

Calli frowned. "You are reaching conclusions I do not find reasonable. Why would you suppose Renne and Nix would be unhappy?"

"She can be no man's wife." Albi snapped. "In just two years, you will be council mother. Are you ready? Today, no, you are not ready. The power to arrange marriages cannot ever be surrendered. Calli, for as long as I live I will always be your adviser. My wisdom, combined with your social popularity, will make us the most formidable force in the Kindred. But only if you do what I say."

Calli's reply was fortunately cut off by Bellu's arrival. Waddling under her first pregnancy, she sighed and plopped down between the two women. "My baby has been trying to kick his way out today."

"Or her," Calli reminded her friend.

Bellu shook her head. "Oh, Urs could father nothing but a boy," she proclaimed sunnily.

Calli looked away. "I suppose so."

"Our husbands went out today to hunt, just the two of them, did you know that?" Bellu asked.

Calli was surprised. "Palloc and Urs?"

"Palloc has been over to our fire several times, wanting to go out alone with Urs. It has been very important to him, for some reason."

"I never heard anything of this," Calli replied.

"The hunt," Albi snorted. "While we do all the work, they run around looking for something to kill, and half the time they fail at it."

Calli and Bellu exchanged a wordless glance.

"Anyway," Bellu finally said, "your mother just fed me a stew. My son must be in my stomach eating everything that I swallow, because I am already hungry again!"

Calli nodded, patting her pregnancy. "I feel the same way."

"I could not stop eating," Albi agreed. "When I was with Palloc, the hunger never stopped."

"Oh?" Bellu responded. "So there was a time in your life when you were hungry?"

Calli stared, shocked at her friend's audacity. Bellu's eyes widened, as if she, too, were surprised.

Albi did not hesitate. Her eyes narrowed and she swung her meaty arm, palm flat and open, and slapped Bellu hard across the face. With a cry, Bellu fell to her side.

Albi sprung up and brought her foot back as if to kick Bellu's pregnant belly, and Calli was in front of her without even realizing she had stood up. "No!" she yelled at Albi.

The two women squared off, Calli ready to fight, and then a dark calculation came and went in Albi's eyes. The council mother had just struck the wife of the hunt master.

Albi had made a very bad mistake.

Brach had summoned Silex: the big she-wolf had been spotted nearby. The two Wolfen trotted side by side.

"Fia wants a child. Children. It is all she speaks about," Silex blurted.

Brach nodded, uncomfortable with the subject. "There has been good hunting lately," he noted.

"What if it is me? What if I cannot impregnate my Fia?"

"I am pleased with my new spear."

"How long before she turns to another man?"

Brach looked shocked. "What? She would never do that! Silex, sometimes at night, well . . ." He cleared his throat. "The sounds coming from where you bed provide inspiration to my wife and I. It does not seem to my ears as if Fia is dissatisfied."

"Fia is the most passionate woman I can imagine," Silex agreed after a moment. "And that is what worries me. Am I enough for her? Of the seven of us who split from the tribe, there are only two women—that feels a mistake."

"If another were to even approach Fia I would kill him myself," Brach pronounced grimly.

"Yes, well, we all know that when a female wolf is receptive, even the most submissive males are restless, often beyond wisdom. It has been two and a half years since we left the others. In that time, the boys have grown the beards and bodies of men. I think, Brach, it is time to find Duro and our brother Wolfen and give our unmarried men a chance to meet their own mates."

"If there even *are* any unmarried women," Brach observed.

"True."

"There," Brach interrupted, pointing.

Silex smiled. It was her, the large she-wolf with the white human handprint on her forehead. Brach stopped, handing Silex a reindeer leg. It was as heavy as a club, laden with meat.

"It has been some time since you have made yourself

known to us," Silex called out softly. Behind her, he spotted several young wolves, shying back and staying in the trees even as the she-wolf approached. Her offspring—she had had a spring litter!

The large wolf accepted the tribute from Silex when he heaved it across ten paces to her, watching him, her eyes on his face.

Palloc carried a club in one hand and a spear in the other. Urs held only a spear. They were out in the area where the Kindred had hunted successfully a few days before, but the herd had moved on, and they were not finding tracks heading in any particular direction. The hard earth made it difficult to discern where they might have gone.

Palloc was not paying much attention anyway. Several times since the night of their weddings he had decided the time had come to get Urs alone and finally fulfill the pledge he had made to himself to kill his nemesis, but the hunt master had resisted every suggestion that they do this, hunt together, just the two of them. Now, surprisingly, Urs had swiftly agreed they should go off by themselves when Palloc again proposed it, and the summer quarters finally were far enough away that they were out of sight of anyone from the Kindred. It was a clear, dry day, and the men moved into a wooded area more for the shade than the likelihood they might encounter reindeer sleeping in the grasses there.

Good. The trees provided additional cover.

Palloc would do it quickly. He would simply fall a few steps behind the other man, raise his club, and strike with all his might. The first blow might not kill him, but it would stun Urs long enough for Palloc to drive his spear into the hunt master's heart. Then he could use the club to finish the job.

Palloc would wait two days and then return to camp and claim a bear had made off with Urs. By that time, scavengers would have been at the body long enough that even if they searched, all the hunt would find would be bones marked with animal teeth. No one would doubt his story.

Palloc fell back. *Now,* he thought to himself. He gripped his club. Urs was taller than Palloc by several finger lengths, but the club would make up for that. The stone tied to the end would crush Urs's skull. *Now. Now.*

Urs halted abruptly, turning so swiftly that Palloc nearly tripped in surprise. "I need to talk to you," Urs said quietly.

Sweating, Palloc nodded. He loosened his grip on his club.

"A spear master is charged with more than true aim. He must be a wise teacher, willing to help the younger hunters hone their skills. He must withhold his throw until sure of a hit, so as not to waste his shot, and to demonstrate patience. When the spear master throws, the spearmen will often follow the action immediately, so it must be right. Understood? The throw must be right."

Palloc blinked at Urs's intensity. Why was he talking about this? These were things that were well known.

"But you have not taken time to help the younger hunters. And your own aim is not true, and is often premature. This disrupts the effort of the entire hunt." Urs shook his head.

Palloc stared at him.

"I cannot have you as my spear master anymore. It is not good for the hunt; everything I do must be good for the hunt. Everything we all do." Urs clapped him on the shoulder. "I know this is hard. But there is no humiliation in facing the truth of one's limitations, there is only humiliation in failure due to overreaching."

Palloc felt as if his club had hit his own head. He was stunned literally speechless.

"I am glad I was able to tell you away from the others," Urs continued. "I will go back now; you wait half a day and then follow. By the time you return, all will know, and it will be my instruction that you be treated with the respect due a spearman of the hunt. This is all for the good. I know you see that."

Palloc nodded dumbly. And that was that: Urs turned and headed back to camp, his head up, his shoulders square. Palloc watched him go, the spear in his hand twitching.

Now, the voice said inside of him. *Now.*

TWENTY-ONE

L ook," Silex called, pointing. The men with him followed his gesture. Far in the distance, the small wolf pack they had been tracking was running in single file, the large female with the handprint marking at the head of the line.

"Must be game in that direction. Do we follow, Silex?" Brach inquired.

Silex was staring at the line of wolves, seeing their tails, their ears.

"There is a difference between pursuing and fleeing," Silex noted. "These wolves are running from something." He squinted at the surrounding hills. "We need to get to high ground."

W hen, one by one, the women of the council heard of the slap that had been delivered to Bellu, they headed immediately to her mother's family camp, everyone solicitously patting Bellu's shoulder and asking how she was feeling. Something was adding up for them, Calli could see. Bellu, the prettiest among them, having her face struck. Bellu, bursting with unborn child, being knocked over. Albi, dispensing rough justice without a council meeting, taking everything into her own hands.

"It is time," Bellu's mother, Ador, said gravely, "to replace the council mother."

Furtively glancing around to make sure they were safely out of earshot of Albi, the women nodded their agreement.

"In two more summers, Calli was to be made council mother," Coco reminded them. "Perhaps the time has come *now.*"

More nodding, amid murmurs of assent. Calli watched all of this with an almost detached air, betraying nothing. She was not sure what she was feeling. *I will always be your adviser,* Albi had promised her. It had sounded like a threat. What would the position of council mother be like, with Albi always around?

"Shhh!" someone warned. The women stiffened. Approaching them was Hardy's wife, Droi, a concerned look on her face.

"I heard Albi struck you," Droi told Bellu. "Are you recovered?"

Bellu nodded hesitantly.

Droi looked around at the other women. "What is everyone talking about?"

No one seemed to want to answer the question. Women awkwardly dropped their eyes.

"Ah. It is about Albi," Droi reasoned. "You want to depose her as council mother."

Still, no one spoke.

"But you do not want to tell me. Albi, who copulates with my husband. You are afraid for my feelings. Albi, who has beaten me with her fists since we were children. You worry how I might react. Albi. My sister." Droi looked at them with narrow eyes. "You think I will warn her, but you are wrong. For me, there is only one day of real happiness left in my life, and that is the day when she falls over dead."

For a moment, no one moved. Then Ador hugged Droi, and Coco joined the hug, and then the women of the Kindred, drawing strength from each other's arms, stood in one large, silent embrace.

Only Renne, on the fringe of the group, did not join the hug. She backed away a quiet step, then another, and then slipped away without making a sound.

Albi was by her family fire, her expression unreadable as she watched Renne approach her.

"Council Mother?" Renne lowered her eyes, standing several feet back.

"What do you want?"

"Some of the women are talking about you. I thought you should know."

Albi considered this. She looked off into the distance, her eyes unfocused, then sharpened her gaze at Renne. "You seek to gain favor with me. Come closer. Tell me what you have heard."

Renne nodded and stepped up until she was within whisper range. In quick strokes, she explained what the women were up to.

"So Calli is moving against me now," Albi muttered.

"Well," Renne corrected, "the women are saying Calli should be made council mother. Calli herself has expressed no opinion."

"Oh no, she is behind it all. My own daughter-in-law betrays me," Albi insisted sharply. "None of this could happen without her approval. She covets. She schemes. She is a wicked person." Albi drew in a breath. "So. You were right to come to me with this, child. Had I called a meeting, I would have been caught off guard by this sedition, and Calli's attack might have been successful. This gives me time to plan my defense." Albi appraised Renne, looking her up and down. "Now, as to you."

Renne stood silent, unconsciously stroking the scar on her face that Albi had put there.

"You are past the age when women usually marry, but without a living mother, there is no one to speak on your behalf to the women's council, and thus no man has been found for you," Albi observed.

"Yes."

"Would you like for me to pick a husband for you?"

Renne nodded, keeping her eyes down.

"Well then. I do not blame you. When I was your age, I thought I simply had to have a husband. Later I realized they have very few uses. When my husband died after stupidly getting in the way of a winter mammoth, it was my day of freedom. Still, you probably want children. So I should say . . . Nix. Bellu's brother. He is a good choice for you."

Renne's face was shining, as if she could not believe her luck. She looked so radiantly joyous it was on Albi's tongue to tell her to forget Nix, she would pick someone else. But bestowing this favor on Renne made sense—it would ensure the younger woman's continued subservience. Albi needed to focus on what was important. It was like the tribe's migrations—not about the day's journey, but the destination at the end of it.

"I will speak to the council about Nix," Albi declared magnanimously.

"He is a kind man," Renne blurted.

"Well, he is not smart enough to be anything else," Albi grunted. "You may go."

Renne turned as if to sprint back to the communal fire. "Oh, Renne?"

Renne paused, turning back, something like fear in her eyes.

"Keep me informed," Albi said, "of anything else Calli tries to do."

* * *

The Wolfen were hiding in the grasses at the top of a rise, peering at the plains below. They spoke to each other in whispers, though they were much too far away to be heard: a party of Cohort had come upriver. The valley tribe was easy to identify—they rubbed black ashes on their face until they appeared fierce and savage. Their robes were simple and crude, mere flaps of hide hanging from rope belts to cover their genitals and, across their shoulders—to Silex's dismay—some wore wolf fur.

Four of the Cohort were advancing slowly, each with spear and club, while on either side of this line two of them went left and two went right, a wide encircling movement. They were hunting something, but what?

"There," Silex hissed. In the middle of the field, hiding in the grass, a family of Frightened were hunkered down behind a mound of earth. The male was hugely muscular and held a club, as did two adolescent children—one girl and a boy. The woman, pregnant, fearfully clutched a small child of perhaps two or three.

"They think they are safe. See? The four Cohort are spread out, and look as if they will walk right past the Frighteneds, who will hide in the gap between the advancing hunters. But the Cohort know they are there, and they are sweeping in from behind, coming up on each side. It is a trap." Wolves sometimes did something similar, splitting into pairs on either side of their prey, but usually not until a hoofed animal took flight.

"What do we do?" one of his men whispered tensely.

"Do?" Brach replied in soft scorn.

"We could run, draw off the Cohort," the man argued.

"For a family of Frighteneds?" another spat scornfully.

"Then the Cohort would come to hunt us," Silex replied.

"The Frightened are large and powerful. They can defend themselves without our help."

But the attack, when it came, was brief and unimaginably brutal. With a shrill, inhuman sound, the Cohort advanced from all sides. The Frighteneds raised their weapons but the Cohort struck with shocking effect. The male went down first, surrounded. The Cohort turned on the older children, viciously pounding their heads even as they dropped their clubs and cowered. Their mother screamed as her toddler was ripped from her arms and thrown to the ground and stomped. And then, grinning fiercely, the Cohort surrounded the woman, pushing her down. She twisted, sobbing, as they pinned her arms and ripped off her skirt, flipping her onto her pregnant belly so the first one could have her.

"We go," Silex said, sickened. "We go now."

They snaked backward in the grass until they were far enough away to stand without being seen, and then they ran, all of them wanting to put the grisly slaughter behind them.

"Why do they do that?" Brach asked Silex later, when the two of them were off by themselves. Brach's face was still pale and sweaty—none of the men had wanted to eat when it came to be mealtime.

"The Cohort? I do not know," Silex said. "They have always been a murderous people. And there is another question."

"Another question?"

"There was a time when the Cohort came out of their valley and attacked anyone they came across, but for several years they have not been seen." Silex gave his friend a searching look. "Is it starting again?"

* * *

Palloc found Calli at the family fire, watching indulgently as her son Dog wrestled and played with Ligo, his four-year-old friend. The two were well matched—despite being one summer younger, Dog was as tall as the other boy.

"We need to get away from here," Palloc informed her. "Take some food; we will spend the day out and return as darkness is settling."

Calli frowned at him. "What? Where were you yesterday?" She struggled to her feet, one arm crooked under her pregnant belly. "Whew."

"Dog!" Palloc commanded. "We are going downstream for the day."

"Good!" Dog shouted exultantly. Whatever they were doing, it sounded as if it would be grand fun—and for Dog, it probably would be. "Can Ligo come?" he asked eagerly as the two boys rushed up.

"No."

The two boys looked at each other as if they had just learned that one of them was to be fed to the wolves.

"Palloc, what is it? Why are you behaving so strangely?" Calli asked.

"Please, Father?" Dog begged.

"All right," Palloc snapped. "If it will keep you out of my way, Ligo can come." He pointed at Calli. "Gather food. We are leaving now."

Albi watched as Palloc and his wife took Dog and Ligo and left camp, headed downstream. For once Palloc was doing something useful for her. She went to the men's side of the camp, signaling for Urs to join her. After what she interpreted as an insulting delay, Urs rose, making his way over to where Albi was waiting. "What is it?"

"Hunt Master," Albi said, speaking formally. "Though the weather has been mild and the hunting good, we must depart immediately for winter quarters."

Urs blinked in surprise. He glanced up at the clear blue sky, then down at her. "I was thinking we had many more days."

"I am telling you that the women believe winter will come early. We must leave in two days. The women are packing." Or they would be, as soon as Albi informed them of this decision.

"Well," Urs started to say.

"Plus there is something else," Albi interrupted. Urs gaped at her as the council mother sank to her knees. "Often, Hunt Master, just as you discipline the hunters, I must impose order among the women."

Urs was baffled. "Order? Among the women?"

Albi squeezed her eyes together in abject contrition. "I fear that in doing so, Hunt Master, I administered a light slap today."

"I do not understand any of this."

"I will accept any punishment, Hunt Master. Strike me with fist or club, at your will."

"*Hit* you?"

"It was Bellu upon whom I administered the council's discipline."

Urs blinked. "Wait. *Wait.* You struck my *wife*?"

Albi, still kneeling, bent so that her forehead touched the ground. "I submit to your punishment."

TWENTY-TWO

Urs regarded Albi's prostrate form, utterly flummoxed. The anger he should be feeling was flustered by her behavior. *I submit to your punishment.* Was he supposed to beat her? Kindred men were forbidden to touch any woman not related by blood or marriage. Something like this was usually handled by the women's council, but Albi *was* the women's council. "Stand up," Urs grated.

Albi rose, and he was pleased to see the fear in her eyes. He thrust a finger at her face. "If you ever touch my wife again, I will . . . I will *kill* you," he threatened.

"Yes, Hunt Master," Albi replied submissively.

Urs realized he was standing there with his finger extended and nothing else to do. Oddly dissatisfied, he snatched the digit back and turned and walked stiffly away.

He did not see the contemptuous smile on Albi's face.

Urs went to find his wife. Bellu was sitting by the Kindred stream, bringing handfuls of water to her face.

"Bellu," Urs announced sternly, "I have just spoken to Albi."

"Oh Urs." Bellu came to him, her pregnant belly between them.

"I told her she may never touch you again. Understand?" For some reason, *now* Urs could feel anger.

"Yes. Thank you, Husband."

"Women are . . ." Urs could not finish the sentence

because just starting it caused all perplexity to flow, like blood from a wound. "We leave in just a few days for winter quarters. I must take the hunt out."

"So soon?"

"I have to find Valid," Urs responded. He was still unaccountably angry.

Valid was waiting for him on the men's side. "Gather the hunt," Urs instructed in clipped tones. "I will tell them you are spear master, and then we go at once to look for game. We leave for winter quarters in two days' time."

"What?" Valid mimicked Urs's examination of the cloudless sky.

"The women want to go. Do not ask me why."

"Palloc will not be able to join us on the hunt," Valid cautioned. "He left with his family and my son. I do not know where they were going."

Urs considered this. "We cannot wait for his return. We leave for the hunt immediately."

A dor and Coco were talking when Bellu came up and breathlessly reported what she had just heard, that they were departing for the winter quarters earlier than anyone expected. Coco's eyes narrowed. "Oh? Such interesting timing."

"What do you mean?" Ador asked.

"We certainly would never select a new council mother during the move, nor when we first arrive at winter camp. There is just too much confusion. Albi has managed to cling to her position for many more days."

Ador nodded. "Of course."

"I am afraid I do not understand," Bellu told them.

"It means Albi is not going to go without a fight," Coco told her. "Where is Calli?"

* * *

It was easier to march ahead of his wife and the two children than to stride next to them and converse, so Palloc kept his eyes to the path and plodded along. Here the terrain along the stream arranged itself in hillocks, sparse trees waving in the light breeze.

"Palloc," Calli called. "You have to stop."

He turned and saw to his irritation that they were fifty paces behind him. Dog was clinging to his mother's side as if his legs had ceased functioning, and Ligo was a further twenty paces back, listlessly dragging his feet a slow step at a time. With a sigh, Palloc reversed course.

"You have to remember that these are little children," Calli scolded him when he came up to her. She wiped a hand across her sweaty forehead. "And I am not suited for this, either. Why are we going so far?"

Palloc picked up Dog, holding the wriggling little boy under one arm. "Just a little farther, there is a place we can stop. Come on, Ligo!"

"Run, Ligo!" Dog called. Ligo ran, a burst of speed that made Dog giggle.

Palloc took her to an area the hunt had found many summers ago: a path led up a long, gentle rise to a place where water came out of the ground, flowed over rocks in a trickle, and landed with a gurgle in a small pond where people could bathe, one person at a time, though the water was frigid. From here they could see the two hundred paces back down to the Kindred stream—the hills here were more heavily treed, making for a secluded, private area.

"This is a wonderful spot!" Calli enthused. She splashed her legs and laughed as Dog and Ligo revived themselves with a water fight. The cloudless sky reflected up at her from the surface of the pond—she immediately looked at peace, as comfortable as she could be with the baby inside of her.

Palloc sat back from them, on a rock, and brooded. He wanted to come up with the words he would use to tell her that he was no longer spear master, but all he could dwell on was the way he had failed to raise his club when he had had the chance. One true blow, and the hunt master would be dead!

Now it was obvious why Urs had been so reluctant to go off hunting alone with Palloc: Urs had been planning this treachery all along, and did not want any friendship to build between them for fear it would make this unfair demotion awkward.

Palloc seethed. Excepting the unexecuted plan to kill him, Palloc had been nothing but loyal to Urs!

He remembered the day the lion attacked Hardy. Palloc was there, but did he get any adulation? Now he wished he had run up and loosed his spear and that it had gone straight into Urs's gut. Urs would be dead and Palloc would be hunt master. Palloc would be married to beautiful Bellu, instead of Calli, who asked too many questions and had too many opinions.

Calli shot him several sideways glances, but Palloc remained distanced from them. "Father, come play!" Dog called to him, but Palloc's expression was stony, and he gave no indication he had heard.

"Shall we eat?" Calli shouted up at him an hour or so later.

"Go ahead, I have no appetite today," he responded.

Calli shrugged, opened her pouch, and tore pieces of cold cooked venison for the boys to eat.

"I want to do this every day from now on!" Dog announced. Calli laughed as her son, grinning, threw a piece of meat into the air and tried to catch it in his open mouth. Ligo soon followed suit, missing about half the time.

"You must still eat it if you get it dirty," Calli admonished.

Dog rinsed off the venison in the water, challenging his mother with a triumphant look.

"Yes, very clever," Calli nodded. "You certainly outsmarted me, Dog."

Calli and the boys dozed during the afternoon, and the sun was just starting to slant when she struggled awake. She saw from the remains that her husband had come to feed while she napped. He was closer now, watching her from a few paces away. His expression was dark and unreadable.

"What is it?" Calli fought her pregnant belly, eventually making it to a sitting position, back against a rock.

"There has been a change in the order of the hunt."

"The order?"

"The hunt has an order. Every man knows his position in the hunt. Most are spearmen, but some are superior to others. Then there is the stalk master, Mors, who scouts ahead for game, and the stalking men who help—each stalker has a place. It is the order."

"I have heard this, I just never heard of it as the 'order,'" Calli replied agreeably.

"I will now be the most superior spearman."

Calli nodded. "I see," she said, not understanding.

Palloc stared moodily into the distance. "Valid, on the other hand, will be the spear master. It is a change in the order, but not much of one."

Calli stared at her husband. She saw the anger in his eyes, but there was something else there, too: this hurt him, she could see, and she felt her heart going out to him. She held out her arms. "Husband. Come here."

His lips twisted and he stood abruptly. "I thought you should know." He stomped off, wandering up the hill until he was out of sight.

Dog and Ligo came out of their sleep as if lightning had struck them, going from unconscious to running around laughing in an instant. Calli sighed, holding her belly.

Far downstream, a black shape moved. Calli caught her breath when she saw that it was a great bear, busily overturning rocks and sniffing underneath them. It was at least a thousand paces away, and seemed unaware they were nearby.

Her husband was out of sight. "Palloc?" she called.

Palloc did not answer. The boys were oblivious, splashing each other and laughing. Calli bit her lip. The creature was either unaware of the human presence or it did not care—the huge beast never once looked in her direction. After a while, Calli relaxed. Apparently there was no danger.

Palloc returned after some time had elapsed. He seemed to have overcome his anger. Calli decided not to mention what they had been talking about.

"I have been watching the bear," she told him.

Palloc's head snapped up. "What bear?"

"It seems a young one—it is not as big as they can get, anyway. See? Way down there. He is digging along the streambed."

Palloc stared at the huge predator. "Did you just notice him?"

"No, it has been since you left. It is okay, though, he has never looked up here at us, or even raised his nose. He is just concentrating on the rocks."

"He knows we are here," Palloc whispered.

"What?"

"Every time you look at him, has he moved a little closer?"

."Yes, but he is just slowly working his way along the stream banks."

"He knows we are here. Hardy spoke to us often of this kind of behavior. He is hunting us."

Calli's heart clenched inside her like a fist. "Oh no."

"Dog! Ligo! Be quiet! Say nothing! We must leave *now*. Do not take anything, just come!" Palloc hoisted his spear and they padded down to the stream bank as silently as they could. Ironically, this brought them even closer to the bear, but the only trail back to camp was along the stream.

"Do we run?" Calli whispered.

"No. A great bear is faster than any man. We walk. Do not look back."

Calli nodded, holding the boys' hands in her hers, but after a hundred paces she could not help herself and glanced behind her.

The bear had closed half the distance. He was sniffing the ground, for all appearances not interested in them, but he must have galloped for a few seconds. Now she could very clearly see the legendary claws of the great bear, who was massive, as tall on four legs as she was on two. "Palloc," Calli gasped, her voice trembling. "He is getting closer."

Palloc risked a look back. The bear shuffled ahead, seemingly just strolling along.

"Stop," Palloc commanded.

She dreaded the idea, but she did as she was told. She turned and looked at her husband, seeing the immense predator over his shoulder, still steadily headed in their direction.

"He is going to charge us," Palloc grated.

Calli glanced at his spear. He shook his head. "No one man can stop the charge of a great bear."

"Then what are we to do, Palloc? I am so scared."

Palloc's pale complexion seemed to have turned as white as a snowbank. He was visibly trembling.

"If we run, he will take us," he murmured.

Calli realized she was going to die. Her gaze turned to Dog. Palloc followed her look.

"If we each pick up a child . . . ," she began urgently, her voice shaking.

"Then one adult and one child will die," Palloc interrupted. "But if we pick up one child, I pick up Dog, and we run, then two adults and one child will live."

It took a moment to register what he was saying. "What? *What?*"

"It is the only way, Calli."

The bear was seventy paces away and had also stopped, seemingly unhurried now that they were no longer fleeing.

"We cannot *leave Ligo*!" she hissed. Tears were flowing now, and she wiped them angrily away. "Palloc! We cannot!"

He bent and picked up Dog. "Ligo," he said, his voice so strange that the two boys stared at him solemnly, "we are going to go ahead, but we want you to wait here. And then when we call, you show us how fast you can run, understand?"

Ligo nodded, grinning.

"No!" Calli shrieked. She snatched up Ligo, who stared at her, frightened.

The great bear was turned, looking back the way he had just came, as if he had just heard something. He raised his nose to the air.

"Go!" Calli snapped. Waddling as fast as she could with her burden, she headed up the path. Within seconds Palloc was even with her, giving her a desperate plea with his eyes, and then he and Dog bolted ahead.

One adult and one child would die.

"Ligo," Calli panted. "If I have to put you down, if I fall

or if something . . . if you see a bear, you need to get up and run and catch up to Dog and his father. Do not try to save me."

Ligo looked at her with wide eyes, frightened, not understanding. Calli tried to smile reassuringly, but a sob broke from her lips instead. "Please, Ligo," she whispered.

Behind her, Calli heard the great bear roar.

TWENTY-THREE

Calli had run no more than twenty paces when Ligo began to struggle in her arms. He wanted down; the way she was carrying him, up high off her belly, was awkward and strange. He needed to get away from this woman with her terrified face and strange instructions.

"No, Ligo," she sobbed. "Please."

"Down!" he insisted, pushing at her.

There was another roar, louder and more terrible than before, and Calli tripped and fell hard, pushing Ligo from her so she would not land on him. She rolled, gasping, as Ligo leaped to his feet and bolted up the trail in pursuit of Palloc and Dog.

All right. Calli placed her hands over her stomach as she struggled to a standing position. Dog was safe. Ligo was safe.

She turned to face the bear.

The great bear was rolling on the ground, bellowing in rage, slapping at himself with his immense paws. Blinking through her tears, Calli saw, to her amazement, a broken spear shaft sticking from the bear's belly, and then, higher up, the stub of a second spear, impaled in the bear's shoulder. Beyond the bear, men were darting out of the trees, running full force at the wounded predator.

The bear, jaws snapping, came to its feet. Its head was low as it charged the hunters, moving terrifyingly fast.

The men, shouting, flung their spears. One hit true, and

another, and another. The bear stumbled, its foreleg crumpling under its body and its face digging into the dirt. The shouts turned to cheers as more spears found their mark, and the bear convulsed, dying.

When the men were close enough to pound the bear's head with clubs, Calli could see who they were. The Kindred, out in force.

Calli started walking toward them, dazed. "Urs," she croaked.

The men looked up at her approach. Urs broke from the hunt and rushed to her, his arms out, concerned.

"Oh Urs," she sobbed. She fell into his arms, kissing his face, unable to stop sobbing. "You saved me. You saved me."

Urs held her tightly, and for a moment it was as if they were still lovers—she could feel him responding despite the round weight of her pregnancy. And then he went rigid, gently but firmly pushing her away. She looked up and saw him gazing over her shoulder, so she turned, too.

Palloc and Ligo were approaching. Palloc was watching the two of them embrace, scowling.

And Calli did not care.

"Ligo!" Valid shouted.

"Father!" the little boy answered, running over and tackling his father's legs.

Valid turned and unexpectedly clasped Calli. "Thank you," he murmured into her ear. His breath warmed her and then they awkwardly broke apart.

Calli turned and watched Palloc approach, her face cold.

"We have been tracking the bear half the day," Urs hailed Calli's husband. "We lost him for a while, but picked up his tracks in the mud by the stream."

Bear meat was no one's favorite, but the fur of a bear made a wonderfully warm blanket despite its coarse feel.

Men liked to collect bear teeth and claws to absorb some of the predator's ferocity into themselves. It was a good omen, to kill a great bear.

Calli turned to Palloc. Her eyes were icily furious. "Where is Dog?"

"I put him on a rock, high up, where the bear could not reach him. I was coming back for you, Calli," Palloc claimed angrily.

"You left him on a rock?"

Urs, glancing at the two of them, backed out of the marital conflict.

"What else could I do? I was coming back for you!" Palloc shouted.

Calli pushed rudely past him and headed up the path. A hundred paces later, she came upon her son, who was, indeed, standing up on a slab of rock higher than a man's head. Some natural handholds gave clue as to how Palloc managed to get him up there.

Her son was safe. Her anger was gone in a gust—this was her little boy, full of life, and she loved him so much.

"Hello, Mother! Look how tall I am!" Dog called to her.

Year Nineteen

Her brothers were gone. The female wolf puppy understood this less as a loss than as a lack; there were simply no siblings to play with. Losing the entire pack would be something else, a life-changing, probably life-ending, catastrophe. But there was still a pack, still a mother-wolf, and the man, who had always been there. Now, when the puppy played, she played with the man.

She was driven by a joyous sense of fun to wrestle with him, to jump on him and nip at him, but there was also an instinct at work, a purpose to the play. Wolves learned how to fight when they were little, teaching themselves technique. When the little female tumbled on the cave floor with the man, she was getting an education. She learned that the hands that fed her were also effective weapons, with a grip like a pair of jaws. Her defense was to go after the arms, above the man's grasp, and clamp down with her little teeth and shake her head.

She also learned something else. "Stop! Release!" the man sometimes yelled. There was pain in his voice, a sharpness, and the hand might shove at her with astounding force, sending her rolling away in the dust.

If she were a normal wolf puppy in a normal pack, she would be disciplined by the elders when she put too much aggression into her play, so she learned a similar lesson from this. And, just as a pup would lick her mother's mouth in utter submission, seeking forgiveness in such situations, the little pup would crawl to the man and lick his face. Then, when he gathered her to his chest and buried his face in her fur, she felt as content as when she curled up next to her mother to sleep.

Year Four

The weather for the migration was clear, dry, and warm. The Kindred stopped often for water from their stream, and moved more slowly than usual, because several women, including Calli and Bellu, were pregnant. Calli was the furthest along, and had been spared the need to carry anything but her unborn child. Whenever Dog complained, his grandmother Coco would scoop him up willingly, even though she was already burdened with dragging the cooking implements they needed.

"You spoil that child," Albi said sternly. "Dog, get down and walk."

"Yes, Grandmother," Dog said obediently. He slid down from Coco's hip, but when Albi turned her back he stuck out his tongue. Coco had to stifle her laugh.

As always, tension began to rise as they approached the point in their journey where the little Kindred stream joined the big river and the waters flowed into the Cohort Valley. They were half a day's walk from the juncture, padding slowly and silently, the hunters all armed with spear and club and alert to any danger, when Coco looked over and saw her daughter's expression.

"Has it started?" Coco asked in low tones. Nix, the hunter closest to her, gave her a sharp glance for risking even this tiny whisper.

Calli nodded. She held up two fingers: two contractions.

As quietly as she could, Coco increased her speed a little, pulling up next to Albi. "Calli's in labor," she said in a barely audible voice.

Albi gave her a baleful look. "We cannot stop now," she hissed back. "Not *here*. We are almost to the place where rivers meet."

"No, of course not."

Calli kept walking. Her waters had not yet come, but the pains seemed to be increasing and coming closer together. With Dog, nearly a day had passed like this, but she was aware of how bad the timing was. There could be no more dangerous place to have a baby.

Coco gave her a drink, and Calli nodded gratefully. A few minutes later, a harsher pain gripped her, so that she inhaled sharply. It held her the way a lion held a struggling deer in its jaws, squeezing her inside.

She bit back her whimper. Her legs turned warm, and she looked down in alarm: her waters had come.

Now the pains redoubled, coming more quickly, nearly toppling her off her feet. She staggered, sweat pouring from her brow, but still she walked, and still she was silent.

Bellu and Ardor came and silently took Coco's load from her, and Coco put her arms around her daughter as another contraction came.

Calli felt it in her back, at the base of her spine, and then throughout her lower body, as if someone had rammed a hot spear into her from behind and was now twisting and jabbing it. The intervals between pain were less. She kept stumbling forward, but she could no longer see or think of anything but what was occurring.

Her vision swimming, she realized someone else was there. Palloc. He was on her other side, supporting her. He had left the hunt to help her. She felt a wave of gratitude that was pushed aside by a contraction so long and hard she could not help the loud gasp that escaped her lips.

They were right at the river juncture, the most dangerous place. Calli could feel the child descending. She knew it would be here soon, and she could no longer support herself. Palloc tried to keep her up, but Coco was sagging on the other side.

"Stop," Calli mumbled.

She lowered her head, stretching her arms to the ground as if diving into water. Her husband and her mother helped her down gently, and Calli knelt, her knees apart, unable to prevent the whimpers from escaping her lips.

The Kindred acted as a single organism, stopping its march without a command. Under a clear, blue sky, everyone silent, Calli bit her lip until it bled, her eyes crossed, pushing.

Coco saw the baby's head, bloody and covered with mucus, emerging from between her daughter's legs. She bent over and tenderly supported the child as its shoulders emerged. The poor thing was crimson faced, and when at last it popped out into the world, Coco saw that she had a new grandson.

The baby cried.

Everyone in the Kindred went rigid at the tiny noise. The hunters raised their spears as if attack were imminent, most of them also clutching a club. The women glanced at each other in alarm. Frowning, Albi strode over to where Calli lay.

"Shhh, baby boy," Coco murmured. She handed the child to Calli, who was still suffering as the afterbirth was expelled.

The baby, as if sensing what was required of him, stopped squalling. Calli held him to her breast, but he did not seem interested in that. He blinked through bleary eyes in the strong sunshine. Calli smiled up at her husband, and Palloc felt his heart swell at her expression. She was his wife, and they had a new child. He smiled back, feeling full of love.

Ignus, Calli's father, joined them, panting because he had been ranging well ahead with the stalkers and had only just heard that his daughter was in labor. He held Dog in his arms and the expressions on both their faces was the same: solemn, wide-eyed, even a bit fearful.

"We have a new grandson, Ignus," Coco whispered proudly.

"His leg," Albi grunted.

Everyone looked at her, then at the baby. They saw what Albi saw: there was something wrong with the baby's leg. Below the knee, it was stunted, twisted, with a small, toe-less foot. The child was deformed.

Calli held her child, her new baby boy, a satisfied smile on her face. She was still sore, hurting too much to stand or walk, but all of that seemed completely unimportant in view of the little person she cradled in her arms. "You have a brother, Dog," she said softly. Dog shyly hid his face in Ignus's shoulder. Ignus, characteristically, had nothing to say.

"The baby is cursed," Albi hissed.

Coco stared. Calli did not seem to notice.

"The baby is cursed. He brings a curse on all of us. The Kindred," Albi insisted in hushed tones.

Palloc looked down at his new son. In a flash, he saw what the boy's life would be. He could never join the hunt. He would be a burden on everyone. During migrations, someone might even have to carry him. People would blame Palloc for the problems the boy would cause.

"He is just a baby," Coco murmured. "Look at him."

"I *am* looking at him," Albi snapped. "He is a curse on us. We need to throw him in the stream."

This shocked everyone. Calli shook her head wildly. *What?*

Albi took in their expressions and her scowling face hardened. "What do you think it means when a baby is born like this? Of course it is a curse. To keep it for even a moment is to invite doom to all of us. Do you realize where we are, how treacherous this place is? Why was he born *here,* of all places? What more proof is required?"

People nearby were giving them censorious glances for even the bare whispers. Calli wrapped her arms protectively around her baby son, wondering what Albi thought she was doing.

She soon found out. Albi reached down. "Give it to me."

"No!" Calli protested.

Albi seized the baby's twisted leg, then let go as if she had touched a hot rock when her hand connected with the deformity. She reached for the other one, fixing Calli with a hard look. "It is for the good of all of us," she insisted as she pulled on the newborn.

"Quiet!" someone hissed at them.

"You have to let it go. Let me take it," Albi commanded, pulling harder.

Calli inhaled. "No!" she screamed, as loudly as she had ever screamed anything in her life.

TWENTY-FOUR

Calli's shrill cry seemed to ring in the air. The Kindred had frozen in shock and were now glancing at one another with bulging eyes. If there was a Cohort attack party nearby, Calli's shout would bring them running.

Urs was by their side in an instant. "Calli!" he whispered urgently. "You must be quiet!" He crouched down next to her.

"This baby has been born cursed. We must put it out of its misery and save the Kindred," Albi informed Urs.

He frowned, not comprehending.

"The *leg*," Albi spat, clearly communicating she thought Urs a fool.

He glanced at the baby's leg and winced. "What happened to it?"

"It is just how he was born," Coco murmured.

"A curse," Albi insisted. "This is not your business, Hunt Master. This is a women's council matter."

Urs considered this. "We must remain perfectly quiet right now," he finally whispered back.

Calli realized he was accepting Albi's argument, that he would let her baby die because *it did not have anything to do with the hunt.*

"I can do it," Palloc said suddenly.

"All the better," Albi agreed.

Coco and Calli stared at each other, dumbfounded at the direction of the conversation.

"No," Ignus objected softly.

It was the first word from Ignus in such a long time that everyone, even his wife, was shocked. For a moment, the mere fact that he had spoken startled them all. Dog turned, his thumb in his mouth, to look at his grandfather as if he, too, was astounded.

Urs stood back up, pointing his finger at Ignus. "It is a council matter. Let them handle it." He nodded at Palloc.

"Urs," Calli said urgently, "if anyone tries to take my baby, I will scream so loudly that my voice will echo for days. I will scream and scream until every human, Wolfen and Cohort among them, is summoned to find out what is happening."

Urs gaped at her, utterly astounded. Albi looked disgusted. Palloc, considering what might happen if she did scream and scream, was frightened.

Calli met her mother's eyes. "I, too, will scream," Coco affirmed, nodding at her daughter.

"And I," Ignus stated calmly.

"You would bring the Valley Cohort to kill us all!" Urs whispered.

"You," Calli replied in low, even tones, "would let Albi kill my baby."

"They would not dare scream," Albi sniffed.

But she did not know Calli the way Urs did. After a long moment, he nodded. "It is, as I said, a council matter," he concluded, "but not something to be decided as we journey south. When we have set up at winter quarters, when we have had a hunt and are secure, then the women may meet and make a determination. Until then, no action."

Albi was shaking her head. "You are not the decider, Hunt Master."

Urs turned on Albi with a ferocity that made the woman take an involuntary step back. "I have *spoken*. Calli, can you stand?"

"I can walk, Hunt Master," she responded proudly.

"Then let us get out of this dangerous place."

S ilex smelled the camp's fires and knew they were close to where the main body of Wolfen gathered along the river. Grinning with excitement, the three unmarried men of their group received a nod from their leader and ran ahead.

"It will be good to see everyone," Silex told Fia. "And good for the men to see some other women."

Fia glanced back at Brach's wife, Ros, who was carrying her newborn son—though even while burdened, they all moved at a quick pace, as was the Wolfen way. "I do not know," Fia answered flippantly. "It has been very entertaining to have so many men fawning over us."

The four of them laughed, but Silex's mirth was forced past his uneasiness.

A bend in the river and they were upon the encampment. Silex instinctively raised his spear: something was wrong. The main body of Wolfen, alerted to their approach by Silex's advance party, had gathered and were standing mutely, staring at him. Silex's eyes darted left and right, trying to find the cause of their obvious distress. All of the men were clearly out on a hunt—aside from a lone old man there were only women and children in the camp. One of them—his sister Ovi—broke from their ranks and came forward. Her breasts were heavy under her tunic, and she held a sleeping baby. Duro, like Brach, but unlike Silex, had been able to get his wife pregnant.

"Silex," Ovi greeted simply. They embraced, but it seemed stiff and formal.

"What has happened?" Silex asked quietly. "Why is everyone acting like this?"

Ovi gestured sadly behind her. "This is all there is," she said.

"I do not know what you mean."

"I mean there is no one else, Silex. The men of the Wolfen are all dead."

The Kindred women and the children spent many days at winter quarters before the hunt returned. The men had come across a great flock of noisy birds chattering by a water hole and had managed to kill armfuls of them until the birds lifted into the sky with a great roar of wings and were gone. When plucked of their feathers, the birds were twice the size of a man's hand. The men had also seen the signs that meant there were winter mammoths nearby— though elusive and bad-tempered in equal measure, enough spears and the great beasts could be brought down. The challenge was always to get close enough for accuracy and yet avoid being trampled.

The men and women hugged each other in celebration, and the festive mood kept them at the communal fire, feasting together even though every hunter brought home a portion for his own family. Calli ate so quickly she felt sick, but the sight of her mother and Dog chewing their meals made her heart lift. They were going to survive this.

Most of the women bolted down their bird meat and experienced similar problems to Calli's, many of them lying near the fire, holding their bellies and squinting their eyes at the cramping pain. The men had taken meals on the hunt, but from the sympathy in their eyes, the wives knew they, too, had been similarly afflicted. It was a lesson difficult to remember: gorging on meat after a prolonged period of involuntary fasting inevitably caused problems, but they rarely could stop themselves.

Albi was one of the first women to make a run to the bushes to relieve herself. When she returned, she regarded the women sprawled on the ground with utter contempt.

"Tomorrow," she said evenly, "the women's council meets."

She turned and stared directly at Calli.

"Tomorrow," Albi repeated. "Tomorrow."

But when tomorrow came, they did not hold council, because Ignus was dead.

Silex was trying to make sense of it: all the Wolfen men dead?

The women sobbed, some clutching their children, pouring out their grief as if they had been saving it for Silex's arrival. It was instant chaos.

Silex acted decisively—if there was danger nearby, he needed to know, but he would get nothing coherent out of these people while they were so emotional. He brought out the food that his group had with him, directing Ovi and some others to cook it, and for all to sit at the fire.

The smell of cooking calmed them, and the surviving Wolfen ravenously tore into the meat. They had eaten very little recently. It was Ovi who explained what had happened, her expression dark and sad. "Four of them went to hunt downriver. They did not return. After several days, Duro became convinced it was the Cohort. He assembled the rest of the men, even the boys, and they went out to drive the Cohort away, to kill enough of them that they would retreat into their valley and never again come onto the land of the wolf. And we waited for them to come back. We ran out of meat, and we ate all of our dried berries. When Duro did not return, we sent Denix."

Silex remembered Denix as a spindly little girl. She was now perhaps thirteen years old, still boyish, but with a long thin body catching up to her gawky arms and feet. Denix looked too fragile and thin to send on such a dangerous mission.

Denix looked at Silex with solemn eyes.

"What did you find, Denix?" Silex asked softly, dreading the answer.

"Their trail went downriver, but not as far as the valley," Denix replied, choking back tears. "I found Duro lying on some rocks. His head, at the back, was crushed, and his limbs were no longer attached. He had been savaged, his body scattered. And there were wolf tracks."

Silex understood why this was so upsetting. "Denix," he said kindly, "you were very brave, and the Wolfen are proud of you. The wolf tracks do not mean that Duro was attacked by our benefactors. We have not fallen out of favor with the wolf. Brach will tell you; we just yesterday paid tribute to the female with the handprint on her head. No, those tracks mean that Duro was very brave, and after fighting the Cohort, he was rewarded and became a wolf himself. His human body, no longer of use to him, was ripped apart by scavengers. You have not been out hunting to see this, but it happens to all animals. Carrion eaters find them all."

Denix was nodding, but her eyes were glassy.

"You saw something else," Silex prompted intuitively.

"Men with fire-black on their faces," Denix whispered. "I hid in the grasses as they came close by, and then when they were not looking I ran away."

"The Cohort," Silex said heavily. He had everyone's rapt attention. "Denix, how close were you to the Cohort Valley?"

"Not far. A day's run."

Perhaps, thought Silex, this was not as bad as it seemed. "The Cohort have not come north in a long time, and it would seem that they were not far out of their territory when they encountered our men."

"The men? Duro took our *boys*," one woman wailed.

"So what do we do, Silex?" Fia asked, loudly enough to direct everyone's attention back to their leader.

Silex looked at the circle of his people, all of them waiting for his reply with desperate hope in their eyes. There were now just six adult men, one of them too old to hunt. They had gone from having too many men who needed wives to being a tribe of nearly all women and children. It would be difficult to muster a hunt and leave the females protected if the Cohort had decided to resume raiding the northern creeds.

They could not survive. They did not have enough men.

His eyes met Denix's. She, like everyone else, expected him to solve this. And Denix, he realized, was essential to the solution.

"Denix," he summoned, evincing more confidence than he felt. "Come forward."

TWENTY-FIVE

T he last words Coco spoke to her husband were, *Ignus, will you come to our fire soon?*

She had much more she planned to say to him. She wanted to tell him how proud she was to have him as her husband, and that she was sorry she had acted so coldly to him for so long. She knew that her abrupt manner with Ignus came from her hurt over his obvious preference to be left alone, instead of craving wife and family. She met his rejection with some of her own, until so many days of silence went by in their marriage it was as if the words between them were smothered with snow. But on the migration south he had stood up for his wife and daughter and grandsons. She wanted to tell him she loved him.

Her imagined conversation made her happy, and she was looking forward to it. When the hunt returned with their bounty of fat birds, she worked hard to catch his eyes as she prepared the communal meal, but as usual her husband was occupied with his inner thoughts and did not seem to notice her glances.

All is good, she decided. This was the man the council had chosen for her. If he needed his solitude, she would allow it and not pretend it was something being done to *her.*

"Ignus, will you come to our fire soon?"

Ignus met her eyes for a brief moment, nodding once.

All is good.

He went to the men's side and sat by the fire and ate

cooked bird meat. Everyone was accustomed to his laconic way—they gave him room and conversed as if he were not there. No one noticed when Ignus put a hand to his throat.

"The hunt should waste no spears for birds in the air, nor as they float," Valid was saying. "They must be taken on the ground like normal prey."

"The Blanc Tribe hunts birds in water," Palloc argued.

Valid blinked at him. "Yes, well, as spear master, I am directing my spearmen to hunt only those birds on the ground, where the Kindred has dominance."

Ignus lunged forward onto his knees and one hand. His face was swollen and visibly red, and his other hand was clawing at his throat. He made a soft sound, like a bark.

"Ignus?" Valid asked, concerned.

"Pick him up!" Urs commanded. "Get him out where Sopho can help him. Mors! Go get Sopho!"

They dragged Ignus out from the men's side to the communal fire. Sopho, the healer, came as quickly as she could. Ignus was on his back, drool flowing out of the corner of his mouth. The sounds from his throat were barely audible.

When Sopho bent to him, Ignus dropped his hand heavily. His face was blue tinged, his lips puffy, his eyes sightless.

Sopho looked up at Urs and shook her head.

It was Palloc who brought Coco to Ignus's side. Calli and the baby were both asleep and he elected to allow them to remain that way.

Coco knelt by her husband. His face was so contorted it did not really even look like him. She took his hand, still warm, and held it.

Urs lowered himself to his knees and the rest of the hunt followed, silent and respectful. "We are sorry, Coco. His throat closed on his food," he told her.

She looked up at Urs, her eyes full of tears. "There was so much," Coco wept, "that I was planning to tell him."

* * *

Albi spent the three days after Ignus was buried with her mouth set in a bitter line, aggravated by the delay. Finally, she could tolerate no more mourning. "The council meets," Albi announced.

When men called the hunt for formal council, they summoned one another with grave portent. The hunt master looked to his spear master and stalk master, who then went to the spearmen and the stalkers, no one joining the circle without the ritual invitation. Once seated, they spoke little, remaining silent until the hunt master began speaking, and then only responding when specifically asked to.

When the women's council met they generally began to drift over to their side of the camp in small collections of two or three, sitting down and chatting easily with one another. To the men, it sounded as if they were all speaking at once. It made them very uneasy, when the women's council met.

Coco and Calli sat defiantly together, the newborn sleeping silently in Calli's arms. Dog was technically no longer welcome at these meetings, as he had been named and was now a full member of the Kindred, but he was a favorite of the women and was laughed at indulgently as he showed off his somersaults in the center of the gathering. Calli knew she should make him leave, but she said nothing, letting it sink in on the women that what they were about to discuss was the fate of this charming boy's brother.

Coco turned to Calli. "Other than condolences, mostly they are talking about how warm and dry it is and wondering why we came so early to winter quarters. Albi has not managed to stir ugly passions against the baby."

Calli nodded. "But that does not mean they are turning against the council mother. They simply do not want to talk about my child. They hate that the topic has even come up."

Coco gave her daughter an appraising look. As was often the case, Calli was demonstrating a special wisdom. Mists and shadows.

"Still," Calli continued, "she will need to walk carefully with that stick, because if she is seen using it too harshly against us, with Ignus's death so fresh, any woman who has ever lost a husband or a father will be offended."

Coco nodded, her expression doubtful.

"Soon the rains will come," Albi pronounced from her place in the circle, speaking more loudly than anyone else. Several women glanced at her, absorbing the statement. Good, they needed the rains.

"And we will have weddings, of course," Albi added. Another good thing. The women exchanged appreciative looks—this meeting was not as unpleasant as they had expected. "We speak for Renne, who has no parents, but who would be a good match for your son Nix, do you think, Ador?"

Ador blinked in surprise. "Well, yes," she said after a moment. Everyone was smiling, now, and Renne was blushing with pleasure.

"May we continue to be favored with fertile couples, good weather, strong hunts, and safe journeys between winter and summer," Albi continued.

This brought nods from everyone except Calli, who was watching Albi with narrowed eyes. *Here it comes.*

Albi now stood, leaning on her heavy stick. "But every blessing can be offset. Just as the great good warms us and lights the day, there is another force that wishes to see the Kindred starve, to be afflicted with disease, and to be taken by the Cohort. Where there is blessing, there can also be curse."

The women shifted uncomfortably at how closely Albi had come to directly referencing the great evil that brought the night, something the Kindred never did. Albi waited until the ripple of movement had stilled. She put a lugubrious expression on her face. "Nothing could pain me more than to know that my own grandson, born not many days ago, brings just such a curse to the Kindred. Why, his birth happened at precisely the moment to cause us the most danger of discovery by the Cohort! And his leg is like a festering wound that brings fever and death. We are afflicted, and we must rip out the tooth." She pointed at several of the women in turn. "And who speaks up for the child? Ignus, who then chokes to death on his words!"

There was a gasp as the truth of this hit home.

"We have a duty. I am heartbroken to pronounce it. But I must," Albi claimed. "The curse must be taken to a watering hole and submerged until it can no longer threaten our lives."

Calli's heart sank as she saw that the women were looking into each other's eyes, but not at hers. Bellu glanced up at her and then quickly away—even her best friend had been persuaded.

Albi's expression turned into a smirk as she turned toward Calli, inviting rebuttal. "A curse, you say," Calli replied loudly, still seated. "And yet despite the fact that we have come to winter quarters when the days are still long, earlier than ever before, the men found birds to feed us. The time of greatest danger, you say, and yet the only threat we suffered was when you came to me with the ridiculous notion that a newborn should be thrown in the river, so that the hunt master had to come and threaten you with death to get you to stay quiet!"

This was confirmation of a rumor that had been flying around, and the women reacted with startled expressions.

"You bring my father's death to the council. A tragedy, but you bend it until you find meaning, the way a wet elk hide, twisted in the hands, will eventually be wrung of drops of water. Did he not choke on our abundance? Is he the first man to die from eating too eagerly? Are we to believe that every person who finds a small bone stuck in the throat is cursed? Yes, it is true, he joined the chorus of hunters who threatened you with spears if you would not stop talking at the river juncture."

"Oh, that is *not*—" Albi began angrily.

"The Kindred," Calli shouted, leaping to her feet and overriding the council mother, "has never put to death one of its own! Not even you, Albi, when your arguing could have brought the Cohort down upon us. Yes, the hunters wanted to kill you, but they ultimately stayed their hands. The *Kindred*," she continued, pointing a finger at Albi, "has a long-standing tradition that until a child has been named during the third summer of his life, he is attached to the breast of his mother and is hers and hers alone. You, Council Mother, would have us defy the way of the Kindred, all to extinguish a curse that you say has led us to such misfortune, though the only evident hardship I can see is that you have brought us to winter quarters too early!"

No one had ever spoken to Albi this way in council, and there was a long, stunned silence.

"She is right, sister," Droi spoke. She turned to Sopho, who was sitting next to her. "Sopho and I are the oldest women in the tribe, and we cannot recall the council ever interfering with a living mother's choices for a child who had not yet been named. Why, remember Mors, your oldest boy, Ador? He would not stop biting the other children, but the council gave you leave to find your own measures to stop him, which you did, and now he is stalk master. This is how it has always been."

Sopho was nodding. "Yes, this is true," she murmured. "And my own father died when he tried to swallow a fat piece of elk meat too large for his throat. He was a good man, a spear master, who loved his family. He was not cursed."

The council mother, her eyes slits, drew in a breath, but she hesitated before speaking, taking in the women's faces in a quick survey of opinion. Calli was clever—faced with a difficult decision, the women would always choose inaction if they could. There would be no forcing this issue now, not with Sopho weeping into her hands over her gluttonous father. "Very well," Albi proclaimed smoothly. "It is of course true that as council mother, I simply speak for us— I do not decide for us. It is evident to me that the women's council's will is that no decision be made concerning the cursed child until his third summer, when he is named, joins the Kindred, and might then do the greatest damage to us."

The tiny infant in Calli's eyes stirred, blinking blearily at the world. She stared back down at her son, smiling.

She had three years.

TWENTY-SIX

Year Nineteen

The wolf puppy knew nothing but the cave. The smells wafting down the crevice were tantalizing and mysterious, but she had forgotten any connection between them and her brief experience frolicking with her brothers outside in the vast world. She knew the cave and her mother and the man.

The man was not here—he had vanished up into the sky, taking his scent with him as he climbed up the shaft.

She was hungry. The last time she had fed, she had tasted blood on the teat and her mother had punished her savagely, turning and snapping at her so that she broke away and ran to the man, leaping into his lap, seeking reassurance.

"You have teeth now, little girl," the man said. "It hurts her too much. And I am sorry to say I have just finished the last of the food from my pouch."

The puppy liked it when the man made his sounds, and she playfully pounced on his hands, chewing his fingers.

"Sharp teeth," he said, snatching his hand away. The puppy watched him alertly, wondering what game they were playing now.

"A lion has a far-ranging territory. We have been hiding in here many days. I cannot imagine it is still lingering out there, waiting for me to emerge. But I need food, and now you need food, too."

And that was when the man stood, pushing her from his lap. He made some more sounds, but eventually he left.

Alone with her mother, the puppy whimpered. She could smell the milk, and it drew her forward, until the mother-wolf snarled and growled in warning.

She did not understand where the man was and she did not understand why her mother would not let her feed. She only understood that she was hungry.

Year Four

The hunt felled a winter mammoth, whose ample flesh pulled the Kindred back from the edge of starvation. Lean reindeer meat could be smoked and dried and would keep for many days, but mammoth, with all its fat, needed to be consumed not long after cooking, though snow retarded spoilage. This meant the families had ample food, but Palloc was nonetheless surprised—and perhaps even suspicious—when his mother invited him to her fire for a meal.

"Did you ever wonder about Dog? His coloring? And your new child, the deformed one, the same is true," Albi bluntly asked her son as he took his first bite.

"I do not know what you are even suggesting to me," Palloc replied slowly, chewing.

"Why, when your skin is so pale, your eyes such a light brown, are both boys so dark?"

"They look like everyone else in the Kindred," Palloc answered, baffled.

Albi shook her head. "Do not be so stupid. Should a boy not resemble his father? Does Bellu's child not look like Urs? Do Bellu's brothers not resemble Pex?"

Palloc frowned. In his mind, Bellu's baby looked like a baby. He tried to mentally compare Bellu's brothers with Pex, their father, but Pex had a deep white scar across his forehead and had lost a lot of his teeth, and that was all Palloc could think of.

Albi made a contemptuous noise. "What about their eyes?"

"Their eyes," Palloc repeated, not understanding.

"Calli's children all have dark eyes. Neither of them have light eyes, like yours."

Palloc considered this. "Calli ate no fish while with child," he reasoned. "That is why Dog and the baby have normal eyes."

"Do you think I ate fish when I was pregnant?" Albi demanded.

He was startled. "Are you saying my father had eyes like yours, like mine?"

"A boy looks like the father. A girl looks like the mother. That is why you men all think Ador's child, Bellu, is so pretty," Albi informed him.

Palloc tried to remember his father, who had died after being trampled on the hunt a long time ago. Truthfully, his memories were fleeting and without definition; glimpses of a heavyset, broad-chested man. Palloc simply could not remember the eyes. He focused on his mother. "Is this true? I have never heard such a thing. Children usually look like themselves."

"Ask any woman who a child resembles and she will tell you," Albi replied confidently.

"And my father . . ."

"You resemble him exactly. As I look at you, I see a younger version of him."

Palloc inhaled. His mother's words hit him hard, like a club to the stomach. Dog, not his son? The new baby?

Urs. He felt the rage heating his face. Palloc always suspected Calli had been with another man before their wedding night. And, in his heart, Palloc had always known who the other man was. The idea that the relationship had continued into adultery made him sick with a vile mix of emotions.

Albi was watching her son with a satisfied expression, which she quickly changed to concern when he raised his hot, wet eyes to hers. "Palloc, my son, I am so, so sorry to be the one to tell you this," she murmured.

Palloc stood. "I am going to kill her," he vowed.

Albi nodded at her son's fury. "Yes, exactly," she agreed. "That is exactly what you must do."

Denix was actually trembling as she went to stand next to Silex, a look of nervous dread on her face. She was still so much a child Silex wanted to hug her and assure her that all was good, but that would not befit what he was about to say to what was left of his tribe.

Silex spoke more loudly than necessary, feeling they needed to hear decisiveness and power in his voice. "I have wondered why the magnificent she-wolf who accepts our tribute is so forthright and bold, dauntless as she approaches the Wolfen. And now I understand, because there is a message in her circumstances. She, like Brach and I, split from the main tribe. And she, not the male, is the leader of a pack, one that grows with a successful litter." Silex put a hand on Denix's thin shoulder. "My father stated that we are People of the Wolf and must always live as they do, but in our hunting we are more like the Kindred, leaving our women behind while the men track game. The message of the she-wolf is that this is wrong. We must consider our resources." Silex moved Denix forward with a subtle push, pausing so everyone could remember how she had gone alone to see what had happened to Duro and the men. What he was trying to tell them was so unorthodox, he could see noncomprehension on almost every face, but he nodded as if everyone had shouted assent. "Yes. Denix. She has proven herself brave as any man, going out to risk her life to see if she could save anyone." Though this was not exactly what had happened, the concept stirred his people, and they were now regarding Denix with precisely the sort of appraising respect he had hoped for. "We cannot ignore such bravery. Denix will go with the hunt."

Silex smiled at Denix, who appeared thunderstruck. The men were glancing at each other and frowning, but Silex ignored them, deliberately fixing his wife with his eyes. "Fia is clever and fast, and she, too, will accompany us, as will any woman who can master spear and club. The children can find the berries and gather the acorns, but, like the wolves, Wolfen—male and female—will hunt together."

Year Nineteen

Her mother's thumping tail awoke the puppy from a fitful sleep—the hollow pain in her little belly prevented anything other than light dozing. The instant her eyes opened she smelled the man and was there to greet him when he landed on the cave floor. She jumped and spun and yipped, overjoyed that he had returned.

"Yes, all is good, little girl. I have something for you, and your mother as well."

The puppy's mouth filled with saliva when the man offered her a small morsel of fresh meat. She chewed it rapidly, swallowing and looking up expectantly.

"I am sorry I allowed you to become so hungry. I was afraid of the lion, though I saw no sign of it."

With the sounds came more food.

"That is enough for you. I want to see how well you fare on a solid meal before I give you any more."

The puppy raised herself up on her rear legs, sniffing eagerly, but backed away when the man knelt at the mother-wolf's head.

"I know you are no longer allowing your puppy to your breast, but will you still eat?" he said softly. He reached out and the mother-wolf accepted a larger hunk from his hand, the puppy watching enviously.

Later, the man put some meat into the fire, an odor both familiar and delicious to the puppy, who could not remember a time when the smells were not present. Then he ate, pushing her away when she thrust her nose at his meal. He did, though, give her another bit of food. And then he sat quietly, so the puppy put her head in his lap as she often did, closing her eyes when his hand stroked her head.

"I am challenged to explain even to myself what I am doing, living in a wolf's lair, sharing my food with two animals. Yet it is as if we are family. When I return to the cave, you both shake your tails with high energy. I know it means you are glad to see me, that you missed me. It is as if I have left one family for another—a wolf family. But what would happen if I allow you to live?"

The man's sounds were as soothing as his hand, and the puppy only drowsily knew he was making them.

"You are little now and I do feel for you as if you are a little sister, a baby. But you will not always be a baby and a grown wolf is a fierce killer. Would you do that to me, little girl? Would you one day see me as prey? If we somehow manage to survive the rest of the summer, evade the lion, and find a way to live through the winter, would it only be to have you turn on me and tear out my throat?"

Year Four

Calli, holding her newborn son, was sitting with Bellu when Palloc strode up to her. Dog was off somewhere—his laughter could be heard over the calls of the other children, playing among some sparse trees.

"Come with me," Palloc commanded curtly. When Calli was slow to rise he reached down and yanked her roughly to her feet.

"What are you doing?" Calli demanded angrily. "You will wake the baby and I just got him to sleep."

Palloc's response was to reach for the child and pull him from his mother. Calli was too shocked to resist. Palloc turned and walked away from her.

"Palloc?" With a wild glance at Bellu, Calli ran after her husband.

Palloc carried the newborn straight to the communal fire, which was crackling merrily as Coco prepared to cook some reindeer meat. Calli's eyes grew—why was he going to the *fire*?

Palloc stepped around the flames and thrust the baby at Coco. "Here," he said curtly. "I need you to watch your grandchild for a moment."

Something in Palloc's face made Coco accept the newborn without protest. Calli caught up to them. "What is going on?" she asked shrilly.

Palloc grabbed her hand. "I need you to come with me."

Several women watched silently as Palloc all but dragged his wife away from the communal area. When Calli stubbornly slowed down, he yanked hard on her arm and it hurt so much she yelped. "Palloc," she gasped, suddenly terrified. "Please. What are you doing?"

Palloc's eyes were fierce, his jaw grim. He did not answer. He kept walking, pulling her with him.

TWENTY-SEVEN

I t is the right thing, what you are doing, Silex," Fia murmured to her husband as they lay together the night after Silex announced women would be joining the hunt. "You are a better leader than even your father."

That seemed improbable. "We would not be in this situation if I had stayed," Silex reminded her, despair in his voice.

"Had you stayed, you would have been compelled to go with Duro, and I would not have a husband. Having women help with the hunt is brilliant."

"We need more sons, Fia. *Males.* Without more males the Wolfen will die out. We could die this very winter."

Fia leaned slightly away from him, and the cool air was as unfriendly as the expression on her face. "And so you need me to produce a son," she stated flatly.

Silex wanted to pull his words back. "I was just trying to say we are in a desperate position!" He dreaded the anger in her eyes.

"There is more you are wanting to say," Fia said tightly. "I can tell."

Though it was not how he wanted to broach the subject, he plunged ahead with what he had been thinking. "In the wolf pack, in times of privation, sometimes there will be more than one female allowed to have a litter."

"Because the dominant male takes more than one mate," Fia finished for him.

"Yes. Exactly."

"And this is your proposal for us. That the men take more than one woman to their beds."

Silex was pleased at how quickly she guessed the solution. "I believe it is the only way our tribe can survive."

"So this is about you and Ovi, then," Fia said bitterly.

"What? *No,* it is not about me at all. I am married. So is Brach. But the three young bachelors . . ." Silex spread his hands.

Fia was staring at him intently. "You are saying that at a time when you might very well argue that you, as our leader, should be lying with all the women of the Wolfen, your position is that our marriage overrules all other consideration? You said that times were desperate."

"I did say that. That is why I need you to speak to the women. Convince them. I do not imagine they will be happy with this, but it is the only way."

Fia shook her head impatiently. "Silex. Do not get on the trail of a different animal. Stay with what is important. Despite circumstances, you wish to honor our marriage, to honor me, above all else."

Silex nodded. "Of course, Fia. What did you think?"

"I think," she murmured, her breath hot on his face and she leaned toward him, "that I love you, Silex."

He felt his anxiety relax as she kissed him, stirring his blood. Fia rolled onto her back, holding her arms out to him. "I want you, Silex. Mate with me, Husband."

Palloc had half dragged Calli all the way to their lean-to, and now he grabbed her with both hands.

Calli was frightened for her life. "Palloc, what are you doing?" she cried.

As an answer he ripped at her garments, violently pulling them off her and tossing them to the ground. She staggered, trying to remain upright. The air felt cold on her nakedness. His face was a stew of dark emotions, his pale eyes intense but unreadable.

Grunting, he all but threw her to the ground, dropping his own skirt. *So this was what he wanted.* Half relieved, she submissively went to her hands and knees, gasping in shock at the brutal way he came at her. "Please," she said in a tiny voice, a sob lodged in her throat.

Palloc was heedless and urgent. And, thankfully, it was over in just seconds, Palloc making a wild choking noise before collapsing against her.

Calli's tears rolled silently down her cheeks. She remained with her head on her arms even when he sprang up, leaving her there.

When she rolled over to look at him, he was gone.

Calli left Dog and the baby with Coco one afternoon late into winter, when everyone was getting restless to migrate back north. She found Albi alone by her family fire, and waited respectfully for the older woman to notice her. Albi was patiently probing at a mammoth joint with a stick, working to get at the sinew so she could chew it off the bone.

"I see that my son spends his nights sleeping on the men's side," Albi stated, not looking up from her task.

"Yes, that is true," Calli replied evenly. This was not what she had come to discuss.

"You two have a little marital spat?" Albi asked nastily.

"Something like that."

"Well do not look to me to try to fix it for you. When a man is pouting, you just have to let him pout. They come back, eventually." Albi did glance at her now, her expression sly. "We have something they need."

"I am not here to ask you to fix my relationship with Palloc," Calli responded woodenly.

"Ah. This is about the cripple, then."

"My baby, yes. Your grandchild."

Albi smirked at her.

"Our arrangement," Calli continued quietly, "is that in a few years, you will nominate me for council mother. We both agree that with your endorsement, my election is assured. But why, when you are still so healthy, should we even think of such a transition now? My proposal is simply this: I will not be council mother. You need not endorse me. You will not resign. All will continue as it is."

"And then the cursed child . . ."

Calli carefully did not react to the provocation. "And then my child will be named in his third summer, and he will do what he can to help the Kindred. He will learn a skill—perhaps he could help tool master Hardy—and life will go on."

"Life will go on," Albi repeated. She was grinning manically, her expression so odd that Calli frowned. "You tell me you would give up being council mother, but do you not realize that the position is no longer yours to give? You insisted on keeping the baby, and I let it be, because I knew that everyone would see that it was cursed, would know you had put your selfish desire to keep a crippled child ahead of the good of the Kindred. If you had not protested, the curse would be ended and the women would have already voted you council mother. *Do not for a moment think I was not aware of your treachery!* But you picked it, a child with a hideous deformity, ending all chance that you could replace me."

"He is *not* hideous!" Calli snapped, her anger flaring.

"You think that over the next three years, you will somehow convince people to love your baby. But that will never happen. He came out of the womb with an abhorrent leg. They fear it and they are disgusted by it. As long as he lives, he is a reminder of something horrible. Can you imagine what an awful life he will lead, now, with everyone hating him so?"

Calli bit her lip.

"And as long as he lives," Albi continued with a smile, "I will remain the council mother of the Kindred. Every time I demand his death, you will fight me, and when you win, girl of mists and shadows, I will have more years in control. The baby is a curse for the Kindred, but he is a gift to me."

Calli left the council mother without a word and went straight to Renne, who watched Calli's determined approach with widened eyes. "Renne, how is it that Albi knew to thwart our plans to vote against her by calling for an early migration?" Calli asked bluntly.

The answer was on Renne's stricken face. "Calli . . . ," Renne started to say.

Calli held up a hand. "I just have one question. Do you still report everything I say to the council mother?"

"No," Renne cried, anguished. "I am not sure why . . . Oh, Calli, all my life I have just wanted a family. I do not even remember my parents; they died when I was so young. And no one on the council cared that I wanted a husband!"

"And now you are betrothed to Nix. You did Albi a great service, and she returned the favor," Calli noted.

Renne hung her head.

"I do not blame you. I am not angry," Calli said softly. "You are right. We were so concerned with everything else, no one was paying attention to your needs. But I can count on your help, now? In three years' time, after my son's naming, Albi will pounce, I am sure of it. And I will be ready for her. But I want to be able to depend on you."

"Yes, Calli," Renne replied, her eyes bright. "Yes you can."

Calli embraced her friend, and then turned to go.

"Calli . . ."

She turned back with a questioning look.

"There's something else," Renne said. "A secret I am not supposed to reveal, but I believe it will help."

TWENTY-EIGHT

Year Seven

D enix had changed in the three years since her first hunt. She was still lithe, with taut leg muscles, but her hips were subtly larger than a child's, her breasts recognizably a woman's.

She did not, though, behave like a woman. She dressed as did all the hunters, in summer skins and winter fox furs. She could throw a spear as far and as deadly as anyone. She deliberately kept her chest covered in loosely gathered folds regardless of the weather, so that the men would not take notice of her femininity.

Silex reinforced her obvious preferences by treating her as he did all the men, though there were times when he clearly favored her. She was with him now, just the two of them, carrying a slab of elk meat in a sling. "Up there," Silex murmured to Denix. "See her?"

Denix instinctively crouched, but when Silex remained erect she leaped back up to a standing position, her cheeks red. "I do see her."

The large she-wolf with the handprint mark was watching them.

"She has had another litter this past spring. See her teats? The pups have not long been weaned, so she is still swollen."

"What do we do now?" Denix asked.

"Let us see if we can get a little closer," Silex responded. Denix glanced at him in amazement but followed as Silex closed the distance to the she-wolf. "You look well and have another litter," Silex called to her. "We heard your howl several nights ago."

The she-wolf watched the two of them come closer. The female human carried a faint scent of blood between her legs and there was fear in her sweat, but her face held the same expression as the man who had been feeding the wolf these several years—eyebrows up, teeth slightly bared, mouth open.

Silex stopped a respectful ten paces away. "Your children are not with you," he noted, "but I have seen the ones from two years ago and some bear the same mark on their forehead as do you."

The wolf tensed a bit when the two humans unstrapped the elk meat, but when it flew in the air, arcing toward her, she did not flinch. It landed in the dirt right in front of her. She sniffed it, then gazed at the man.

"She is thanking us," Silex told Denix, who stared. Silex grinned at her expression. "I know. It is the same for me, every time." He took in a deep breath of cool, dry air. A perfect summer day—he felt exultant. Denix smiled back and he knew she shared his mood.

Back at camp, Fia was standing with her arms folded, awaiting their return. "You fed the wolf, though hunting has been very poor lately," she greeted crossly.

Denix ducked her head and slid past Fia, who gave the younger woman a cold glare. "Husband," Fia said, halting Silex as he tried the same maneuver, "you and Denix were gone a long time."

Silex was hungry and looked longingly at the fire, where the hunters were eating cooked elk steak and dried sweet berries for breakfast. "I knew the wolf was out there, but she has had a litter and probably did not want to stray far from the den, so she was not close," he explained.

"And you do not think what the men might say when my husband heads off for the entire morning with young, un-married Denix?" Fia's face was hot.

Silex was baffled. "Denix?" He looked over to the hunters. There were now enough babies back at the gathering site that the women no longer came on the hunt, except for Fia and, of course, Denix, who in Silex's mind was almost a man.

"Denix," Fia nodded, her face stern.

Silex sighed. Twice Fia's pregnancies had ended prematurely, both times on the hunt. Since the second loss, Fia's joy seemed to have left her—she still had passion, but she expressed it mostly as anger.

"I did not consider such a thing and I am sorry," Silex replied.

"Father!" Cragg, age five and along on the hunt for the first time, rushed up to them. Orphaned when Duro took the boy's father to fight the Cohort, Cragg had been more or less adopted by Silex, with Ovi acting as the little boy's mother. "Did you feed the wolf?" he asked eagerly.

Silex seized the boy and swung him up onto his hip, glad for the interruption. "I did, yes." He turned his grin on Fia, but she was already walking away.

"Did you see a lion?"

"I did not. I do not want to see a lion, Cragg."

"I do."

Silex looked indulgently at his son.

"Father, if I throw a spear and it does not hit anything, why does it fall down? Why does it not keep going until it strikes an animal or a tree?"

Silex pondered this one as they walked through the tall grasses to the fireside. "It is," he finally replied, "as when a wolf gives chase to a young deer. If unable to take the prey in, the wolf will break off and lie down to rebuild its strength. Once a spear has found no target, it does the same, coming to earth so as to be ready to take flight again when needed."

Cragg nodded, thoughtfully regarding the spear in his hand.

"Kindred!" someone hissed. "Over there!"

As one, the Wolfen instinctively ducked down. Silex looked in the direction the hunter was pointing and spotted them: about two hundred paces away, a group of perhaps fifteen Kindred men, their spears raised, were splaying out in a ragged line, standing rigid as they stared at Silex.

"Why have you come to our side of the river, Kindred?" Silex asked quietly. But he knew the answer. There had been so few rains, this odd, cool summer, that most game had vanished. Even from where he stood, the Kindred looked thin with hunger.

With this head start, Silex knew they could easily evade an attack—they were Wolfen, able to run faster and longer than any other creed, especially the lumbering Kindred. But they had Cragg with them—the boy would have to be carried.

His hunters all appeared terrified. "There is no reason to fear," Silex said sternly. There was, but acknowledging the fact would only be as adding small sticks to a fire. He strode briskly to where everyone crouched, his eyes fixed on the Kindred, who had not moved. "We grab the food, our weapons, and Cragg, and run upriver. They will not pursue us very far," he stated calmly.

"They are very close," one of his men breathed.

"Steady," Silex replied. "All is good."

"I will lure them," Denix blurted. Silex glanced at her but before he could even reply, Denix was up and running, holding her spear at her side. She was headed straight for the Kindred.

"Denix!" Silex yelled in frustration.

Dog was tall for his age, tall and lean, but Calli's three-year-old son was the opposite: he had big bones and his one good leg was oddly muscular, as if the spirits who had twisted his weak leg had given favor to the other.

It was time for the naming: all the children who had survived to their third summer would be given their legends, their formal names, and then, of course, their nicknames. When the hunt returned, the Kindred would all gather in the common area for a ritual that was nearly as joyous as the winter weddings.

When the hunt returned. Calli sighed. Most married women greeted their husbands with relief and happiness, but when Palloc came home he never even acknowledged that Calli was there. The entire tribe was made tense by their arrangement, with him sleeping on the men's side like a bachelor. Since that day he had so brutally taken her three years ago, he had not touched her or spoken to her. When Dog went to see his father, the boy usually came back bitter and sullen: he, too, was part of the odd separation.

No man had ever done this—willingly left the bed of a young, fertile wife. There was no precedent and the women's council had never discussed what, if anything, should be done, because Albi would not allow the subject to be raised.

"The hunt should return soon, I hope they have found reindeer!" Calli said to Bellu.

"My son has been so sick," Bellu replied glumly.

Calli nodded soberly. Bellu's own child, who had been fussy at the breast and who seemed to cry most nights, had been through a rough winter. He was often unable to keep his food down, and recently had fallen somehow, getting a weeping wound under his eye that had taken all summer to heal. "Is he well, now?" Calli asked politely.

Bellu wiped a tired hand on her brow. "I am doing all I can do for him," she replied.

Calli searched for something to say. "Your mother must be excited for the naming."

Ador would be busy: as the oldest living female in her big family, she would name Bellu's son, her son Mors's daughter, and her son Vent's male child.

Calli's son would, of course, be named by the oldest female in her family—Albi.

Every time I demand his death, Albi's voice whispered in her head.

For three years Albi had made no such demand, to the point where the women's council had become accustomed to the uneasy truce between Calli and her mother-in-law. But Calli knew Albi had not given up—she was merely waiting for the right moment to raise the issue of the curse again, use it to tighten her control of the council, which was growing weary of Albi's mercurial temper and authoritarian rule. As far as they knew, this was the year when Calli would ascend to the leadership role—everyone had heard of the marriage bargain.

Albi, of course, would never let it come to a vote. But how far would she go to prevent it? And Calli's plan—would it work?

The Wolfen hunters were all motionless, staring in shock as Denix ran straight toward the Kindred hunting party. Silex needed to get them moving. "Go!" Silex barked, scooping up Cragg. They took off, while from behind there was a shout as the Kindred prepared themselves for what appeared to be a mad rush by a Wolfen. Silex risked a look over his shoulder and saw Denix hurl her spear.

She was so clever, Silex thought. Her throw was from too far away to land even close to the Kindred, but it galvanized them and, as one, they gave pursuit. Silex slowed to a pace that the Wolfen could maintain for half a day or more. "They have been drawn off," he told his tribe.

The Kindred were led by a tall man, and Silex recognized him. It was the same Kindred who had tried to spear him near the stream less than five years ago. Now he wanted to do the same to Denix. *I will kill you someday, Kindred,* Silex vowed.

He watched Denix's retreating back, proud of how fast she could run. She truly was the most swift of all the Wolfen. The Kindred were too stupid to realize she was deliberately keeping her pace just slow enough for them to gain on her a little with every step, enticing them forward. Soon Silex and his group would be out of sight, and then Denix would increase her speed, while the Kindred grew breathless and exhausted.

It was precisely the maneuver he would have wanted, with just one problem: Denix was leading the Kindred hunters directly toward where they had last seen the great she-wolf.

TWENTY-NINE

The she-wolf had gorged herself lazy on the meat from the man. She was still lying in the summer grasses where she had fed, the sun keeping her drowsy. Back at the den, she knew her pups were playing under the watchful eye of Mate. Thanks to the man, she would furnish a meal for her five offspring, who would soon be old enough to travel with their parents and rejoin the pack. She and Mate were the dominant pair.

When she heard the odd running sound, the she-wolf leaped to her feet. Astoundingly, the female human from earlier in the day was dashing through the grass, while behind her in apparent pursuit was a ragged line of male humans, many with long sticks. They were coming almost directly at the she-wolf.

Naturally, her instinct was to flee, but instead she was arrested by the bizarre sight of this chase, something she could make no sense of. She could smell the humans now, even though they were downwind, and hear their harsh panting.

As the female human drew close the she-wolf began running, but instead of fleeing for safety, she veered over and burst through the grasses directly in the female human's path. Loping ahead of the woman, hearing her shocked gasp, the wolf for a moment felt as joyous as when she ran with Mate when they were juveniles. It was play; running with this human.

Denix almost stumbled in her surprise when the wolf appeared in front of her, scarcely ten paces away and matching her speed exactly. For a moment her pursuers were forgotten—all Denix could focus on was the beautiful, plush fur of the huge wolf, the gorgeous tail whipping in the wind. Denix was *running with a wolf.*

Then, with a peek over her shoulder that looked somehow gleeful and sly, the she-wolf streaked off, disappearing at breathtaking speed.

Denix glanced behind her. The Kindred were tiring, but had managed to close the distance until she was nearly within spear range. Denix decided to follow the wolf's example and stepped up her pace: Silex and the rest of the Wolfen must be far away by now. She had successfully teased the would-be killers along until they were no longer a danger.

Denix ran on, not bothering to see if the Kindred were trying to keep up. They would fade back; no one could catch a running Wolfen.

Denix had run with the great she-wolf. This was something that would not seem real until she told Silex about it.

Whenever Silex and Fia came together as husband and wife, he clutched her to him, amazed each time that he might embrace such a woman. His hands trembled as he stroked her face and her breasts, feeling the heat of her skin, as if his palms had a special sensitivity. When they were finished he would gaze at her and marvel at her beauty—she was never more lovely to him than just after they had mated. Especially now, when she was swollen with his child.

"Such a nice way to finish the day," Fia remarked, laughing softly.

"Oh yes."

Fia rolled onto her side and raised herself a little, supporting her head on her hand, her elbow crooked. He mimicked her move, so that they were face-to-face. This was usually how they held their most intimate conversations, often after mating, and Silex sensed there was something important she wished to discuss.

"Why do you suppose the wolf ran with Denix?" she asked.

He was surprised at the topic—though the Wolfen had spoken about nothing else for days, Fia had remained rather aloof on the subject. "I do not know, but I believe it is a good thing."

"Could it be, perhaps, that the wolf was trying to tell us something about our direction?"

"Our direction? That we should stay the path, perhaps?" Silex liked the idea.

"Or change, maybe. Maybe we need to change something."

"Oh?"

"You have stopped bringing women on the hunt with us," Fia pointed out.

"They all have young children, now. And nearly all the babies are boys." If anything, this success only proved that Silex had led them in the right direction.

"No, there are women who are neither married nor have babies."

"When I allowed women to hunt, the Wolfen needed something drastic to cling to, give hope for the future," Silex pointed out. "But that was three years ago. Much has changed."

"And now we have gone back to the old way, and a wolf appears on the path and leads Denix as she runs away from the Kindred, who also bar their women from the hunt. So the wolf is telling us to leave the Kindred's way behind."

Silex marveled at the way his wife's mind worked. "None of this occurred to me," he admitted.

"So we agree we should return immediately so that you can take the unmarried women out on the hunt," Fia concluded.

Silex frowned. "Immediately . . . ," he repeated.

Fia sighed. "I must return, Silex. I, too, need a new path."

"What are you saying, Fia?" he whispered, alarmed.

"Oh Husband, the look on your face!" Fia blurted, laughing. "What do you think I am saying, that I am tired of you? Especially now, when I carry your child? I only mean that twice before I have been pregnant, and both times I had a bloody and unformed discharge, not a baby. And both times I insisted on being with you on the hunt. This time must be different."

Since Silex had suggested this very thing several times, he kept his expression neutral. "Of course," he murmured.

"And Denix. I would like her to remain behind with me."

This also surprised him. "What? Why?"

"Is it not clear that the wolf delivered the message to her, and not you, for a reason? She, too, must need to change course. She needs to remain behind. She can help Brach protect the women and children."

Silex frowned over the idea of losing his best hunter. "I do not think—" he started to say.

"Silex!" Fia snapped, her eyes flashing. "Hear me on this!"

"I just do not understand," Silex protested, dreading his wife's sudden anger but truly mystified.

Fia sighed. Her expression lost its heat and became caring and sympathetic. "Silex, you do not see how she looks at you."

"Who? Denix?"

"Denix. She respects your marriage, but that is not what

her heart desires, Silex. I do not want her out on the hunt with you if I am not there. The other women—I do not worry so much about them. They are all afraid of my wrath."

Silex shook his head. "You are mistaken."

Fia gave him a pitying smile. "Oh Silex," she said softly. "So wise, so smart, and so completely oblivious."

The hunt brought back meat, though not as much as all had hoped. Still, there was food, and the good spirits carried over to the gathering of all the Kindred for the naming.

It began with Ador, who picked her girl grandchild first. She told the Kindred that the girl was lucky, finding ripe berries on her first expedition, finding pretty flowers whenever she looked. That was her legend, and her long name, "She Always Will Be the First with Luck" was shortened to "Felka Novus." The Kindred applauded as the little girl raised her hands in triumph.

Ador then gave Urs and Bellu's son a legend describing him as a boy who was always sickly and clumsy when young, but he had healed from his broken arm at age two, he had struggled back from many stomach illnesses, and he would grow to be a man of incredible health. Salus Masculus. He also raised his fists in the air.

The short forms of their names were intuitively obvious: they would call the girl Felka and the boy Salu. Vent's son would always be pushing his way out in front of others as they marched, so he was Markus Trudo. He mimicked his cousins, holding arms up in triumph. Markus.

Next was a boy who was supposedly fated to be unde-featable in battle, and his name would be shortened to Vinco. He, too, held up his tiny fists and strutted around.

The Kindred all laughed and clapped, no one more so than Calli. *It was going to go well. Everyone was so happy.*

And now it was time for the next child to be named: Calli's son.

Alibi stood and waited for quiet.

THIRTY

Fia's labor came alarmingly early. The women of the Wolfen rallied around her, building up a fire for warmth and keeping her as comfortable as possible, while Silex sat with his friend Brach and pensively chewed a meal by a much smaller fire.

Brach had two children, but he intuitively understood there was no sense in telling Silex not to worry. Nothing left a man feeling more inadequate and powerless than when a woman went into labor.

A cry of pain from where Fia lay turned Silex's face ashen. He leaped to his feet. Brach stood also, putting a hand on his friend's shoulder. "Steady. It means the child comes soon."

Silex stared at Brach with glassy eyes. "I do not care about anything but Fia. I do not need a child, I need my wife."

"Sit, Silex."

Nodding, Silex sat back down. At the next cry, and the next, his face flinched.

Brach felt a rising dread. In his experience, after much waiting, there would be a few shrill cries from the pregnant woman, and then not much longer after that the women would all cheer and the father would be invited to visit the mother and new child. But even after the shouts of pain ceased, the women remained silent, long enough for Brach to throw wood on Silex's fire twice. Still no baby.

Silex's mouth was open in terror, and he looked to the fire without seeing. Several times Brach patted him on the back, but he did not seem to feel the gesture.

"Silex."

It was Ovi. She stood over her brother, her lips trembling. Silex staggered to his feet, dread in his eyes. "No Ovi," he whispered.

"You should go see your wife now."

"Is the baby—"

Ovi shook her head, interrupting him. "You should go see your wife now, Silex. *Now.*"

A lbi waited until there was complete silence—it was so like her to let the sense of drama rise, to relish the moment.

"There is much good in this world," Albi finally stated. "The reindeer. The elk. The rains that summon our food in winter. The grasses, the seeds, the berries, the sunshine. All of these are their own spirit, but they all work in harmony. They feed us and keep us warm.

"And then there are the things that array against us. The bear, the wolf, and especially the lion. The cold that descends, the snows that extinguish, the darkness that swallows us at night, the stillness of death. We may not speak of the evil forces behind these."

A stir went through the Kindred. She *was* speaking of them.

"We, the Kindred, are chosen to be in the middle," Albi continued obliviously. "We accept the blessings, and we fight the darkness with our fires. We listen to the spirits, who suggest to us when it is time to go to winter quarters, who lead the hunt to prey, who release fragrant smells to guide us to berries and roots. This is why we are Kindred, and all other creeds are animals. *Because we pay attention to the signs.*"

All the Kindred were listening rapturously, hanging on Albi's every word.

"What we must never do. *Never,*" Albi stated, looking from man to woman to child, holding up a bony finger, "is ignore the spirits when they communicate a message to us. To do that is to invite disaster and ruin."

Several people were nodding.

"And so it is that a message comes," Albi intoned. "Not from the good spirits, not of the sunshine and the fruits and the herds of prey, but from the dark. From the cold. From the *twisted.* A curse we must listen to or we will surely suffer. And it comes to us in the form of a boy. A boy whose leg is a horror. This is his legend. And his formal name is *'He Who Brings a Curse upon the Kindred with His Leg and Must Be Put to Death for the Good of All of Us.'* Cursed leg. *Mal Crus.*"

Calli's gasp into the silence was so loud it almost sounded like a scream. She wept openly as her son, who no doubt had been anticipating jumping up and raising his arms in triumph like the other children, rose uncertainly to his feet. He stepped forward, as the others had done, and Albi dramatically backed away from him, as if her little grandson brought great danger. Not really understanding what was happening, he turned to face the Kindred, tentatively raising one hand.

Calli had been focused on the council meeting, but Albi had outsmarted her and made her move at the *naming.*

"Mal," Calli choked, struggling to break from the crowd and rushing to her son. She went down on one knee. "Your name is Mal. It is a good name," she told him, her voice hoarse. She stood, lifting him, facing her tribe with hot eyes, holding him so that he could not see their cold faces, their revulsion. "My son," she said more firmly, speaking to everyone before her. "Mal. My son is named Mal."

The circle of women parted for Silex as he made his way to Fia's side. No one would look him directly in the eyes. He knelt by his wife, grabbing her hand, which seemed clammy and cold. Her eyes were focused on nothing, her lips pulled back, her breathing in short gasps. And everywhere was blood, a huge dark stain on the animal hides on which she lay.

"Fia . . . ," Silex choked. She did not register his presence. He glanced wildly at the women. "Why is there so much blood? Is there supposed to be so much blood?" His heart was pounding, his head filled with the wild thought that he was being punished for violating his father's deathbed wish.

No. He could not lose her. Could not live without her. The women were soundless. "Fia!" Silex shouted.

Fia blinked. Her eyes swam in her head, finding him. She licked her lips. "Silex," she whispered. Then she wheezed, arching her back, gripping his hand in hers. It was as if some animal held her in its jaws and was clamping down, and it went on and on, robbing her of breath. Her eyes rolled up, showing white.

"Oh no. No Fia," Silex moaned. He wiped away his tears. "Please, my love. Please no."

After a time, Fia's vision cleared. She focused on her husband. "Silex," she whispered. "Promise me."

"Please, Fia," Silex begged. "You cannot leave me. Please."

"Listen to me," Fia replied. For just a moment her fire was back, her eyes gaining sharp focus. Silex bent down to listen.

"Promise me you will marry Ovi. Raise Cragg and Tok as your own. Have another child, a girl, and name her Fia. Promise me this, Silex."

Silex could not speak. Sobs wracked his body. He shook his head. This could not be happening. He could not lose her!

"Silex," Fia murmured. And then another pain hit her and her body went rigid, her tongue falling loosely from her mouth. Silex watched in horror as she suffered.

"Can you not do something?" he yelled at the women. Their reaction was to take a fearful step back, retreating from him when he needed them to *help*.

Thankfully that was the last pain. Fia's breathing changed, its pace rising and falling, as her hand went slack in his. He called her name, but she did not look at him. Her eyes, half lidded, stared at nothing.

When her breathing stopped, Silex felt strangled, and his ears were filled with a strange, harsh sound, so loud it blotted out all else, every sensation.

It was him, he realized numbly. The noise came from him.

He was screaming.

Year Nineteen

The mother-wolf twitched in her sleep, then awoke when she sensed her lone pup sniffing her dry teats. The cub still nuzzled her, but no longer sought milk.

The mother-wolf's front legs had stopped working, and strong pains gripped her insides. An instinct as old as her species told her that she was dying. The determination that had kept her alive despite her injuries was loosening its grip. There was nothing more she could do for her offspring.

Her cub whimpered, a lonely sound she often made when the man was out of the cave. The mother-wolf was right there, but it was the man that the pup craved more than anything.

The mother-wolf was content that she was not leaving her cub alone, that the man was caring for her. And then when she heard the familiar sound of the man's feet hitting the cave floor and her pup fled her side to greet him, yipping in excitement, she felt a happiness rising up within her. She remembered chasing an elk long ago, loping with her siblings, and what she experienced then was what she felt now, the sheer joy of being wolf.

The man put his hand on her fur. For a moment, her thoughts escaped into a confused dream, and she thought it was her mate's head, lying across her neck in the den as they waited for her pups to arrive. When he stroked her, it was her own mother's tongue, cleaning her when she was herself just a pup. Then she remembered another human, and her affection for him when he gave her food.

"Oh, wolf. You have been such a good mother to your pup," the man murmured. "You are so brave. We will miss you so much." The man leaned in closer, and she peered at him blearily. It was the way, with some humans, to stare into a wolf's eyes.

"You were willing to do battle with a lion, to save your pups. My own mother . . ." The man's voice broke, and the pup nuzzled him. "My own mother has sacrificed for me, as well. She is the reason we have meat to eat. At great risk to herself, she has given me food all summer. She feeds me, I feed you, and you have fed your little girl-wolf. We are family, the three of us, and I will protect your pup. I do not know how I will survive the winter, but if I do, your wolf-child will survive as well. I may regret it when she is old enough to do me harm, but I somehow doubt it. You accepted me; I believe she will do the same.

"Regardless, I will do it for her, and I will do it for you, because I feel a kinship toward you. You see, we are very much the same." The man stroked her head and she closed her eyes again.

"Very much the same, with bad legs. We are both cripples. See? I was born this way, and if not for my mother, I would have died long ago."

The mother-wolf felt the strong emotion in the words, and, her eyes closed, settled back into a gentle dream. She had never felt so at peace. Her pain was gone, now. She would lick the man's hand if she could, but her tongue was unresponsive and her vision gone dim. They were her pack, her pup and the man, and she felt them running beside her, full of elation for the hunt.

They were chasing an elk across alien ground, where the land was permanently frozen in winter. As the horizon unexpectedly dropped away, the mother-wolf did not break off her pursuit. Instead, she followed the elk calf to the place where the dazzling ice met the sky, and floated over the edge, soaring through the air, young and alive and free.

PRESENT DAY

The sommelier serving the American professor and his companions was unable to keep the annoyance off his face as he was waved over to their table. James Morby pointed to the empty bottle and with a dismissive, crass gesture indicated they wanted another bottle of Château Siaurac. Morby's friend Bernard Beauchamp, observing their server's stiff acquiescence, smiled knowingly.

"What is so funny, Bernard?" Morby wanted to know.

"Our sommelier believes you should not have any more wine because you are too drunk and too American."

"Ah. Well, because I am the former I will insist I am not the latter."

Both men gave the mild joke more laughter than it deserved. The graduate student, Jean Claude, joined in, but he wasn't drinking, and his mirth was expressed as something closer to a polite chuckle. "He does not know that you are celebrating, Professor," he noted a tad obsequiously.

Morby regarded the younger man. In the classroom Morby was famous for reading the expressions of his students, and his hazel-colored eyes now brightened despite the dulling impact of the alcohol. "I take it you have a question for me, Jean Claude?" he asked suggestively.

Jean Claude blushed, but, getting an approving nod from Beauchamp, plunged ahead. "Yes. It's about the wolf. The first dog, you said, but it isn't a dog, not really," Jean Claude stated awkwardly.

"You saw the collar," Beauchamp chided gently. "What is the conclusion you draw from that?"

Jean Claude seemed ready to apologize.

"No no no, let the young man speak, Bernard. Please. Yes, Jean Claude, as you say. A wolf. *Un loup.* Yet did you know that every dog alive today has a little wolf DNA? Not just huskies, who often look like wolves, but pugs, corgis, poodles? Chihuahuas—they sometimes act like they still are wolves, and they are fundamentally correct, down deep in the double helix."

They paused to watch the steward present the bottle, the cork, and go through the rest of the ritual. Morby played the part with serious concentration, but his performance did not seem to redeem his reputation.

"*Oui,* yes, I understand this, Professor Morby, but that happened over thousands of years. What you propose is that one day," Jean Claude snapped his fingers, "a wolf decides to obey man, becomes a dog. Like that."

Morby and Beauchamp exchanged glances. "Saltation," Beauchamp offered with a sly grin.

Morby smiled back. "Indeed. A man with the gloriously absurd name Étienne Geoffroy Saint-Hilaire penned the theory that a species might evolve in giant steps. You've read Saint-Hilaire, Jean Claude?"

Jean Claude nodded to assert that he had. Morby could see in his eyes that he had not. But this wasn't class and he wasn't here to skewer the young man, so Morby spoke as if confirming something Jean Claude had said. "Exactly. From the Latin *saltus,* meaning 'leap.' Saltation. Darwin, of course, ultimately won out against this idea that perhaps a hippo might give birth to a modern day pig, and so on," Morby continued. "We now know that evolution is an excruciatingly gradual process, *n'est-ce pas*? So consider this dog, who is, admittedly, nothing but a rather large wolf with a red collar. Could it be saltation at work? Saint-Hilaire's last laugh? One day a wolf, the next day a dog? I think not. Even today, after thousands of years of encountering humans all over the planet, when we have literally killed off the hostile and aggressive ones, wolves do not easily become pets. They see us all the time, but there's never been a documented case of a wolf running up to a human and requesting amnesty from the wild. No, adopting a wolf puppy requires a unique set of circumstances for it to grow into a family pet—often the adoption fails to blossom into anything beyond an uneasy acceptance. So something must have happened, some sort of acclimatization, socialization, for our wolf to wind up with the red collar. Evolution cannot be hurried, cannot be rushed."

"What? What could have happened?"

"Well, Jean Claude. I have pondered that for a long time." Morby reached for the wine bottle, oblivious to the spasm of distaste on the sommelier's face, who hurried over and wrestled the thing away before Morby could commit the gauche act of pouring his own refill. Morby surrendered with a bemused smile. "How did it happen," Morby said softly. He held his glass up to the candle, watching a dancing ruby flare across the bowl. "I try to imagine humans and wolves out on the steppes, competing for the same food, the wolves only discouraged from hunting *us* by our spears— and if there were enough wolves, or if they were hungry enough, I don't think spears would do the job. It's hard to imagine a friendship developing—why would either species be interested? There would be no immediate benefit evident to either one. Food was scarce, would a human really feed a random passing wolf? Were we handing out meals to bears, lions, foxes? How long would we do such a thing before we, ourselves, were eaten?" Morby took a sip of wine. "Part of me thinks it *was* a sort of saltation, that at least in evolutionary terms, it happened in the blink of an eye. I can't imagine any other way. But honestly? I have no idea. No idea at all."

BOOK

TWO

THIRTY-ONE

Year Seven

The day after the naming, the women's council came together slowly after the first meal, the women drifting in reluctantly. This might be necessary, but it would not be pleasant. They sat and spoke in uncharacteristically quiet tones. Albi's naming of Mal Crus was forcing them to face an issue they would have ultimately preferred not to address.

This is the reason, Albi thought with satisfaction as she glanced from one grim expression to another, *that there is a council mother.* The women of the Kindred required a strong leader, a stone point at the tip of their spear when they needed it. Was it not true that nearly every important decision was made by the council mother and endorsed by the women, and not the other way around? They dithered. They could talk a subject to death. They hated finality.

Albi had been wrong about the cripple. Some, perhaps even most, of the Kindred viewed the little boy with repugnance, but others seemed charmed by his cheerful personality. Instead of a mounting disgust, there was a steadily building approval, and Albi's vitriol against the curse was, with each passing day, less effective.

But she had certainly changed everything, had she not? After this day, Albi knew, there would never again be a challenge to her authority.

He Who Brings a Curse upon the Kindred with His Leg and Must Be Put to Death for the Good of All of Us. Not much anyone could do, not with a formal name like that laid upon the child. Albi doubted there would even be a debate.

She was strong enough to do it herself, she knew. She would only ask that Calli be restrained. The women might lack the nerve to drag the boy down to the stream, beat him with a rock, and hold his face under water, but they would cling to Calli and suppress her screams long enough for Albi to get the job done.

Everyone was here except Calli—perhaps she lacked the nerve, or maybe she and the boy were running, which was even better. Let them be found by the Valley Cohort—Albi would argue that they had been taken by the dark spirits once the curse had been chased out into the open.

"We have something to talk about," Albi announced quietly. She loved being able to speak in such soft tones and having it silence everyone, as if she were the hunt master speaking to the men.

"We do," came a voice from behind her. Albi turned and scowled as Calli strode into the circle, arrogantly standing, as if she were equal to the council mother.

"Something very important," Calli affirmed.

The women were staring in something like shock as the two women, open enemies, stood next to each other.

"Why not take your place," Albi suggested evenly. She knew that if she maintained a steady voice and cool temper, the difference between her and the high-strung Calli would be obvious.

"In the tradition of the Kindred," Calli continued as if oblivious, "on a day when the council has called a meeting, we may, in first order, discuss replacing the council mother, if there are two women who ask it. And I am asking."

"And I ask it as well," Coco called promptly.

No one else spoke, and the brief jolt of worry Albi had felt over Calli's confidence melted away. Calli had no one else but her stupid mother.

"Then let us get this over with. Who among us would replace the council mother?" Albi asked.

"But first," Calli interrupted, "we have a discussion."

Albi sighed, giving the assembled circle a "see how patient I am?" look. "All right. Discuss."

"Thank you, Council Mother." Calli turned and faced the women. "You all are concerned about a curse. We have heard much about this. But what is the curse? Since the birth of my son, times have been both lean and fat, the way it has always been. But now we have good hunting, the men returning with as much food as they could carry. Of course, some of us were fat even when the Kindred were starving," Calli noted slyly. Several women gaped at her boldness.

"This is off topic," Albi snarled.

"Oh, you are right, Council Mother. Forgive me. Because what we need to speak of are the ways of the council—and what is the most important rule, the one thing no woman must do?"

There actually was no formal ranking of rules or even, really, any promulgation of the "ways of the council"—so most of the women looked mystified.

"That is right." Calli nodded, as if someone had called out an answer. "Under no circumstances must one woman ever, *ever,* interfere with the marriage of another." Calli let them ponder that for a moment, allowing it to sink in.

Albi's lips twisted sourly. *Hardy.* Had the old fool talked to other men, who then told their wives? The council mother considered her position. Well, widows had always been allowed the latitude to fornicate, and no one thought they restricted their favors only to unmarried men. This was a desperate and doomed attempt, and Albi decided to let it proceed so that no one could later argue she tried to stifle Calli's challenge.

"That is right." Calli smiled at them as if they were children learning the Kindred's traditions. "So let me answer the question that has been on everyone's mind for several summers—why is it my husband, Albi's son, sleeps on the men's side? Why is my bed cold?"

No one—not even Albi—had seen this turn coming, and everyone was silent. Calli glanced at Renne, who nodded encouragement.

"Because," Calli continued, "Palloc was told by his mother that the reason my children have normal eyes instead of light eyes like his is because they were fathered by someone else. She told him that a son always resembles the father, and she told him that Palloc's father, Albi's husband, had light eyes. That this is why Palloc has light eyes. And so my marriage was destroyed. All because of what she said."

Albi opened her mouth to speak.

"It is a lie," Sopho said, rising creakily to her feet. Everyone turned to look at her. "I remember Palloc's father very well. His eyes were normal, the same color as everyone in the Kindred."

"Albi lied to my husband," Calli concurred. "And that is why I have no marriage anymore."

"Yes," Sopho affirmed.

"You are all but blind, old woman," Albi spat.

"I remember him, too," Droi, Hardy's wife, agreed. She, too, rose to her feet. "His eyes were the same color as everyone else's."

There was a long silence. Albi registered how, one by one, the women were looking away from Droi and toward the council mother.

"It is not the only time Albi has interfered with a marriage," Droi continued. "For many years, she has come to my family fire and fornicated with Hardy. My own sister, and she forces me to leave so that she may lie in my bed with my husband." Droi took a shuddering breath, her face collapsing in tears. "She has ruined my marriage, the way she has ruined Calli's," she lamented angrily. "Now, when I try to love my husband, all I can see in my mind is the two of them together."

Albi stared at her sister, unable to believe the betrayal.

Renne rose. "When I was younger, Albi's son Palloc went to his mother and asked if the council would approve of him marrying me. And she denied his request, which was her right. But then she sought me out, and she beat me with her . . . her *stick*. It is why I have this scar on my face, and why I cannot chew food without pain in my jaw. I consider myself lucky to be alive. Everyone knew Albi had done it. Do you remember what I looked like?" Renne sought out their faces, and many women guiltily turned from her glare. "No one stood for me. No one defended me. Albi might have killed me. So I ask this of you now, this one thing. Take away this woman's power before she uses her club on some other woman, or ruins another marriage, or *kills someone's child*." Renne turned and locked eyes with Calli.

Albi's heart was beating loudly, but she was hardly ready to quit. The distress of the women was plain upon their faces—at this juncture, they could be turned in any direction. Mostly they just wanted the conflict to *stop*. "And what?" Albi demanded derisively, sure of herself, now. "You would have Calli be council mother? Her child is a curse upon the Kindred, and you would elevate her to such a position? You insult the spirits and you will be punished!" Albi thundered.

"Of course not," Calli responded calmly.

"What?" Albi replied suspiciously.

"Of course I should not be council mother."

A Wolfen wedding was largely a wordless ceremony. After a man declared he was taking a woman for his wife, the adults of the tribe danced together, the men attempting to put their arms around women from the rear, and the women twisting away, laughing, to face the men, defying their wishes. Wolves mated in a similar fashion, the female flirting but not allowing mounting, touching faces and climbing up on the male's back, then turning playful, bowing down. When all of the married Wolfen had managed to embrace their wives from behind, the last couple, the one getting married, engaged in their own teasing dance, the rest of the tribe cheering them on. It was a true celebration of marriage, a reminder of how important fidelity was to wolves and man alike.

Silex went through the motions of his wedding dance with Ovi, his heart heavy. When he and Fia did this dance, there had been only one couple—Brach and his wife Ros—to participate, but the happy thrill of that night had stayed with him ever since. Adding more people to the dance did nothing when one subtracted Fia.

Ovi, too, seemed unenthusiastic. Was she remembering her wedding to Duro? Had she been joyous on that occasion?

When finally they were the last couple and Silex had his arms around Ovi, the Wolfen came together and lifted their voices into the night in as close an imitation as they could manage of a wolf's howl. After each howl, the tribe paused, listening. Tradition had it that an answering call from the wolves meant that the marriage was blessed. Three times, the tribe howled, and three times, the attempt was met with silence.

Brach clapped Silex on the shoulder. "The wolves did not howl for me, either, Silex, but I have been happy."

"All is good," Silex agreed.

Stirred by the dance, the couples were eagerly leaving to go to their beds. Silex lingered by the fire, not ready.

"I am very happy for you, Silex," Denix murmured to him, smiling shyly.

"Thank you, Denix."

Something happened to her smile, a brief tremble in the corners of her mouth, and then she nodded curtly and left the fire. Soon it was just Silex and his new bride.

"And so finally, Ovi, I have fulfilled the promises I made upon the deaths of my father and my . . . and of Fia," Silex told her as they went together to her bed area. The women had decorated Ovi's animal skins with smooth, shiny pebbles from the river, arranging them around the blanket's borders.

"And I promised our father as well, Silex," Ovi pointed out.

Silex looked down at the bed. He remembered Fia's hot skin, how the longing inside him made it impossible to do anything but reach for her when they were together. And he looked at Ovi and felt none of that.

Sighing, Ovi went to her hands and knees, facing away from him, hiking her skirt. He closed his eyes, imagining Fia, calling to his lust, willing it to come out and help him do his duty. He had made a pledge, and now he needed to fulfill that pledge. They would have a daughter, he and Ovi, and they would name it after his first wife. He would complete the assignment given him at death by his father.

He opened his eyes.

Ovi, was watching him blandly over her shoulder, waiting for him to do something. "What makes you happy, Ovi?" he asked compassionately.

"Why do you always ask that, Silex?"

"Because you are my sister, now my wife, and I want to see you be happy."

Ovi exhaled impatiently. "I do not like the question. Are we going to mate, Silex, or not?"

THIRTY-TWO

Albi stood with her mouth open, the black holes where she had lost teeth in plain view. "I could not possibly be council mother," Calli continued. "With your lies about the curse, you have caused so much doubt and fear, no one would ever feel secure under my guidance. No, obviously the person who is council mother should be of the new generation, should be someone we all like and can support. The new council mother clearly must be Bellu, the hunt master's wife."

The announcement so surprised the women that several laughed and clapped. Bellu, of course, Bellu! She was beloved and beautiful. And she had suffered so with Salu, her ill child—this would give her just the lift she needed! She was not a strong leader, but she was married to one. After years of the autocratic and cruel Albi, she was exactly what the council required.

"Bellu! Bellu!" they called, and when she stood, giggling, they surrounded her, kissed her hands for luck.

Calli watched her friend accept the accolades with a sense of detachment. She had long coveted council mother but this was better—Mal was safe. Bellu was beaming, everyone was happy, but all that mattered was her child. Calli turned to see how Albi was taking it.

But Albi was gone.

* * *

The former council mother stalked away from the meeting with her mouth in a sour line. This would not stand, she could not let it stand, but at the moment she was stymied. Her sister! Renne! Her enemies would be made to pay for this. *Calli.* Albi seethed with hate for the woman who thought in mists and shadows. And her son, who spoke to her of his conspiracies but had thus far been too much the coward to do anything about either Calli or Urs—her son was so weak!

So intent was she on her rage, Albi did not even see Nix, Renne's husband, until she had nearly bumped into him. Albi looked up, startled—he was standing by Albi's family fire. What was he doing here?

"Hello, Albi. I came to speak to you," Nix greeted. He was grinning, but it was a strange expression, somehow cold and mirthless.

"I am not wanting to speak to anyone at the moment," Albi muttered. She went to push past him, and then gasped when she felt his rough hand on her arm.

"But I am wanting to speak to you," Nix replied softly.

Albi went to pull her arm away, but Nix held it more tightly. She stared at him, alarmed.

"I am wanting to speak to you about the time you used your stick on my wife," Nix continued.

"That is not . . . she was not your wife . . . this, you cannot . . . ," Albi stuttered.

"I was thinking I might beat you to death with my fists," Nix said casually. "Do you believe I could do such a thing?"

Eyes wide, Albi nodded.

"But my wife asked me not to do so. So, to please her, I will not beat you to death with my fists. What I will do is tell you that if, at any time, you in any way displease my wife, if you insult her, if you take her food, if you treat her children poorly, if you even look at her with an unpleasant expression, I will beat you to death with a rock. See? Not my fists. A different thing. I will still be obeying my wife's wishes, but your skull will be smashed and your brains will run into the dirt."

Albi's mouth tightened. He would not ever really do this, she realized. It was a threat intended to scare her. Well, he was misjudging her. She drew herself up.

"I will tell the hunt master of the threats you have made here today," she hissed. "You have violated the way of the Kindred—"

She got no further. Nix lifted his hand and slapped her across the face with such force it blinded her. Staggering, Albi fell back. Her ears rang and her jaw felt as if it were broken. Stunned, she stared at him.

"I do not want you to speak unless I invite you to do so. And I am not wanting you to speak at the moment. Do you understand me?"

"No man," Albi gasped, "may touch a woman except her husband or—" That was as far as she got. Nix slapped her again, and Albi cried out.

"I asked: Do you understand me? Otherwise I am not wanting you to speak at the moment. So, do you understand?" He lifted his hand up as if to deliver a third blow.

Albi nodded hastily, her eyes tearing from pain.

"You are correct. Normally a man must not touch another woman, but there is a new rule for when the ugly hyena strikes a man's wife with a stick. You see, I did not come here without first speaking to Urs. He told me I could beat you, but I was not to kill you. Not today. Not unless you insulted my wife, and then I could crush your head with a rock." Nix smiled at her pleasantly. "I hope you remember this new rule, but if you forget, I will do you a favor and let you pick the rock I will use to open your skull. See the favor? I will let you pick the rock."

* * *

A ripple of tension went through the pack, passing from wolf to wolf. Instantly, the large she-wolf, old now but still formidable, alerted to the social stress. She eased to her feet.

They were at the howling site, the place where the wolves gathered when they weren't out hunting. Some newly weaned cubs were lying at the she-wolf's feet—the entire pack would take shifts protecting them and ensuring they didn't wander off until they were old enough. Though their markings were unimportant to the she-wolf, one of the puppies, a female, was significantly larger than her siblings, and had a small white patch on her forehead.

Mate had died a few winters ago. The she-wolf had therefore stopped reproducing, but could still hunt and was still the largest of her peers, even if she was no longer the dominant female. When she lay curled up at night, memories of running with Mate came to mind, and often during the day she would sniff for his scent, expecting to find it on the air. They had been together for so long she often forgot that he was gone. When no sign of him came to her nose, she would remember why, and sometimes she would whimper almost silently, missing him.

This spring was unusual because there were two litters in the pack, which had seen its ranks thinned by disease after three cold summers with little to eat. There had been more luck the past winter, and so the dominant male had mated with more than one bitch. One of those mating females was the large she-wolf's direct descendant, her daughter from a litter five years ago, whose size nearly matched that of the she-wolf.

The she-wolf had discovered through successive litters that some of her offspring were simply too intimidated to go with her to accept meat from the man, while others accompanied her without concern.

Something else was unusual this year: her daughter's litter, when it was escorted to the howling site, was brought by a single parent, the male. The she-wolf's daughter was not with them. Her offspring smelled like their mother, but something had happened.

The she-wolf neither dwelled on the loss, nor mourned it. Her instinct, though, was to spend all of her time with her descendants, protecting them and caring for them as if she were their mother.

And now her inner sense told her something grave was about to occur. The mother of the other litter was a black wolf, not as large as the she-wolf but young and strong. Black Wolf was pacing back and forth nearby, her ears back, her tongue out. The black wolf was eyeing the pile of sleeping puppies at the she-wolf's feet—three males and the one large female.

This was why there was suddenly anxiety in the pack. Black Wolf saw this litter as competing with her own. She was the dominant bitch and had come to eliminate the competition.

The big she-wolf stood her ground and pulled her upper lips, revealing her teeth. Her low growl awoke the pups, who were confused when the old she-wolf, chest stiff and tail high, disciplined them, cowing the pups into shrinking down in humble submission instead of spreading out to play and explore. The she-wolf needed them to remain in a defensible group.

The black wolf growled, not backing down, circling, calculating.

Restraint soon broke among the pups. One of the males scampered away and the black wolf instantly streaked after him, head down as if pursuing a rodent. The old she-wolf ran straight at Black Wolf, cutting off the attack and slamming into Black Wolf with brutal impact and the two wolves went up on their back legs, swiping with their paws and slashing with their fangs. It was a vicious and savage fight. Biting and snarling and ripping at each other, they did not give ground.

The rest of the pack milled in confusion and distress.

Black Wolf was young and fast, the old she-wolf larger and more experienced. The black wolf yelped as the old she-wolf drew blood from an ear, and then, when the she-wolf managed to gain a crushing grip on the black wolf's throat, the conflict was suddenly over. The black wolf went limp and compliant.

The old she-wolf let the black wolf get up to flee, and one of the younger males of the pack actually lunged and bit the retreating female as she ran away.

For her part, the old she-wolf felt no compelling instinct to try and destroy the black female's litter.

The pups had already forgotten the fight and were playing joyously with one another, but the pack was confused. The old she-wolf, so long the dominant bitch, was apparently in that position once again, which felt wrong because she had not mated, nor had she smelled receptive to it during the winter.

The situation was so odd that, as if on signal, the adult wolves raised their noses and howled, the ululating cry traveling far on the wind. Astounded, the puppies sat and stared, and then tentatively they raised their own heads and added their tiny voices to the chorus.

THIRTY-THREE

B lack Wolf did not attempt to harm the litter again. The she-wolf remained both dominant and vigilant, protecting them as they grew sleek and strong over the summer. The largest one, the female, was an especially powerful wolf. Running with them, teaching them and guiding them, the old she-wolf gradually forgot they were her daughter's litter, and not hers.

The she-wolf was hunting with the juveniles at summer's end. The younger wolves sprinted ahead, intoxicated by the scent of the reindeer they were chasing—the prey had taken a wound, somehow, and was bleeding slightly, the aroma of it filling the air so succulently they could taste it on their tongues.

When the unmistakable smell of ice wafted to her, the old she-wolf slowed. A memory tickled her now, from long ago. For a moment the recollection was so overwhelming she forgot where she was, and could only remember a pursuit along these same grounds with Mate and Brother, and the ice, and the way the prey vanished from sight.

She slowed. There would be no kill, the she-wolf knew. The reindeer would attempt to escape across the frozen ground and would vanish where the ice met the sky.

The memory brought another association: the man who had for many seasons brought her food. She missed him, suddenly, and found herself oddly yearning to be fed by him.

She sat and waited. The big female pup was the first to

return, and she nosed the old she-wolf in confusion. How was it that the prey disappeared at the end of the world?

Not bothering to wait for the rest of the litter, the old she-wolf turned to find the scent of the man, her granddaughter at her heels. The males would simply have to catch up.

The winter migration the year Mal was named was miserable for the Kindred. After they moved silently through the Cohort territory at the river juncture, the weather turned dry and chilly and they were unable to find anything to eat. The herds of southward migrating reindeer must have all turned into the Cohort Valley, where the Kindred dared not go. The hunt went out and came back empty-handed and frustrated.

The supply of dried berries, intended to last well into the snows, were sacrificed. The nuts and seeds painstakingly gathered all summer were swiftly depleted. Their progress slowed while they dug for insects along the way. They were almost desperately hungry when they arrived at the Blanc Tribe settlement, willing to trade everything they possessed for food. Urs even gave up the skin from the great bear that had stalked Calli.

Calli and Coco, the cooks, were grateful for the fish and the waterfowl the Blanc Tribe provided, though the fish, as usual, tasted odd compared to the red meat the Kindred preferred. And the water plants were so bitter, but it seemed impolite to refuse them.

"They are very welcoming, though," Coco remarked.

Calli agreed. "Perhaps their odd appearance makes them less likely to turn away others—they, themselves, would normally be turned away."

Coco saw the wisdom in this. "Though we do have some

pale-eyed among the Kindred," she pointed out. Then she bit her lip—no one ever spoke of Palloc around Calli. He still had not returned to the family fire, too proud to acknowledge that the story of his wife's adultery had been discredited. Or was it fear of his mother?

Coco saw the disturbed expression on her daughter's face and decided the time had come to reveal something she had long kept secret. "Ignus," she blurted, pulling up short after the one word, suddenly reticent to continue.

Calli gave Coco a curious look. "My father," Calli prompted, wondering why her mother looked so distressed. "Is there something wrong, Mother?"

"There is a reason you have no siblings. Your father was not . . . He was unappreciative of the warmth of my bed."

"What do you mean? He always . . ." Calli's words trailed off. "Oh," she said in a quiet voice.

Coco nodded. "Your father was a good man and he did sleep by our fire, but I knew his reluctance the way I knew his silence. He just seemed to prefer to be by himself. He provided for me in many ways, but not . . ." Coco made a gesture.

Calli nodded thoughtfully, and then her eyes widened. "Never?" she exclaimed, shocked.

Coco pursed her lips. "What I am trying to say to you is that I know what you are going through. I know what it is like to have a husband who does not give of his affections."

"Mother?"

Coco closed her eyes. "You must never tell anyone. The shame would be too much."

"Who?"

Coco opened her eyes and gave Calli a sad smile. "Hardy."

"What?"

"It was after his first wife died, and before he married Droi. I went to him because he was the new hunt master. I wanted his advice on what to do about Ignus. Hardy offered . . . more than just advice."

"Hardy is my *father*?" Calli felt tears on her cheeks, though she was not altogether sure why.

"He had such strength, such power, and was so smart. Calli, please do not hate me. I was young. My husband would not touch me and I sought confirmation that I was still an attractive woman. It does not mean I did not love your father."

Calli looked over, trying to find Hardy among the men of the hunt. Being with the Blanc Tribe meant there was no formal men's side or women's side, but even still the sexes naturally segregated. "Does he know?"

"Hardy? No, I never told him."

"I am not sure what I am feeling, Mother," Calli said honestly.

"I wanted you to know that it is not unheard of, what is happening between you and Palloc. I know how it is. And I know the temptation of the other man, the strong and powerful one. What Albi said . . . I will never tell another of you and Urs, never."

"Are you saying you believe Albi, that Mal is not Palloc's child?"

"No, Calli, I am saying I know that even after Urs and Bellu were promised, you would sneak off with the hunt master. And I do not care to know how long that continued. Because someday Palloc might change his mind, and come back to your bed, and it would no longer be as cold and empty as mine."

Calli took a deep breath. "You misunderstand. I do not want him to change his mind, Mother. I want things to remain as they are."

Coco's expression turned mournful. "I am so sorry, Calli. Perhaps I should have attempted to prevent your wedding. I thought I was doing what was best for you."

"No, Mother. Albi is formidable. She wanted me to agree to leave her leadership unchallenged for five years, so she brokered a deal using her own son. Just as she now uses Mal to attack me."

"All you say is true. I feel so stupid. You mean the world to me—you, and Dog, and Mal."

Calli hugged Coco. "It was Albi," she said again, but she was thinking of something else entirely.

Hardy was her father.

There was but one wedding that harsh, frigid winter; a couple who waited impatiently for the damp cold to lift so the ceremony could be held. When finally the long-anticipated break in the weather came, there was scarcely the morale for a celebration. People were exhausted.

Something curious happened when the circle finally gathered to bless the marriage: a little girl joined her voice to the traditional song. She was daughter to Valid and Sidee, a couple who had lost two children to disease but had a son, Ligo, who was Dog's closest friend. The little girl had been born during Mal's first summer, and thus she was not named because she had not yet had three full summers.

The men were stamping somewhat listlessly and the women were humming with similar hesitance when the little girl, full of childish excitement, starting singing *words.* "Wedding! Happy!" she cried in her tiny voice. "Happy!"

No one had ever thought to chant words in a song before.

Everyone was so astonished that for a moment all went quiet, and then the Kindred roared with laughter. Valid picked up his daughter and kissed her, and in that moment, the wedding ceremony seemed to find its authenticity, its power to pull the Kindred into celebration.

They were Kindred, superior to all the northern creeds. They would survive.

Year Nineteen

Are you sad, little girl?" Mal asked the pup, who was sniffing intently at the place where the mother-wolf had spent nearly all of her time in the cave. It seemed to Mal, too, that the odor of the adult wolf still hung in the air—or at least, Mal sensed something, as if in some way the mother-wolf were still there. He sighed. "I know that I am sad. I miss the way she would tap her tail in the dirt when I climbed down the crevice. I did not fully know it, but I had come to love her."

Mal took a deep breath and reached for the puppy, gathering her into his arms. She wriggled and squirmed around so that she could lick his face, and his sadness lifted instantly. They play-wrestled until she tired. She lapped up some water and then lay down with a sigh. He put a hand on her head.

"I do not know if you will be upset when I am finished with your mother's pelt and bring it back in," Mal said after a time. "I am using the mixture made from tree bark to cure the skin now. It bakes in the sun. I hope you understand that I did not kill your mother. The lion did that, though your mother was like stone inside, and fought death as fiercely as she fought her killer."

Mal thought of the vow he had made to protect the wolf
The lion was still out there somewhere, and thus Mal

cowered in the den, venturing out only to meet his mother for food, his heart pounding the whole time.

The little girl-wolf depended on him.

What would happen when winter came?

THIRTY-FOUR

Year Twelve

S ometimes Calli would stare into still water, looking
for some sign of Hardy in her own face. Of course,
she could not really tell what Hardy's face would
look like without the mass of scars disfiguring him. And
Calli simply was unable to remember the tool master before the lion attack that nearly killed him.

She was gazing into a small pool when Valid and his
daughter came across her.

"Calli, good summer," the girl greeted shyly.

Her name was Lyra, because she was the child who had
sung at a wedding and then, at her father's insistence, sang
almost every time the Kindred gathered together. The songs
were mostly just lilting words and tended to repeat "happy"
and "summer" a lot, but the beaming expression on Valid's
face indicated he thought the melodies were sheer brilliance.

"Good summer, Lyra."

"What are you doing?" Valid asked curiously, peering
over Calli's shoulder into the water. "I see nothing there."

Calli was embarrassed. "Does your wife never look in
still water?" Calli knew she did.

"Look in the water? For fish?" Valid replied, baffled.

Calli regarded the spear master with a bemused expression. "Have you not noticed that when you gaze into water,
your own face is there gazing back?"

"You look into water and see my face?" Valid responded. Calli laughed. He was teasing.

"I want to see, I want to see!" Lyra chimed.

"Then come here, Lyra. Lean down." Calli guided the little girl's head until it was positioned over her reflection. Lyra's mouth opened in astonishment. "See?"

"That is what I look like?" she demanded.

"This would be a good subject for a song, I think," Valid noted.

Lyra frowned. "I do not like my hair." She gazed up at Calli. "Would you teach me to braid it, like yours?"

"Of course."

"Well," Valid objected, "maybe when she is older. I do not want my daughter wearing the hair of an adult woman."

"Please?" Lyra begged, turning solemn eyes on him.

Calli smiled as the man visibly wilted under his daughter's pleading. "All is good," he grunted. "I will just have to explain it to your mother."

So Calli pulled Lyra close to her and started to work on her hair. The little girl, at her father's urging, sang a quiet song.

This is what it would be like to have a normal family, Calli thought to herself. *A husband who loves his wife. A father who speaks to his daughter. A little child in my lap who everyone loves and no one sees as anything but a joy.*

She smiled at Valid and he smiled back. Conventionally a Kindred woman would glance demurely away after a moment, but Calli let her gaze linger on the man until he blushed.

She was not sure why she did that.

Silex made sure that no one in the Wolfen suspected, no one knew. To all appearances, Silex went to his wife's fire and slept with her and the two of them might someday have a child. They did not know that when Silex gazed at Ovi's sleeping form he felt dead between his legs, and in his heart there was no joy or longing.

He and Ovi rarely discussed it after their wedding night. He caught her crying once and raised the subject, asking her if raising the adopted boy Cragg and her own son, Tok, Duro's child, was enough. Did she want more than just the two children?

She assured him that her tears were just because she was sad, that day, and had no specific cause. She was willing to make the attempt for more offspring, though, which was part of the problem for Silex—Fia had come to him *wanting* him, her excitement stirring up his own. Ovi gave him none of that.

But Silex liked sleeping next to his sister—near enough to feel her body heat, but not touching her. It reminded him of easier times, when they were very young children and their parents took care of them. Those days, those long ago days, when he had no responsibilities and spent his time running and running with no particular destination in mind. Lying next to his sister, thinking of his childhood, gave Silex comfort in the night.

Mal was eight summers old when things started to change.

He was too young to remember his best friend Salu, Bellu's son, who died the winter after his naming from a sore that puckered and oozed and eventually rotted like a log despite his mother's constant care. He understood only that Bellu was council mother and a sad woman who spoke constantly about wanting to have another baby. No, for him his best friend in the world was his brother Dog, so that was the first change, his eighth summer: Dog no longer wanted to play every day. He suddenly wanted to be with older children.

At eleven summers, Dog was as thin as a flower stem, but oddly strong, as if his muscles, stretched taut to keep up with his growing bones, got their power not from mass but from length. His brother was growing in precisely the opposite direction—though three years younger, Mal already carried heft to his shoulders and arms.

Mal ran with a pack of boys around his age—literally ran, his bad leg giving him a stuttering gait, and no one seemed to mind he was slower than the rest. They ambushed tree trunks and dirt mounds with spears. They tested their literal boundaries, daringly crossing the Kindred Stream when no adults were watching, sharing the thrill of breaking the rules.

Dog and his friend Ligo, Valid's son, wanted to be spearmen to the hunt, which is all any boy wanted to be. Stalkers were important, they knew, but it was the glory of the spear they craved. To let a weapon arc through the air and bring down a massive elk, its rack of antlers as big as a man, or kill a winter mammoth, the earth shaking with the impact as it fell—they all lusted for it and talked of nothing else. They felt bonded, almost as if they were a hunt, all by themselves.

And then the boys began looking at him differently, that eighth summer. The good-natured teasing they gave each other seemed to carry a touch of malice when it was turned on Mal.

Vinco had always been Mal's best friend, but lately had started spending more time with Grat, who was a summer older than they were. And it was Grat whose derision cut the sharpest, telling the others that Mal's leg stank, or that when Mal was alone he walked in circles until he fell down. Mal laughed along with everyone else, but there was a dark light in Grat's eyes when he loosed his mockery on the boy with the cursed leg. Grat was a handsome boy with heavy eyebrows and, because he had lost a front tooth, a grin that always resembled a leer.

Mal had spent the morning impatiently helping gather firewood for Bellu, a job that rotated among the children, boys and girls alike. Bellu managed the fire for the Kindred, a good assignment for her, everyone agreed, because she was still so heartbroken over losing her only child.

Finally released from his chore, he tore off in pursuit of the boys, finding them trying to catch some mice that lived among the rocks in the woods. Mal's heart sank—the activity took nimble feet, so his leg would impede him every time he tried to dart after one of the rodents. He had often fallen among the rocks.

Markus, who had been named the same night as Mal and Vinco, held a dead mouse in the air as Mal approached. "Got one!" he shouted.

"And here comes the cripple," Grat advised, noticing Mal.

"Good summer," Mal replied cheerfully as he walked up. "That is a fierce beast, Markus."

Markus grinned. "I think I will make a robe out of its fur," he proclaimed. The boys laughed.

"We should make the cripple boy eat it," Grat suggested.

"Delicious! But I would share the feast with everyone," Mal replied jovially.

"Only if we cook it, first," Vinco laughed.

"No, we would hold him down and make him eat it," Grat repeated. Everyone dropped their grins.

Swallowing, Mal looked away. He had been held down and forced to eat things before, but always by older boys—not by his friends.

"Why not come hunt with us, Mal?" Vinco invited after a moment.

"Yes, we love watching you fall in the rocks!" Grat hooted.

This time, everyone laughed. Mal forced a smile. "That does sound like fun. I was thinking instead of throwing stones at the stream." It was a game they all enjoyed: a piece of wood was tossed in the water and then the boys threw rocks at it as it floated past. "Vinco," Mal said to his friend, "would you like to throw stones at the stream?"

"No, he does not want to throw *stones at the stream*," Grat replied in a mocking baby voice. "We are hunting mice. You should leave—when we have enough to feed you a good meal, we will find you, cripple boy."

Mal felt his hands curl into fists. Grat, a bigger boy, looked delighted at the anger on Mal's face. Then Mal blinked it off. "Well," Mal observed, "if this is our hunt, I suppose we should follow the rules of the hunt." Members of the hunt were prohibited to fight. Mal glanced at the other boys and saw them nodding at his words—this was not the first time he had reasoned himself out of an altercation.

"This is not *our* hunt, because we started without *you*," Grat countered. He had lost support, though, and bit his lip angrily.

"We should go back to hunting," one of the other boys remarked, turning over a rock to look for rodents underneath.

"Well, I am going to throw stones at the stream," Mal announced. He raised his eyes at Vinco, who did not happen to be very good at catching mice, either. Vinco glanced away.

At the Kindred Stream, Mal told himself that he was having more fun by himself—all of the shots that hit the floating sticks were definitely his, so there was none of the credit stealing that went on when other boys were there. But he was fairly listless about it.

His mother told him all the time that he was no different than the other boys, but he knew it was not true. His leg made him different.

Suddenly there was a splash in the stream—someone behind him had thrown a rock into the water. He turned, grinning delightedly, but did not see anyone. "All is good!" he shouted.

A movement in the trees caught his eye and another rock arced toward the stream. This one came so close to his head that Mal had to duck. "Ha!" he laughed. "Who threw that?"

He saw Markus, just for a moment, and another rock soared overhead. Mal followed it with his eyes, looking blankly at the splash it made when it landed in the stream. There was nothing floating to aim at.

His back was still turned when the stone hit it, right between his shoulder blades. He looked up at the sky, now full of lethal-looking missiles, and gasped with the shock of realization. They were throwing at *him*.

THIRTY-FIVE

Mal dodged several stones and scanned the trees behind him. Now that he knew where to scrutinize he could see the boys, though they were making an effort to stay hidden. Several more rocks split the air and Mal dove to one side. He bent and snared a stone and fired back, but he was throwing uphill, and he was known for having a weak arm.

"This would be more fun if I had some men on my side!" Mal yelled. He tried to make it sound as if he were laughing but there was a strange noise in his throat, almost a sob. A stone struck his hip and the boys in the trees cheered. "All is good, you got me!" he shouted, feigning delight. He felt sick, almost ready to vomit. The rocks did not stop. Another hit him in the shoulder, and another in the arm. "You win! Someone else's turn!"

There was no place to go but into the stream. He hated wading where the current was fast and deep because his withered leg gave him so little support. He dreaded having the boys laugh at him if he fell in the water. He ducked, taking another rock. "All is good!" he cried desperately.

Then there was a different sort of cry from the trees—real pain. Mal glanced up and saw, to his amazement, Grat, who was bent over, clutching his stomach. Most of the boys turned and ran, two of them taking rocks in the back as they fled, rocks thrown so hard Mal could hear the thuds. One of the boys who had been struck went down with a cry.

Mal tracked the trajectories back to their source and saw Dog and Ligo, who were thirty paces away, picking up rocks and throwing them with stunning force. Vinco, cowering behind a tree, put his hands up to protect his head. Grat bit off a scream as a stone bounced off his shoulder.

Mal ran up to his brother just as the older boys advanced, reaching the trees. "So, Grat," Dog hissed, fiercely angry, "should I let you start running before I throw the next rock?"

Vinco looked terrified, while Grat appeared sullen and somewhat defiant. His eyes changed, though, when Dog hefted a stone the size of a man's fist. "Do you want me to wait three breaths, or two?"

"Dog," Mal urged, "it was only a game. All is good."

"A game," Dog repeated dubiously. He looked down at Mal from his great height—he was now as tall as some of the Kindred men. "You are bleeding, Brother."

"It was a game of throwing rocks," Mal insisted. "It was Grat's turn next."

Dog regarded his brother for a long time. "Grat's turn," he repeated finally. "Do you want to take your turn now, Grat?" he asked softly.

Grat shook his head. "Not if you are going to play."

Ligo and Dog both laughed at this, and after a moment, Vinco and Mal joined in. Grat just stared at the dirt.

"Such a stupid game," Dog said dismissively. "Mal, come with me. We will throw spears, like real men."

Cragg was ten years old, Silex thought wonderingly to himself as he watched the boy focus on pulling feathers off one of the several geese they had killed. Ovi's son Tok was eight and saw Cragg as his big brother, the two of them inseparable. They were a family: Silex, his sister, and the two children. He was happy.

He heard someone approaching and turned. It was Denix, still their most capable hunter. She looked different, Silex thought as he watched her come. She had used the curved rib bones of a badger skeleton to unsnarl the natural knots in her hair and wore it tied at the end with a bow of leather thong—Silex had seen enough women combing themselves to recognize the effect, oddly feminine on such a masculine female as Denix. He also could not remember her ever putting a flower in her hair, but she sported one now, just over her right ear.

"Could I speak to you, Silex?" she asked in low tones. She seemed tense, for some reason.

"All is good," he agreed. He motioned for her to follow him, and soon they were on a well-worn path, trotting at a steady pace.

Denix seemed relaxed, now that they were in motion, though he could tell something was bothering her. "We are having a good summer," she observed after a time, breathing easily. She kept one hand loosely resting on her pouch, slung over her shoulder with a thin strap, so that it would not bounce too much as they ran.

This was not, he sensed, what she wanted to say, but he nodded agreeably. "After three such lean years, it is nice to find food and enjoy better weather."

"I want to talk to you about Hena," Denix continued, naming one of the female children in the tribe. "She is the same age I was when you took me on my first hunt, Silex."

"Yes, but you are a rare person, Denix."

She gave him a small smile. "I was given a rare chance."

"You are saying we should bring the older girls out on the hunt. But they will be women soon. I do not imagine the wives will be happy about such an arrangement."

"They accept *me*," Denix pointed out.

Yes, but you are like a man, Silex did not say. "Times were different," he said instead.

"Oh no," Denix exclaimed suddenly. She stopped, groping for her flower, which had come loose. She seemed flustered, which was so unlike her.

"It is a pretty flower," Silex remarked.

She gave him an intense, indecipherable look. "Thank you. Silex . . . You are right, times are different. Our men are all married, now."

"You are right: the Wolfen are still rebuilding, and if the girls are willing, we should let them hunt."

"Well . . . we were speaking of the married men."

"Yes, of course. The wives will not like it that the girls are out on the hunt, even though none are yet old enough to mate. It is an issue I have confronted before. I will handle that."

"No," Denix said, looking frustrated. "When I said all of our men are married I meant that there are no *single* men. I am the only adult woman who has never been married, Silex. I have never . . ." She trailed off helplessly.

"You have never been married," Silex finished for her. "Yes, I know."

Denix was fumbling with the flower, but it kept drooping over her ear. "I cannot make this work," she said in disgust.

"Would you like me to help you?" Silex offered politely.

Denix nodded wordlessly. Silex took the flower from her fingers and gently threaded it into her hair, which was straight and black, so different from Fia's curls. Denix was watching his face as he concentrated.

"Silex," she said quietly.

"Shhh," he whispered, looking over her shoulder. "Turn slowly."

Denix turned and saw where Silex was pointing. The

large she-wolf with the handprint markings, her muzzle grey with age, stood next to a tree, staring.

"I did not think to bring tribute," Silex muttered mournfully.

"I have some bird meat in my pouch," Denix informed him. Silex gestured and she swung the pouch around and pulled out a goose breast and offered it to him.

"No," he decided, "this should be your honor."

Denix's eyes widened in surprise, but she followed Silex as he approached the massive wolf, who waited impassively.

"I have not seen you in some time and was worried you might have perished," Silex called.

Denix caught her breath when she saw a juvenile wolf dart out from the trees. There was no mistaking the lineage—not only was this young female far larger than most, she had a white mark on her forehead, very visible and, if anything, more distinctly hand-shaped than that of the older she-wolf. The two wolves touched noses.

The Wolfen pair halted twenty paces away. "This cub is so bold! She looks us full in the face, just like her mother," Silex remarked, awed.

"Should I throw the food?" Denix asked anxiously.

"Not just yet."

And then, astoundingly, the young wolf left the older wolf's side and trotted up to the two humans with supreme self-confidence, stopping just a few paces away and staring at them curiously. The juvenile raised her nose and sniffed when Denix brought the tribute out and laid it reverently on the ground, and when the two Wolfen backed away respectfully, the juvenile picked up the bird meat and stood with it in her jaws, watching them. The sight gave Silex a shiver.

The wolves vanished into the woods with the goose breast and Silex and Denix stared at each other with wide eyes. "She all but received it from your hand," Silex exulted.

"What does it mean?"

"I will have to think on it," Silex replied. "I do not know what it means. But it can only be good."

"Silex," Denix said, touching his arm. "You and I have shared something together that no one else has. As is so often the case, the wolf approaches when it is just the two of us."

Silex nodded, pondering this. "You are right, Denix," he agreed, grinning. "We need to tell the others!"

He turned from her and ran, heading back to the Wolfen camp. Denix bit her lip and then followed, catching up to and matching his pace.

After a time, the flower dislodged from behind her ear and fell to the ground.

Calli put more force into her command. "Mal! Come! Now!" she yelled into the gathering gloom. When Mal finally emerged from the darkness, she was angry. "Why did you not answer when I called you?" she demanded.

"I am sorry, Mother," Mal responded in dead tones. He made to brush past her to go lie down in his spot, but she grabbed his arm to force him to look at her, then gasped when she saw his face.

"What happened to your eye?"

"Nothing," he muttered. His left eye was swollen and weeping, completely shut. Even in the firelight, Calli could see the multicolored bruises rising above his cheek.

"Who hit you, Mal? What happened?" Calli pressed.

"We were playing," he told her woodenly.

"What? No. Playing. Who hit you? Was it Grat? Vinco?"

Mal pulled his arm out of her grasp. "I said we were just playing," he insisted harshly. "Leave me alone, Mother. I can take care of myself."

Calli blinked at the ridiculousness of the statement. Take

care of himself? He was just eight summers old, he could not *take care of himself.*

And yet, she realized, boys always played rough, and it was not the mother's place to control them. That would be Palloc's job—the fathers dealt with such matters.

If Palloc would *do* his job.

"All is good, then, Mal," she murmured resignedly.

He sullenly turned away from her and found his way to his bed. His eye hurt, throbbing in concert with the bruises his mother had not seen on his ribs and shoulders. His mouth could taste the blood from where the knuckles had found his lips.

Mal lay down, wincing, trying to ignore the pain.

"We were just playing," he said aloud, so softly his mother, five paces away in her own bed, could not hear him. He felt the sob in his throat, but he *would not cry.* "Just playing, just playing," he repeated. "My father and I were just playing."

The Kindred were migrating to their winter quarters when they heard wolves howling in the day. The Wolfen, miles away, tracking the same herd of reindeer as the wolves, heard it, too.

Neither tribe knew what the howls meant. To the Kindred, the wail of the wolf at night was the voice of the spirits who could never be spoken of directly, the evil that fought the sun to death every evening. Women Kindred clutched their husbands, and around the fire on the men's side, bachelor hunters glanced uneasily at one another, unwilling to show the fear they felt so strongly. For the Wolfen, the howls represented the mystical song of their benefactors, the wolves who modeled how they should live and who led them to game.

Only other wolves could hear the high yowls and ptula-
tions and ascertain the true meaning: a member of a pack
had died. Any wolves within hearing distance stopped what
they were doing and raised their own voices to the sky.

The old she-wolf had lived longer than most, helped
through times of deprivation by offerings from the Wolfen.
She had seen four litters of her own in that time, and her
granddaughter, who had been traveling with her and had
taken food directly from human hand, was the dominant
bitch and had mated recently. The pack was healthy, thanks
in no small part to the old she-wolf.

Her passing was that rare occurrence among the wild, a
natural death. One evening she was listlessly without appetite, and the next morning she lay breathing in short pants,
her eyes closed. The dominant bitch refused to leave her
side, so the pack wandered away and then returned, confused and restless, touching noses. As the moon rose well
before sunset, the she-wolf took her last breath. The pack
knew of it instantly, the knowledge moving like a scent from
wolf to wolf. As one they sat down, raised their noses to the
afternoon sky, and sang the song of the great wolf's passing.

THIRTY-SIX

Year Eighteen

D og patiently retrieved the three spears Mal had just thrown. The target, a large, lone tree trunk with buds just emerging on the tips of its branches, was largely unmarked, though Mal had been attacking it all day.

"I am tired. I do not know why we have to do this anymore," Mal whined churlishly.

Dog grinned down at him. At seventeen summers, he was now the tallest man in the Kindred, while his brother Mal was shorter and stockier than normal. "Because," Dog responded, "we migrate soon and this will be your fourteenth summer. It is time for you to take your place among the Kindred as a man."

Dog was a spearman and, many said, as good as Urs. He could send his spear flying with such force and accuracy that it was often his weapon that struck the target right after the hunt master's. Even Valid, the spear master, spoke of Dog's special skill.

"Now," Dog said firmly. "Again."

Frowning, Mal picked up the first spear with his right hand—his man's hand. Normally, a man would put his woman's side foot forward and use that as a pivot while lifting the man's foot off the ground to give the spear extra lift, but Mal's left leg was his weak one, so they had developed a technique of throwing with the right while stepping off the right. Man hand, man leg.

They were thirty paces away from the tree trunk. Concentrating, Mal threw as hard as he could manage, but the spear simply had inadequate power behind it, and fell to the grass in front of the target—accurate, but short.

"Again," Dog instructed. "We drill until perfect."

"Arghhhh!" Mal yelled. He picked up the next spear and tossed and this one went forceful but wild.

"If a cave lion were charging us right now, your throws would have us be killed," Dog remarked.

"If a cave lion were charging us right now, I would hide behind you," Mal retorted.

Dog handed him the spears. "I am serious to you, Brother. Nothing will make me more proud than when you are out on the hunt by my side."

"All right," Mal muttered. He knew his brother—the only male member of the Kindred utterly unbothered by the crippled leg—loved him and only wanted him to succeed. He threw one set of spears, then another set, then another. Dog had him lower his man's side elbow, then raise it, but nothing seemed to be able to provide the power Mal needed to slam the spear point into the wood. Mal's frustration began to rise again, sweat matting his hair.

"Again," Dog murmured.

Mal stood ready, a spear in his hand, two more at his feet, and then his shoulders slumped. He relaxed his grip and let the spear fall to the ground.

"I cannot do this, Dog," he sighed.

"You must." Dog bent down and picked up the spear. "Take it."

"No."

"Mal. Please!"

"No."

"Take it!"

"I cannot!" Mal shouted. He yanked the spear away from Dog with his left hand, spun, and hurled it into the woods.

Dog's mouth dropped as the weapon soared high, vanishing in the forest.

Mal stood panting, his eyes hot. Dog started to laugh. Mal frowned. "What is it? What?"

"Did you see how far that went?" Dog exulted. "Mal, we have been using the *wrong hand*!" Dog began running to get the spear, taking leaping steps. "You nearly hit the sky, Mal! You just need to use your other hand!"

Mal watched his brother cavort. Now that he considered it, he realized that he tended to do everything with his woman's side hand, especially if no one was watching. Perhaps having a twisted leg on that side gave him more strength in his left arm to compensate.

"You are going to be a spearman! A spearman!" Dog was calling from the woods.

L yra found the two boys later that afternoon, lying in the grasses and laughing and talking about nothing. She carried with her several pieces of cooked meat impaled upon a stick, as well as a pouch full of eggs that Calli had allowed to simmer in hot water all morning.

She was a pretty girl with a shy smile, just a few months younger than Mal. She liked to take small stems and chain them together and weave them into her braids, an exotic new style that some of the older girls had started to emulate. Dog and Mal scrambled to their feet at her approach.

"I brought you some food," she greeted. "Calli said you were out here practicing hunting, but I see that instead you are lying around doing nothing."

Dog laughed, but Mal's grin was tempered by a sense of injustice. "We *were* practicing," he objected.

"When on the hunt, then, do you lie in the grass and wait for a winter mammoth to step over you so you can spear it from below?" Lyra asked.

"That is exactly how we do it," Dog affirmed.

"Well then. Please eat. Clearly all I thought I knew about hunting has been wrong," she said agreeably.

They sat cross-legged on the ground. Lyra offered the stick first to Dog, then to Mal. Both young men noticed she had fashioned a vine around her wrist, something they had never seen.

"Thank you very much, Lyra," Dog said formally.

"When you crack the eggs, you may find the centers are still warm," she advised.

Mal looked impatient for his brother to share their news. "We have been trying a new technique for throwing the spear," he told Lyra.

Dog nodded, but did not elaborate on Mal's statement.

"It is going very well," Mal continued forcefully.

Dog was assessing Lyra. She met his gaze and he flushed.

Boys were named men when they were in their fourteenth summer but females were deemed adults when the women decided the girls were capable of bearing children—though how they knew *that* was a mystery to the men. "So Lyra, this coming summer or the next you will be taken into the Kindred as an adult. What will be your craft?" Dog asked.

"We are assuming I will be a spearman," Mal interrupted almost desperately.

"I am hoping to apprentice to Renne. I like making rope," Lyra answered with a soft smile.

"Because you are very good at cooking," Dog told her, smiling through a mouthful of meat.

"Let me show you," Mal exclaimed, bounding to his feet.

When he threw the spear, it went nearly thirty paces before striking a tree. It did not stick, but fell to the ground. Still, a triumph. Mal turned back to his brother and Lyra, and they clapped.

Lyra had known Mal her whole life, and could not remember a time when he appeared so happy.

Two days later, the Kindred left for their summer quarters. The departure was so different than the migration made at the start of winter—they were excited, looking forward to a bountiful season, better food, and gloriously warm days spent in a far more beautiful place.

Dog, as a spearman, did not need to help his mother anymore, but he still came to take the travois from her, a respite Calli was grateful for. Coco did her best but had weakened in the past few years and simply was not up to the task, and Mal—Mal always tried, but for him, just keeping up with the Kindred was challenge enough.

"Thank you, Dog," Calli said as her tall older son unburdened her. "Just for a while, and then I am happy to take it back."

Dog grinned and nodded. He was always grinning—he made everything seem as if it were fun. He was so tall and was finally filling out a little. Calli looked often at his arms, wondering if they might someday fill out like Hardy's, but mostly he was lean, tall and lean.

They walked side by side in contented silence, and then Calli gave her son an appraising glance. "So, Dog, the women on the council have been talking openly about who you should marry. As your mother, they naturally are eager for my opinion."

As she spoke, Calli's eyes involuntarily found Albi, who struggled along as far away from Calli as could be managed, leaning on her walking stick more than ever. Things were so much better with Bellu as council mother. The women talked uncensored, they aired differences, they achieved consensus. How it must gall Albi to see everyone so much happier!

"Well, I do not know about marriage," Dog replied.

Calli searched his face. "Are you afraid what has happened between your father and me will happen to you?" she asked softly.

Dog cocked his head, considering. "No, I do not believe so. My father has turned against all of us because of his mother. My own mother only cares about me."

They smiled at each other. Calli reached out and touched his arm.

"Also," he continued slowly, "the one girl I would be interested in is not yet eligible. She has yet to be declared a woman—perhaps this summer."

Calli's jaw dropped. "What? Who? Who?" she demanded. She began mentally listing the girls she thought might make sense, but then stopped—it was obvious. "Lyra?"

"Shh," Dog replied, his face turning red.

Calli smiled. What a wonderful choice. She decided she would speak to Council Mother Bellu about it soon, as well as Lyra's mother, Sidee, and make it known among the council, so that when the time came, Dog might have the woman he desired. It was not the same as allowing a couple to determine for themselves, but it was so much better than when Albi decided everything.

"I think you are probably right. It may not be much longer before Lyra will be eligible to marry. I would like to be a grandmother."

Dog laughed at her radiant expression.

"What? Why do you laugh?" she demanded, shoving his shoulder lightly, but she was laughing, too.

* * *

The water in the river was frigid this time of year, though the ice had recently melted and moved out. Silex shivered at the thought of bathing in it, but he liked the feel of his skin when it was freshly washed.

He was fond of a place upriver where a series of low sandbars trapped the stream in pellucid pools. He made sure he let people know he was going there in case he was needed, but he headed there alone, wanting time to think. His sons Cragg and Tok thought bathing was torture and were happy not to be invited. The sun was warm and high in the sky—he would lie on the rocks and bask until dry.

Just as he was reaching his favorite spot, Silex started in surprise. Someone was already there. Instinctively, he ducked behind some foliage.

It was a woman, standing naked in water up to her ankles. She was reaching down and cupping water with her hands and ladling it on herself. Her back was to him, her skin smooth and buttocks taut.

Silex took in shallow breaths, his mouth dry. He should turn away, he knew, but he found himself frozen in place, enraptured. His pulse pounded as he watched the trickles flow down her body, dripping from her breasts. He knew who she was.

Denix.

The intense feelings now startled alive within him had been dormant since Fia died: the longing and the lust, the pull. This was not just mild attraction, this was an instant hunger that wracked him, consumed him, compelled him. When she turned her head, it was as if she had known all along he was there, had known he was watching. She met his eyes, her eyebrows raised.

Silex bolted, turning and fleeing as if being chased. The

run helped, redirecting his blood flow, the uneven ground demanding his attention and diverting it away from the image of Denix standing naked in the water. But when he made it back to the Wolfen gathering site, she was all he could think about.

He was married. *This is not good,* he admonished himself sternly. *Not good at all.*

THIRTY-SEVEN

The Blanc Tribe considered the Kindred to be a harbinger—when the migrating tribe arrived, it meant it would soon be summer, when fishing would be so much better.

The Kindred had fresh meat, and the Blanc Tribe immediately set out to put on a feast, the women mingling easily while the men withdrew to examine each other's weapons. The children were soon a running melee, brown-eyed and pale-eyed mixing without tension.

Not all children played. Those about to be accepted as adults: Vinco, Mal, Markus—were uneasy, eyeing the teen members of the other tribe, not sure what to say or do.

For Mal, being somewhat apart from everyone gave him an interesting perspective on the mingling of the tribes. He watched as the Blanc Tribe traded items of questionable value, such as the shiny shells they somehow pulled from their lake, for choice cuts of meat. They even brought out the bearskin that Urs had given them years ago and successfully traded it back—it had been fur for fish and now it was fur for meat, as if the fish had been directly traded for meat, in an exchange spread out over several years.

Several women from the Blanc Tribe swarmed Bellu, who had recently given birth to a little girl. They passed the child, bundled in fur, from hand to hand, cooing over the pretty little thing, who seemed to have the same eyes as her mother.

"She cries most nights. I never sleep," Bellu told them. They nodded sympathetically. "And she is sick all the time."

Not long after the Kindred's arrival, a light-eyed man found Calli. As was true of all the people in his tribe, he had shells throughout his hair. "May I ask of you if you are the mother of the one with the leg that is twisted so badly?" the man inquired.

It took Calli a moment to shake off her reaction—in the Kindred, no man would walk right up to a woman and speak without a proper introduction. "Mal, he is my son," Calli affirmed, deciding to ignore the man's faux pas.

"Mal. Of course. I remember when I first saw him. He is always playing, as if his leg were not so horribly deformed."

Calli crossed her arms in front of her chest. "Yes?" she prodded, more coldly.

A girl a year or two younger than Mal peeked out from behind the man. "I must introduce you. This is my daughter. Ema."

Ema looked up at Calli with tentative light eyes. Calli smiled politely at the girl, somewhat mystified. What was going on?

"Show her, Ema," the man urged impatiently.

Reluctantly, Ema stepped completely out of her father's shadow. A less sensitive woman might have gasped—Ema's arm on her woman's side ended above the elbow in a mass of scar tissue.

"Her hand was pinned beneath a great rock," the man explained. "We could not move it. The only way to save her was to use an ax." He swallowed, nodding at Calli's horrified expression. "First we tied a cord around her arm and wound it tight with a stick until her flesh was blue. And then we chopped just below the cord, separating the joint as cleanly as we could. I had hoped she would pass out, but she was conscious during the whole thing, my Ema," the man continued, his voice roughening. "Then, we packed the wound with mud and spiderwebs, and left the rope in place for several days. Her skin grew hot and she spoke in a strange language—we think she was talking to the spirits in the lake, who were trying to decide whether to take her. But the wound healed. Now she is healthy. And what a strong heart! So much pain, and still, she lives."

Calli could not imagine what that must have been like for the girl. She regarded Ema with sympathy and admiration. A strong heart, indeed. It reminded her of her son Mal, always living his life as if he were not afflicted with a deformity.

"But now," the man whispered, leaning forward, "no one from my tribe will marry her. Who would, with that arm? It is hideous."

Ema was listening, her expression bland. Calli felt her anger stir that he would speak so bluntly and unkindly in front of his daughter.

"But your son. Perhaps he will have the same problem? You see? Ema is thirteen years old. Next time you come, on your way to your winter quarters, perhaps we can have a wedding."

Calli looked at Ema, who gazed back solemnly. "Do you know my son, Ema?" Calli asked softly. The man seemed surprised at the question, but Ema nodded, smiling a little. "Does he seem like the sort of boy . . . the sort of man you would like as a husband?"

"Yes," Ema replied. "Yes, he does."

"And where would they live? With the Kindred? Or here, eating fish?" Calli wanted to know.

The man shrugged. "Perhaps he is happy here, perhaps he is happy with the Kindred. My wife is dead, so there is no woman to pine for grandchildren. I would be satisfied to see my daughter when the Kindred comes through to trade meat, and perhaps one winter or two they stay here if they wish."

Calli could see it, and it made her smile. A wife for Mal. She thought of the Blanc Tribe and their accepting ways, always welcoming, and of the bruises Mal tried to hide from his mother—bruises administered on a regular basis by his "friends." She knew Albi's influence among the women had all but evaporated, but she saw the older woman sometimes sitting and talking to Grat and some of the other boys, as if she were a kindly aunt. Calli suspected Albi was giving the boys malevolent ideas.

Calli pictured stopping here twice a year to see her son and his family. Her happy son and his happy family. "Yes," she found herself saying. "This is a wonderful idea."

Year Nineteen

When the man was in the den with the wolf puppy, they would play games together. Often they simply wrestled, but there were other games, such as when he made recognizable noises and gestured with his hands, over and over, until she reacted with a behavior that he praised and rewarded with a succulent morsel from the pouch he kept out of her reach. Sometimes she was to sit down. Sometimes she was to wait for him while he left, not moving from the spot where he put her until he returned. Her favorite, though, was when he called to her and she ran to him. She loved these games, and she loved the man.

"Before I can take you out of this cave, I have to know you will come to me when asked, or remain where I tell you, to keep you out of danger. I do not want to lose you."

One day he put something on her neck. The smell was familiar—he had something with the same scent looped around his waist. When he stood and her neck was yanked, though, she did not understand and rebelled, twisting and pulling, choking, getting frantic.

The man threw his arms around her and she calmed.

"I think this will work. With the rope on your neck, you will not be able to run off. Please. We will walk around the cave. You only need to become accustomed to it."

After some time, the wolf understood. It was another game. Tight, the cord choked her, but if she followed next to the man's heels, the rope dragged on the cave floor and he gave her meat. Not a fun game, but they did it over and over again.

That night, the man brought in something very strange—it was somehow the mother-wolf, with her scent and soft fur, but the pup's mother herself was not there. The pup smelled it up and down and whimpered, more out of bafflement than fear.

Later, though, the man lay on the mother fur and the wolf pup drowsily put her head on his chest, feeling content. The presence of the mother-smell gave her comfort.

"Tomorrow," the man said, the vibrations in his chest filling the young pup's ears, "we will go outside. I will carry my spear. I hope I can protect you."

Year Eighteen

The Kindred stayed with the Blanc Tribe for two days. Calli found Mal in an isolated group of Kindred adolescents, and called to him to help her. When she had her son aside, Calli pointed to a group of girls who were fussing with a tangle of ropes called a "net." Many of the women of the Blanc seemed to spend a lot of their time building or repairing the things, which were somehow used in catching fish.

"See that girl there? Her name is Ema. The one with the arm?" Calli asked.

Mal stared. "What happened to her arm?" he gasped, looking repulsed.

"What happened to your leg?" his mother responded sharply.

Mal looked up at her, shocked.

"How do you feel when people react with such dread to your leg?" Calli asked more gently. "Think how she must feel when people are unkind to her because of her arm."

Mal took this in and, to his credit, seemed to understand.

"Her father asked that you help her and a few of the other girls do something. I want you to go with them."

"Her father?" Mal repeated dumbly.

"Mal. Just go with them. The girl's name is Ema, and she is two summers younger than you, I think. Maybe just one. The Blanc use years instead of summers, so it is always a little difficult to calculate."

"Yes, Mother," Mal replied.

"And while you are out with Ema, ask about her. Find out about her. Notice how pretty she is."

"How pretty she is," Mal echoed without comprehension.

Calli sighed. "I just think that someday a woman like Ema could make a good wife for a man like you."

"Oh," Mal responded, his vision clearing of doubt. "No, Mother, I have already decided who I want to marry."

"You have?"

Mal nodded vigorously. "Lyra, of course. We are in love."

M al did as he was told, escorting the Blanc girls on their mysterious mission. At first he was irritated as he followed the well-worn path. The girl Ema walked serenely next to him, while her two companions, older by a couple of years and each carrying a rolled-up net under an arm, skipped ahead and then glanced back over their shoulders at them, laughing as if there was nothing more hilarious than a Kindred carrying a club. But then Ema said, "Thank you for protecting us," and Mal instantly changed his perception of what they were doing. No wonder Dog had suggested the club. These girls from the Blanc Tribe were going somewhere, and Mal was there to protect them from predators.

"I like it when the Kindred comes. You always bring meat, and everyone is always happy," Ema observed. She ran a hand through her hair, which was even lighter in color than most of the Blanc Tribe. The motion made a small rattling sound as the decorative shells threaded into her locks clicked together.

Mal nodded. He was older and thought he should say something wise in response to this, but he could not think of anything. She *was* pretty, he saw. Small dots of darker color stippled her pale cheeks, as if her skin was trying to turn to a more normal brown color, a tiny bit at a time. Her arm was less revolting than interesting, once he became accustomed to it.

He liked how tranquil and composed Ema was, nothing at all like her tittering friends, who were walking backward now so they could laugh openly at the two of them. It made Mal want to throw something at them.

"I think something is going to happen today," Ema blurted.

He glanced at her curiously. "Happen? What?"

She regarded him intently, her pale eyes full of energy. "Something wonderful," she whispered.

THIRTY-EIGHT

The path soon turned toward a small rocky bluff. The two older girls darted ahead and left the trail and bent over, gathering dry, brown grasses in their hands. Ema did not help them, so Mal did not either.

At the top of the trail, a cave waited, wide open and tall enough at the opening for a man to walk in upright. Several club-length tree branches were piled at the entrance, some of them blackened at one end. The older girls had wound the grasses around the tips of three of the branches. One of the girls was huddled over a rock with a piece of flint, her tongue in the corner of her mouth while she worked to strike a spark. Mal waited, more and more impatient, as the girl continued her inexpert efforts.

"Would you like me to try it?" he finally interrupted.

The girls all glanced at each other and, naturally, giggled. But he was handed the flint and he set his club aside and leaned down and found out that what he had seen Bellu do countless times was actually rather difficult: he struck and struck, but the few sparks he made flew in random directions and then flared out the way the vividly bright blood drops of the sun sometimes streaked across the night sky and vanished.

"I have never done this before and it is not as easy as I thought," he admitted. He looked up and saw the girls staring at him in something like shock. "What is it?"

They exchanged glances. "It is just so seldom that a man admits a mistake," Ema observed.

"Or that he cannot do something," one of the older girls added.

Mal did not like the idea that he had made either a mistake or an admission of a lack of aptitude, and did not see why they were speaking to him as if it were a compliment. Just then, his efforts made a spark fly and land on the head of one of the torches, and he leaned over and blew on it as he had seen Bellu do, until a little flame started in the grass.

To Mal, this proved the girls were all wrong. He looked up at them proudly.

"Though you never attempted it before, it came to you easily," Ema praised him, completely getting the point. She reached out and touched him with her one hand as he stood, and, of course, the girls giggled.

There was plenty of illumination from the girls' torches. A few feet into the cave, he was surprised to see the walls coated with ice, and the temperature plummeted.

"It takes nearly the summer, but eventually it will all melt," Ema told him. "Then the walls are wet instead of frozen. And back there, the ice never melts, because all winter long the women come and break off ice tongues and throw them back here."

"Ice tongues?" Mal frowned, trying to picture it.

"When water flows in the winter, it forms a tongue to lick the earth," she explained.

"I have not seen such a thing."

"Maybe you should stay here next winter!" one of the older girls suggested. Barely had she spoken than the two girls were laughing so hard they had to clutch each other, their torches wavering and sending mad shadows dancing on the walls.

Ema turned to them. "Why would you try to ruin my life?" she asked softly.

It was as if the two girls had been slapped. They stared at Ema, speechless, while Mal tried to figure out what was happening. There was no laughter now. One of them nodded. "I am so sorry, Ema," she apologized.

"Sorry about what?" Mal asked curiously.

The girls did not reply. They lowered their eyes and went deeper into the cave. Another few feet and a wall of ice greeted them, an odd wall that looked as if frozen logs had been stacked up on top of each other. The ice tongues, Mal supposed. Here there were several odd clubs lying on the ground, their stone heads placed so that the blade pointed straight forward from the top, like a spear tip but thick and heavy like an ax.

"Would you help us?" Ema asked, touching his arm again.

The older girls demonstrated and he quickly got it: the point of the club was thrust at the frozen ground, cracking it. Most of the earth had been turned this way before, Mal saw, and once he broke the few inches of ice the soil underneath, while frozen, yielded fairly easily into chunks. Proud to show how strong he was, he attacked the task without questioning why he was doing it.

"That is good," Ema praised. The girls all dropped to their knees and, to Mal's astonishment, began pulling fat fish out of the earth, each one as long as the distance between elbow and hand. They threw these fish on the nets they had brought, piling it up.

"Do they live in the ground?" he asked, bewildered.

This time even Ema laughed. "All summer long, we bring fish here and bury it where the ground is always frozen. The ice tongues melt a little. These fish are frozen solid. See?"

Ema thumped on one with her hand. "But when they are cooked, they will feed all of us. This is why we always have fish for the Kindred."

The older girls trussed up their nets and slung the heavy loads over their shoulders. "Thank you for helping us," one of them said in Mal's general direction. Once they were out of the cave they tossed their torches to the dirt and ran ahead, so that Mal and Ema were alone. He picked up his club and the two of them headed back.

"I can go faster," Mal told Ema, conscious that her pace was deliberately slow.

"But then we would be home much more quickly," Ema replied.

Mal pondered this. Yes, that was true. But so what?

"Most of the Kindred are so thin, but you are like us, with muscles on your arms and shoulders," Ema remarked.

Mal glanced at his arms. "I have always noticed that the Blanc people have bigger bones," he admitted after a moment, "but I have never seen myself as anything but a boy with a bad leg."

"I remember the first time I saw you," Ema replied. "Even then, you were stronger than all the other Kindred boys your age."

Mal doubted that anyone who saw him noticed anything but his limp. He glanced down at his tiny, toeless foot. No one would ever miss that, he reflected bitterly.

She caught him looking at his own leg. "Does it hurt?" she asked him quietly.

"No. Never. In fact, I have trouble running over rough ground because the leg is a bit numb," Mal replied, shocking himself with a confession he had made to no one.

"My arm hurts. Even though it is not there anymore," Ema told him.

"I am sorry," Mal said after a moment. It seemed an in-adequate sentiment, but what do you say to a girl with a mass of scars where her arm should have been?

They walked with each other in silence, but Mal could feel her next to him, watching his face, and when he glanced her way she gave him that pretty smile.

"I am sorry that you will be leaving in just one or two days," she said.

"We have to get back to our summer settlement. There is good hunting there, a clean stream, and caves to live in," Mal replied.

"I would love to see it."

He looked at her. It was as if she were talking about something else entirely, having a conversation he did not understand.

At the edge of the Blanc settlement, Ema stopped. Mal turned toward her questioningly.

"This has been a wonderful day for me," she sighed.

Mal nodded, a bit bewildered. "Good," he finally replied.

"I have a secret, would you let me tell it to you?" she whispered. Mal nodded, and she beckoned for him to lower his head to hers. He bent down, and her breath warmed his ear and sent a tingle down his backbone. Her hand came up and touched the back of his neck, pulling his head down farther, and then her mouth moved from his ear to his lips.

A warm sensation flooded through him like hot water. Shocked and enthralled, he dropped his club and stood with his arms hanging limply, his heart pounding. When she released him he stared at her pale eyes, his mouth open, and then she turned and ran away.

She had kissed him. Kissed him! Elation flowed through him now. He was a man who had been kissed!

He went to find Dog—this was news that had to be shared, and at once.

He had been pretty good at it, he decided. He and Ema had stood, locked together, for a long time. He felt his blood heat up just remembering it. Now that he had kissed a girl he could do it again, and he would, soon.

He would kiss Lyra!

For the only time in anyone's memory, there were still pools of snow in the shadows at the summer settlement. The trees were budding but the leaves were not yet out in the open, and no tender shoots of grass were feeling their way toward the sun. The Kindred regarded each other solemnly. Perhaps this explained why they had not seen any prey in several days—until the grasses rose from the soil, nothing would venture this far north.

The hunt went out and did not come back for two days, and then three, and then four. For them to stay out meant that they were finding nothing.

The women foraged. They found insect larvae and tender roots, and the buds of some flowers, though often bitter, could be eaten. Still, hunger cramps seized the women and their children.

On a day when the rain contained pellets of ice, a scream tore the morning air. The women ran out to find Bellu sobbing, collapsed by the communal fire. "My baby!" she shouted hoarsely, her mouth sagging in horror. And then she began screaming again, holding the limp, lifeless child in her arms.

Tragic though it was, this was not an infrequent situation for the Kindred, and indeed it was the reason why they waited so long to give children their names. Bellu's child was not yet a person in her own right, but was simply of the mother, as a hand, or a leg. There would be no assembly of the Kindred for burial—this was an event that occurred often enough that common practice mandated that the mother take the baby away and bury it a discreet distance from camp. But Bellu had thrown herself into the mud and was inconsolable, unable to communicate with any coherency, and so Albi volunteered to dispose of the tiny corpse. "As a kindness," she explained in a murmur, gently tugging the baby out of Bellu's reluctant arms. "I will see to it." The other women gathered around, many of them veterans of the same sort of tragedy, while Albi scooped up the child and left camp.

Calli fell asleep that night holding Bellu cradled in her arms. During the night she awoke, shifting painfully with the weight of Bellu slumped against her. It had stopped raining, the air cold and still. The men, she realized drowsily, must be nearby, because she could smell cooking meat in the night. *Good*. They would be home with food.

They did not come home, however, not that day, nor the next. Bellu remained despondent, sitting listlessly, barely acknowledging when Calli brought her some thin soup—*her* soup, Calli's ration, because Bellu had already consumed her own. Feeling a sharp anger rising within her, Calli bit off what she might say and left camp. She had no direction, she just kept walking, thinking perhaps she would never stop. Just walk out into the plains until exhaustion took her down, then await her fate.

After too many paces to count she was far from camp, though the fires still flavored the air with smoke. Calli felt broken and numb, walking more and more slowly because it seemed less and less important that she keep moving. Then she heard something, a noise that made her head snap up alertly despite her lethargy. She instinctively made her way in a crouch to a large mound of dirt: the noise seemed to come from just the other side.

It was a snuffing sound, slightly wet. Curious, Calli cautiously crawled to the crest of the mound, lifting her head to see.

It was Albi, sitting on a stone next to the blackened remnants of a fire. Her hands were to her mouth.

She was eating.

W ith the bullying Grat now a member of the hunt—he had been made a stalker the previous summer—Vinco and Mal and Markus were back to being inseparable, a relationship made all the more fraternal by the knowledge that this was the summer they would be made men before the Kindred. Restless with their growing bodies, they threw spears and rocks, they chased younger boys, they told themselves wild tales about the bears and lions they would kill. Theoretically they were also the home guard, and they did carry their spears, but they were too bored to hang around the settlement and were often out in the woods together.

The hunt was back, though—bringing a few rabbits and a vile-tasting badger—so they dared not abandon their posts, and thus they were even more itchy than usual.

"We should go see what Lyra is doing," Mal suggested.

Vinco and Markus rolled their eyes at each other. This was not the first time Mal had come up with this brilliant idea. Lacking something better to do, though, they struck off toward the family fires to see if they could find her.

As little boys they had had free rein to wander the men's side, but once they were old enough it was explained to them that until they were adults, they were prohibited from going there. This meant that Mal rarely saw his father, so he was surprised to see Palloc striding toward them. Palloc's pale features were scowling and he seemed focused on an internal struggle of some kind and did not notice the boys.

"Father!" Mal called. He left his friends and ran forward with his awkward gait, dragging his bad leg with each step. "Good summer, Father," Mal greeted as he approached. "I am happy to see you today."

Palloc stood motionless. Mal politely dropped his spear and raised his hands, palms out, as he had been taught to do when addressing another man. "I am hoping that the hunt will be good when you go out tomorrow."

"Do not call me that," Palloc said darkly.

Mal was startled. "What? Call you what?"

Palloc took four steps and knocked Mal to the ground. Mal's head bounced on the hard earth, and odd little dark spots flew around in his vision, like sparks rising from a fire.

"To you I am Spearman. Understand?" Palloc hissed. He turned away.

Mal leaped to his feet. "Why do you hate me?" he pleaded to his father's back. "I am your son."

Palloc whirled, making a sound deep his throat, and strode back. Mal raised his arms to cover his head and Palloc hit him solidly in the chest, rocking him back so that he had to take his weight on both legs and nearly fell. When Palloc hit him again Mal crumpled.

Markus and Vinco turned to each other in horror. They were children and had no right to interfere, but the savagery of this attack was unlike any family discipline they had ever witnessed.

"We have to get Dog," Vinco breathed.

Markus nodded and the two boys ran to find Mal's brother.

THIRTY-NINE

Calli sent word to Urs through Nix that she urgently needed to speak to him. Urs found her waiting for him upstream, not in their forbidden rendezvous place but well south of the Kindred's self-enforced border.

"Good summer, Calli," he greeted formally and, to her ears, awkwardly.

"Good summer, Hunt Master," she replied. Anyone watching would see two people standing two paces apart, not touching, merely talking. Nothing improper. "Thank you for coming to meet with me, Urs. I wanted to speak to you about my son."

Urs regarded her carefully. "Dog?" he asked, because he did not want it to be the other one.

"No, not Dog," Calli replied patiently. "Urs, soon we will have our summer gathering and Vinco, Markus, and Mal will receive their assignments."

Urs was already shaking his head.

"Just listen," Calli urged. "Please. They will receive their assignments. The boys will join the hunt—"

"I cannot," Urs interrupted. "Not Mal."

"But Urs . . ."

"I am sorry but I have to do what is good for the hunt. A man needs to be able to run."

"Dog says Mal can throw a spear farther and more accurately than anyone else."

"I have seen him throw," Urs grunted. "He uses the wrong hand."

"What does that matter?"

"Calli!" Urs said sharply. "You are not to question *me* about matters of the hunt."

She stood there staring fiercely at him for a moment, and then her shoulders slumped. "If he has nothing assigned to him, he will have no purpose. It will kill him."

Urs watched her, the slight wind blowing her hair. She was not much different than the first time they went upstream together, into forbidden territory, forbidden passion. His own body had changed, marked by scars, his face weathered, but Calli remained a beauty.

She caught the way he was looking at her. She had influence with this man, she realized, and she needed to use it. "Then I have an idea. Something to spare my son the humiliation of living in the Kindred as a permanent child, without a purpose. And you must do this for me, Urs, this one kindness, as amends for vowing to marry me and then abandoning your vow and putting lie to your words. Do this, and I forgive you. Deny me this, and I will never speak to you again."

Urs was thunderstruck. "But Calli, I told you at the time, I had no choice, it was arranged . . ." He trailed off, helpless before her hard expression.

"You broke your vow and now you must make amends. Will you do it, or not?"

Urs raised his hands, then let them fall helplessly. "What is it you would have me do?" he asked.

Mal lay in the dirt where his father had knocked him down. The blood in his mouth was thick. He looked up and Palloc was standing there panting, fists clenched.

It did not seem that another kick was coming. Mal pulled himself up, struggling into a standing position. His mouth did not even hurt, he realized. His ribs ached, but his face felt numb.

"Fa—" Mal croaked. The word stuck in his throat, tripped up by his bloody lips.

"What did you say?" Palloc demanded.

Mal spat in the dirt. "Father," he whispered defiantly.

The moment he said it, he was sorry he did, did not know *why* he did, but the word was out and Palloc's eyes widened and then narrowed. Mal ducked his head and raised his arms as his father hit him savagely in the ribs with his fists.

"Stop!"

It was Dog, marching toward them. Mal was doubled at the waist, dribbling more blood, feeling oddly like crying now that his big brother had arrived.

Palloc watched Dog approach with contempt in his eyes. "This is not your business," he said. "Go back to kissing your girl."

Dog did not even slow down. He walked straight up to Palloc and punched him hard on the shoulders with both fists, knocking him back. Palloc was too surprised to do anything but stumble. "What—" he started to say. Dog kept walking and shoved him again and this time Palloc fell, staring up at Dog looming over him.

"There is no fighting among the hunt," Palloc protested, still lying there.

"Get up, and we will see about that," Dog replied, his eyes cold.

"This is a family matter. I am applying discipline."

"This *is* a family matter," Dog agreed. "And I, too, am applying discipline. If you ever touch my brother again, I will beat you until your broken ribs protrude from your sides. Do you understand the discipline? Unless you want to stand up and finish it now. I am ready *now*."

"That is against the rules of the hunt," Palloc insisted.

"Stand up and fight and then let us see what is our punishment," Dog suggested. "Perhaps I will be forced to stay with the women for the summer, serving you soup while your broken bones heal."

Palloc did not reply. He looked away. Dog turned to his brother. "Are you badly hurt?"

Mal drew himself up again. This time, when he spat, it was more for dramatic effect. "No. He could not hurt me. He hits like a girl."

Dog looked at his bleeding brother and a small smile came to his face. "You are a hard stone, Mal."

Palloc crawled a few feet and then stood and left with a haughty set to his shoulders. Dog put an arm around Mal, and Mal grinned through bloody teeth. Brother to one of the most beloved men in the tribe, Mal felt accepted and normal, a man in all but formal name, soon to join the hunt and contribute to the Kindred.

Three children were in their third summer and were named by the eldest woman in the family—all boys, which was seen by all as a good omen for the tribe. No one mentioned the lone girl, Renne's child, who had come down with a fever and died over the winter, but Coco, who had lost three children in such a fashion in her own life, sat with Renne and squeezed her hand.

After the naming, Urs stood to announce the hunting assignments for the fourteen-year-olds. Calli drew in a breath, nervous despite the bargain she had struck with the hunt master. Her eyes sought out Valid, and the smile he gave her was calming.

"The way of the hunt is to stalk the prey, to spear the prey, and then to cook what we need and bring the rest back to the Kindred," Urs began ritualistically. "Today we invite a new stalker into the hunt. Markus, please come forward. A man of the hunt, stalking man—stalker."

Markus stood, clearly unhappy. Stalker was a far less admired position than spearman. Nonetheless, he stood and faced the Kindred, all of whom applauded. Soon the men would line up and, one by one, welcome the new hunter to manhood.

"When a powerful arm is needed, our new man of the hunt, man of the spear, will be there," Urs intoned. "Vinco, spearing man, come forward."

Vinco bounded up to stand next to Markus, grinning at the applause.

Then a hush fell on the Kindred, a hush that seemed to carry a small dread in its silence. There was one adolescent left. People darted glances at Mal, who was sitting next to his mother.

Urs took a deep breath. "When we cook our kill so that we have the strength to hunt and to return to the Kindred, our fire is made from the smoking horn that one of us wears. Always in the past, this horn has been packed by the fire maker." Urs nodded at Bellu, who nodded back, looking ready to weep because her dead son, Salu, would have been named to the hunt today. "But now we have a situation where the fire maker is also the council mother. It is not a good . . . ," Urs searched for a word. "Thing," he finally came out with, "for the council mother to make the fire horn." Urs threw a glance at Calli. "We need a male to prepare the fire for the hunt. Not to go with us, but to make sure the hunt is properly outfitted, the way the tool master is a man who makes our spears. Mal, step forward."

Mal had been following Urs's rambling speech with

growing alarm, and now he stared with disbelief. Numbly, he stood, searching for Dog with his eyes.

"Mal, you will be our fire . . ." Urs faltered. "Our fire boy," he finally finished.

Mal flinched. He did not see his mother behind him, glaring angrily at Urs.

The applause was loudest for Mal, perhaps because everyone was relieved that Urs had so wisely found a solution to the problem that had been worrying them all.

People were standing and heading back to their fires. Vinco and Markus were already on the men's side—traditionally, a new hunter slept there his first night. The men were queued up in a single file line to give Vinco and Markus their formal welcome.

Calli caught Urs as he was trying to slide away to the men's side.

"Fire *boy*?" she hissed at him. "You were to make him a man."

"I just could not . . . it did not sound right."

"Did not sound right?" she demanded incredulously. "You denied him a man's place because of the *sound* of it?"

"A man has to be in the hunt, Calli. I am sorry, but that is how it must be. He cannot hunt. He has an important job, as you asked of me, but nothing I can say or do can ever give him a good leg, and without two strong legs, he is not a man."

"No," Calli snarled, her eyes down to slits. "*You* are not a man, Urs. A man keeps his vow, and when he breaks it and promises amends and then breaks *that* promise, he is shameful and weak. You betray me because all you care about is being hunt master. Because you like the way it *sounds*."

* * *

Mal was waiting for Calli at their family fire. "You did this," he accused.

Calli bit her lip. "Mal, I am sorry."

"Where am I going to sleep tonight? I cannot sleep on the men's side, because I am a boy, the fire boy. But now I have been given a job, so I cannot sleep here, with my mother, like a child, can I?" Mal sneered. "And can I now marry? Have my own family? No, because I am a boy."

"You are right," Calli said. "This is not the honor you deserve."

"It is because of my leg! Everyone hates me because of my leg!" his voice filled with anguish, his face red. "It *is* a curse. It has ruined everything!"

"They do not hate you," Calli replied faintly, wishing it were true.

"I should go." Mal turned and stared out into the darkness, as if contemplating spending the night away from the protection of the tribe.

"Perhaps you should," Calli said.

Mal whipped back around and stared at her with wide eyes. "What did you say?"

"Mal . . . The father of Ema, the girl with the, with the arm, the Blanc Tribe. He came to me and suggested you might live with them."

"With them?" Mal repeated, dumbfounded.

"That you might take Ema. As your wife. And live with them. They have no history with you. They have never heard of Albi's curse, any of that calumny. They only know that Ema needs a husband."

Mal remembered Ema kissing him, the shock and the pleasure of it. He regarded his mother blankly. "But I am in love with Lyra," he objected.

"If only it were that simple. If only it were about love. But Mal, the council will never let you marry Lyra."

"Why would it stop us? We are in love!" he insisted.

For a moment all Calli could do was stand there and re-member mating with Urs, thinking, *He loves me, he loves me,* when the heartbreaking truth was that it was probably never true, never true at all. The illusion, the story she told herself, had been the most sweetly satisfying thing in her life. Should she really deny Mal the joy that came with such jubilant delusion? Her vision focused on Mal's tormented face.

"Mal. Are you sure Lyra feels this way, too? Has she told you this?"

"She does not have to, Mother. I know the truth of it. She spends all of her time with me. We laugh together."

"And Dog," Calli added softly, committing herself. It sickened her, what she was about to do, but she needed him to see that the arrangement with Ema was the absolute best for him.

"What?"

"You spend all of your time with Lyra and *Dog*."

"Yes, my brother is my best friend in the Kindred."

"And you are sure that it is you that Lyra is spending her time with, when it is the three of you. That she is with you—and Dog—because she loves *you*."

Mal looked horrified. *"No,"* he whispered. "You are wrong."

"When we visit the Blanc Tribe this next winter, why not consider staying with them," Calli urged gently. "Spend time with Ema, and learn their ways." She wiped her eyes. "You could stand in the water, your powerful spear . . ."

"You are wrong, Mother. Lyra loves me. She loves *me*!"

FORTY

Dog came upon Lyra sitting on a rock by the Kindred Stream. "Well good summer, Lyra! I did not know you were here," he hailed her, smiling broadly.

"Why did you come here, then?" she replied.

Dog's habitual grin slipped a little. Though he was seventeen and a member of the hunt, this girl just three and a half years younger always seemed to confound him. "I was just seeking a drink of water," he finally explained unconvincingly.

"Pretty far to come just for a drink," she observed. "Are you sure you did not want to see me?"

"No, of course," Dog answered.

"I am not at all sure what you mean by that statement," Lyra returned lightly. "Of course, or of course not?"

"I mean yes, of course not."

Lyra laughed. "Where is Mal today?" she inquired, looking past Dog as if expecting his brother to be shadowing him.

Dog's face fell a little. "He is not doing well with being made fire boy. He sleeps off by himself and does not speak to me."

"It is not your fault, Dog. You cannot protect him from everything," Lyra said softly.

Dog grunted, hearing the truth in her words. "Someday, though," he started to say, and then broke it off.

Lyra gave him a speculative look. "They do say you are our best hunter. Someday, you may well be hunt master, and then your brother will finally be able to take his place with the men."

Dog was nonplussed at her correct reading of him. She smiled at his expression, then stood and gestured to her garments. "What do you think?"

She wore a light tunic made from reindeer skin, exposing her bare arms, which had tanned from the summer sun. As she posed with her hands on her hips, Dog could see that she had tied small bits of leather thong to the front of it, the hide pierced and gathered at each knot.

The design was eye-catching and unique. Each knot was the same distance from the one before it—five across, and five down. For Dog, accustomed to the sprawling chaos of nature's constructions, such uniformity was nothing short of astounding. He simply had no words for what he was seeing. "They are . . . I have never seen such a thing. What do you call it?"

Lyra cocked her head at him. "Call it? I am not sure. What do you say when the reindeer return to the same place every year?"

"We say . . . it is a habitual pattern," Dog replied.

"Just so. This is a pattern, then."

"It is very pretty."

"Pretty?" Lyra raised her eyes at him. "A bold thing for you to say to me."

"What? No, I just meant to compliment you."

"That is why you sought me out, to compliment me," Lyra noted. "All is good."

Dog was blushing furiously. "That is not what I meant."

"You are a man." Lyra gazed up at him. "The tallest of the Kindred, everyone says."

Dog drew himself up. "Thank you."

"Oh," Lyra laughed, "was that a compliment?"

"This conversation is following a pattern," Dog replied. "This is how we always talk to each other."

They held each other's eyes for a moment, smiling over something shared. "So as a man, do you believe you will soon be married?" Lyra finally asked. Then she laughed at Dog's startled reaction. "I am sorry, did I alter the habitual pattern of our conversation?"

"The council has not yet said anything to me about marriage."

"So *that* is why you came to gift compliments upon me," Lyra speculated.

"I thought we said you would compliment *me*."

"So what are we going to do?"

"Do?"

"I am not yet a woman."

"I am not able to track the pattern of our conversation."

"No, I am serious now, Dog." Lyra gazed at him levelly. "Have you thought about the problem? I am not a woman so the council cannot propose me as a wife. Are you willing to wait for me?"

"I just came for a drink of water!"

"Dog. Will you wait?"

"Why," he asked plaintively, "cannot the council just declare you to be a woman *now*?"

Lyra threw back her head and laughed. "That is not how it works. Do you seriously not know?"

"Not know what?"

"This is a topic for you to bring up with your mother. I am not going to tell you."

"When boys turn fourteen summers, they are named to the hunt as men," Dog insisted stubbornly. "It does not matter if they have no beard. Most, in fact, do not. But they are deemed old enough. I do not understand why women do not adopt this sensible solution."

"We have a different, uh, pattern," Lyra admitted. "We must be ready, and it is not up to any person, but rather something inside the woman herself, that determines this. So: I am not yet ready. Will you wait for me?"

Dog nodded. "Yes, Lyra," he replied.

"Well, that is the right answer." They were back to smiling at each other. "So we cannot marry yet, but you will speak to your mother? And I will speak to mine."

"I may have already raised the subject."

Lyra's eyes danced across Dog's face. She held a hand up to touch his cheek. "Exactly," she told him softly.

After just a few moments with Bellu, Mal could strike a spark with a single strike of the flint. Learning to pack moss and sticks into the severed tip of smoldering hollow bison horn was just as easily accomplished—and this was what Bellu was given as a full-time job? As council mother, Bellu seemed to turn to Calli for guidance whenever any sort of decision was required of her. What did Bellu do all day?

Now that he had a job, Mal was no longer free to run around playing all day, and it gave him a new perspective on life in the Kindred camp. The pine nuts they ate in winter, of which there always seemed to be an inadequate supply, turned out to be tremendously time intensive to harvest and prepare. Mal went with his mother and several other women into the pine forests, and Calli taught him that the trees they sought had both open and closed pinecones—the open ones meant the seeds were ripe, the closed ones still had their seeds. Then the cones themselves were set out on hot rocks by the fire until they opened, and then Calli and Coco smashed the cones with rocks, so that small pieces fluttered out, each with a tiny seed. The seed itself was encased in a shell that could only be cracked with teeth. No wonder they always wound up with so few!

As fire boy, Mal wore the horn around his neck with a loop of leather, or carried it in his hand by the strap. Every so often he would blow into the wide end of the horn to assure the fire was still smoldering, and he fed in tiny sticks and more dried moss whenever it seemed appropriate.

If any of the boys he ran with knew that his job entailed "finding moss" he would be completely humiliated. The term was fraught with significance and was even considered something of an insult—young boys often accused each other of having to go find moss without have the slightest idea what it meant.

The whole fire boy thing was a colossal exercise in nonnecessity. There were fires burning all over the Kindred encampment. Even a drenching rainstorm would leave some coals. And the hunt always carried some of these fire horns with them, assigning them to the most junior members.

Mal sourly regarded the horn around his neck. At times, it was too hot to hold, and when it was not, Bellu said that meant it was time to blow on it. Mal doubted she knew this; it struck him as something she had made up.

At the small end, another hole had been chipped in the horn, allowing air to flow in from both sides. It occurred to Mal he might blow in this end, rather than the other one. Did that not that make more sense? He could fit the small end entirely in his mouth.

He put the small end of the horn to his lips and blew, but his wind was blocked. He blew harder, and still could not get any air into the thing. He expanded his lungs, held tight to the horn, and blew as hard as he could.

The contents of the horn exploded out the large end, igniting instantly when the embers hit oxygen. Mal blinked in amazement at the cloud of fire he had created, which rained down to the ground, still burning.

Using a stick, he managed to shove some coals back into the horn and patiently reconstruct the fire. He was grinning, though—he doubted anyone in the Kindred knew what happened when you blew in the small end of the fire horn.

It felt good to have some secret knowledge. Allowed him to be less a boy, somehow.

I love our summer quarters," Bellu told Mal.

He could see why: as hunt master, Urs was allowed an actual cave for his family, a small one that sat above the large communal cave, like a tiny nose over a huge mouth. Even more delightful than the commanding view was a natural, scooped-out depression in the rock near the mouth of the family cave, as if a large egg had been pushed into mud and then the mud had become rock. Filled with water and then warmed with stones from the family fire, it was a place where Bellu could bathe, stretched out, her face above water. Nearly every single day Bellu was found in her bath, especially now that she had a fire boy to carry the heated rocks with a hollow log and drop them in the water for her.

Her hair reacted to the daily rinsing by becoming soft, so that all the men of the Kindred were giving her the same sort of glances she had earned when she had been young and unmarried.

Bellu lay back in her bath and sighed. "Would you warm the water, Mal?" she requested lazily.

Mal was wearing the most neutral expression possible. He used a branch to manipulate a rock from the fire into the hollow of a log, then carried the rock to the water and slipped it in. It sizzled and Bellu moved her legs so it would not touch her.

"Thank you, Mal."

Mal nodded, not looking at the woman considered the most beautiful in the Kindred as she floated naked in the water.

She splashed him playfully. "This is not such hard work, is it?"

"No," he agreed. "Though sometimes a man *wants* to do hard work."

"If he can," Bellu responded.

"Yes," Mal responded evenly.

"A man," Bellu said idly.

Mal nodded and made to leave.

"Wait. Stay for a moment. Look at me."

Mal glanced at her face, then away.

"Mal. Look at me." Bellu spread her arms. Her nipples were touching the surface of the water, and from where Mal stood, down by her feet, he could see between her legs. She was watching him, seeing him look at her. He glanced away again. "Mal," she repeated. Her knees separated slightly, and the tip of her tongue slid out from between her lips. Mal could not help himself; he stared openly, feeling a hot sensation start in the pit of his stomach and move down. "Not such a bad job, being in charge of keeping my bath warm," Bellu observed.

"No," Mal croaked.

"I can see I am making quite the impression on you." Bellu smiled.

Mal dropped his hands to cover his crotch. He turned away, feeling his face burn. Bellu laughed.

"I must leave," Mal told her. The sensation between his legs was painful and pleasurable and perplexing, and his heart was pounding. This was far from the first time he had

had a hard penis, but there was something new about this one, something complex and mysterious.

That night his dreams were vivid and wild, with an exotic pulsing element to them, so that when he woke up he wondered if he had a fever.

He had planned to go sit with Hardy, who let him observe toolmaking and did not object when Mal seized a rock and shaped a stone ax head. But in the end he wound up climbing up to the hunt master's cave, to see if Bellu wanted another bath.

FORTY-ONE

S ince Mal had so little work to do, he took to wandering around looking for prey, carrying a spear with
him. He hoped for rabbits but instead discovered a
tree with little green fruits that crunched when he bit into
them, his mouth puckering at the sour taste.

"They are better when they are not so green," a voice
called behind him. Mal turned and it was her, of course, the
one person he did not want to see: Lyra.

"You have been so busy I have not spoken to you in many
days," she remarked, joining him at the base of the tree. She
idly reached up and plucked a fruit from a low branch,
examining it. "Yes, still too early yet."

"I have been very busy," he agreed coldly. She wore flowers in her hair and also spliced into the vines she had woven
around her neck, vividly colorful.

She met his eyes. "I think you are deliberately busy for
some reason having to do with me."

"No, that is not it. My job is just much harder than anyone realizes," he corrected sternly.

"Of course it is."

He inhaled. "I can smell the flowers you are wearing."
He meant to continue that the smell was too much—
overwhelming, unseemly—but he bit off the lie. In truth
the bouquet enraptured him.

She smiled. "Thank you. We should talk about what else

besides your job has you too occupied to spend any time with me. To go from speaking to you every day to speaking not at all is very strange."

He did not reply for a moment. "Well . . . ," he began reluctantly, "my mother says you and Dog are . . ." Mal trailed off.

Lyra, nodded, considering. "Is that why you have been avoiding me?" she asked.

So. She did know how he felt about her. For some reason it made him glad and sick in equal measure.

"Mal. I am not taking your brother away from you, even if we marry someday. He will always be your family."

No, she did *not* know. Mal felt even worse. "My mother," he finally replied, "says you speak your mind and are wise for your age."

Lyra blushed. "That is a very nice compliment."

"I do agree that you speak your mind but sometimes I think you are a stupid hyena."

Lyra stared at him with shock and hurt in her eyes. Mal looked away, not sure why he had said that, or what he was doing.

"Well," she said finally, "in this case I will not speak my mind, because what I have to say to you is that you are trying to ruin our friendship because your brother and I are in love. You do not seem to understand that this was bound to happen, your brother would eventually want to start a family with *somebody,* but instead of being glad that he wants me, you insult me. You are a spiteful, mean boy."

He watched Lyra walk away from him, his dissatisfaction gnawing at him. *I am not,* he wanted to shout, *a boy!*

But he was. He was Mal Crus, the fire boy.

*   *   *

Silex took cooked deer heart with him to Brach's fire, wordlessly squatting next to the other man and handing him a piece. For two men to share the organ was considered a sign of deep friendship.

"You have done wrong, Brach," Silex finally said.

"I know this," Brach sighed regretfully.

"You are married. Men, like wolves, mate for life," Silex continued. "When we had a good supply of bachelors, I encouraged unmarried mating because I wanted to rebuild our tribe. And it worked; we have children. But as was predictable, strong bonds developed and love flourished and people married and they, like you, must not commit adultery."

"Silex. It is widely said you and Ovi do not share a bed at night. Do you not get cold sometimes, by yourself?"

Silex sighed wistfully. "There are times when I miss Fia so much," he admitted after a moment, "and that longing is often for her in that way, as well as so many other ways."

"I am sorry, Silex."

"But despite that, I cannot violate my vow."

"You have never had a child of your own. Is Ovi unwilling to receive you at night? My wife says she is consumed with a peculiar melancholy."

"It is not Ovi, but my own reticence, that keeps me from her bed."

"Then . . . we have young women with no husbands, plus the two older women, Kele and Mili, who I . . . whom my wife found out about. All of these women are anxious to have children."

"It is a problem," Silex admitted.

"Cragg is sixteen. He could help fill the, the need . . . with your permission," Brach continued.

"I have noted he spends considerable time looking at the women with some appreciation," Silex responded. "I have been meaning to tell him how things work between husband and wife, but it is a difficult subject to raise."

"If you do not raise it I believe Kele will do it for you," Brach noted.

Silex looked at him appraisingly, and Brach nodded sheepishly. "She brings a certain enthusiasm to a man's bed."

"You are right, then. I will speak to my son."

"Silex, we still have the problem of the unmarried women who need men. So what is the solution?" Brach pressed.

"It is not to commit adultery, Brach," Silex said sharply.

Brach raised his hands. "I do hear you saying this. I speak now not for myself, but for the good of the tribe, and for you. If you and Ovi are not lying with each other as a wife lies with a husband, how would it be adultery?"

A lbi sent word to the men's side and Palloc answered her summons. He looked wan and exhausted, his ribs showing and dark circles forming under his eyes. "When will the hunt go out again?" she demanded.

Palloc collapsed into a sitting position as if lacking the strength to stand. "I do not know, Mother. The hunt master does not consult with me on such things."

"We need to eat. I am *starving*."

Palloc sighed.

"This would be a good time for you to show leadership. The hunt must go back out."

"Leadership!" Palloc snorted in disgust.

"You never listen to me, which is why you are like a hyena, always arriving late to the glory, always feeding on rotten meat."

"You are an old woman."

"And you should respect that. Does it not occur to you that the curse has finally been flushed into the open?"

Palloc frowned at her in noncomprehension.

"It is as I foretold. By harboring the crippled boy, by giving him a job in the Kindred, we have given great offense, and that is why the hunting is thin. Urs refuses to address the issue and has proven himself unable to find food. And Bellu," she continued, "has turned the cripple into her personal servant. Do you know she lies naked before him while she bathes, in ways that a woman should only lie in front of her husband? Ah, I see *that* bothers you. Bellu, the beautiful woman that you could not have, and she offers herself to Mal Crus. Do not worry, the boy has not enjoyed more than just the view—she thinks to taunt him, though I imagine he is more grateful than tormented. Bellu is stupid and the men who pant after her, you included, are even more stupid. What is required now is discipline. Whether the council votes to rid the Kindred of the curse and then replaces Bellu as council mother, or they make me council mother first—either way, it will happen. But only if you remove Calli as a factor! As council mother, I can manipulate Urs. You will soon be back to being spear master, and all will regard you as the logical choice when they finally see Urs for the fool that he is. Only Calli can stop me, so you must stop her!"

A hard determination was on Palloc's face. "I may kill the hunt master first," he declared.

Contempt flickered on Albi's face. "Yes, you have said that before, and never once taken action. What matters now is Calli. Understand? *Calli.*"

The hunt had been out for four days and had not spotted any game except for some horses, far distant. Unlike the stocky reindeer, horses were skittish and impossibly fast.

Men lusted to spear them, but no Kindred had ever gotten close enough to try.

The grass was sparse; this summer, the air dry and considerably cooler than was normal. Urs was getting worried—his men were growing as gaunt as they did in winter, but this was summer, when they should be putting on weight. His wife had complained to him about being hungry, though as hunt master his share of any kill was always the largest. Where were the reindeer?

When Markus, the least experienced of the stalkers, failed to report back to the hunt when he should have, Urs sent four men—Nix, Nix's brother Vent, Palloc, and Dog—out to find him.

Palloc could feel Dog insolently watching him as they followed the elusive trail Markus had left in the dusty ground. Palloc scowled. He had not spoken words with Dog since the two of them had fought, and being this close to him now made him uncomfortable. Palloc endured it as long as he could, finally deciding he had had enough. He stopped walking. "I have a question for the hunt master," he declared.

The other men halted, regarding him curiously. Dog's expression was more of a smirk, and Palloc turned away from it, feeling his face grow hot. "I will return to the hunt," Palloc announced stiffly. He walked back the way from which they had come.

"What is he doing?" Nix asked as Palloc's back retreated.

"He has a question for the hunt master," his brother Vent replied.

Dog shrugged. "He is not a good tracker. We can do just as well without him."

The men nodded and followed Dog, whose head was down, trying to see a sign of where Markus might have gone.

There were coniferous trees here, and the terrain was hilly. The pine needles on the ground were much like the color of rouge, the powder that could be used to turn things red. The men lost the trail, but pressed on anyway.

"If he came here, he found no game," Dog remarked. "There is no grass."

Nix nodded, then stopped. "What is that?" he asked.

The other two men halted, cocking their heads. They heard it again, a shrill, piercing noise, like a bird might make but unlike any bird they had ever heard. A whistle, answered by another eerie whistle from behind them.

"It is like the call of the elk during mating season," Vent observed. And it was, indeed, a little like an elk. A novice like Markus might have thought he was on the trail of a herd of the big mammals, but there was a sharper quality to this sibilant trilling.

Another whistle from their man's side, and an answering one on the woman's side—piercing and different, two notes from one, three from the other, and then a long one from behind them.

Whatever was making the sound was getting closer.

The three Kindred men frowned at each other. It was as if they were surrounded by some unseen creatures. Dog peered around, but could see no movement.

The men reflexively tightened their grips on their spears. They were in a small clearing but the trees were thick all around them.

The whistles came even closer, and then with a sudden, single drawn out note, they went completely silent. The men waited.

"They must have left," Vent noted. Nix nodded.

"But how? Are they birds and have flown off?"

Nobody knew. Dog scratched his head. "I wonder what they were," he murmured.

And then he turned at a sudden motion, seeing men move silently out of the trees. Strange men, with faces smeared with charcoal and rouge so that their eyes appeared starkly white. Hideous, wild-looking men. Men carrying clubs.

Cohort.

FORTY-TWO

Palloc did not get very far when he thought better of his plan to return to the hunt. Urs would be angry with him for disobeying instructions, and probably intended for Palloc, as the senior man, to lead the search for Markus.

It had just been too much to bear. Dog evinced obvious but unstated contempt—clearly, he felt that he had somehow bested Palloc. Dog might be much taller, but Palloc was broad shouldered and in an actual fight might have easily defeated his adversary. In fact, he could imagine it, could practically feel his fist upon Dog's jaw, knocking the younger man senseless.

But they were not children and a fight was forbidden. Punishment might include banishment from the hunt, essentially turning Palloc into a woman. And Palloc had no doubt it would be *his* punishment, and not Dog's, even though it was all Dog's fault.

Bitterly, Palloc turned and went back the way from which he had come. Dog, Vent, and Nix were easy to track. He would advise the three hunters that he had spoken to the hunt master and returned. What was said was no one's business but his.

No, that made no sense: he could not have made it back to the hunt in so little time.

Scanning ahead, Palloc could see that the three men had entered a pine forest. On his woman's side, a tall hill bristled with deciduous trees. If he climbed a tree at the top of the hill, he could see into the pine forest and much of the surrounding countryside. If Markus was lost, wandering in circles, or injured, Palloc would spot him from up there. Palloc would be the hero. The hunt and the Kindred would admire his initiative and celebrate his success.

Palloc had not climbed a tree since he was a child, and he was startled at how difficult it was. His arms were soon trembling from the effort, and he dropped his spear when he had to make a panicked grab to keep from pitching head-first onto the ground. He was right, though: from the crest, he could see far in every direction. Why did the stalkers never think to climb trees? Palloc decided that he would keep this idea to himself, so that when he was hunt master someday, his first command would be to climb the trees at the top of hills to spot for game, and everyone would agree he was a wise leader who should have been made hunt master long ago instead of Urs.

He could see into the pine forest, where Nix, Vent, and Dog had stopped and were standing around talking. Clearly, once Palloc left them, they became confused as to what they should do next.

A movement caught his eye, something darting from one tree to another. He frowned. It was dark and big and was now invisible. A bear? But no bear would behave like that, hiding behind a tree.

All the way on the other side of the pine forest, he saw two men, their movements not furtive, but out in the open. Palloc swallowed. They were not Kindred. The two strangers were looking at something on the ground, and after a time Palloc realized what it was: a human, lying motionless, its head a bloody mess. Palloc recognized the garments.

Markus.

Palloc turned to look at the other Kindred. "Nix!" he shouted. But he was too far away and the wind pushed his voice aside. He could see men flitting between the trees, eight of them, closing in on the Kindred hunters.

Cohort. They had to be Cohort.

And then they were right there. Palloc gasped as one of them stepped up to Dog and swung a club. Dog instinctively ducked, rolling away. Vent and Nix just stood watching him, transfixed, and did not see the men rushing up behind them. The Cohort hit both brothers with clubs simultaneously, viciously cracking them on their skulls. Vent went down, while Nix staggered and turned to face his attacker. Dog jabbed with his spear and managed to pierce the chest of his opponent, but then two of the Cohort closed on him and savagely beat him. Dog fell to his knees and they hit him in the head again and again. Nix was down now too, and the Cohort pounded at their skulls, which split and bled in the pine needles.

When they were done, the Cohort circled the dead Kindred. Their faces were blackened, which made it possible for Palloc to see their grins. The one Dog had stabbed still had the spear high in his chest, the end of it down on the ground. One of the Cohort reached out and snagged the spear and yanked it from the wounded man's chest, and he shouted angrily and the rest of them laughed.

Palloc clung to the tree, feeling sick. It had all happened so fast. Four Kindred hunters were dead. Dog, who he had held in his arms as a baby, slaughtered. And why? For what reason?

They were talking to each other, and then, to his horror, one of them said something and to a man they all turned and looked in Palloc's direction, finding him in the tree and staring at him.

They knew he was there.

Panting, Palloc scrambled down the tree, scraping his skin raw on the bark and not caring. The minute his feet hit the ground he snagged his spear and was stumbling and falling as he fled down the hill, running as fast as he could. Were they behind him, pursuing him? He did not dare look back. He ran, bushes ripping at his skin, heedless, and when he tripped and sprawled a sob broke from his lips. *No!* He was back up instantly. He was making so much noise he could not tell if his pursuers were close.

Palloc did not stop running until he burst into camp, the hunters leaping to their feet in alarm when they saw him.

He was trembling, coated with sweat, dizzy with lack of oxygen. Valid grabbed him, holding him up, while Palloc bent over and sucked in air. "What is it? What happened?" Valid demanded.

"Cohort," Palloc panted.

Instantly the hunt was on alert, snatching up their spears and instinctively closing ranks into a tight circle. Urs seized Palloc's shoulders. "Palloc. Speak now. What are you saying?"

"Cohort. More than ten of them. They . . . they had Markus. They got Dog and Nix and Vent."

"Got them?" Urs demanded. "What do you mean, 'got them'?"

Palloc looked at the hunt master and the answer was in the misery written in his eyes.

"How did you get away?" Urs asked. "Why were you not with them? Why did you run?"

Every member of the hunt was staring. Palloc swallowed.

"If you had stayed with them, perhaps you could have fought off the attackers!" Urs accused.

"No!" Palloc shook his head wildly. "There were too many."

"So you fled."

"It was not like that! I had climbed a tree."

"A tree?" Urs repeated incredulously. "Our hunters were under attack and you climbed a tree?"

"That is not what happened!"

"We should go. Perhaps they are still alive," Valid urged.

"Right," Urs decided. He turned away from Palloc in a move that spoke of utter contempt. "Be ready. Grat, you go to the back and watch for attackers from that direction."

The hunt now acted as if Palloc were not standing there in their midst. Though he had barely escaped with his life, they had no feeling of relief, and had completely miscon-strued events.

Yet only Palloc knew where to go, so Urs motioned for him to be up front with him. They started at a run, difficult for Palloc after his crazed dash all the way from the hill, but he kept up.

"They came from all sides," Palloc panted.

"Just focus on where to go," Urs snapped back.

Palloc saw the hill to his left. "This way," he said, point-ing, his eyes so full of bitterness they burned.

A trail of blood led off into the woods, but it was getting dark and Urs eventually called off their pursuit. They needed to get back to camp, much more easily defended than the strange territory they were on.

As they turned back, several of the Kindred raised their heads and stared off into the distance. They had heard some-thing, something far, far away. Something strange.

Some sort of whistling.

Calli was combing the bushes for berries, hating harvest-ing the tiny, immature fruits before they were sweet and swollen with a full summer's ripening, but having no choice—sour and small as they were, they were food. The Kindred needed food.

When she heard the sound she was not sure, at first, what it was, but it came from the direction of camp and instantly alarmed her. Heart pounding, she abandoned her collection of berries and ran toward the noise.

Screaming.

She rushed into camp and saw that the hunt had returned. The screaming was coming from the women who, as usual, had gone to greet the men as they came back: women wailing in pain, falling to their knees, clutching their husbands. Several women were bent over Renne, who thrashed in the dirt.

"What is it?" Calli asked, joining the group. "What happened?" She saw her mother, and Coco shook her head, not knowing.

"Cohort," someone said.

"Nix!" Renne screamed.

Calli understood, then, and the horror made her legs buckle. Bellu and her mother, Ador, were sagging against each other, sobbing. Urs stood nearby, grim.

Calli scanned the men. She saw Palloc, who appeared oddly wooden faced, watching the Kindred grieve with a curious lack of emotion on his face. Calli saw Mal approaching, looking bewildered and frightened, then swung back to find Dog.

Dog.

"Valid," Calli gasped, her voice so weak with dread she could barely speak. "Where is Dog?"

Valid looked her in the eye, and she knew.

It fell to Mal to tell Lyra. She was coming up the path to the camp a few hours after the hunt had returned. Still in shock, Mal noticed she was gone, and he waited for her on the downstream path, where he had often seen her go.

"Lyra," he called.

Things had not been left well between them when they last spoke, but her uneasiness fell from her face when she saw his expression, changing into something more like fear. "Mal, what is it?"

He tried to tell her, but his breathing became labored, and his lips trembled. "Dog," he finally whispered.

Her eyes went wide. "What? Tell me!" she pleaded, clutching at him in panic.

"They were attacked by Cohort."

And that was all that he needed to say.

They clung to each other, crying, her head on his shoulder. He wanted to be a man but the thought of losing Dog made him feel like running to his mother. *Dog dead.* It was impossible to understand it, to cope with it.

They did not see that they were being watched: Grat had come down the trail and spotted them, his mouth drawing a bitter line as he observed their embrace. From where he stood, despite the circumstances, it was not difficult to mistake their movements for passion. His face held a black rage to suppose that Mal, the crippled fire boy, had won the affections of Lyra.

He turned and walked away before either of them noticed him standing there.

One word repeated itself in Palloc's head: leadership. Very well, he would show his mother leadership. He went to Grat and suggested the two of them go hunting. Yes, the Kindred were convulsed in grief, and the hunt master had issued a strict edict against straying from camp lest the

Cohort take more hunters, but they would draw great admiration if they showed courage, risking themselves for the good of all. Grat had eaten so many bugs his throat ached; he was not difficult to persuade.

Palloc and Grat did find prey, a den of weasels. The creatures were small and the meat was tough, but at least the Kindred would eat something. Palloc grinned fiercely. They would be heroes.

"Food!" Palloc shouted as they returned. People streamed into the communal area, the two hunters holding their kills aloft, beaming with pride. "Food!"

Coco and Calli accepted the small corpses listlessly and without thanks. Palloc frowned at his wife. Did she not understand what this meant to the tribe? She and her mother immediately set about skinning the animals, and Palloc was gratified to see that some children gathered to watch in greedy anticipation.

There was a commotion as Urs and Valid pushed their way forward. Palloc turned to face them. "We bring weasel meat, Hunt Master," Palloc greeted respectfully.

Urs never slowed down. He walked right up to Palloc and struck him hard on the side of the head. Palloc spun, gasping with shock and pain, and saw Grat fall to the ground as Valid slapped him in the face.

"You were forbidden to leave!" Urs bellowed.

Palloc stood himself tall, biting back the hatred roiling inside him, resisting the urge to grab a club and beat the hunt master bloody. "We needed food," he protested.

"You knew you were not to leave the settlement!" Valid shouted at him.

Grat lay where he had fallen, too stunned to be enraged. This should not be happening—the rule against fighting among the hunt was inviolate. It was what kept them unified. But what could one do if the hunt leaders were the ones breaking the taboo?

Palloc folded his arms so that no one would see his trembling hands. "We needed to hunt," he insisted weakly. He searched for his mother, but Albi was nowhere to be seen.

"Yes, and because of you, the hunt has been delayed two days," Urs snapped back.

"We thought you had both been taken by the Cohort," Valid growled. "We did not dare leave until we determined what had happened. Did it not occur to you to tell anyone you were going on an unauthorized hunt?"

"We have wasted two days," Urs repeated. He looked ready to hit Palloc again and Palloc braced for it. Then the anger went out of Urs's eyes, and he relaxed his fists. "Palloc," he said sadly, "you just do not think before you act. It is why I could not have you as my spear master."

Urs turned away from him then, the rest of the hunters following suit, leaving Palloc to stand there with Grat his only ally. Grat stood, dusting himself off, and the two men exchanged looks. Palloc was ashen and looked ready to cry, but Grat's expression was black with hate. "Urs will regret this day," Grat vowed. "He will regret it."

FORTY-THREE

The mother-wolf, granddaughter to the great wolf who had first accepted tribute from the man, was still the dominant bitch. Her pack's range had grown, leading to challenges from other packs, but the wolves in her pack were larger than most others, and the dominant female was largest of them all.

She still took food directly from the hand of man. None of the wolves from her two litters had the courage to do this, but they did not skittishly flee when they spotted humans out on the plains, either. They all knew by scent the man who provided the mother-wolf food, and the people who traveled with him were familiar, too. Other packs of humans were aggressive to the wolves, as were the larger, darker people who lived in the forest. The mother-wolf had learned how to discern the difference between friendly humans and those who meant harm, how to smell their emotions and predict their behaviors based on their movements and gestures.

Her pack was healthy. Much of their prey this year were sick and frail from the lack of forage—something the mother-wolf did not fully comprehend, of course, but she could smell the weakness coming off the ungulates, spot the ones they would take for their meals.

Still, when the scent of the man was close, she liked to break away and find him and be fed—not just for the easy meal, but because there was something about the man that drew her. She saw him now, and he was standing with his frequent companion, the human female. The mother-wolf approached them boldly, seeing their eyebrows rise and their mouths open—something the mother-wolf knew meant they had brought meat.

She would eat.

A pall lay over the Kindred that summer, even as hunting greatly improved and the gaunt hollows under their eyes receded. Death was not unfamiliar to the tribe, especially when it came to children, but losing Nix and Vent, who were fathers, and the younger Dog and Markus, hit especially hard. This was not due to a disease or accident, this was a tragedy deliberately inflicted by other humans.

Calli craved her son, needed Mal to be with her, but Mal could not seem to bear a single day by the family fire, and was often by himself. When he saw his mother, he thought of Dog. And when he saw Lyra, he thought of Dog. There seemed to be no safe place to rest his eyes, because everywhere he looked he expected to see Dog coming toward him.

"Please Mal," Calli blurted to him once.

He turned his eyes to her, puzzled. "Please what, Mother?"

Calli could only shake her head helplessly. She did not know what. She wanted them all to stop hurting. She wanted her sons to both be alive and healthy.

As the shadows advanced out from the trees earlier each evening, Bellu did not call the women to council, and Calli realized her friend did not want to migrate. Bellu had always despised winter quarters—a common feeling among the Kindred, but more often articulated by Bellu, who had lost a baby to disease and two brothers and a nephew to the Cohort and was comforting herself by taking daily baths.

Calli approached her directly. "Bellu, the night is gaining strength, and air brings chill. It feels past time to migrate to winter quarters."

Bellu was in the bath. She sighed, putting a hand to her face. "This has just been such a hard summer for me. I am not feeling ready. No one seems to understand that I just lost two brothers and a nephew."

Calli pursed her lips. "Yes, and I lost a son, Bellu," she reminded her friend quietly.

"I have had two children die!"

"I know."

"I just do not want to leave yet."

"But you know it will be harder still if we stay too long."

"I do not know that," Bellu responded petulantly. "Why do we always leave? Because we have always left."

Exasperated, Calli sought out Urs.

"It is time for us to leave for winter quarters," Calli declared.

"Is that what the women's council wants?" he replied, looking relieved.

"Yes," Calli affirmed. "Well . . . not Bellu. But we all know it is time; the days are growing short."

Urs nodded. "But we cannot depart if the women are not ready."

"The women *are* ready," Calli shot back. "You just need to talk to your wife."

"Well . . ." Urs shrugged, grinning condescendingly. "You know, sometimes women are not easy to talk to."

"No, I do not know," Calli snapped. "She is your wife. Why are you afraid?"

Urs's eyes grew hard. "I am not afraid," he corrected icily.

"Then talk to Bellu."

"Do not tell me what to do, and do not presume to instruct a hunt master in what to say to his wife."

Calli stared at him. "What happened to the man I used to meet upstream, in a bed of grasses?" she finally asked softly. "He was not afraid of anything."

To his credit, Urs's fierce glare eventually dropped, and he seemed to honestly contemplate the question. "Everything seemed so easy then," he finally responded, looking defeated. "I felt that I could conquer all. But now . . . now it is my job to lead the hunt, and if we find no food, the Kindred starves. Yet we must stay together for protection. I cannot send out the stalkers, not after what happened. You are right. I *am* afraid, now."

"Would you like to do it?" Silex murmured to Denix as they watched the gigantic mother-wolf come toward them.

"No. You are the one, Silex," Denix replied in a hushed voice. The mother-wolf was approaching them so casually Denix wanted to laugh. The wolf and Silex were *friends*.

He knelt and Denix sucked in her breath. He offered the meat and the wolf took it out of his hand, as if there was nothing unusual about a man feeding an animal, holding the gift in her jaws as she turned and trotted away.

"I will never become accustomed to that," Denix professed in a shaky voice.

"Yes!" Silex agreed. "I know what you mean." He stood back up.

"You honor me, Silex, when you bring me along to pay tribute. Why am I the only one you invite, now? You no longer bring Brach."

They started running together at an easy pace.

Silex thought about it. "Brach does not actually like it. And you are our best hunter. Everyone looks up to you, Denix. And . . . I just, I just appreciate having you with me," he finally admitted. He glanced over at her, trotting at his side, and saw she was staring at him. "What is it?"

Denix put her hand on his arm to stop him. "Silex. There is something I need to tell you."

They stood, breathing easily. The grass around them was all brown and dead looking. It made it easy to spot prey at a distance, but it also made the Wolfen easy to stalk. Twice Silex had seen a lion in the distance. He was anxious to get back to the hunters, as much for his own sake as theirs. The more hunters, the less likely they would be attacked.

"Silex," Denix said, biting her lip, obviously struggling with something. He glanced at her mouth—there was something about the way that it was shaped, a perfect circle, which always drew his eyes.

Then he noticed that her face was flushed as if they had run much farther than they had, and was jolted with a sudden concern. "We should keep going."

"No, would you please just listen to me?" she pleaded.

Silex raised his eyebrows. He thought he *was* listening.

"Do you mean that? You appreciate me being with you?" she asked.

He was not sure why, but looking into her plaintive brown eyes, he suddenly remembered her bathing, the water trickling down her beautiful naked body. It was an inconvenient moment for such an image to burst into his mind, because she obviously had something portentous to tell him about the hunt—but, if he allowed himself the truth, the fact was that he thought about what he had seen that day with a repetition bordering on obsession. Often it was the last vision he took with him into sleep at night.

"Why are you looking at me like that?" Denix asked him in a whisper.

Silex shook himself out of it. "I am sorry."

"Do not be *sorry*, Silex. Tell me," she urged.

Silex had the apprehensive sense that she knew exactly what he had been remembering. "I am not sure what you want me to tell you, Denix."

"What you are feeling, Silex. How you feel about *me*."

Something was loosed in Silex then. It was as if a herd of animals were startled within him and now was stampeding through his blood. Denix's chest, rising and falling, made him remember Fia's breasts, and there was no mistaking the hot hunger growing in her eyes when she registered where he was looking. "We cannot do this, Denix," he whispered in despair. He turned, shaking off her hand when she tried to stop him.

"Silex!"

When Silex ran as fast as he could, there was only one person in the Wolfen who could catch him: Denix.

But she did not try.

Lyra knew she was supposed to view the blush coming to the tree leaves as a sad thing. The trees were joining a battle to hold back the dark and the cold, shedding blood in the effort, some leaves already curled in death. But in truth she loved the time of year before migrations, and did not mind that Bellu was keeping them at summer quarters so late into the year.

Her grief was supposed to be a secret, just as her love for Dog was kept hidden away from the prying eyes of the council and Sidee, her mother. So she spent most days off alone, and had created work for herself, a labor requiring such industry she could forget about Dog's death until she crawled exhausted into bed—and this, too, was a secret.

She tracked Mal, saw him working up the nerve to speak to her, and knew why it was so difficult. Several times he seemed to approach, and then he would break away, his eyes haunted.

Finally, the separation was too much for the both of them. "Where do you go, most days?" Mal asked Lyra softly.

Lyra gave him an oddly pensive look. "I have a special place."

Mal nodded, as if the answer was as complete as anyone could ask for. "It is cold," he observed, pulling his thick furs around his shoulders and glancing up at the grey skies.

"I miss him so much," Lyra replied. Her face twisted and she began weeping. Mal held her and let his own tears flow. With Mal, she felt safe revealing her full feelings. He understood her in a way no one else did. He was, she realized, her dearest friend.

I saw you talking to Felka yesterday," Lyra told Mal several days later. There was something teasing in the way she said it, an implication in her voice.

Mal blushed, but his heart fell. How could she kid him about another girl? He must mean nothing to her. "I have no interest in Mors's daughter," he said tersely.

"Oh, I see," she responded lightly. It was the first time Mal had seen her smile so unreservedly since Dog died.

"I am promised to someone else," he informed her. He wanted this revelation to hurt, but Lyra exhibited nothing but surprise.

"You are?"

"It is all arranged," he affirmed.

"With who?"

Not a bit of jealousy or disappointment, Mal noted sourly. "With a girl named Ema, from the Blanc Tribe. Their way is for the father to speak for a woman, so he approached my mother. I do not believe that the women's council has been informed, but I will live with the Blanc People so it does not matter."

"But . . . you mean you would leave the Kindred?"

"Yes. Well, perhaps just in winter. We will have to see. No one in the Blanc Tribe thinks I am cursed."

"And how do you feel about this Ema?"

Mal thought about kissing her at the ice cave. "She is in love with me. She kissed me. I liked it."

Lyra laughed.

Mal blushed. "I am happy to have her as my wife. I think of nothing but the day I will see her again." This last part was not true, but Mal felt some strange need to exaggerate his affections.

"Mal, I had no idea of this!" Lyra exclaimed. "I am so . . . I do not know what you say. Are you truly in love?"

Mal reflected on the irony of this question coming from this girl. "Yes, Lyra, that part is true," Mal said gravely, looking directly into Lyra's eyes. "I am in love. I am surprised you do not know this."

A slow surprise built on Lyra's face. She glanced away from the intensity of Mal's gaze. "Oh," she replied softly.

Mal wondered if she were thinking of his leg. They sat in silence for a long, awkward moment, Mal nearly choking on his self-loathing. He was behaving so foolishly, humiliating himself in front of Lyra.

After a moment, Lyra turned back to him. "Would you like to see my secret place?" she asked.

FORTY-FOUR

Lyra took Mal far downstream, into an area where large boulders lay partially buried in soil and grasses. She asked Mal to make a torch, which he was able to do expertly, using the smoldering peat from the horn he carried. The little fire was comforting—the day had grown even colder, as cold as Mal could ever remember being at summer quarters. Then she led him to a small hole at the base of one of the rocks. "It is hard to slide in, but it is a much bigger cave than it looks," she advised him.

Mal could see that she had scooped a lot of the earth away from the hole, but it would still be a tight fit for him.

Lyra went first, and Mal handed her the torch before backing into the cramped space. At one point the rock ceiling was pressing down on him, holding him to the ground, and he felt a rising fear that he might get stuck. But then he wriggled free.

They were inside a cave so large that their torch could not penetrate all the way to the back. One wall was light-colored stone, and Lyra motioned toward it with a shy expression on her face. "See?"

Mal frowned, trying to make sense of what looked like a series of dark marks on the rock. Some of the marks were red, rubbed into the stone with rouge.

"See? Look, it is a bear. And here, these are reindeer," Lyra explained, stroking the marks with her finger.

Then, just like that, Mal saw that she was right. It was

as if a herd of reindeer were there on the rock, except they were flat, and it was just their outlines. Mal gasped, his mind reeling. "How is this possible? There are animals in the stone!"

"I pressed them into the rock with charcoal and rouge."

"You did this? But how could you make animals?" Mal was dumbfounded.

"I dragged charcoal across the surface and bent the resulting marks into the shapes of animals. Do you like them?"

"I could never have imagined anything like this." Mal was not entirely sure how he felt about it—the marks made him dizzy.

"This is what I do. It makes me happy."

"It is the most amazing thing I have ever seen," he told her sincerely.

Lyra gave a light laugh of delight. "You are the only one who knows, Mal."

He regarded her in the flickering light. He should tell her, right now, that he loved her, but he did not. The words made it all the way to his lips, but there they died, the way the heat from his torch flickered and then faded before it warmed their skin.

They were on the path back to camp when Grat emerged from the trees. "Where have you been?" he demanded bruskly.

Mal blinked at the harsh tone. "Why, has something happened?"

Grat ignored him. "You should not wander this far without a hunter," he lectured Lyra. "These are dangerous times."

"I was with her," Mal pointed out.

"What were you doing, anyway?" Grat asked, still not looking at Mal.

"We were walking," Lyra replied slowly, her voice sounding angry. "Why?"

"Your father asked me to make sure you do not come to harm."

"My father? No he did not," Lyra said.

Grat shook his head. "It was on the hunt," he insisted. "You would not know of such things." He gave a condescending glance at Mal. "Neither would you, obviously."

"I do not believe it," Mal challenged.

Grat's eyes narrowed.

"Perhaps you misunderstood my father," Lyra interrupted, putting a cautionary hand on Mal's shoulder.

"Members of the hunt are prohibited from fighting," Grat stated pointedly. He stared at Mal. "But not you."

"What is that?" Lyra interrupted suddenly. She gestured into the trees, which were vanishing into a grey-white cloud. A windlike tumult was quickly upon them.

Snow.

The Kindred left summer quarters in a panic. Never before had this happened—no one, even those most concerned about how long Bellu was tarrying—thought it would *snow*.

The blizzard continued unabated for days. Soon every step was a struggle, the wind whipping their faces. The hunters took turns walking up front, breaking down the calf-high snow so that the rest of the Kindred could step in their tracks. It was exhausting.

Hardy was the first to die. They were laboring on a day with particularly vicious winds. Then a thin, reedy scream whipped past, a wail that seemed to have no direction. Everyone halted, backs to the storm, glancing around for the source of the raw keening.

Calli and Coco found Droi on her knees in the snow, holding her husband's head. His ruined face was frozen in the odd sneer left by the lion, his rheumy eyes clouded and dull. The women sought to comfort Droi, but she thrashed away from them.

Urs came back to see what the commotion was about. "Oh no," he said sadly. He exchanged a look with Calli, then turned to Droi. "We must keep moving, or we will all perish," he told her gently, pulling her up.

"Could we not make camp and wait out the storm?" Calli suggested.

Urs shook his head. "This is not a storm, this is *winter*. If we do not get south, we will die on the trail."

They did not bury Hardy—there was no time for such niceties. Coco and Calli gazed down at him and then at each other. The wind whipped away any feelings either of them might have shared.

Calli was despondent. Now she had lost two fathers—yet what she mourned most was the missed opportunity. Why had she spoken so seldom to either one of them when they were alive? Her reason—that they had not ever spoken much to *her*—seemed a thin excuse, now.

Urs was right: winter had arrived. The next day was thankfully clear but bitterly cold. They squinted in the stark sunshine bouncing off the snow, which was unbroken as far as they could see. Not a prey animal in sight.

Calli felt the hunger seep into her, made worse with the cold. She could not stop shivering. They were taking frequent breaks now, and Mal was busy making fires whenever they halted. No one said it, but they were grateful for his help. Bellu, nominally in charge of the fires, had completely abdicated, and sat staring into the flames whenever Mal lit some wood.

"We need meat," Urs declared urgently. No one answered

him—they all knew this to be true. If they came across tracks, Urs had vowed to pursue them and find the animals that had made them—but so far the snow was undisturbed.

"We should never have left this late," Albi remarked. No one answered her, either.

The next morning, Droi was slow to wake up, and fell so far behind the main group she was lost from sight. Finally Albi waited for her to catch up.

"You need to move faster, my sister," Albi observed.

"I am trying," Droi protested weakly.

"What is it you are carrying?" Albi asked, pointing at the ball of elk hide hanging from a strap around Droi's shoulders.

"It was Hardy's," Droi explained. She stopped, putting her hands on her knees, while the pouch swung from her shoulders.

Albi watched the motion of the pouch, fascinated. "What is in it?"

Droi shrugged.

Albi turned and looked at the Kindred, now so far ahead she could no longer identify the people in the rear. "I remember that Hardy always liked to carry a bit of cooked, dried meat to chew on," she mentioned casually. "Is that what you have, there?"

"It is all that I have left of my husband's. There are a few items, some bear teeth, things like that."

"Plus, perhaps, some food," Albi insisted.

Droi stood. "We should keep moving." She determinedly pushed past Albi.

"Droi," Albi murmured.

Droi turned and the walking stick caught her full on the side of the head. With a cry, Droi fell into the knee-high snow. Splayed facedown, she struggled to find purchase to push herself back up. Albi stepped forward and put her knees on Droi's shoulders and her palms on the back of Droi's head. Albi bore down, keeping her sister's face in the snow, while Droi weakly bucked and turned, trying to get her off.

Albi waited. After several minutes, Droi lay still, but Albi continued to hold her down. Finally she released her sister's head. Albi found the pouch and rooted around in it, grinning in triumph when she located the hard piece of meat, only slightly moldy. She shoveled it into her mouth, using snow to add moisture so she could swallow it more easily.

The Kindred were still a day out from the Blanc camp, and they were starving. Eyes dull and gait reduced to a stumble, almost no one spoke.

They grieved their dead. Two days after the Kindred noticed that Droi was gone, Coco came to Calli to say that Sopho, the oldest woman in the Kindred, had not awakened. Then Ador, Bellu's mother, fell down, could not get up, and was carried by her sons for a day and a half, until she breathed her last. Worse were the children—three who had not yet been named were gone, as well as a boy of six summers whose formal name had ironically referred to long life.

The snow, melting, heavy, and wet, was untracked all the way to the horizon. Sun bounced off it and stabbed their eyes until they were all weeping from the glare. No game, no insects, no worms. Their hopes lay with the Blanc Tribe. The pale-eyed people would feed the Kindred, who would trade all they had—even Urs's treasured lion skin—for food.

Despite the lack of wind, they could not smell the fires of the Blanc Tribe on the still air, and the morning the Kindred stumbled into camp they found out why: they were gone.

The silence was eerie, even menacing. Where were the happy people who always ran to greet them, calling in friendship, offering fish and fowl? All that remained was black mud throughout the settlement, mud wet with snow-melt and riddled with a hundred footprints.

It was all so wrong that the Kindred instinctively hud-dled together around Urs, though it was a stalker—Grat—who figured out what they were seeing. "Blood," he asserted. "See? It is all blood."

Urs did see. Splattered everywhere was old blood, in pools and smears. "Something happened to them."

Calli put a hand to her mouth. "What is it? What are you saying? Why did they leave?"

"I do not think they left," Urs replied grimly.

Mal pointed to the churned up earth. "See how the smaller footprints are here, behind the larger ones? This is where the men stood to protect their children. This is where they fought and bled. And there is the direction the children ran." Mal pointed toward the lake, a hundred paces away, looking starkly blue and beautiful under the cloudless sky. He limped over to the footprints. "Here the feet are placed far apart. These other men were chasing the children." He squinted at the lake, then turned back to look at Urs, who was nodding. "Cohort," Mal finished. "The Cohort came."

Calli stared at her son. "The Cohort were *here*?"

"Why are you even talking?" Grat demanded contemp-tuously.

"He is right," Urs replied.

"But there are no scavenger tracks," Palloc pointed out. "If what you are saying is true, we would see their prints. Oth-erwise the bodies would still be here."

"Not if the Cohort took them," Urs replied. "As they took Dog, the day you were hiding in a tree."

Palloc flushed.

"What do we do?" Valid asked.

"We cannot go on today. We will stay here for a bit. Perhaps the weather will be warmer tomorrow," Urs answered heavily. His shoulders slumped in defeat.

Calli fell to her knees and wept. They had been such good folk, open-hearted and welcoming to all who traveled through—why would anyone do this?

"Stay here? Stay *here*?" Bellu cried in a panicked voice. "What if they come back? Urs, what if they come back for *us*?"

"I do not know but we can go no farther today," Urs mumbled exhaustedly.

So hungry he was dizzy from it, Mal built a communal fire, then set some outlying fires for the families. He was remembering Ema, her smile, and her kisses. She was to be his wife. It had been arranged.

He tried to mourn for the girl with the missing arm, but in truth he could scarcely remember much about her.

Though the sun was as high in the sky as it would get that day, people were already curling up as if for the night, staring at nothing. The fires seemed to bring up the scent of blood—it was sickening, and yet it called to their empty stomachs, drawing out the ache and making it all anyone could think about.

Mal saw Palloc tossing aside one of the Blanc Tribe's nets, and he went to get it, remembering the two girls carrying it as they went to the ice cave, the day of the kiss. No one in the Kindred had ever had use for such a thing, and Mal looked at it curiously, seeing how each strand was tied to several other strands.

The net reminded him of something, a memory that came to him after a moment.

The ice cave.

FORTY-FIVE

Mal looked around. The way people were settling in, it was apparent no one wanted to move, and yet if they did not, if they stayed here, they would all starve.

Unless there was food in the ice cave.

He told no one where he was going, taking only the net and a smoldering horn for fire. At the mouth of the cave, he found the dead grasses piled neatly, and used them to fashion his torch.

It was starkly cold in the cave, the walls glistening white with ice. He carried the pick with him and grunted when he got to the back of the cave: here the mounds of ice and snow were piled knee-high. He set to work, his exertion sending clouds of smoke from his mouth.

When he dug out the first fish he tore into it with his teeth, crunching the ice, feeling the flesh become slimy as he chewed. He allowed himself just the one, knowing that the cramps would be worse if he ate more, and then pulled out one fish after another, stacking them on the net.

He staggered under the weight of the load, easily enough to feed the entire Kindred.

No one looked at him with more than listless interest when he returned to camp. He found his mother sitting and staring blankly at the communal fire, Coco's head in her lap. Coco's breathing was raspy and labored, and as Mal limped up to them, Coco was wracked with a hoarse, painful-sounding cough.

"Mother," Mal greeted. He dumped the net down in front of her and Calli looked at it without comprehension. "Food," he said. He picked up a stick and thrust it through a frozen fish's mouth, holding it out over the fire, where the ice melted off and hit the coals with a sizzle. "Food," he repeated. "We can eat."

Calli's eyes cleared. "Mother," she whispered to Coco. Coco focused dully on Mal. "Food," Calli said wonderingly. She stood, embraced her son, and then turned to the Kindred. "Mal has brought food! Food! Food!"

The reaction was muted at first: people roused themselves and stared in confusion. Not until the odor of the burning fish meat hit their noses did they react, and then they surged forward, grasping for their own meal.

Urs came to the fire, his eyes wide in disbelief. "Mal has brought food," Calli informed him, beaming. He was hunt master, so she held the first stick out to him, and he accepted it in wonder. "Mal did it," Calli repeated. "Mal."

The assumption was that Mal had taken the net and gone to the frozen lake and somehow caught frozen fish, and he did nothing to dispel the rumor, though when he went out for another load of fish he was trailed by a dozen children and then the secret was out. Still, it was Mal's actions that saved the Kindred, and everyone knew it.

"I do not care what happens to my eyes," Valid remarked happily at his family fire. "I will eat all the fish the fire boy brings."

"Odd, though," his daughter Lyra observed. "He is old enough to be a man, but we call him a boy. He saves the Kindred, and yet he cannot join the hunt."

"He is a boy because his leg prevents him from being a man," Valid reasoned. His sons, seventeen-year-old Ligo and ten-year-old Magnus, nodded at the logic.

"I think I will go thank the *boy* for doing more to feed the Kindred than was managed by any *man*," Lyra retorted.

Valid stared after her as she stomped off. "You let her get away with too much," Sidee, his wife, remonstrated.

Valid shrugged. "She has always been a little stubborn."

"Because you allow it," Sidee insisted. "Tolerance is not a good thing with her."

Valid shrugged again.

Lyra tracked down Mal fussing with the net. It had become tangled, and he found it impossible to straighten out. "Here," Lyra offered as she walked up. "Let me."

Mal willingly handed it over. Lyra frowned at it, then started to work with the weave. "It forms a pattern," she murmured.

"A pattern?" Mal queried politely.

Lyra was staring at the net without seeing it, thinking of another day, but at his response she raised her head. "Thank you, Mal. You have saved the Kindred," Lyra told him as her fingers worked with the tangle.

"Well," Mal grunted, embarrassed.

"And you have lost so much," Lyra continued, her face softening in sympathy. "Your brother, your grandfather, and now your wife."

Mal swallowed and nodded.

"I am sorry. You do not deserve such things," Lyra said. She reached out and touched him on the leg, and he stared as if stunned: his bad leg, she was touching his bad leg, seemingly unconcerned.

* * *

Silex had correctly gauged the severity of the winter and had moved the Wolfen south along the river until it flowed into the Cohort Valley, where he turned east. Coincidentally, much of the trek was over the same ground as the Kindred traveled during their migrations, but Silex was not aiming for a specific destination—he was tracking the wolves, listening to their songs at night, hoping they were celebrating a kill.

He sought Denix's eyes with as much urgency as he hunted for food. He wanted to experience that surge of feeling again, the exciting thrill of eye contact. He stared at her over the fire at night, trying to connect. But she would not meet his gaze, nor engage him when he maneuvered close to her for a conversation. Her eyes were down and her responses to his gambits perfunctory, and she made sure they were never a moment alone.

When the snows lashed at the Wolfen they made their way toward a ridge of rocks for shelter and stumbled upon a cave bear, and this kill kept them alive while the storms howled. They burned old mammoth bones plus gnarled, stunted trees that gave off a fragrant smoke.

When they could move again, Silex saw the huge motherwolf, granddaughter to the first wolf to whom Silex ever paid tribute, in the distance, up a rocky hill. She was alone and staring at him, though she did not react when Silex waved his hands. They had some bear flesh left to offer, but she did not come forward. Instead, she trotted up the hill, then stopped and looked over her shoulder. When it seemed as if she could see Silex watching her, she moved a few more paces uphill, then looked again.

"Brach," Silex called. "Stop. Everyone!"

Brach yelled for the Wolfen to stop moving. They were all in a ragged line headed downhill, where instinct told them they might find food, but Silex was transfixed by the wolf. He had seen adult wolves tracking prey with juveniles, looking over their shoulders at their young ones to make sure they were paying attention.

"I want us to climb that hill," Silex announced, pointing.

No one was particularly enthusiastic about the idea, but they did as Silex commanded. It took them nearly half a day, and the mother-wolf vanished from view the moment the Wolfen headed in her direction, but eventually they reached the summit.

On the other side of the hill, a slender stream grew fat at an obstruction, widening into a pond that had not frozen over. From where the Wolfen stood gazing down, it was a thin black line in the snow, leading to a teardrop. And around the pond, a herd of reindeer pawed at the wet ground, seeking fodder.

"She led us to food," Silex breathed. He turned to look at Denix, to share this wonder. And Denix, of course, looked away.

Palloc had been shadowing Grat and had seen the younger man spying on Mal and Lyra, who were sitting together like lovers. Now Grat's face was full of furious revulsion as he strode angrily away from the couple.

Palloc joined him, matching his pace. "You and I go off and hunt and bring back food, and we are reviled for it," Palloc observed. "The cripple does the same thing, and he is the hero."

Grat stopped and stared, looking surprised. The parallels had clearly not occurred to him. Nor to Palloc, actually—his mother had primed him for this conversation with Grat. Her plan made sense: there was a dark violence in the younger hunter, something that Palloc could use to his advantage. He was like a club—*Think of him as a weapon,* Albi had urged. What she did not say was that it was clear that despite his threats, Palloc lacked the courage to kill anybody. He had failed with Urs, he had failed with Calli, and he never even tried with Mal Crus.

"Why do we even need a fire boy?" Palloc continued. "We have a fire maker, and it is the easiest job, one best left to women. We drag him with us on migration, an extra mouth to feed, when we are starving and people are literally dying. He cannot hunt, and anyone could have found those fish. I am sure either one of us probably would have within the day."

"I was planning to explore the area," Grat agreed.

"So for that, everyone thanks him. We are publically humiliated by the hunt master and his toady, but the cripple with the cursed leg is celebrated. Does no one understand that if it were not for him, the Blanc Tribe probably would have been fine? That it would not have snowed, that we would have found game on the trail?"

Grat thought about it for a moment. "This is the curse your mother speaks of, then?"

"Exactly. We nearly all perished on the way here, what more proof do you need?"

Grat peered at Palloc. "You are the fire boy's father."

"He is a curse. His father is the spirit of darkness." Palloc sneered at Grat's expression. "Oh, do I shock you when I mention spirits? My mother says nothing can be worse than letting the curse remain with us. *That* is what should scare you, not talk of evil."

"I am not afraid," Grat responded coolly. "He is a crippled boy. I am a man of the hunt."

"Then what will you do, man of the hunt?" Palloc mocked.

Grat's lips twisted in contempt. "What will I do? I will rid us of the curse."

Year Nineteen

Mal removed the loop of leather from the pup's neck and held it out to her. She sniffed it, unimpressed.

"See? I rubbed rouge into it. Now it is red, a red neck-band for you. This is your special day, your naming day."

The pup yawned, scratching at her ear with her left rear leg.

"You are always happy, always joyful, always playing. This was my brother Dog. You are like him in that way. So you are now, 'She Who Is as Happy and Carefree as My Brother Dog.' And your short name is 'Brotherly Dog—*Dog Fraternus*. And I will call you Dog. All is good? Dog, your name is Dog. Now, sit still for a moment, Dog."

Mal fastened the loop back around the pup's neck, tying the long rope to it. "Now we will go outside, Dog. I will un-block the entrance so we may both squeeze through."

Dog was ecstatic to be outside. Mal kept a firm grasp on her leash, and spoke strongly to his wolf when she pulled too hard. She was perfectly named—when Mal's brother was a boy, he was as tall and skinny as this wolf cub, whose legs seemed ridiculously long.

After some time of steady progress, the left fork of the stream that fed the Kindred became disorganized, splitting into smaller tributaries, independent little creeks. The terrain was now more extreme, with rocks and boulders and cliffs, the brook often choked with deadfall that made passage difficult. What a strange and wonderful place! The stone walls, and the way the creek fought obstacles in its path, frothing a white that flashed in the sun, were all starkly beautiful. When Mal stepped into the ankle-deep water, he was shocked at how much colder it was, as cold as any he had encountered. Why, with summer full of strength, did this stream now flow with the chill of full-on winter?

"You are pulling me farther upstream than I have ever been, Dog. These are the northern wilds—no creed lays any claim to this territory."

He was conscious of the sun climbing higher. He knew he should turn back soon, but every bend in the creek lured him forward with new sights.

"All of this is mine," he declared out loud. He spread his hands and lifted his face to the sun. He felt so much joy that moment he wished Lyra were there so he could sing *her* a song!

The sound of falling water, at first a muted, muffled rustling sound, then a louder roar, like a solid rainstorm, drew him forward. The sun still held dominion over the sky, but was beginning its descent toward the horizon. He needed to get back, but he was curious—what could be causing rain on a cloudless day?

What he found left him awestruck. A sheer rock cliff, many men high, was the source of the sound. Capping the rock wall was an immense pile of white ice, ice that reached all the way to the ground and built a small mountain there: ice tongues, as big around as a mammoth, with water cascading down them and splattering the surrounding rocks.

Could this be the birthplace of winter? Did the ice heaped high at the top of this cliff eventually reach to the sky and hand the clouds snow to drop down on the ground?

Dog's nose was to the ground, sniffing at the frigid, wet earth.

The rocks surrounding this astounding area were treacherous, slippery with both water and often a thin covering of ice. The cold here was breathtaking, and soon Mal was shivering despite his garments. He was fascinated, though, his mouth open as he took it all in.

Something halfway up the ice caught his attention, something sticking out of the frozen wall that did not belong.

Frowning, Mal stared at it, trying to make sense of what he was seeing.

It was an elk leg, thrust at an odd angle out of the ice. The flesh had rotted away, but the bones and hoof were unmistakable.

How did elk bones grow out of the wall? A shiver unrelated to the cold crept up Mal's spine. He knew he should not contemplate such things, but he could not help but regard this as the work of the same evil spirits that caused winter. What other obscene things might sprout from the ice, so defiant of summer that it remained frozen despite the sun?

FORTY-SIX

Year Nineteen

Hunting was not good for the Kindred, that winter. Though it was cold, the rains were sparse and the water holes did not attract the usual amount of game. Tay, Vent's widow and mother to three children, was one of a dozen people to have a toe turn black and fall off, but in her case the foot turned a deep crimson and she died of fever. Her infant son soon followed her into death. Mors, Vent's older surviving brother, said he and his wife would care for the two living children. Bellu could not very well do it—she was prostrate with grief, virtually unresponsive when the women's council gathered around her to suggest that the days were finally long enough to head back to their summer quarters.

Mal was miserable. All of his childhood friends were cold and hostile toward him, especially Grat and Vinco, who always seemed to be hanging around Lyra, effectively blocking his access to her.

Calli could not bear to tell him that the common wisdom was that the curse of Mal's leg had finally extracted its due from the Kindred, leading Dog and the others into ambush by the Cohort and bringing the harsh winter.

Bellu seemed to have forgotten that it was her decision to linger at summer quarters that brought disaster upon the tribe—she was as eager to ascribe it to Mal's leg as everyone else, telling Mal she did not need him to help with the fires, that she had plenty of assistance from the other children in gathering kindling. No one was particularly grateful that Mal had found the fish that staved off starvation at the Blanc settlement. It was as if no one even remembered.

The day the Kindred arrived at summer quarters, they were dismayed that once again pools of snow were still gathered in the shadowy areas, that the Kindred Stream was swollen with icy water, and that the berries and buds were tiny and green. Bellu was devastated. The days had been just the right length, the sun winning more and more time every morning it rose triumphant in the sky making her sure it was the correct moment to migrate. She collapsed, crying, and could only manage a daily bath, too distraught to help with any other chore.

Everyone was grim faced. What would they eat? And more and more, as they chewed leather and ate any green thing they could find growing, their eyes were hot and accusing when they focused on Mal—"*He Who Brings a Curse upon the Kindred with His Leg and Must Be Put to Death for the Good of All of Us.*"

Silex could remember being a young boy and listening to his father tell of what a thrill it was to approach a wolf pack gathering site. Great care was taken to maintain silence, and the wolves were always observed from a tree and at great distance. Detection might cause the wolves to flee, or to turn aggressive, but the wolves were at their most social in their gathering sites, and much could be learned from them there. When a mating pair's cubs were old enough, the parents would bring the pups to the gathering site to be cared for by the pack.

But this pack was different than the one Silex's father told stories about. The wolves had grown accustomed to the Wolfen presence and to the smell of man on their dominant bitch. They reacted with no alarm and little interest to Silex's scent as he squirmed through the grasses to get a closer look.

"The granddaughter with the white handprint markings has departed to give birth!" Silex exclaimed. "She is again a mother-wolf!" He turned a delightful grin on Denix—but she was not there. He found her twenty paces back, regarding him with a sullen expression on her face. "They are very playful today," he told her. "You can see them if you just crawl up to that hummock."

"Are we going to give tribute?" she asked.

"No. The mother-wolf has left to whelp."

"Then I think we should go back," Denix declared coldly.

"Denix." Silex reached out and grabbed her before she could start trotting away.

She spun on him. "Why did you ask me to come with you, Silex?" she demanded, her eyes flaring angrily.

For a moment he hesitated, struck by a memory of Fia, how angry she was when he first pursued her. Finally he shook himself out of it. "I wanted to speak to you alone."

She crossed her arms. "Then speak."

"Does it have to be like this? You have avoided me since the end of last summer. Everyone has noticed how you shun me. I do not understand."

"I agree you do not understand. Is that what you wanted to say, that I have avoided you?"

"No." Silex sighed. "Brach came to me with a disturbing revelation."

Denix's hard gaze grew defiant. "Oh," she said. "That."

"Is it true you approached him and suggested the two of

you might . . ." Silex could not bring himself to finish the thought.

She watched him fumble with a mocking expression. "He does have a history of such behavior," she pointed out.

"Why would you do that?"

Denix laughed harshly. "Oh Silex. How can you be so ignorant?"

"Watch what you say to me, Denix," he warned angrily. "I am not ignorant. I am aware there are no eligible bachelors, but you may not take another woman's husband to your bed. Wolfen mate for life."

"So what is your plan?" Denix asked, abruptly plaintive. "Am I to wait for someone to die in childbirth, or to be eaten by a bear, and then I take the surviving widower, no matter who he is? I am twenty-eight years old! I will soon be too old to have children!"

"But why Brach?"

"I told you. He has a history."

"He is my best friend," Silex protested, anguished.

Denix stared at him. "So the offense is to you, then."

Silex drew himself up. "The offense is to the Wolfen," he answered severely. "It is about adultery."

"Brach is your best friend. Which makes the adultery worse."

Silex swallowed. "No, of course not."

"Well then," Denix continued in reasonable tones. "What about Tok?"

"My son?" Silex responded, horrified.

"Since Cragg married, he is the only single male, and I imagine soon enough he will be ready for a woman's bed," Denix said deliberately. "Has that not occurred to you? And he is not married. So you do not have any reason to object."

"He is but half your age!"

"I assure you that if that does not matter to me it will not matter to him."

Silex was speechless.

"Right? So it is settled."

"No. Not it is not settled," Silex fumed.

Denix turned from him and started to run, so he hastened to keep up. "Denix, we are not finished."

"Yes we are, Silex," Denix said in mocking tones. "It is settled. *Settled.*"

Lyra was sitting on a rock by the stream, talking to friends, as Mal walked by on the path, and she called to him. He waited stiffly, reading the derision in the girls' faces as they whispered to each other, but Lyra's smile was open and welcoming as she approached him.

"And there you go, ever mysterious, off by yourself," Lyra told him, her eyes sparkling.

"I just have something I need to do," he explained tersely. He could not help it—standing close to her, his feelings roiled, an odd mixture of joy and dread. He saw that Lyra was wearing a leather strap around her neck, and that it was looped through one of the largest of the shiny shells the Blanc Tribe once used for trade, one the size of a child's palm. She had fashioned a hole in it somehow, though the shells were delicate and easily fragmented. He pictured her working with a rock, patiently scraping until she had worn through it.

"Let me go with you, Mal."

No, that was impossible. He could not bear to be with her—he was a boy, so he could never court her, never marry her. "All is good," he agreed helplessly.

Lyra waved at her friends, who waved and then immediately went back to whispering, their hands over their mouths. Mal scowled at them.

"They laugh that you are wasting your time with the crippled boy," he said, sounding more curt and unpleasant than he had intended.

Lyra gave him a puzzled look. "Why would you say such a thing?"

He turned and began walking, Lyra easily keeping pace. "I have heard many such sentiments my whole life, Lyra. It is not a concern."

She touched his arm and it was as if a warm breeze blew through his whole body. "I am sorry. But I promise you, that was not what we were saying when we saw you on the path."

She was staring at him intently, willing him to look into her face, and when he did his heart raced. Her eyes were shining. He remembered kissing the girl with the missing arm, Ema, and ached to take this woman into his arms.

"Mal, you have a very handsome face," she told him matter-of-factly. "You remind me very much of your brother."

Dog. Mal pulled back from her, and did not care when he saw her momentary hurt and confusion. Then realization dawned on her. "Mal, I did not mean . . ."

He was already marching up the path. "I have something to do, Lyra."

"Because you resemble your brother does not mean I do not appreciate you. You do know that, Mal."

"I need to go and I do not want you to accompany me," Mal responded icily. Something inside enjoyed punishing her even as he regretted it.

Lyra stopped walking. "All is good, then, Mal. You are not using adult reason, so I do not want to accompany you, either. But your brother was a man I admired, just as I admire you!" she called to his retreating back.

Striding away, Mal felt trapped by his decision to be petulant. He wanted to turn around and say something to Lyra, but he had no words to give. She *admired* him, she said. "I love you, Lyra," he whispered. "I love you."

Lyra turned and slowly walked away. Soon she encountered Vinco and Grat on the path, heading in the direction from which she had just come.

"Good summer, men of the hunt," she greeted formally, not wanting to talk. They halted, though, so she did, too.

"They said you were with Mal," Vinco told her in a tone that sounded almost accusatory.

Lyra drew herself up. "Yes, that is right."

"Where is he now?" Grat inquired, an odd eagerness in his voice.

She involuntarily glanced over her shoulder in the direction Mal had taken, then looked back at the two men. "What do you want with Mal?"

"Oh," Grat informed her with a tight grin, "we have something very important to tell him."

Lyra felt a chill. "I am sure he will return soon," she said quietly, thinking she needed to slip away and warn Mal to be alert.

"No, we will find him," Vinco replied. He pushed past her rudely, but Grat stopped and leaned in intimately.

"I have something important to discuss with you, too," he whispered. Lyra stared at him, trying to read what was going on with his grin and the wild look in his eyes. His tongue was pressed into the gap where he was missing a front tooth—it looked like a worm in a hole, repulsing her. Then he, too, was gone.

When they were half a dozen paces away from her, still following Mal's trail, they broke into a run.

FORTY-SEVEN

Mal realized he was being tracked. There was a sound to the forest, a different feel, somehow, that let him know something or someone was back there.

He immediately swung from the path, crossing the stream and wading into the deeper brush.

He felt that he knew who they were and, as soon as he emerged from the thick undergrowth and into a thin pine forest, he was able to confirm his suspicions. Mal stopped. Grat carried a club and Vinco a spear, but Mal had no weapon, only the fire horn slung from the strap around his neck.

"Good summer," Mal called.

They did not reply.

Mal waved at them, attempting a careless gesture, but his hands were trembling. He turned as if he had no worries, but began walking as quickly as he could. Up ahead, a row of bushes pressed against some large rocks. It was not much, but perhaps if he could make his way there, he might find a place to hide.

He could hear them now. Vinco and Grat were doing what he could not—they were running.

Just as Mal came to the bushes and was preparing to throw himself into them, something astounding happened: the branches shook and then a Frightened burst from the leaves, his face open in terror. He nearly ran into Mal, and then he was past.

Taller, larger, and darker, the Frightened was an imposing figure, but like all of his kind, ran from humans. With a whoop, Vinco and Grat took off in pursuit. The Frightened was faster, but lore had it they were easily tired. It had been many years since any Kindred had even seen one, much less killed one. Mal watched the chase enviously, not for the first time wondering what it would feel like to have both legs working in concert in a headlong dash through the woods.

A small noise attracted his attention. Mal turned to the bushes from which the Frightened had emerged. There was something there. An animal? Mal bent forward, peering into the foliage, gingerly parting it to get a better look.

What he found was a female Frightened and two youngsters. The female's chest was heaving, and her children, both of them under the age of ten, hid behind her, peering at Mal in terror.

The woman held a rock, and she raised it, shaking it at Mal in a clear threat.

"No," Mal whispered. "I will not hurt you."

The Frightened did not speak the Language, and she did not appear to comprehend. Mal pantomimed holding his hand over his mouth. *Quiet.*

The woman seemed to understand. Mal held up his empty hands, then cautiously backed away from the family of Frighteneds.

As quickly as he could, Mal headed back toward the Kindred.

He was not quick enough.

Grat and Vinco caught up with him in a clearing. They were panting, making enough noise that Mal had plenty of time to hide, but there really was no place to go at that point—the trees were too far ahead, and there were no boulders, nor even tall grasses, just thin, sandy soil with a little scrub growth clinging to it.

Mal turned to face the danger.

Vinco was breathing hoarsely and looked ready to collapse, but Grat seemed filled with a dark energy. He was grinning at Mal, and his eyes held an unmistakable bloodlust. He had failed to kill a Frightened, but the pursuit had put him in the mood to destroy, to annihilate.

This was not going to be another beating, Mal realized.

This was to be a killing.

Vinco was there to watch. He hung back, letting Grat take the lead. Mal glanced at him and Vinco, his childhood friend, would not meet his eyes.

Grat's face held a feral grin—when he attacked, it would be in a frenzy. Without a club, there was nothing Mal could do but try to dodge. His leg allowed no retreat.

"Fire boy," Grat spat, his face full of sneering repugnance. He glanced at Vinco, who gave a confirming nod. Mal was not of the hunt. There was no prohibition against fighting.

As if to validate Grat's statement, Mal raised the fire horn and blew into the wide end, stoking smoke and glow. Grat ignored this: he was looking at the spot on the side of Mal's head where his heavy cudgel would strike the first blow. Grat was a stalker, experienced with using the club with deadly effect. He stepped forward, lifting his weapon, while Mal drew in a huge breath as if getting ready to scream.

Mal drove himself off his good leg, closing the distance to Grat in an instant. Grat blinked in surprise, unable to swing his club with Mal right up against his chest. Mal put the small end of the horn into his mouth and blew into it with all his might.

The embers exploded out of the horn and directly into

Grat's face. With a cry, he dropped his club and swatted at his face. His eyes were full of grit and live coals spilled down inside his tunic, searing his flesh. Grat fell to the dirt, rolling and yelling in rage. Vinco jumped on him and tried to pat out the smoking cinders in Grat's hair.

By the time Grat had stripped his clothes and shoved his face into the stream to rinse the ashes out of his eyes, Mal was gone.

When Calli saw Mal burst into camp she raised a hand to her mouth. She had never seen her son look so terrified. "Mother!" he called, as if he were still a little boy. Panting, he ran to her, and she reached out to hold him.

"Mother," he gasped, breaking from her embrace. "Grat means to kill me."

"He . . ." She tried to make sense of this. "Did you have a fight?"

"Not a fight. Listen to me. He was stalking me. He and Vinco. With a club. He tried to hit me with it. He wanted it to be a fatal blow!" Mal sketchily explained what had just occurred, and Calli paled.

"What am I to do, Mother?" Mal implored.

Calli felt weak with fear. She reached for her son's hand. "Come with me," she said, trying to sound confident. She turned and walked him toward the women's side of camp, pulling insistently when he hesitated. "It is the only place, Mal," she insisted. "Come."

Reluctantly, Mal stepped over the line, following his mother into female territory. Almost immediately, Albi was there, glowering at them. "What are you doing? What is he doing? He cannot be here," she snarled.

"He is a boy, remember? A mother may bring her boy to our side."

Albi scowled, but stepped aside when Calli pushed past her.

Calli directed her son to hide among some large rocks. Other than Albi, they had drawn no attention, and Calli could think of no reason to change that. "Just stay here," Calli directed.

"Where are you going?" Mal asked, panic in his voice.

"I am going to talk to Urs."

Urs came out of the men's side with an impatient look on his face. "I know you are preparing for the hunt," Calli told him, "but I need to speak with you, Urs. Privately. It is urgent."

With a curt nod, he followed her down the path until they were alone. Calli bluntly described what was happening, and Urs's frown deepened.

"I am sure your son exaggerates," he soothed.

"I am sure he tells the truth," Calli retorted.

"Calli," Urs said in exasperation, "this has nothing to do with the hunt."

"If Mal were a member of the hunt . . . No, Urs, just listen to me. If *he were a member of the hunt,* Grat would not be allowed to hurt him."

"That can never happen."

"Do you not remember that when we were starving, it was Mal who found food for the Kindred?"

Urs shook his head. "It was *fish.*"

"What does that have to do with anything?"

"It was not meat, Calli. Finding a pile of frozen fish in a cave does not make a man a hunter."

"Then make him tool master! I have seen his work and it is clearly superior to many."

"Calli. Tool master was something Hardy declared for himself. There has not been such a thing before or since."

"But there could be! As tool master he would be a man. He would not have to go on the hunt with you, but he would be protected. Can you see how this will fix this? Can you see how this will save my son?"

He shook his head again. "They are saying I am a bad hunt master," Urs advised gravely. "They say that I allow a curse to remain with us even as our food supply dwindles."

"You know there is no curse."

"I know only that our hunts have been poor, that the weather has been evil, and that there is open talk that perhaps I am not the man to lead the hunt."

"And that is more important than my child's *life*?" Calli demanded angrily.

Urs's expression hardened. "If you want protection for your son, you need to speak to his father. That is the person who rightfully protects children from harm. A father is allowed to intercede and to prevent any action by Grat."

"Palloc," Calli spat contemptuously. "He will not help."

"It is not my business, what happens between and man and a wife," Urs observed, "but I believe you should go to your husband and apologize for whatever you have done and beg him to take you back. Perhaps then he will speak on Mal's behalf."

"Palloc will not do that because he believes Mal is your son," Calli hissed.

She hated him then for the look of revulsion on his face. How could she ever have loved this man, who felt such contempt for her boy?

"That is ridiculous," Urs said scornfully. "He obviously is not."

"Well of course he is not," Calli snapped. "But Dog was, Urs. Dog *was*."

When she returned to camp, something had changed. Several women were gathered at the communal fire, though there was nothing cooking. They averted their eyes when she approached, as if ashamed to look at her.

Trying to quell her panic, Calli hurried to the women's side. When she arrived, she saw Grat and Vinco standing at the boundary, lingering there. Grat held a club in his man's hand. He looked wild, his hair wet, his beard burned away in spots that were erupting into blisters on his face. Vinco poked Grat and nodded in her direction, and Grat turned and fixed her with cold eyes.

"We need to speak to Mal Crus," Grat announced imperiously. "Get him."

Calli ignored the chill that went up her spine. "I do not know where he is."

"Yes you do. He was seen entering the women's side," Grat replied.

"Lots of women saw him," Vinco volunteered.

Calli stared at them. "What are you two doing? Do you really intend to try to slaughter a member of the Kindred? Do you really suppose you will not be punished?" she asked softly.

Vinco dropped his eyes, but Grat's expression was hard and unmoved. "Get Mal Crus," he repeated.

"I will not." Calli moved to step past him and Grat seized her by the arm.

"Get him or I will get him myself."

"I am a married woman. *You must never touch me.*"

For a moment it appeared he was going to strike her—she saw it in his face, his eyes. Then he wavered, releasing her arm. Calli restrained herself from rubbing the sore spot that remained. She turned and marched away, feeling sick to her stomach.

"We need to put an end to this!" Grat shouted after her.

Calli looked over her shoulder and was horrified to see Grat step over the line, following her into the women's side.

It was just Grat: Vinco could not bring himself to trespass on forbidden ground. When Calli realized she was leading Grat straight to her son she veered sharply away, and Grat followed.

Her heart was pounding and she did not know what she was going to do. She headed back toward the communal area, horrified that everyone was deliberately turning from her. They were going to let this thing happen. Grat was going to kill her son right now, and *nobody would help her.*

Grat had halted, confused by her change in direction. He turned and looked back toward the women's side, then straightened in surprise. Calli followed his stare and felt her breath leave her.

Her son was walking calmly toward his killer. The weak terror had left his face, and his broad shoulders had straightened with resolve.

"Good summer, Grat," he said. "Let us not do this on the women's side."

FORTY-EIGHT

As if he had no cares at all, Mal walked right past Grat, who could easily have raised his club and smashed in the back of Mal's head, but who instead followed Mal. "All is good, Mother," Mal assured Calli.

This broke her. Sobbing, she trailed after him, her knees buckling, as her son and his enemy crossed over into the communal area.

"So, Grat," Mal said. His voice was steady, even if his hands were trembling.

Grat stepped forward, raising his club, and Mal braced himself.

"Grat! Vinco!" Urs shouted sternly. Startled, everyone turned. Urs stood several paces away. "The hunt leaves now. Come."

Grat and Vinco froze in indecision.

"Grat!" Urs shouted again. "We are leaving. Come *now*!"

The hunt always departed in the morning. No one could remember them ever leaving in the midafternoon.

Vinco reacted first, breaking into a dash. Grat lowered his club. Before running after Vinco, he turned to Mal. "We will be back," he promised.

The water at Silex's bathing place was like ice, reflecting a summer that still had not taken firm hold of the world. He splashed himself hurriedly and then lay on a warm black rock, gloriously alive, his skin tingling. He thought about the times he had seen wolves stretched out on soft grasses, luxuriating in the day. This, he reasoned, was what it must feel like to them—worries momentarily forgotten, bellies full, nothing chasing, nothing to chase.

Silex lingered far longer than he might otherwise, allowing himself a lapse in what he experienced as a daily struggle to ensure the Wolfen's survival. When finally he reached for his skirt of fox fur and tightened it around his waist, he raised his eyes sharply, feeling a human gaze.

Denix came out of the foliage. Her hair was wet. She walked toward him with a deliberate calm, and Silex flushed, realizing she possibly had been there, observing him, the whole time.

"If you had come before I bathed, you could have watched me, as you did that other occasion," she remarked.

She was fixing him with the intent stare he so coveted, and naturally it unnerved him. He wanted that look, craved it, but when he got it, the feelings it stirred were like a meal too rich, a light too bright. He turned away from it, his face hot. "I did not watch you on purpose," he protested weakly.

"You did not glance elsewhere. You stare your eyes at me when I am not looking in your direction, but then when I return your gaze you turn away." She reached up and ran a hand through her hair, shaking it so that small droplets fell on her brown arms and glinted there like stars. "Why is that, Silex? What do you want from me?"

Silex watched, fascinated, as Denix stepped right up to him and raised a hand to his face. The moisture on her palm was cool on his cheek.

"You are so like my Fia," Silex murmured. "Your passion." He felt the strength of that passion now, calling to him, raising his own like a wolf howl.

"I am not like your Fia," Denix corrected sharply. She

let her hand fall and Silex's face ached to have it back. "She was horrible to me. So jealous and mistrusting."

"Fia? I did not know this," Silex said apologetically.

"*Everyone* knew this. The two of you were so suspicious and jealous of each other. It did not seem a marriage based on love, though I know it felt that way to you. When she died, as life left her, she made you promise to marry Ovi because she knew Ovi would never love you the way Fia did. Even in death, Fia begrudged you any woman who might bring heat to your bed. Ovi is your sister, but she does not love you the way a wife would. The way *I* do, Silex."

"Oh Denix."

"The day you picked me for the hunt, there was but one man for me."

Silex closed his eyes. "So, then. What of Tok? What you said."

"I would never fornicate with Tok, Silex. He is your son. I would not have let Brach touch me, either. Nor any man. I just attempted to cause you an aggravation."

He stared at her. "Why would you want to do that?"

"To get you to do something, Silex! I know you want to!" she shouted, anguished.

Silex licked his lips. "Yet you know I cannot. I, especially, must set the example."

"But it is killing me, Silex. I tell you this with all my heart—a woman desires a man's touch. Without it, she is as dry and brittle as old bones in the sun. But it must be the one man who touches her, the one to whom she has silently given everything. I have wanted forever to tease out the longing in you. I have done all that I can." Tears flowed down her cheeks. "Just one time, Silex. I beg you, please let me know your love just one time. There is no one to see us." Denix lifted off her simple garment of elk hide and stood before him naked, her small breasts reacting to the cool air, her dark nipples firming. "*Please.*"

"I cannot do this, Denix," he choked almost inaudibly.

"Just once," she insisted. She took a step forward and he watched her as if fascinated. "I promise, I will then leave you alone. Just this one time."

He felt his resolve give way to a desire stronger than any hunger. His limbs were trembling as he reached for her. It was sudden and irresistible and he gave into it with undeniable joy. They eased themselves down on the warm sand, their mouths pressed together, panting. Denix made to roll over on her hands and knees, but he stopped her, and, lifting his skirt, showed her what he had learned from the Kindred, that they could look into each other's eyes as he moved on top of her.

She opened her legs to him but Silex, despite the urgent calls from deep inside, held back. This would be her first time. He put his lips to her breasts, kissing them, letting his tongue play there until she moaned and closed her eyes, seizing his head with her hands to pull him up for a rough, frantic kiss. He took a gentle finger and felt down between her legs, touching her until she was slippery and thrusting her hips up at him insistently. Then they finally came together, and she gasped.

Her tears flowed again, but inside the interior of their kiss, she was smiling.

Mal was safe only a single day. The morning after the hunt left, Calli went to Bellu's family cave and found the council mother crying, her head in her hands. "Bellu. What are you doing? Why are you hiding? Albi has called for a meeting of the women's council. *Albi.*"

Bellu would not look at her.

Calli bit back her frustration. "Bellu, you must come out of your cave and address this. Only you may call a meeting. Do you see? By hiding up here, it is as if you are saying that Albi is now the council mother."

Calli reached for Bellu, who shook her off.

"Bellu. Albi means to have the council vote to have Mal . . ." Calli swallowed. "She wants to kill him, Bellu." It sounded ludicrous, but Calli could picture how it would happen. Albi and a few of her closest allies on the council would approach Mal and, though he was a man, he would not fight them off—it was prohibited for any Kindred male to raise his hand to a woman not related to him. The women would do to him what Grat had intended.

"I have tried. But it is too hard," Bellu whispered. "I cannot be council mother when there is a curse."

"What?" Calli cried.

Bellu raised red eyes. "I am sorry," she choked.

"Bellu. Do you realize what you are saying? You no longer want to be council mother? You give up your position, you give up your baths, your favored place in the meals, your ability to protect your husband from the conspiracy to make Palloc the hunt master? You give all that up?"

Bellu's eyes were glazed, as if Calli had said too much to think about.

"The only way you can remain council mother is to come to the meeting," Calli urged. "You need to be there for yourself, and I need you there, too. I need you to speak up for Mal. Please, Bellu. Save yourself, your husband, your family—and my son. Please come with me now."

Something briefly glowed in Bellu's eyes, and then the light faded. She shook her head. "No," she whispered. "I cannot."

* * *

The rest of the women were already assembled in a circle when Calli arrived, Albi strutting in the center, unable to restrain herself from exuding pure glory. The other women eyed Calli as she took her seat.

"Is Bellu coming?" Renee asked anxiously.

Calli wordlessly shook her head.

Albi snorted. "We have a lot to talk about," she stated, firmly seizing control of the meeting. "We must do something about the curse that has followed the Kindred, the curse that has taken our game and our men and even the warmth of the summer from us. The curse we have tolerated far too long."

Calli looked around the circle. Not a single woman would meet her eyes, now. They stared at Albi as if transfixed. Calli had lost. They were going to go through with this.

Calli was out of options. She stood, and immediately she had their attention. "Yes," she said simply, nodding. "You are right. It is time to do something about the curse."

Every woman in the council stared at Calli in silent shock. Nothing she might have said could have surprised them more. Even Albi was mute, her eyes slitted.

"I have spoken to the council mother," Calli claimed. "I come from her cave. She is in agreement. A curse has been placed on the Kindred, and that curse has found its way into my son's leg, which it has poisoned." Calli looked at the women sitting around her. "And we must deal with the curse in a way that ensures it will never return."

"What we must do . . . ," Albi began, finding her voice.

"What we must do," Calli echoed loudly, nodding, "is what the council mother says. If we were to try to rid ourselves of the curse by killing Mal, could we be sure the curse was truly defeated? Right now we have the curse where we can see it, but if Mal was dead, who knows where it might land next? Clearly the curse started with Hardy, our brave hunt master, who had it put in him by the lion. Remember how crippled he was? And then it moved on to my unborn son. Who else will it take? Whose child?"

"That is enough," Albi declared.

"What the council mother says is that the curse must be driven out of the Kindred and sent into the forest. We must banish Mal from our camps." Calli wiped her eyes. "Can you see? Only by forcing the curse to leave can we be safe."

Albi thumped her stick into the ground, and several women reacted to the sound with a wince. They were, Calli realized, remembering exactly what it was like when Albi ran things. "This is *not* the will of the council," Albi stormed.

"And you speak the will of the council?" Calli demanded, as much scorn in her voice as she could muster. Albi's face flashed hot.

"Yes," Albi hissed. *"Yes!"*

"No," came a soft voice.

Everyone turned. Bellu had come up quietly from behind.

"I am the council mother," Bellu said. "What Calli says, I think she is right. Mal should take the curse and go off into the wilds with it, take it back to the lions."

It was the strongest declarative statement Bellu had made as council mother in a long time.

"Calli is right," Bellu repeated. "Mal must be banished."

FORTY-NINE

Mal stared at his mother. "I do not understand," he whispered.

Calli bit back her tears. "This is the only way, Mal. Albi has convinced the women you are the reason so many bad things are happening to the Kindred. She wanted to see you . . . to see you killed."

"Do *you* think I am the reason?" Mal blurted, anguished.

Calli looked at him and once again saw not the man he was becoming but the child he had been, so wounded and vulnerable it was everything she could do to prevent herself from pulling him to her in a protective hug. "Mal. Neither you nor your leg has anything to do with anything," she replied in a low, even voice. "This is an attempt by a wicked, wicked woman to twist things to her own advantage. Understand me?"

"Then why must I go off by myself? It's ridiculous. No one can go off by *himself*."

"It is the only way you can escape the danger," Calli pleaded, swallowing down her feelings. If she thought about her son out there alone, it made her wild with fear. "Until I can talk to Urs. Until things are better for the Kindred. Or until . . ." Calli gestured with a hand. "Until Albi dies. She is an old woman now; when she falls into death there will be no one remaining to argue that a curse exists. But until then, you must live away from us, Mal."

Mal shook his head stubbornly. "I want to speak to my father about this."

"Mal . . ."

"I said I want to speak to my father!" he yelled.

Calli blinked in the face of his sudden fury. She understood it, though. Her shoulders fell. "Your father will do whatever his mother says," Calli told him quietly. "You know this, Mal. You know the kind of man Palloc is. I am sorry."

Mal *did* know. Slowly, the anger faded from his face. He lowered his eyes. "All is good, then," he muttered resignedly.

Nothing had ever hurt Calli as much as the way her brave boy accepted his fate now. The unfairness of it all made her sick.

She told him to take food and weapons. "There is a place upstream, beyond the boundary, where large boulders meet a flat bank covered with grasses. On the third day, after the midday meal, I'll bring more food to you there." Calli realized that she was trying so hard not to sob aloud that her voice sounded strange, as if caught in a hiccup. She forced herself to take a breath. "Mal? Do you understand me?"

Mal found Lyra exactly where he knew she would be: at her painted cave. He could hear her singing to herself in there, and for a moment he lingered outside and simply listened. The words were something about eating food by the fire.

Her head emerged, smiling, when he called softly past a thin scent of smoke into the space under the rock. "Mal," she greeted, climbing out on her hands and knees.

"Good summer, Lyra," he replied.

She picked up something in his voice, and her eyes widened when she examined his face. "What is it? What is wrong, Mal? Why are you carrying both club and spear?"

He swallowed. "There has been a decision by the women's council," he began, relating in a halting voice what his mother had told him.

Lyra grew more and more dumbfounded as Mal spoke. "I was not told of any meeting, and I spoke to Bellu immediately before I came here," she protested.

"Albi convened it."

"Albi?" Lyra sputtered. "There is something seriously wrong."

"My mother says this is the only way."

"But Mal. No one can live *alone*." Lyra turned and looked north, contemplating what it meant.

"I will miss you, Lyra," Mal whispered hoarsely.

Lyra's mouth trembled. "This is like the day Dog died. Hearing it does not make it something I *understand*. I just cannot imagine this thing happening."

"I know." Mal now also looked north. He needed to get moving.

Lyra read the resolve in his face. "Wait," she said. She ducked into her cave and was gone a few moments, reappearing with a braided leather thong that easily measured three times the distance from the ground to Mal's head. "Here. I just finished making this."

Mal examined the tight weave. "This is a fine rope, Lyra."

"Take it. You may need it for something."

"All is good," Mal agreed. He coiled the rope and tied it to the one around his waist. "Thank you, Lyra."

He stood and stared at her. There seemed to be so much

to say to this woman, but he could not find any words within him.

Lyra wiped at her eyes. "Mal."

"Good-bye, Lyra," Mal said. *I love you,* he did not say to her.

"Good-bye, Mal," Lyra replied.

She watched his retreating back. His asymmetrical gait was so familiar to her; she had seen it her whole life. Heartbroken, Lyra fell to the ground with her face in her hands. This was *exactly* like the day Dog died. The pain was the same, the nightmarish sense of unreality was the same. And now, as then, she felt she would give anything for just one more moment to be with him.

But she did not run after him, and soon any opportunity to catch up with Mal had passed.

Mal found the area his mother described just as the sun entered its fatal battle with the night, gloom rising up from the forest floor like a fog. There were two large boulders a person could squeeze through, and he built a fire in front of these, hunkering down in the cramped space. He wanted to feel confident—he was a man, no matter what the Kindred said—so it surprised him when he began sobbing, wanting nothing more than to be back at his mother's fire. He could not do this. No one could.

He was going to die out here.

The next morning Mal moved farther north, spear ready to take any game. He would spear an elk, or even a bear! In a few days' time, he would return to the Kindred with furs and food and prove there was no curse.

He was watching the ground for animal tracks when he heard the unfamiliar grunting and hissing noises and came upon vultures feeding on a wolf corpse. After driving them off, he realized there had been two wolves fighting a lion, and, tracking the blood, he came to a small cave mouth, back from the stream.

The wolf was in there.

C alli," Coco called to her daughter gently.
Calli blinked, focusing on her mother.

"Your face was so angry, but you were looking off at nothing," Coco said.

Calli smiled bitterly. "Everyone wants to pretend life is normal. My son has been living by himself all summer, yet he is forgotten, and I am treated the same, as if nothing happened."

Coco sighed. "It was the same when Ignus died, do you recall? No one knows what to say, what words would be welcome, so they say nothing at all."

"I am sure it is not the same, Mother. My son could be starving, and no one cares."

Coco did not take offense, watching as Callie carefully slipped a few days' worth of reindeer meat into her pouch. Every third day, Calli took food to her son, crossing into forbidden territory and meeting him at the same place where she had once met Urs. Coco could see the strain of fear in her daughter's eyes—Mal had been unable to hunt or even successfully forage. Without Calli's regular deliveries, he would already be dead. "You are right," Coco murmured. "It is not the same at all."

The hunting had been good, and everyone in the Kindred was relaxed and happy. After the midday meal, most people were drowsy, retreating to their family areas for a nap. Calli slipped away unnoticed.

She had barely started up the path when she heard her name being called. She turned and tried not to gasp: Palloc stood there, regarding her with unfriendly eyes.

"Where might you be going, Calli?" he asked softly.

"I decided to see if I might find some berries," she answered after a moment.

Palloc came closer, closer than he had been in several years. "A woman should not venture out alone. Are you forgetting the Valley Cohort?"

"Of course not," Calli replied. "Are you forgetting they killed my child? One of my two children, who have both been taken from me?"

He looked her up and down, working his lips in an amused fashion, and Calli had to force herself to endure his examination without reaction. "What is that in your pouch?" he finally asked her.

"Nothing."

"Let me see."

"What? No. Leave me alone."

He grabbed her arm roughly, snatching the strap off her shoulder. "Let me see," he repeated forcefully.

Helplessly, Calli watched as Palloc found the cooked reindeer meat. "Ah," he said. He looked at her and of course he knew who the meat was for. "Well, no, my wife, I think you probably meant to give this to your husband." He lifted a hunk to his mouth, grinning at her, and bit off a piece. "Good," he declared as he chewed. "You are a good cook, Wife."

"I am not your wife."

"No?" He grinned through his full mouth. "You do not think so?"

Calli fought the chill that came over her then. The look in Palloc's pale eyes unnerved her—she had seen that feral expression on his face once before. She turned. "All is good," she said over her shoulder. "Eat it, I do not care."

Palloc nodded. "Oh, I will eat it and you do care. You meant this meat for someone else, and I know it. But you will not leave the Kindred, Calli. I will watch you every day, that you do not go anywhere."

She kept walking, feeling safer but also sinking into despair. The hunt would not go out for many days, not with the most recent success. Could Mal survive until then?

FIFTY

It was the third day, but his mother did not appear when she was supposed to, missing her appointment for the only time that summer.

Mal waited for her until nearly evening. He was out of food because Dog's appetite was ravenous and Calli did not know her son was sharing his rations with a wolf. Neither he nor Dog had eaten since the morning of the day before.

Hunger bit at him sharply, and he spent most of the rest of the day upending logs along the stream, searching for worms and insects. What few he found did nothing to take the edge off the pain in his stomach, and, of course, Dog lapped up the few worms instantly and then stared at him with utter expectation. "I am sorry, she was not there, for some reason," Mal apologized.

Dog hated to be left alone, and often yipped and yowled when Mal climbed up the crevice—the ground-level entrance was thoroughly blocked with rocks. But he had given it much thought: yes, a predator could take Mal, and then poor Dog would be trapped inside the cave and would eventually perish where her mother did. But starvation, as cruel as it was, would be far more merciful than what would happen to a wolf who was too young to hunt on her own—sooner or later, Dog would be eaten. The dull fade into unconsciousness that would be her death inside the cave was surely preferable to that.

The next day, Mal ate some grass in the morning. He saw

some tiny fish lazily lying in the shadows along the stream banks, but neither his spear nor his club could kill one.

Again, his mother was not at the secret place at the chosen part of the day. He lingered for as long as he could, watching the sky with increasing despondency. Where was she?

Cramps seized him on the way back to his cave, and his stool was watery as he squatted, leaving him breathless with the pain. When he was done, he was dizzy, which is why he stared at the rabbits without recognition for a moment, his thoughts too fuzzy to do anything but numbly register their movements. There were several grey rabbits in the low shrubs, venturing out in the fading light to feed on some tender grasses by the stream.

Food.

Mal hefted his spear, his arm shaking as he took careful aim. He knew he would only have a single shot—his throw would scare them back into their holes.

"Careful," Mal whispered to himself. His heart was pounding and his mouth was open. When he loosed his spear it went hard and true and missed by a finger length, but his prey was darting for the bushes the moment the weapon buried its head in the dirt. Mal never even saw where they went. They simply vanished like rocks tossed in dark water.

His wolf greeted him with yips of joy when she heard his feet hit the floor of the crevice, and rushed to his hands, licking them eagerly.

"I have nothing, Dog. It will have to be tomorrow."

Her eyes met his and he felt guilt stab him like a spear.

Calli did not come the next day. Mal was exhausted by the walk down to the rendezvous point, but he did not dawdle this afternoon—it was urgent he find food. He went to the small clearing where he had spotted the rabbits, but they were not in evidence. Again, he moved on.

He headed upstream, hoping he would see something he could eat. After a time, he realized he had stopped thinking and looking, that he was just plodding along with his head down. In this condition, he might walk right past a reindeer without realizing it. He decided to lie down, to rest just a moment, but when he collapsed it was with the saturating weariness that he remembered from the days when the Kindred migrated, walking all day until every muscle ached.

He lay on the ground and regarded the sky with dull eyes. Some part of him wondered if he would have the strength to get back up again.

A twig snapping brought Mal into full, frightened consciousness. He sat upright, his heart pounding. What was he doing, sleeping out in the open? What if the lion came across him sprawled in the dirt, an easy meal?

This far upstream the cliffs were taller than at the wolf's den, and as he walked he occasionally craned his neck to peer upward, which was how he spotted the owls—a huge flock of them, small and grey, circling out from the rock face the way insects sometimes swirled in clouds over murky water. Tracking them, Mal could see small pockets of twigs stuffed into cracks in the wall—nests.

Eggs?

This was not at all like the climb up the rocks to the smoke hole entrance to his cave, where only a precarious ledge interrupted the succession of easy hand- and footholds. Mal left his club and spear at the base of the rock wall and began a nearly vertical ascent. He fumbled for handholds, straining, his arms trembling with the effort, making slow progress.

When he looked down he gasped—he had never been this high; could not imagine what would happen to him if he fell. His vision was distorted, everything impossibly small, as if captured on the walls in Lyra's cave. From here he could see the smoke from the Kindred's fires, and the great river that separated his tribe's territory from the Wolfen.

When something struck him on the cheek, he assumed it was a falling rock, though the sensation had been oddly soft before the pain bit him. When another one slashed at his scalp, he realized he was being *attacked*. The birds were on him, using beak and talon in full fury.

What sort of birds hunted humans? They fluttered in his face, pecking at his skin, opening a cut under his eye. He slapped them away and lost his balance, desperately grasping for a hold as he slid, nearly falling to his death.

"Yahhh!" he shouted in pain and frustration. He could barely see from the intensity of the onslaught.

He climbed, finding a ledge where he could wedge himself securely. He waved his arms furiously and gained a respite, looking about in wonder. More birds were in the air than he could count, grey owls with their strangely small beaks and squashed-in faces. They circled and swooped, oddly silent, their cold eyes intent, trying to get at him. When he batted at them they veered away, but they came right back, determinedly pressing their offensive.

Mal was looking for a loose rock to use as a weapon, and that was when he spotted a small nest of twigs wedged in the cracks in the cliff a few arm's lengths away. The nest clutched a couple of tiny, dull eggs, each about the size of the tip of his thumb. Eagerly, Mal shuffled sideways, groping for handholds, and shoved his fingers into the nest. He cracked the eggs and sucked them dry, seeing another nest, and another.

A bird cut his forehead, another lacerated his scalp, a third drew blood from his hands, but Mal went from nest to nest, looting them, gathering eggs. When he had swallowed enough food to break the cramp in his stomach, he collected the rest of his harvest in his pouch, wiping the blood from his forehead as the birds conducted their relentless aerial assault. It was a dangerous, grim business—trying to fend them off, grab the eggs, and stay wedged in the cracks high above the ground. When he was done he had depleted all the nests he could reach, but the pouch hung heavy from its strap.

Climbing down was, for some reason, more frightening. His good leg probed for cracks that would support his weight, his tiny foot on his woman's side unable to do much to help. His hands were torn and sore, and the owls kept up their murderous assault until, just as suddenly as they had begun, they broke off, swirling away in a grey swarm.

He was so intent on clinging to the rock that when his foot hit the ground he jolted in shock. Panting, he went to his knees, fighting the nausea and trembling that overtook him.

The blood, he knew, was dangerous—the scent could draw predators. Lugging his swollen pouch, he went to the stream and cleaned himself as best he could, then collected his weapons and peered at the horizon.

He had spent much more time on the wall than he had realized. The day's fight with the night would soon end with the sun's blood smeared across the sky. He would not make it back to his cave in time.

Mal ran as fast as his leg would allow. He did not remember hiking so far. As the shadows deepened, the terrain seemed less and less familiar. Only the sight of the stream to his side as he ran gave him comfort that he was not lost, but that meant having to follow every bend, not daring to strike out in a straighter line as the watercourse meandered.

The gloom descended, malevolently leeching away Mal's vision. Large black mounds of soil, ripped from the ground as trees were uprooted in storms, looked like bears waiting for him to draw closer. Rocks were wolves, a thick tree trunk a crouching hyena.

For a time a wild panic drove him in blundering, stumbling flight, but as the night triumphed over the last of the day and the winking droplets of the sun's blood emerged scattered across the sky, reason returned. Panting, Mal halted. He found dried grasses and twigs and wrapped them around the end of his club and summoned sparks with his flint, giving himself a torch.

The fire was at once help and hindrance. He could see the ground, but the darkness rushed up to the perimeter of light cast from the flames, so that he could distinguish nothing beyond the wavering circle of torchlight. He could not run, now, he had to walk.

He made sure he kept the torch aloft, so that the flames would lap upward and not consume the club. He gathered more grasses as he walked, more twigs, feeding the torch and keeping the flames bright.

A bend in the stream and then the rocks started to look familiar. He was close, now. Not much farther.

And that was when he heard the lion.

Mal whipped his head around in the direction of the rustling sound he had heard, swinging his torch and gasping when he saw the lion's face low to the ground, its shoulders hunched, eyes glinting in the firelight. The great cat, a huge female, could close the short distance in a flash. She was large enough to hold Mal's head in her mouth, her claws as long as his fingers.

Instinctively, Mal gestured with the only weapon he had, his flaming torch, and not only did the lion not pounce, she seemed to flinch slightly. She was afraid of the fire!

Mal realized he was holding his breath, and let it out slowly. He backed up a step, and then another, and the gloom descended around the cat, until all that remained were two winking reflections of the torch—the lion's eyes, watching, tracking.

Mal cautiously made his way down the path. There was a slight sound and Mal knew the cat was stalking him, staying in the bushes, looking for an opening. Mal halted again, and this time, after remaining silent and unseen for more than a moment, the lion let out a quiet, low moan. It sounded like frustration: here was this soft animal, no horns to fight with, unclawed and unfanged, lacking even the protection of other herd members, but to take the kill would mean getting a face full of fire.

Mal fed the flames some more fuel, keeping his focus on a deep pool of shadow where he felt sure his stalker was lurking. The torch responded, spreading more light.

They made their way down the trail like this, predator and prey, Mal keeping the fires going, the lion always audibly near, just out of sight in the undergrowth. Then finally the rocks to his man's side resolved themselves into the familiar formation of the cliffs up to his chimney: home.

Now he had a dilemma. Lions could climb; Mal had seen it. But Mal could not, not with the torch in one hand. He would have to drop the light—he would need both hands when he got to the ledge. Could he get to the top and run to the smoke hole fast enough to evade the lion, once he had lost the protection of the fire?

No. No, he could not.

He took a deep, shaky breath, considering. He had a pouch full of eggs weighing him down—food that might distract the lion. If he dropped it now and made his way as best he could up the rocks, carrying the fire that was keeping the beast at bay, she would eventually emerge from the shadows and plunder the day's take of owl eggs. While she was eating, Mal could attack the part of the ascent that required two hands.

With more than a little regret, he slid the pouch off his shoulder and dropped it on the ground. Then he started to ascend with just one hand probing for holds, the other clutching the torch. It was awkward and slow, but he made steady progress, tightly clutching the wooden handle of his torch. If he dropped it, he was dead.

Nearly halfway up he was stuck. Just as he had thought, he needed both hands to make it any higher, now. He looked down at the ground: he was up a little more than the height of three men. The lion could climb it in virtually one leap. Just above was the ledge where he often rested. And below him . . .

Below him the lion came out of the undergrowth, sniffing the ground as if puzzling where Mal went. Then she looked up. No, she knew where he went. Knew it and was trying to figure out how to get to him.

The eggs! Mal wanted to shout. *Take the eggs!*

The lion was not concerned with the eggs in the pouch. She was interested in the living prey.

His torch would not burn all night. When it flickered out, the lion would come up to get him.

FIFTY-ONE

He was trapped, unable to ascend without using both hands, but safe only as long as he held the torch.

Below him the lion made another low moan, and to Mal's ears it sounded less like frustration than satisfaction.

The thing to do, Mal decided, was to throw the torch up onto the ledge overhead, then pull himself up there as swiftly as possible and pick it up again. If the lion tried to scale the rock wall she would find herself poked in the face with flames: any luck and she would tumble to the ground.

Mal swallowed. The lion was actually sitting and staring at him, the very tip of her tail twitching. She seemed to be thinking about climbing up after him, despite the small fire he carried.

Time to move. Breathing raggedly, Mal swung the torch out and flipped it up toward the ledge. The throw was high and wide: a second later the flames were coming right at him, sparking when the torch hit the rocks. He dodged it and then, with a flash of heat, the light fell past.

Mal took only an instant, less than a second, to see the lion spring away from the falling flames, and then he was groping for his handholds, hauling himself up on the ledge. Without hesitation he kept climbing, hating the noise he was making, inadvertently glancing down when his frantic scrabbling sent a shower of small stones bouncing to the ground.

The torch had fallen into the rocks. The lion's frantic retreat had lasted just a few seconds—now, with the flames impotently flickering in a crack between two stones, she was emboldened. She came forward and seemed to lock eyes with Mal before her shoulders bunched, ready to leap.

Gasping, he struggled to ascend as quickly as he could, lunging for holds he knew were there and thrusting with his good leg at every opportunity. Moonlight now guided him. This was taking too long; he was going too slowly! He folded himself over the lip of the bluff and that was when he heard it: the sound of claw on rock, coming fast. The lion was in pursuit.

He was on the flat area at the top of his cliff. In the time it took him to stand and dash for the hole that led down to the wolf's den, the lion scaled the rocks. With a clatter it was at the top, and Mal knew it would close the distance to him in an instant. When he reached the dark mouth of the crevice he leaped, aware of the lion right behind him, and then he was falling, desperately reaching for a handhold to break his descent.

When his fingers found a crack he was yanked to a stop with enough force to jar his entire body, but then he was out of danger. He clung to his handhold, gazing up at the circle of moonlight at the top of the chimney.

The lion was standing there, face completely obscured as she stared down at Mal.

The lion knew where he lived, now.

Dog virtually tackled him when he landed on the cave floor, but Mal's focus was on one thing: snatching up his fire horn, he blew flaming embers out into the circle of rocks that held the twigs and grasses he had assembled that morning.

The lion could always decide to follow him down the crevice.

When the fire was snapping and popping and smoke climbing up to the sky, he allowed himself to fall back and accept Dog's licking. They wrestled together, but Mal's heart was sick. The food he had brought back to his wolf was outside where he could not reach it.

"Lions hunt in the evening," Mal told Dog. "Tomorrow morning I will fetch my pouch." But he thought he saw real desperation in Dog's eyes—she was waiting for him to provide food, *trusting* he would do so. "Oh Dog," he said mournfully.

After a time, he remembered when he was a young boy and some of the older children, making fun of his leg, held him down and forced him to swallow mud and grass. As he had turned away from them, on his hands and knees, and dug the obstruction out of his throat with a finger, he had brought up the contents of his stomach. Each time he had tried to clean out his throat, he had retched up more, while all the other children laughed at him.

Mal pushed his wolf cub away from him as he sat, smiling softly when she came right back, climbing on his leg. "All is good, then," he advised her. He turned and stuck his finger down his throat, gagging a few times before his egg meal emerged and landed on the cave floor. Mal wiped his mouth. "Now you eat," he told Dog. "Eat."

At last the hunt assembled itself to go out. Calli observed them while trying to appear as if she were too distracted by other matters to pay any attention, biting her lips in impatience when their unconcerned pace of preparation put the hunt far enough behind that Urs decreed they would allow the day to pass, so that it was yet another morning before the men bade good-bye to their wives, sternly charged the older boys with guarding camp, and gathered on the men's side to leave. Calli busied herself with preparing a soup from pieces of reindeer viscera, internally pleading with the men to just *leave.*

She sensed Valid's quiet approach behind her and turned, his expression faltering when he saw her face. Lately he had come often to the communal fire, always with a clear reason, such as asking if it were yet time to gather the late-summer berries or to remark that her rabbit stew had been particularly delicious, but usually they just stood and chatted pleasantly. She enjoyed their conversations, but was not in the mood for idle talk today.

"What is wrong, Calli? You seem unhappy."

"No, all is good. I am just concerned that the hunt delays its departure."

He regarded her oddly. It was an unusual observation for a Kindred woman to make, and for a moment Calli felt that Valid was peering right past the mists and shadows and knew exactly why she wanted the men to leave. Indeed, the spear master glanced up and over at Palloc for a moment, then back at her.

"Spearmen! Make ready!" Valid called without turning from her gaze. Calli drew in a breath. The spearmen hustled to close ranks on Urs, who nodded, taking their movement as impetus. Within moments Mors summoned the stalkers, and Valid turned away from Calli with just the ghost of a smile on his lips.

Valid *did* know.

At midday, while the women and children of the Kindred ate, Calli was hastily packing her pouch with meat, and she left with the knowledge that she was far from unnoticed. She did not care; her anxiety was like a suppressed scream within her, a fear as strong as any she had ever felt as she ran to where she had promised Mal she would meet him, so many days ago.

He was not there. Calli looked to the sky, trying to convince herself she was earlier than they had arranged. All was good, her son would be here any moment, she just needed to linger a bit longer.

She waited. After a time she went to the stream and waded in, letting the cold water make her as numb as her thoughts. She simply would not allow herself to contemplate what would happen if Mal did not come.

It was here, right here, where she had clutched Urs to her. Everything had been clear and bright for them then, a future easy to see, a life welcoming them. What had happened? How could it be that here she was, all but a widow, with a son dead, and another driven from her?

"Mother."

She spun and stared at her son. He carried a club in one hand and spear in the other. He was cut and scratched along his arms and face, smears of dried blood mixed with dirt in his hair. His ribs pressed hard against his skin, his eyes were dull, his lips swollen.

Yet it seemed he was comforting *her,* when they embraced. She clutched her bony, starving boy and it was he who had the strength to keep them from toppling over.

"All is good, Mother," he murmured to her. "Did you bring food?"

He snatched the pouch from her when she offered it, and his first few bites of reindeer steak were feral and wanton. He closed his eyes, swooning with how good it tasted. Then he pulled back, gaining some control. He actually offered it in her direction.

"Would you like some?"

She shook her head wildly, laughing. "Oh no, Mal, no. It is all for you."

He took another bite, chewing more slowly, and then went to the stream for water.

"Mal, you look—"

"I am well, Mother," he interrupted. "All is good."

She stared at him. All was, of course, not good, but there was something different about him, stronger, some sort of determination in his gaze she had never seen before.

She told him the hunt was out, and explained why she had not been able to come before. Mal was not surprised to hear that his father had prevented Calli from coming upstream. "He is probably right. There is danger up here," Mal acknowledged.

Calli could hardly believe Mal would say such a thing. "You are not suggesting I not come!"

Mal gave her a rueful smile. "No, I am not suggesting that," he admitted. He told her he had managed to raid some birds' nests, leaving her with the impression he had been up in the trees and not high on the cliffs. "But the eggs were very small and the birds took offense. Would you mind if I kept this pouch? I have lost mine—it was not where I left it last night."

That evening Mal lay on the flat ledge halfway up his rocky cliff from the ground. Next to him, her legs trussed with the rope Lyra had given him, his little wolf puppy was very unhappy, her whimpering growing louder as she realized she could not escape her bonds.

Mal had let pieces of his mother's reindeer steak fall down the rocks below. Now he lay in wait, his woman's hand, his strongest, clutching his club. Sitting right nearby, propped where he could quickly snatch it, was his spear, the chiseled stone head lethal at the tip. From where he lay he could see the dense growth along the streambed, and straight below was the clearing.

Mal thought he had seen a bit of movement in the bushes a few moments ago, though there had been nothing for a little while. But Dog's cries were getting louder—if the lion were near, she would soon hear them.

Mal hoped the scent of the reindeer and the distressed calls of the wolf puppy would be tantalizing to the lion, who could easily bound up the near-vertical slope to where Mal waited in ambush. The first thing to clear the ledge would be the lion's head, and Mal intended to put all his strength into his club strike, crushing the lion's skull before she could react. If the lion were still alive when she fell back to the ground, Mal would impale her with the spear—he could hardly miss at such close range.

A good plan, as long as he did not consider that if anything went wrong he and Dog would be trapped on a narrow shelf of rock with a gigantic, furious killer. Mal's hand shook as he gripped his club, and he glanced at the spear for at least the tenth time, mentally rehearsing the weapon exchange in his mind. If he hit the lion but did not kill her, the spear would be their only chance.

There was the movement again. Mal focused, seeing the shadows resolve themselves into the sleek profile of the massive lion. *Oh yes,* she knew Mal was there. But human flesh was lion food, the same as wolf puppy. She knew Mal was there and she wanted to feed on both of them.

Dog was staring at Mal in distress and finally began crying in earnest, a trapped, wounded wail that was unmistakable to any animal. His heart ached when he looked at her little trusting face, so unhappy, beseeching him to come rescue her.

The lion reacted to the infant distress call, easing out of the underbrush. She crept forward cautiously, the unique circumstances making her unsure. Mal dropped his head as low as he could, behind some rocks keeping the beast in sight. She was an enormous creature, a *monster*, with gigantic, wickedly sharp claws and a mouth full of lethal, frightening teeth. He pictured those teeth tearing into him and briefly shut his eyes. They said when the lion attacked Hardy, it closed its jaws on his *entire head*.

"I do not want to die, I do not want Dog to die," Mal whispered out loud, his pulse giving his voice a weak, throbbing quality. But there was no living here with the lion remaining close enough to be summoned by Dog's cries. They were trapped. The lion would eventually kill them both if Mal did not kill her first.

The lion sniffed suspiciously at a piece of reindeer that had fallen to the ground, eventually eating it.

She raised her eyes. Mal lowered his, ducking all the way down and breathing hard. He could feel her down there, thinking. The baby wolf's cries were so loud he was worried he might not be able to hear the lion's ascent—it was critical he knew when her head was going to be within striking distance. It all came down to the timing. If the lion made it onto the ledge, they were finished.

The lion was adding it all up, Mal knew. The blood smell. The trapped infant. The man. Prey. Just up there in the rocks.

How long would it take the lion to climb up here from the ground? He pictured her nimbly leaping from rock to rock. When he heard her coming, that was when he would swing his club.

FIFTY-TWO

Mal waited, his club ready, holding his breath. The puppy wailed. There was no sound from below. What was the lion doing? Was she coming? Should he risk taking a look?

And then the lion's head appeared over the ledge, *right there.*

"Ahhh!" Mal screamed in surprise. The lion's front paws gripped the lip of the rocks and Mal swung his club and hit the lion on the side of the head and the lion *did not fall.* Still screaming, Mal swung again and the lion snarled, reaching out and snagging the club with her claws and wrenching it from his grasp, batting it aside. It bounced against the rocks and vanished over the ledge. The lion took just a moment to glance at the cowering puppy and Mal thrust his hand out to his spear and had it up and there was no time to throw so he just lunged, aiming for the neck.

The lion turned back and Mal missed the neck as the lion snapped at the spear point, biting down on the shaft. Mal was still driving forward and the lion twisted away, jaws clamped down on the weapon, and now she did fall, pulling Mal helplessly after her.

Mal held on to the spear with all his strength because without it all was lost. They tumbled together, man and beast, and when the lion slammed onto the ground Mal fell with his chest on the butt of the spear, doubling over it and gasping with pain as it cracked his ribs, and then he was *on the lion herself,* feeling her fur and blood and claws, and he rolled blindly away. His club, *there.* He desperately threw himself at the club, snatching it, powering himself up with his good leg, raising the weapon high.

The lion was not moving. She had fallen to her side, the spear still sticking out of her mouth, from which she drooled dark blood. Her eyes were open and staring, but lifeless.

She was dead.

Mal dropped his club and slid to his knees, suddenly so weak he could no longer stand. He lifted his tunic and the welt on his ribs where he had landed on the back end of the spear was already turning an angry dark red, and when he touched the tender spot he gasped with the pain.

The force of Mal's fall had driven the spear straight through the roof of the lion's mouth.

Wincing, he stood. He knew his side would ache for many days, and he felt sick. But they were safe. He put his hands on his knees, ill and trembling. *They were safe.* Gradually, his nausea subsided, and he stared wonderingly at the gigantic predator he had just killed. He, Mal Crus, cursed, crippled fire boy, had just killed a lion.

Overhead the puppy was silent, no doubt still cowed by the brief appearance of the ferocious cat right there in front of her. When he hauled himself up on the ledge, though, she became ecstatic, struggling against her bonds and crying in joy. He tried to untangle her and she just made it worse, spinning in circles, licking his face, climbing on him and whimpering.

Mal knew that he would feed for several days on the lion, though his stomach might rebel against the unfamiliar meat at first. And he resolved to skin the beast at first light. He would find the tree bark Lyra had shown him, smash it to a pulp and heat it in hot water, pouring the thick mixture on the hide and leaving it in the sun on the rocks to cure, just as he had done with the mother-wolf's fur. Among the Kindred, it would be Mal and Urs alone who wore lion fur in the winter.

"All is good, little girl," he laughed delightedly. "Hold still and I will untie you."

Calli was frantic. A nice herd of reindeer, close by camp, had made it unnecessary for the hunt to go out as a collective. Instead, smaller groups might venture out onto the plains every couple of days, but never with Palloc, who seemed content to feed off the efforts of others. He hung around the communal fires, watching Calli with lazy eyes. Only when she seemed to be heading out of camp did he move, and then it was to follow her at close distance, not preventing her progress, but tracking her so that if she met her son she would be leading Palloc straight to him. She knew she could never allow that to happen.

The effect of the reliable food supply was magical. The tensions rippling through the women's council dissipated—Albi might be wandering around with a baleful look on her face, but everyone else was happy and relaxed.

Calli went to speak to Bellu, hoping to convince her to talk Urs into sending the full hunt out. "We should be building up our supplies of cooked, dried meat," Calli explained.

Bellu waved her hand languorously. "Urs will decide," she said dismissively. "I have better news."

"As council mother, you can tell him the women are concerned," Calli insisted.

"I am pregnant," Bellu announced. "Wonderful!" Her mouth open and eyes wide in anticipation of Calli's joyous squeal.

"That is good, Bellu."

"You do not seem very excited," Bellu pouted.

"No, of course, I am very excited. I just worry, though, that we will not have enough food for the migration south."

"That is not for some time."

"But to run out of food, while you are expecting a child," Calli pressed.

A shadow entered Bellu's eyes. "Are we in danger of running out of food?"

"Well, yes we are, if the hunt is unable to continue to find game," Calli equivocated slowly.

"I see," Bellu said. She tapped her teeth with her nails. Because of her frequent baths, Bellu had the only clean nails in the Kindred, and they looked odd without dirt under them.

Calli left Bellu's fire convinced the hunt would soon be assembling, but another two days passed before Urs summoned the men for a conversation that went all day, the men laughing raucously many times. They were in excellent spirits. Their wives had plenty of energy for them in the night, their children were not crying in hunger, and the reindeer were easy to find.

"The hunt leaves tomorrow," Renne mentioned to Calli that night. Since the death of Dog and Renne's husband, Nix, Renne seemed to seek out Calli for conversation when she was lonely.

"All is good," Calli replied, relieved.

"Mostly, women will miss their husbands," Renne noted haltingly. She appeared to be wrestling with something. "But you and Palloc are different."

"Palloc and I are married but only in name," Calli replied. "He did not care for my children, and he does not care for me as a wife."

"So you are not offended that Palloc might visit the widows at night?"

"No, I am happy that he does not bother me," Calli replied, pushing a fleeting memory of Urs from her mind. The men might avail themselves of the widows, but there was no one in all the Kindred who was in Calli's unique position. She might avail herself of no one.

Her eyes sought out Valid. He was sitting with his daughter and actually letting the girl do something to his hair, pulling it back and treating it with sticky tree sap so it would not blow in his face. Lyra was singing to her father, and Calli guessed that was the trade for the indulgence—he would allow Lyra to groom him but only if she made up a song in return. Valid was a good father, a good man. His wife, Sidee, often complained about him, in that way that so many wives in the Kindred talked about their men, an attitude that caused Calli to marvel to herself how such small issues loomed so large in the minds of women who had every reason to be content.

Only later, as Calli drifted off to sleep, did something occur to her.

Renne, asking her if it bothered her that Palloc visited the widows.

Renne, who was herself, a widow.

Whenever Silex returned from the hunt to wherever the Wolfen had established their gathering site, he slept in a bed made comfortable by laying an elk hide over grasses gathered in the spring. Ovi slept nearby, though not too near because at night she made snorting sounds that could keep him awake. So her eyes widened in surprise when Silex came to her sleeping place and lay down next to her. There was still enough daylight left to see him, though the gloom was starting to reach out of the shadows to envelop couples in their beds.

"Ovi," Silex whispered.

She propped herself up on one elbow so that she could face him with a questioning look.

"There is something very important I need to speak to you about," he continued.

"Yes?"

He peered at her but saw no suspicion, no sign she knew he had committed adultery. "An important topic," he stalled.

Ovi merely waited.

Silex sighed. "We have never laid as man and wife, not once in all the years we have been married."

She looked at him carefully. "Is this something you want to do now?" she replied cautiously.

He pursed his lips. "Well . . . has it bothered you?"

"Bothered me?"

"Do you want me to, Ovi? Because I will. I do not wish to deny you my attentions if you desire them."

"What is this about, Silex? I have told you in the past. It was never something I enjoyed."

"What *do* you enjoy, Ovi? What makes you happy?"

"I hate it when you ask me that. Why are you always asking me that? What has brought on this concern?"

"I have recently learned that a woman might harbor desires, but feel constrained from revealing them, and that this might be a cruel thing."

"That is simply foolish. A woman does what she must, there is no *desire*," Ovi replied with just a hint of scorn. "There is just the needs of the day. And the next day. And the next, until the final peace of death. I have never felt you were cruel to me, Silex. You just do what you have to do."

"I just want you to know that I am willing, Ovi. I want to be a good husband."

"You are a good husband, Silex. Will you be sleeping here next to me tonight?" she asked neutrally.

Silex looked into her tired eyes. Nothing in their conversation had assuaged his guilt. "No, I will go back to my own bed now," he replied.

The next morning he left early, his conscience burdened, and headed toward a place where some logs had been laid against a rock, forming a protective shelter. Inside this lean-to was a sleeping area made of animal hide laid on summer grasses, and lying on the bed was his lover Denix, her arms and legs open and welcoming.

Mal skinned and butchered the lion. The meat was tough, dry, and stringy when fresh, and the strips that he hung over the fire to shrivel in the smoky air were so difficult to chew he took to softening them up in hot water before he bit off a piece. Dog, though, seemed to love the stuff, and would gnaw happily on a hunk.

The first night, Mal cooked the lion's heart over the fire on a stick, and it was the best meal he took from the animal. He was not able to make much with the rest of the organs, coming up with a stew so strong smelling that even Dog shied away from it.

"This meat will not last all winter, Dog. We must find prey, now that my mother has stopped coming."

Mal had little doubt that his mother wanted to come, and he thought he knew exactly why she was not bringing him food—somehow, Albi was preventing it.

Mal was not at the rendezvous point the first day, nor the second. Calli refused to believe he was dead—their agreement was every third day. He would come.

But the hunt returned in the morning of that third day, laden with meat, grinning with victory. At that moment,

Calli would have given anything for another time of hunger, but the Kindred were fat with their kill and unlikely to venture out for more for several more days.

Calli resolutely butchered a reindeer for the communal meal, feeling as she did a pair of eyes on her. When she looked up it was Palloc, grinning triumphantly, as if he knew exactly what she was thinking.

FIFTY-THREE

og went with Mal every day to walk through the forest, tagging along with the leather rope tied securely around her neck. Mostly, they ate worms and bugs, supplemented with chunks of tough, smoky meat. She was hungry, but the only food she ate came from Mal's hands.

When they came upon a herd of reindeer, Mal could scarcely contain his excitement. Mal proceeded on his hands and knees through the late summer grasses, silent and slow, dropping his head whenever one of the reindeer glanced over in his direction.

Dog was too short to see the prey at first, but she smelled something, and Mal's behavior enlivened her. Dog sniffed at Mal's face, panting in his ear, and gave a soft whimper.

"Shhh!" Mal warned.

Dog cocked her head, hearing something in Mal's tones but not understanding it.

And then Dog saw the reindeer. She went completely rigid, her eyes opening wide. Mal was completely unprepared when she unexpectedly lunged forward.

The rope slipped from Mal's grasp. "Dog!" he hissed, but it was too late. Scampering forward on feet too big, Dog joyously plunged directly toward the center of the herd. Mal put a hand to his mouth: both female and male reindeer had antlers—what if they lowered them to Dog, would she know to evade them?

When the ungulates saw the wolf they reacted with a panicked scramble, milling momentarily before charging off, straight toward Mal.

Gulping, Mal stood up, his spear at the ready. The motion alerted the stampeding animals and they veered, but several were close and Mal let fly and, to his shock, solidly struck an adult female in the hind quarters.

The reindeer stumbled, but then righted itself and thundered off with the rest of its herd, Dog streaking off after them.

"Dog!" Mal wailed at her retreating form. He ran as fast as he could, chasing the dust and the animal tracks.

This was his worst fear: Dog, barely bigger than a puppy, off on her own, where countless predators might view her as an easy meal, or other wolves might swoop in and eliminate her as a threat.

The reindeer, he knew, could run a long way, and would definitely do so with a wolf on their heels. Dog, on the other hand, was tired and hungry—how long would she go?

Some distance, Mal found. The sun had noticeably moved in the sky when without warning the grasses parted and Dog bounded up to him, her tongue lolling out of her saliva-flecked mouth.

"Dog!" Mal called in relief. He tackled the wolf and the two of them rolled on the ground for a moment, his face buried in her fur. "Do not run away like that again," he scolded happily. But he gave her the last bit of lion meat from his pouch. They were now out of lion altogether. He scooped up the rope. "Let us find our kill, Dog. We will eat reindeer meat tonight."

No, they would not. The herd was easy enough to follow, even when they slowed and their hooves no longer chewed the soil. There was a nice blood trail, and at one point they came across Mal's spear. "They will stop soon and the female I speared will lie down," Mal reasoned aloud. Reindeer were grazing animals who would drop their heads to the grass as soon as the immediate threat of the wolf passed, but for some reason they kept moving on this day, and after a time Mal found out why.

A bear had taken the wounded reindeer. Its chuffing sounded mocking and triumphant as it tore at the kill. Mal put his hand on Dog's snout, willing her not to growl at the sight, and he did not linger, but turned and walked away immediately, lest the bear's bloodlust find them and decide to add man and wolf to the dinner.

"We will find some worms along the stream," Mal murmured to Dog. "Do not worry, we will eat something."

They found very little before the darkness forced them to retreat to their cave. They entered through the back way, Mal moving aside the heavy stone he had put in place to keep other animals out, returning it to its position once they were inside.

They settled on the wolf fur, Dog curling up and putting her head on his chest. He ran his hands over her soft fur, grinning with the pleasure of it.

As he fell asleep, his empty stomach growling angrily, Mal remembered something: the bones of an elk leg, thrusting up out of the wet, white ice far upstream. The meat had long ago been stripped off by birds and the eroding forces of sun and wind, but the bones might contain marrow. It would certainly be better tasting than the fat purple worms he had just eaten. He could break the bones and see, anyway.

Tomorrow, Mal thought to himself. He would go tomorrow.

* * *

Some days Silex's conscience would disturb his peace, forcing him into uneasy wanderings close to the gathering site. He did not know what he would do if his secrets were revealed, nor what the Wolfen would do. He felt shame and anguish and yet could not even contemplate being without Denix.

The air was dry and cool and Silex carried his spear with him when he came upon the hyena. It was on the other side of a field, just on the edge of the woods. Silex sucked in a breath, staring, feeling his heart rate increase.

The spiritual opposite of the beautiful wolf, the hyena was an evil canid, ugly and sly, who made humanlike sounds and fed on rotting meat. They were fortunately extremely rare and Silex had never laid eyes on one, though the day many years ago, when his father had stumbled and shattered his ankle, on that black day, his father claimed to have seen a pack of the beasts stripping the flesh off a dead bison.

And now Silex had stumbled upon one, a hundred paces away—just one. What did it mean, to see a lone hyena? No campfire stories ever told of the predators as anything but pack animals. What horrible thing did its appearance portend?

The hideous beast was feeding on what looked to be a dead marmot. It was aware of Silex and kept shooting him baleful glances. Silex tightened his grip on his spear. Should he try to kill it?

There was something wrong with its front leg, Silex realized. It limped as it moved, not letting the right foot touch the ground. Was that why it was hunting alone?

Silex realized he had no choice. He needed to kill this hyena, because if he did not, surely he would return to the gathering site and find his tribe standing in condemnation against his adultery. That had to be the message that the canid was here to deliver. The tribe might even demand Denix be punished, though none of this was her fault—it was all his weakness that kept him returning to her bed.

Without a sound, Silex charged across the field.

The hyena snarled, making its grotesque, snuffling noises. Silex raised his spear, still too far away, and the beast picked up the marmot in its bloody jaws and turned, dashing for the woods in an awkward three-legged gait.

Silex followed into the woods and stopped, panting, looking about in disbelief. The hyena had vanished as if swallowed by the trees.

This was truly a grim adumbration, far worse than if the ugly animal had merely gotten away.

Dismally, Silex turned back toward the gathering site. He knew he would tell no one about what he had just seen, not even Denix.

Mal tied Dog to a tree near the base of the wall of white ice, and then stood looking uncertainly at the leg bones poking forlornly at the sky. He had no idea what it meant that the bones were there, nor any good plan for breaking them out. The ice was hard and coated with a thin layer of water, making climbing all but impossible.

The ice lay against a steep, rocky hill. Clutching his club, Mal gingerly worked his way upward, rock to rock, testing each move before he made it.

Below him, Dog yipped, and when Mal glanced down the wolf spun in a frustrated circle. "No Dog, all is good. Stay quiet," Mal told her.

When he was a little more than four men high, Mal was parallel to the bones. He was able to slide sideways along the rock wall until he was right next to them. This close, he could see a dark shadow inside the ice just below where the bones tilted skyward. The knee was just visible in the ice.

He swung his stone-headed club, which bounced off the ice wall with a spray of particles. He wanted to hit the knee, to sever the leg cleanly, but his awkward position made it difficult to swing accurately. He shifted his good leg and tried again, giving it several hard whacks.

He did hit the knee, but mostly he hit the ice. He stopped, frowning. He had exposed something near the knee with his errant club strikes. He leaned closer, wiping irritably at a trickle of cold water that dripped onto his forehead.

It was elk hide.

Mal stood, considering. Could there be more elk beneath the frozen water? How was that possible?

He threw himself into an attack on the ice, grunting as he bashed the hard, slick surface, which yielded grudgingly. When he fatigued, he leaned forward and wiped away the accumulated crystals and water. He had exposed a little less than half a finger length's worth of elk, but it was enough to see that under the ice, there was more than just bone.

"Meat!" Mal called down to Dog. "I have found us meat!"

He began bashing away with abandon, throwing all his strength into it, and was rewarded by a cracking sound and tremors traveling up and down the frozen surface. What if there was not just a leg, but an entire elk in there?

Suddenly there was a bang as loud as thunder and the ice fell away, striking Mal on the back. He toppled forward, hitting the cold, hard surface, and tumbled with it, sliding and bouncing and shouting. There was no way to stop—his club fell from his hands and he cried out, digging for purchase, tumbling toward the ground.

* * *

Dog did not understand. She was frantic to follow the man, who was above her, playing with a heavy stick. Loud thumps sounded each time he swung the branch, releasing a spray of wet drops that brought his scent cascading to the ground.

She had grown accustomed to the leather strap and even had come to regard it as something that attached her to the man, but now it restrained her attempts to get to him.

When, with a loud crack, the ground fell away and the man slipped, she could sense the fear in his voice. His slide stopped at her feet and she jumped on him, licking his cheeks. "Dog!" he laughed. He sat up and reached for her, and she nuzzled him in relief. She did not like this game, but she craved being hugged by him. "I love you, Dog," he said.

The warmth that flowed through her at his embrace was reminiscent of the sensation of nursing from her mother.

Mal retrieved his club and surveyed what he had done. In his fall he had imagined the entire wall of ice collapsing, but from his perspective now he could see that he had only managed to dislodge a chunk the size of a few men.

His elk had fallen with the avalanche and would be much easier to access now, but that was not what drew Mal's astonished stare. Instead he was looking up where he had just been, focused on a dark shadow that appeared close to the surface of the translucent ice, entirely visible and identifiable as belonging to an elk.

There was another one.

The ground around the ice wall was frozen—Mal used a stone to smash a hole, filled the evacuation with chunks of ice, and stored his frozen bounty there, planning to return to hack off pieces and thaw them for cooking as needed.

Meanwhile the wall itself yielded up more than just another elk; chipping away, Mal found a young reindeer. For some reason, the animals up top were venturing too close to the edge and sliding off to their deaths, eventually being buried in the steady accumulation of frozen water. The white wall was actually nothing other than a huge number of ice tongues, many as thick as a man's chest, but many thin and breakable. When he threw these to Dog, she pounced and crunched them up as if they were bones.

With food in hand, Mal and Dog worked on the commands that would keep her safe. "Dog! To me, Dog!" he called to her many times a day. They also worked on "remain," which seemed to go against Dog's nature. With frequent repetition, though, she came to understand both the word and the accompanying gestures, and also to obey the command "away."

Now he could have her run away if there was danger, and call her back to him when the threat had passed. When they hunted, he would be able to control her, keep her from harm.

She was gaining weight, though Mal could still easily pick her up. Her feet were ridiculously large for her body and she seemed to trip over them when she ran, but standing on all fours her head was above Mal's knees. She followed him everywhere, so he knew she would be upset when he walled her in the cave one morning. "I will be back before sunset," he promised her. Dog curled up on her mother's fur and watched alertly as Mal wrestled a heavy rock over to block the back exit, but sprang to her feet and whimpered when he climbed up the narrow crevice, yipping at him, heartbroken, when he pulled himself up at the top.

"I'll be back, I promise," he told her. "Remain!"

FIFTY-FOUR

Lyra had spent the better part of the morning in her cave, working on the project that had consumed her that summer—painting a herd of reindeer, one animal at a time. Her fingers were black from the carbon she extracted from fires and ground up into a paste with a little water, and her nails were red from the rouge, an effect she found she actually liked. Now she squatted by the stream, lightly singing to herself as she patiently washed her hands, trying to rinse enough off so that her hands merely appeared dirty.

She stood abruptly when she heard something approaching from the north. Should she run, or hide? Frozen in indecision, her legs tense, she held her breath.

"Lyra," someone called.

Kindred. A male. She sighed the tension out of her lungs. "Here," she called back. She waited by the stream and was shocked at who emerged from the bushes. "Mal!"

He grinned at her. "Good summer! I hoped I would find you here. It was not easy; I had to make a long path to avoid the Kindred camp."

She looked around wildly. Her expression was anything but welcoming. "You should not be here!"

He blinked past his hurt. "What do you mean?"

"Grat and Vinco often wander down here looking for me."

"Oh." Mal shrugged. "I am not afraid of them," he

claimed, prevaricating only a little bit. He did not want to talk about Grat or Vinco, he wanted to talk about himself and Lyra. His heart was beating a little, thinking of what he might say to her.

Lyra came up to him, her eyes searching his face. "You have gotten taller."

Mal drew himself up. "I have?"

"Yes, and bigger." She gestured to her own shoulders.

"What happened to your hair?" he asked. Somehow, her hair was both short and blunt, ending in an outlandishly uniform fashion.

Now it was her turn to look hurt. "You do not like it?"

"I have just never seen this. What do you call it?"

"I do not call it anything, it is just my hair. I lay down on a flat rock and Felka poured wet sand around my head. Then she laid a flaming stick on the dry hair and burned it off. See? It is not as long and I like that the ends are all even."

"Do all the women do this now?"

"Why would that matter?"

He frowned. She seemed angry at him. "I think it is very beautiful," he finally said.

A smile twitched onto her lips. "Thank you. My mother is not happy with it, though."

"Well. You do not often seem to care what your mother thinks."

Her smile grew broader. "And you look . . . well, you look well. Mal, I have been so very worried about you. How are you able to eat?"

"I, uh, hunt." Mal surprised himself by lying. "I killed a lion, too." Doubt crept into Lyra's eyes as she sensed duplicity, and Mal was angry at himself. Obviously she thought he was untruthful about the lion and honest about hunting, when the reverse was true. But to explain would be to waste time. "I wanted to see you," he said simply.

Her look softened. "I wanted to see you, too. But the women's council has decided we cannot." Lyra glanced involuntarily at Mal's leg.

"Yes, I know. The curse," Mal agreed flatly. "But I think of you, Lyra, I think of you often, and I, I . . ." Words fled from his mouth and he stood there unable to say more.

"It is so strange to contemplate you living by yourself. But I believe your mother did the right thing—Albi is an awful woman with a powerful obsession."

"Do you believe I am a curse?"

"I do not, no."

"Then perhaps I do not need to live by myself," he suggested boldly.

He hated the look in her eyes, read it as pity, as a woman telling a man that his affections were hopeless and unrequited. He glanced away. "I suppose I should leave. Good summer, Lyra."

"Wait."

He turned to her. Her eyes were grave. "Think of what you are suggesting, Mal. Are you telling me that this is what you would want for me? That I would leave my family, my parents, and the Kindred? That I would be safe and happy?"

Mal sighed deeply. "You have always been so forthright, Lyra. I admire you for it. No, I cannot promise any of those things. But I will not always be banished. I will think of a way to return."

"What you should do is follow us a day behind when we migrate."

He shook his head. "Why does everyone assume I cannot survive on my own? You forget—with no one else to feed, a single kill of a hoofed animal can last me a long time." Of course, he did have a voracious young wolf to feed, but he was not going to tell her that.

"I did forget," she admitted.

"When I return to the Kindred next summer, everyone will be astonished I have prevailed over winter and I will be accepted as a true hunter."

She pressed her lips together, presenting a fragile smile. "Do you have the rope I gave you?"

"Yes. It has been very helpful to me." He wondered how Lyra would react if he said, *I use it to restrain my wolf.*

With summer ending soon, Mal took stock of his preparations. As he had told Lyra, an entire elk was a lot of food, so much that he felt rich with it. It gave him time to accumulate other provisions—he found the dark berries that would dry well in the sun, eating his fill as he pulled them from the bushes. Dog saw him putting food in his mouth and stared expectantly, but when Mal tossed her a berry, the wolf spat it out, wrinkling her nose and looking so disgusted Mal had to laugh.

The acorns proved to be more problematic. Calli had shown Mal how there were similar-looking nuts that were actually poisonous, so he knew which ones to gather. But the act of building a pile, soaking them in water made scalding by adding sizzling rocks from the fire, then cracking off the thin shells with his fingernails, took many days and when he was finished he had so little to show for his labors he finally understood why the Kindred always quickly went through their supply of nuts every winter. Mal had always assumed it was because the women harvesting the small acorns were lazy—now he understood just how hard they were working. At least Dog ate the nuts, though, crunching them up eagerly. If he ran out of meat, the nuts would give them something to eat.

Until he ran out of nuts.

Mal allowed Dog off rope more and more often, guiding

her not with the leather strap but with voice and hand. It gave both of them more freedom to explore the northern wilds.

In search of more elk in ice, Mal and Dog climbed a steep hill not far from the white wall where he had found the frozen animals. Once at the peak, he gazed in astonishment at the terrain: despite the many days of summer, he had found a place of winter. As far as he could see, ice lay on the ground, much of it cracked and jumbled. To the left, a forest of dead trees grew out of the ice, most of the trunks canted at a steep angle, as if arrested in the act of falling over. A cold wind blew off this desert of frozen water, though that was not the only reason Mal felt a chill—this was a bad place, a place where neither sun nor summer could defeat evil. As quickly as he could, the two of them climbed back down.

Lyra did not understand why she cried so brokenly when Mal left her. She saw herself as a smart person—her father, Valid, had always praised her wit and intelligence. She knew that there was nothing that could be done for Mal at the moment—the "curse" was a wicked and guileful manipulation by a wicked woman, but the others on the council lacked either the courage or sagacity to challenge Albi's assertions. Yet that did not mean she should leave her family fire and, at age fifteen, go to live with Mal.

Her father would never approve of any relationship with a cripple. Her mother would declare against it in council. Her affections for Mal were familial, originating with the assumption that she would marry his brother, and she often sternly reminded herself that he could never be more than a childhood friend. She was smart enough to know this.

So why was she crying?

When she heard her mother, Sidee, calling for her, Lyra hastily wiped her eyes. "Here, Mother!" she responded, running down the path. "Coming!"

Sidee was standing with her arms folded. "What were you doing?"

"Nothing."

"I have come because the women's council has decided it is time to migrate. We leave in three days."

"But, it seems so early!" Lyra looked around her at the trees, which were not yet even beginning to change colors.

"Bellu is nervous about having her baby during our journey, though we all know it is too soon. But Albi says it is not worth the risk."

"Oh Albi. I see." Lyra looked in the direction Mal had gone.

"Grat tells me you come to this area all the time."

"Grat," Lyra repeated contemptuously. She made to move past her mother and head back to the settlement, but Sidee stopped her.

"Lyra. What are you doing here?"

"Just . . ." Lyra shrugged.

"Show me."

"All is good," Lyra agreed. No one knew about her cave drawings but Mal. It would be nice to include her family—they would all be so proud of her. She led her mother to the cave mouth. Inside, the torch was still burning, and it brightened when Lyra added some grasses and blew on it. She gestured proudly, the flames dancing across her deer, her rhinoceros, her mammoth. "I put the images on the wall using char from cold fires."

"What are these things?" Sidee demanded stiffly, her face cold.

"They are animals. See?" Lyra traced her elk with a finger.

"This is horrible."

"What?" Lyra replied, dumbfounded.

"I have never felt so betrayed."

"Betrayed? What do you mean?"

"We must leave this place and you are never to come here again. Do you hear my words? These treacherous, despicable marks are unforgivable." Sidee's eyes were hard. "You make your garments different from anyone else's. You wear"—Sidee gestured at Lyra's necklace—"decorations. You burned your hair! You are disrespectful and deceitful to your mother. From this point forward you may wear nothing different than what I wear, you will stop burning your hair, and you may not put flowers in it unless I have first done so. *You will stop acting as if you are better than me.*"

For the second time that day, the tears were flowing down Lyra's face. "No, no," she pleaded. "I have never said I was better than anyone else."

"Your name is derived from the day you added words to a wedding sing. Now every wedding has these words. It is humiliating to be your mother."

"Mother," Lyra begged, weeping.

"I will be glad to have you leave our family area to live with your husband."

Lyra froze. "What do you mean?"

"That is the other news. It is decided. This winter, at the weddings, you will be married to Grat." Sidee turned her back on her daughter. "You are his problem, now."

FIFTY-FIVE

The Kindred's journey south progressed well, Albi remarking casually that the main difference was that the boy with the cursed leg was no longer with them.

Calli cried brokenly as they left camp. No one spoke to her, or tried to comfort her. She was in pain, but they all knew it was for the best.

Grat, as a stalker for the hunt, was up toward the front during the day, but when the Kindred halted he sought out his betrothed, Lyra, who responded to his conversational gambits by fleeing to her family fire.

"He is following me, Father, everywhere I go," Lyra hissed to Valid.

"As he should. You are to be his wife," Sidee interjected. "Go back out there and sit with him."

"He is a cruel man and I will not."

Valid pursed his lips unhappily. "He was cruel to you?"

"Not to her," Sidee corrected angrily. "She means to the cripple."

"I am sure it will be soon that he will do the same to me," Lyra asserted.

Valid straightened. "He may not do that."

"Oh Valid, you are letting her lie to you. He will not touch her in any way not appropriate and we all know this to be true," Sidee snapped.

Valid's eyes were warm with sympathy for Lyra. Sidee

wanted to scream at him. Instead she called to where Grat lingered at a respectful distance. "Grat! Please come join your family."

Smiling broadly, Grat trotted over. "Mother," he greeted. "Father." He took a breath and turned to Lyra. "Wife," he said softly.

Lyra turned from his grin and stared north, back in the direction from which they had come.

While Silex and Denix were searching for the missing she-wolf with the handprint marking, a storm swept through, and they had holed up in a small cave for shelter, kept warm by a fire and each other. Separated from the rest of the Wolfen, it reminded Silex of when he and Fia were together—a comparison he could now contemplate without guilt or guile.

After mating Silex and Denix would remain locked together, her legs around his back, his arms hugging her shoulders, their breath warm on each other's faces, his beard brushing her cheeks. "When I was a boy my father and some men went hunting and found nothing for a full six days," Silex confided to his lover as they lay thus embraced one afternoon. "I have never been so hungry, and when we at last found some fat geese who could not fly and chased them down, we cooked the meat and burned our lips on the food. I was compelled beyond reason to feed myself, consumed with it like a fever. This is like that. Meeting you here. Lying with you."

Denix smiled into his eyes. "So in this telling, I am a fat goose who burns your lips?"

Silex laughed gently. "Your kisses scorch me, yes. But I crave them all the same." He traced her lovely mouth with a light fingertip. "Your kisses are perfect because your mouth is perfect," he murmured.

They gently decoupled, the cool air rushing to fill the space they had emptied between them. Silex reached for their furs.

"Silex," Denix said in a low voice. "It is very important to you to keep this secret, is it not? Us, to keep us secret from the rest of the Wolfen."

Silex regarded her gravely. "You have brought this up before, and you know it is. I have made much of the need to keep wedding vows inviolate. If we were to be found out, it would be seen as a great hypocrisy."

"And then what would happen? No one would challenge you, Silex. You would still be our leader."

Silex sighed. "We have cause for optimism, but we are not yet of sufficient numbers to survive as a tribe. So few children live to the age where they can hunt. I believe that if people's faith in me should falter, it might be the one thing to defeat us. Every pack needs a dominant male—when he becomes old or sick, a new leader is required or the pack fails. Cragg is not yet old enough to lead, and I see no one else to take over should I falter. Well, except you."

"What?" Denix responded, astonished.

"You are still my best hunter. I do believe that if something were to happen to me, the Wolfen would be best with you as leader."

"You are serious," Denix stated.

"Of course."

"You have always seen more in me than anyone, Silex. This is just one of the reasons I love you so."

He reached out and stroked her hair. "And I love you, Denix."

Her expression turned serious. "Yet if, as you speculate,

people found out about us and it led to them losing faith in you, they certainly would not turn to me instead."

"No, that is true," Silex agreed. His gaze was intent. "What is it you are leading me to, Denix? I feel as if you are stalking a subject but have not yet pounced."

"I have not bled for some time, Silex. I believe I am pregnant with your baby."

Dog had come to build such a strong association with the utterance "Dog" that when she thought of herself she heard the sound in her mind. Dog. She was Dog.

She did not like it when the man took the lion-thing and wrapped it around himself. Dog had become accustomed to seeing him put on and take off animal hides and it no longer mystified her—he had furs and sometimes carried them around all day on his back. This, though, was different, causing her mild distress—she was made uneasy with the smell of dead lion, especially when it moved with him. Nor was she pleased when Mal looped the rope around her neck: of late, she had been spending more time off leash, playing the game where she tried to figure out what Mal wanted her to do and, when she was successful, he gave her a morsel of meat. On leash, they did not play the game as often.

For Dog, even more rewarding than the food was her man's affection and approval. She would squirm with pure pleasure when he put his hands on her and stroked her fur and brought his face to hers.

"I am going to my home, to see the Kindred," he told her. "To convince them I am no threat, before they migrate and we are left behind." He shoved aside the heavy rock blocking the exit and together the two of them crawled out into the early morning sunshine.

The man carried the thick branch with the rock at the end.

"I will approach them as if I were a member of the Blanc Tribe. I will offer to trade this dried elk meat for some nuts." He patted the pelt at his side and an enticing flood of odors met Dog's nose. "They will see me wearing lion, and that I have meat—I am a man, not a boy. A man who walks with a wolf, though I will not reveal that today, but will have you remain nearby. I will stay only a moment, so they understand I do not need them. They will realize the extent to which they underestimated my ability to survive. And they must allow me to see my mother. And Lyra. And eventually, after many visits, they will let me back in. I will be unbanished."

They walked a path, and Dog could smell the animals that had been there before, and the scents her man had laid down. Sometimes the stream was close, and other times it went away, but Dog could always smell the water. When she stopped to take a drink, her man stopped with her, and she sensed him caring about her and it made her want to stop for water more often, just to feel his affection in those moments.

After the better part of a day, Dog felt her man's rising anxiety, and it made her tense. "Why are there no fires in the air? What are we walking into, Dog?" Her man looked up at the sky. "It is too early for them to have left on migration."

They came to a place where many dead fire smells mingled with people odors. "No!" her man shouted. Dog yawned nervously, panting, unsure what was happening, why he was so distressed.

"They left, Dog. They are gone. We are now truly on our own."

Silex awoke at dawn. His first thought was of Denix and her unborn child, the pregnancy that was only beginning to pronounce itself. He would have to tell Ovi soon.

He yawned. During the night he had been aware of his sons returning to camp, and was looking forward to hearing about the wolf pack. The young men had gone out with the intention of seeing if the massive female with the white markings above her eyes had brought her young to the howling site.

His sons Cragg and Tok were sitting by the fire. Their faces were grim, alarming Silex. "Has something happened to the pack?" Silex asked anxiously.

The young men glanced at each other. "Father," Cragg said, "we have seen something repugnant."

Silex crouched next to them, warming himself. It was still early enough in the day that the light from the fire flickered in his sons' eyes. "Tell me."

"There is a man, a Kindred, and he has captured a wolf."

Silex frowned in noncomprehension. "Captured? What do you mean?"

"The wolf is fastened to a rope that the Kindred carries in his hand," Cragg responded.

"A rope?" Silex repeated incredulously. "How would a rope save a man from a wolf?"

"The rope encircles the wolf's neck and perhaps it chokes her air," Cragg speculated. "We do not know why the wolf does not turn on the Kindred, only that she is forced to remain captive."

"We stalked them for three days," Tok added.

Silex sat back, his face a study in disbelief.

"It is an abomination. He has enslaved the wolf," Cragg stated emphatically.

"Could this man, could he be a wolf as well, Father?" asked Tok.

Cragg shook his head impatiently. "I have been telling Tok that this cannot be. The man is evil, an evil aberration."

"What should we do?" Tok asked respectfully.

"We must end this horror," Cragg argued.

"It *is* unnatural," Tok agreed, "but I am unsure, Brother, that it is our place to interfere."

They all looked to their father. Silex rubbed his jaw thoughtfully. "An enslaved wolf," he murmured. "I question whether you correctly interpreted what you saw. Such a thing defies my mind."

"The man has a stunted leg," Tok added.

Silex gasped. "*Are you sure?*"

His sons seemed taken aback by his reaction. "Yes, Father."

"A lone man with a stunted leg holds a wolf prisoner," Silex summed up, his face grim. The vision of the hyena in the field made sense to him now. "You can find this man, if you go back out?"

"Of course," Cragg replied simply. They were Wolfen; they could track anything.

"Then we must go find this abhorrence, and we must kill him and set free the wolf," Silex answered. "It is the only thing to do."

The Kindred were well practiced at moving swiftly upon dawn's light. Mothers took charge of their children, while the men of the hunt arrayed themselves at the front of the migration. Valid was therefore somewhat surprised when his youngest son, Magnus, trotted breathlessly up to him when the sun was overhead and the Kindred were starting to walk more slowly, anticipating the midday meal. Magnus was eleven summers old and not yet a member of the hunt, so his appearance was irregular.

"Father," Magnus panted.

"Slow down, Son. What have you come to tell me?"

"Mother said we cannot find Lyra. Your pouch, and our

family's food, is also missing. She does not know how to feed us."

"I do not understand what you are telling me, Magnus. Where is Lyra?"

"I do not know. Mother said that is what to tell you. We cannot find Lyra and Mother does not know how to feed us."

Urs approached. "What has brought your son to the front?" he asked Valid.

Valid shrugged. "I am not sure. Sidee has somehow lost our food, and Lyra is once again evading her."

"It is not unusual for a woman Lyra's age to have disagreements with her mother," Urs observed, smiling.

"This is even more true in our family," Valid agreed ruefully.

"Would Lyra have hidden your food, out of anger, perhaps?"

Valid shook his head. "That, no, does not seem like her." He turned toward his son. "Lyra might be accomplished at concealing herself from her mother, but you and your friends can easily catch her. I am sure she is lurking nearby." Valid gestured to the sparse trees, well spaced but thick enough to hide behind. "Tell your friends that the one who finds her will be gifted a wolf's tooth from my collection."

"All is good. We will search again."

Magnus turned to sprint away, but Valid held up his hand. "Wait. What do you mean? Have you already looked for her?"

"It is what we have been doing all morning."

Valid and Urs stared at each other. Then they both turned and looked north.

"She cannot have run off," Valid whispered. "Surely she would not do something like that."

FIFTY-SIX

S idee had collapsed and Calli was at her side, holding
her hand. Word had swept through the Kindred: Lyra
had run away.

Valid and his sons Ligo and Magnus were assembling
their weapons, and men and women were gathering around
to watch. Urs assessed the grim determination in his friend's
eyes. "Valid. You cannot leave. We must continue south."

Valid shook his head. "I have to do this, Urs."

Urs turned a furious glare on the onlookers. "Leave us!"
he bellowed. They dispersed hurriedly, scattering away and
forming smaller groups to eat the midday meal, glancing
over at Valid and Urs as often as they dared.

Grat rushed up. "I have just heard," he declared.

"We leave now," Valid replied.

"I will go with you," Grat stated.

"No you will *not*," Urs corrected icily. "Valid, I cannot
allow this."

"Please, Valid, you cannot leave me alone!" Sidee
pleaded.

"She is our *daughter*," Valid snapped.

"She has left to be with the cripple! It is her choice, Valid,"
Sidee responded. Grat stared at her, shocked. Calli's eyes
widened.

"Listen to me now," Urs said forcefully, his voice hard.
Valid's sons stared solemnly at the hunt master, and even
Valid seemed unsettled by his friend's tone. "This is not

allowed. You are spear master and needed here, with your tribe."

"Urs. She slipped away just before there was light in the sky, and she must be following our tracks back. She cannot be more than half a day behind us. We will close on her within a day or two at the most," Valid reasoned.

"And then what? In two days' time, we will be much farther south. You will not be able to catch up with us for the rest of the migration. No, Valid, you may not go."

"Urs, do not ask this of me," Valid begged.

Urs stepped closer. "Valid. I have lost a child and I know the pain that comes with it. I cannot tell you how sorry I am. And I promise you, when we return next summer you may take all the men you want and go kill the cripple, if he survives. Kill him and, if she is alive, retrieve your daughter."

Calli stared in horror. Urs seemed to have forgotten she was there.

"But for now, this is the way it must be. I must have you with your tribe now, Valid. With the hunt. There will be no going back."

Calli glanced down and saw triumph in Sidee's eyes. Suddenly filled with loathing for all of them, she dropped Sidee's hand and stood. Valid gave her a pained look, parting his lips as if to say something, but Calli walked away without a backward glance.

After the midday meal, the Kindred reorganized and fell back into step. The momentary flurry concerning Lyra was gratefully forgotten—they were migrating, as they always did, and there was comfort in this.

Calli found she could meet no one's gaze. She plodded along, her expression blank, eyes dark. If Lyra managed to survive and find Mal, the two of them together might stand a better chance of enduring the winter, but then in the summer the men of the Kindred would track them down and kill her son. Either way, her son would perish.

L yra spent most of the first day glancing back over her shoulder, watching for her father.

She knew exactly what would happen. At first light, Sidee would notice her daughter was missing and alert her family. The Kindred would pause the migration and Valid would grab Ligo and come get her.

When he caught up with her, she knew her father would be furious. She would accept his anger and any punishment, but then he would see how serious she was. She would rather come out here and die than marry Grat.

Her father would not let that happen.

She was deliberately slow as she retraced well-tracked ground along the river, lingering for a long time over her midday meal. The farther she went, the angrier her father would be.

At a pretty spot by the stream, she sat and composed herself, waiting. She had rested fitfully the night before and her muscles were tired from days of walking, so it was not long before she had drifted off, sleeping in the sun.

When she awoke, the light in the sky was orange. Shocked, she realized she would have to spend the night alone. She quickly gathered as much wood as she could find, striking her flint so that when night came, she had the stream to her back and the fire warding off the darkness in front of her. She tamped down her fear by reminding herself that Mal had lived alone the entire summer.

She slept a little, but awoke when she heard wolves howling in the distance. She put more wood on the fire and stared at the flames, hugging her knees. For the first time, she allowed herself to contemplate that her father might not be coming.

D enix found Ovi standing by the river. It was as Silex described it—Ovi seemed to be watching the waters, swollen with recent rains, as if waiting for something. Denix observed her staring, not moving, for a long time before finally calling out.

"Ovi."

Silex's wife and sister turned, blinking. She did not respond or raise her hand in acknowledgment.

"I was told you might be here," Denix greeted, walking up to the other woman. "I think we have a lot to talk about."

Ovi turned back to look at the water. "We do?"

Denix frowned. Her whole life, Ovi had been such a mystery to her. "Silex advised me he told you about . . . about my pregnancy."

A black branch floated slowly past, and Ovi watched it. "Yes," she agreed softly. "He told me."

"Ovi, I am sorry. I never wanted to hurt you."

"All is good."

"No, Ovi. Please talk to me. Are you angry?"

Ovi gazed at Denix, her expression implacable. "I am not angry with you, Denix. What would be the point? It is done."

Though it was ridiculous, Denix found *herself* getting angry. "I have fornicated with your husband and gotten pregnant as a result. I do not believe you when you say you do not care."

"Oh, I care," Ovi responded faintly. "You have given me a gift."

Denix paused, puzzled. "I do not understand. A gift?"

"A release. Is the river not beautiful, this time of year?

So deep and dark. Standing here, I often see ice floating on the surface."

"Ice."

"Whatever feeds this river must live in winter. Did you know I fell in at the end of summer, when I was a small child?" Ovi asked. "It was this time of year, and here, where it is unusually deep. My father saved me. I remember how numb I was in the water. No pain. No feeling at all. Just the dark current, pulling me along."

"I did not know about this. It was before I was born."

"It was a long time ago," Ovi affirmed wistfully. "Times were so easy then. Not like now, where every day is such a struggle. I am so weary of it all."

"I was hoping we could talk about what to tell the others. Silex is very concerned that the Wolfen will react badly, but I believe it has a lot to do with how *you* behave, Ovi. He has shared with me that you and he have never been together as man and woman in your bed. If you would tell everyone that you have no objection to me filling that role, I think my news will not cause the harm that Silex fears."

An ironic but unreadable twitch touched the corners of Ovi's mouth. "I think all is good. No harm will be caused by this."

Denix nodded. "That is good of you, Ovi. Perhaps—"

"I really want to be left alone now," Ovi interrupted. She fixed Denix with bland eyes. "I like to look at the river."

"All is good," Denix replied. "I will let you have solitude."

Denix withdrew. Ovi turned back to the river, nodding. "Solitude," she repeated to herself. It was a good word to describe what she craved. She stepped out of her garments, wincing as she waded up to her ankles in the shockingly cold water. She stood for a moment, then took another step.

The numbness came after a time, encouraging her to go deeper, swim out into the currents.

Solitude.

On the second day, Lyra added wet wood to her fire and let it cloud the air with thick black smoke that rose high, visible for miles. Now her father would know exactly where to look. As the day grew long, though, Lyra ventured north, remembering some small caves where her tribe always made camp during their migrations. They were farther upstream than she recalled, but there was still enough sunshine when she came upon the place to allow her to find wood for her fire. After eating from her dwindling supply of food from her father's pouch, Lyra crawled into a small cave and put her hands over her face and sobbed until she slept.

She awoke and faced two choices: go north, back to summer quarters, and try to find Mal, or trek south in pursuit of her tribe, taking her past the entrance to the Cohort Valley. Either way, she would likely run out of food, and she had no way to hunt for herself, though she knew some trees along the stream would still have fruit on them.

She could no longer be sure of her father's support in her stand against marriage to Grat. He had not come after her! Grieving, she remembered sitting in his lap and singing him songs when she was a little girl. Her tears turned bitter, though, when she thought of her mother. Perhaps Father had not tried to find her because Sidee would not let him.

She made up her mind and went north. Mal knew how to survive in the wilds on his own. He would take her in. She smiled when she imagined how he would react to her unexpected appearance.

Then her eyes widened as she let her thoughts float farther along on the fantasy. They would spend the winter together, perhaps in Bellu's cave. It would be as if she were married to Mal, instead of Grat.

Married to Mal. No council to prevent it, no mother to trade her off like an elk hide. Was that what she wanted?

When Lyra thought of her life, Mal was always there, entwined into her memories like the delicate flowers woven into the vines around her wrist. He was a man like her father, thoughtful and kind. He had Dog's smile and seemed so wise compared to others his age.

When the Kindred returned and she rejoined her family, there would be no question of Lyra marrying Grat, because she would be married to Mal.

Yes. It was what she wanted.

She began singing as she walked, interweaving "Mal" and "marriage" into her happy tones. Breaking free of Sidee had liberated her feelings. She was on her way to be with Mal.

She abruptly went quiet when she heard something large rustling in the woods. Unbidden, scary stories from her childhood came to mind—though she was far away from the river junction that marked Cohort territory, the fierce man hunters were said to be lurking everywhere, seeking to snatch the defenseless and take them away. She was far from home, a woman alone out in the forest. Heart pounding, she peered into the thick trees, catching her breath when something big and dark moved ponderously, snapping a twig underfoot. A cold eye regarded her and she exhaled—just a reindeer, a big male. Some females became visible with their motion as well. Just a herd.

Then Lyra remembered something her father told her—where there were prey animals, there were often predators tracking them.

She was not safe here.

Lyra ran and her terror ran with her, pursuing her like a

hungry lion. She imagined wolves and bears and horrible fangs and vicious claws. She wanted her father, her brothers, her tribe to come save her. She wanted Mal.

She found a place where she could lean branches on some rocks and crawled in underneath and lay trembling. The fire she built did not quite give her comfort, and thinking of Mal no longer warmed her. Nothing was worth this, not even being able to marry the man she felt sure she loved.

She had made a terrible mistake.

She barely slept—every noise in the night had been something coming for her, and the leaping shadows from her fire seemed deadly living things. No singing, this day. She could only keep marching forward, with no thought but getting to Mal.

The next day presented her with a choice: the stream bent away from her, off to her woman's side, but the Kindred always marched straight along the path. Her father once told her that if they stuck to the stream it eventually rejoined the path, but they always chose to spend the day away from water, though mothers would soak elk hide and squeeze it into their children's mouths whenever the sun was hot.

She could last the day without refreshment—she needed to make progress. She hated, though, that this meant leaving the trees. She strode along under the cloudless skies, exposed in yellow grasses that came up to her knees in some places. Any predator could see her, here.

She had settled into a dull plod for some time when she glanced back to check her progress, and she gasped in surprise. Far in the distance, some men were coming toward her. Father? She held her hand up to shield her eyes and stared. There were three of them.

They were not Kindred. Even at this distance, she could

see that their garments were crude, simple flaps of hide tied at their waist. They carried clubs and at least one spear, and they were running. Running straight at her. Their faces were oddly black, as if rubbed with dirt or ashes.

She realized who they might be.

FIFTY-SEVEN

Dog focused intently on Mal's hands. It was a routine they had gone through countless times over the summer, and Dog clearly looked forward to it, looked forward to the praise and food she would receive for doing a good job.

Mal swallowed. This was it, their first try at the strategy he hoped would help him hunt this autumn, building up food supplies before the snows came and drove away all the game.

The lesson of Dog running heedlessly into the middle of the herd of reindeer and causing them to bolt in panic toward Mal was not lost on him. If she could cause such a reaction as a pup, what would happen now, when she ran with the smooth speed of an adult?

She was not yet full grown, but Dog was already larger than many wolves Mal had seen.

A small herd of nine reindeer, probably split off from a larger group nearby, grazed comfortably fifty paces from Mal and Dog. All summer Mal had been training Dog for this moment, teaching her hand signals to replace the verbal commands he used first.

His plan was to send Dog to the woman's side until the wolf was roughly parallel to the herd. Then he would have Dog charge the herd and then, as they had practiced, Mal would wave a hand sign and Dog would come to him in a coursing, back-and-forth manner that had taken many days to master. The reindeer would run full at Mal, and he would take one square in the chest with a spear, hopefully bringing the animal down with that one shot, though he had fashioned himself another spear he could use if the opportunity presented itself.

Dog was on alert for Mal's command, unaware of the prey. Mal raised his woman's hand and Dog tensed, her mouth open slightly, eyes widening. Mal pointed. *Away.*

Dog bounded away, turning to glance back repeatedly until Mal held up his hand. *Remain.*

Dog stopped and sat, staring at Mal. Then a scent found her and she whipped her head around, noticing the herd of reindeer for the first time.

"No, Dog," Mal whispered.

Dog seemed to have forgotten Mal was there. She focused intently on the ungulates.

"Dog, remain!" Mal shouted harshly.

The reindeer raised their heads as one at this, and the action was too much for Dog, who broke training and streaked toward the animals with undisguised glee.

Mal watched in disgust as the herd swung their antlers and fled, headed in exactly the opposite direction. All the hours of lessons, tedious and repetitive, and Dog had forgotten everything.

"Dog, come to me!" Mal called. "To me!"

After an alarming amount of time, Dog finally came racing back to him, her tongue out and her mouth open, looking joyous. When she was a few feet from Mal, though, she stopped, her ears drooping and her tail down.

"That is right. I am angry at you," Mal scolded.

They went back to the cave and dined on some of the meat from the ice wall. Dog sensed something and came and rested her head in Mal's lap until he gave up and stroked her soft fur, but he remained pensive, thinking of the day's failure. They would train again tomorrow in the same spot, and perhaps the memory of reindeer would help Dog understand what was required of her.

It was very important she learn, because Dog ate so much, and long before winter's end Mal would run out of food.

D enix squatted next to Brach at the fire. "It has been three days since we found her clothing by the stream. I am afraid Ovi must have drowned."

Brach's mouth formed a sad line. "I grew up with her, she was like an older sister to me."

Denix nodded respectfully. "I have fond memories as well, though I never believed she should be wife to Silex."

"No, what you say is true."

"Silex described to me where they have gone—north of Kindred territory, along the stream. I plan to cross the river at first light and tell him, and tell Cragg and Tok about their mother."

"Be careful of that river."

"I will go to the shallows."

"I do not understand why Ovi would bathe there, where the water is so deep and the current so malevolent," Brach said finally. "This seems less an accident than a deliberate act."

"There will always be things about Ovi we will not understand," Denix ventured.

"Yes," Brach said, looking into the fire. "I do agree."

O ther than having Lyra run off, the winter migration went as well as any within Kindred memory. They were well past the river junction and therefore out of Cohort territory, so Urs took the hunt out for fresh game, allowing the stalkers to range out ahead. Soon a small noise among the spearmen told Urs, without even looking, that one of the stalkers had returned. They would have fresh meat.

It was Grat. He looked as if he had been running some distance, and he appeared agitated, his eyes wide. The scars on his face from where Mal's horn had seared him made his beard odd, the black thick hair missing in the spots where the flesh was pink. Urs always found himself staring at the burn marks, but something about Grat's expression focused Urs's attention, and he waited for Grat to catch his breath, oddly tense. This was not going to be about reindeer.

"Cohort," Grat panted.

A shock of alarm went through Urs, and he involuntarily gripped his spear. "Where?"

"Ahead in a clearing. Many hundreds of paces."

"How many Cohort?" Valid pressed, his face pale with fear.

"Four," Grat replied, holding up that many fingers.

"'Four,'" Urs repeated. "Four? Just four?"

Grat nodded. "Four. They did not see me."

Urs and Valid stared at each other. "There are many more of us," Valid observed carefully, opening and closing his hand three times to illustrate. "There are only four of them."

"They are fearsome," Urs responded.

Grat was looking back and forth between them, scowling at Urs's hesitation.

As if sensing Grat's disapproval, Urs turned to the younger man. "You think we should attack," Urs stated.

"Yes!" Grat exulted. "We should kill them. I almost did so myself."

"They are only four," Valid reminded Urs.

"You agree then, Spear Master? We should kill them, stab them with spears and beat them with clubs?"

"They killed our men," Valid replied.

Urs fell silent, thinking. The two men watched him, Valid respectfully, Grat impatiently.

"All is good," Urs finally said decisively. "Call the hunt together. We will attack these four Cohort. Attack them and kill them."

Dog growled softly. "What is it, Dog?" Mal asked. He followed his wolf's intense stare, but did not see anything in the bushes on the other side of the Kindred Stream. Nonetheless, Dog growled again.

A lion? Mal's grip on his spear tightened. He regretted he had left his club back home.

As if on signal, three men stood from the brush. They carried clubs. Mal gasped, startled but not afraid. They were not Cohort—their faces were not painted, and they looked unsure of themselves as they stepped forward.

"Good summer," Mal greeted evenly. "I am Kindred."

The men glanced at each other. This would be the time for them to set their weapons on the ground, but perhaps they did not know this, for they approached until they were standing on the opposite stream bank, some twenty-five paces away.

"Wolfen," the oldest of the men stated, sounding almost reluctant. They were gazing rapturously at the wolf at his side.

Dog had not moved—she was sitting, rigidly staring at the strangers. When the first of the three men took a tenuous step into the water to cross, Dog stood, and when the other two joined the first in the water, she growled, deep and menacing, which appeared to unnerve the men.

"She will not hurt you," Mal assured them. "Dog. Remain!"

Dog sat, her eyes still focused on the strangers.

Again the Wolfen glanced at each other. Seeming to reach a decision, they waded the rest of the way across, stopping when they climbed up the bank, now just ten paces away from where Mal stood. Their expressions were full of an odd intensity, and they were all three pale and sweating.

Suddenly, Mal knew why they were there.

They were staring at Mal and he was staring back. Dog was growling so softly only Mal could hear her. They had clubs. He had a spear. His was a distance weapon, and once loosed it was gone.

But he would do whatever he had to do to protect Dog.

For several moments no one spoke, and then Mal cleared his throat. "I have been in a situation such as this before," he advised, his voice remarkably steady. "A man named Grat, and his accomplice Vinco, came to kill me. In Grat I saw a determination lacking in humanity, but for Vinco I could see how difficult it was to summon the will to murder. You three are, in your bearing, more as was Vinco. This will not be easy for you to do, yet it is your purpose, this day."

His words seemed to have shaken the three men, who stood mutely.

"Why do you do this, Wolfen?"

"Do not speak to him," the older man whispered. "He is hyena." The younger men nodded and, grimly, the three of them advanced.

They have courage, Mal thought to himself irrelevantly. He had a spear in plain view—one of them was going to take a grievous wound.

He lifted his spear, and that was when Dog lost control—though commanded to remain, this threat was simply too real. With a lunge that caught Mal by surprise, she was at the end of her leash, snarling and snapping with such fury that all three men stumbled backward. One of them fell and, inspired, Mal stepped forward and allowed Dog to move a little closer to the man who had tripped.

The Wolfen lay sprawled in the dirt, staring in mortal terror at the enormous wolf poised to rip out his throat. She was so close that a fleck of saliva from her white jaws flew at him, and he trembled, feeling her hot breath.

Mal kept a firm grip on the leash, letting the fallen man see how close he was to death. Dog snarled and snapped, enraged. The other two Wolfen had retreated and were standing up to their knees in the stream, their expressions desperate.

"Dog, remain," Mal commanded. "Dog! Remain!"

"Please," Silex called. "Do not hurt my son."

Dog brought herself under control. She sat, but the fur was still raised on the back of her neck, and her lips were pulled back from her sharp fangs. Mal regarded her wonderingly. He had been thinking of her the wrong way, as his charge—almost as if she were a helpless child. He thought to protect her, but Dog, with her fangs and claws, could also protect *him*.

"I ask again why you do this," Mal said in a strong voice after a moment. "If you do not tell me, I will spear this one where he lies, and my wolf will pursue and kill you two as you try to run for the woods."

Tripping over unseen obstacles, Lyra had run through the night, more afraid of the Cohort than any nocturnal predator. When the sun roused itself to do battle with the day, though, it was in the wrong place in the sky. She did not understand how that could be, nor did she comprehend where she was. To her woman's side should be rocks, trees and the stream, but instead all she saw were open grasses.

She tentatively struck out for where she knew the stream would be. When she found it, the waters would lead her to the Kindred summer quarters.

Here the unfamiliar terrain was rolling, low hills covered with sparse grass. She ate the last of her food as she walked, anxiously watching the sun climb higher. What might under other circumstances be a welcome stretch of warm weather seemed fraught with terrible threat, as dangerous as the night.

When Lyra topped a rise, she stopped, jolted with fear.

Across a wide, grassy field were the three men of the Cohort.

They were much, much closer.

FIFTY-EIGHT

Grat scouted ahead and came back nodding: the Cohort were still there. Once again, he held up four fingers.

Valid and Urs exchanged grim looks. This was like nothing they had ever attempted before. They were hunting men, now, not the lone Frightened. Armed humans.

The Kindred hunters clustered around their leader. Palloc regarded Grat with cold eyes. He knew that at the end of this day, somehow Grat would be heralded, though as stalker all he did was run around ahead of the Kindred looking for game. Palloc was a spearman—it would be up to him to kill one of the Cohort, which he would do without mercy, but he knew with a bitterness born of life experience that no one would notice his bravery.

They would attack as they would conduct any hunt: the spears would fly and then they would charge with clubs. Urs swallowed, wiping the sweat from his eyes. To do this, he had to picture his people being murdered by this same tribe. The rage helped; it kept hesitation at bay.

The men were waiting. Urs noticed how their eyes seemed larger than normal, how their skin shined with perspiration.

"Just over the rise," Grat whispered, gesturing to the small hill in front of them. "They feed, no fire. Clubs, no spears."

"Only four," Valid pressed.

"Just four." Grat nodded.

There were four Cohort, compared to a hunt of three hands' worth of men. "All is good," Urs murmured.

They crawled to a place just before the lip of the small rise. Urs closed his eyes briefly, thinking of Bellu, heavy with his child. And then, as often happened, he thought of Calli. The girl of mists and shadows. The woman he should have married.

Valid's hand closed on his arm. Urs opened his eyes and nodded.

Now.

The men of the hunt boiled over the top of the hill and there were the four Cohort, sitting on their haunches less than forty paces away. They sprang up, staring with eyes white in their fiercely blackened faces.

It was too soon to loose spears, but they flew anyway, arcing through the air, thrown hard and true. "Not yet!" Urs hissed, but only Valid heard.

Palloc did not throw, either: he was at the very back of the hunt, trailing, and did not yet have a clear shot.

The spears fell toward the Cohort, who astounded the Kindred by watching the weapons arc through the air, flinging themselves to the side just as it seemed the spears would land. Most of the spears fell short, but the rest the Cohort managed to evade simply by dodging out of the way.

The Cohort turned and, lifting their clubs, faced the charging Kindred.

Valid heaved his spear with such force that even though they dodged, a Cohort was clipped on the leg. The Kindred roared, raising their own clubs. Palloc stopped to throw but dared not because the hunt was nearly upon the Cohort savages.

The Cohort had spread themselves an arm's length apart and were waiting with their clubs ready. The Kindred jostled with one another as they closed the final few paces, literally falling over amongst themselves.

Urs, out front, swung his club, and the Cohort savage unexpectedly held up his own club with two hands, crossways and high before his chest so that it took Urs's mighty blow. The shock of the impact traveled down Urs's arm and his momentum carried him forward and the man from the Cohort Valley pivoted and slammed Urs viciously in the side.

Urs went down.

Valid had the same experience: the Cohort fighters somehow knew to block the club's descent and then to turn and strike, turn and strike. Valid took a blow to the hip and stumbled. A sharp pain bit his other leg and he rolled, staring at the spear splitting his calf.

Pex fell to the ground next to Valid, his head bouncing as it struck the earth. His eyes were glassy. "Pex!" Valid shouted, but the man was dead.

Valid looked up. One of the Cohort lay still, another was on his hands and knees. The other two fought on, but they were outnumbered and Mors hit one from behind and Palloc picked up a spear and ran it into the stomach of the other, and then it was over.

Men were groaning, including one of the Cohort. Valid looked over to Urs, who was writhing in the dirt. Mors turned and tried to grin at Valid, but there was blood running from where his teeth used to be.

Panting, Grat approached the Cohort who was on his hands and knees. With an intent look on his face, he lined up his shot and struck the man with sickening impact at the base of the skull.

The one Palloc had stabbed was lying on his back, and Grat dispatched him with so many blows to the face that Valid had to turn away.

The other two Cohort appeared dead, but Grat used his

club on them, too, and then stood breathing through his mouth, his face flecked with Cohort blood.

Of the fifteen Kindred who had come over the hill, half were badly hurt, and five were dead. The Valley Cohort were *warriors*. Valid did not understand how so few of them could have inflicted such damage.

"Palloc," Valid croaked. "Good work."

Palloc blinked at him. It was obvious that Valid did not realize that the spear in his leg had been Palloc's, thrown recklessly into the battle at precisely the wrong moment. Instead, Valid only knew Palloc had picked up a spear and killed a Cohort.

"Grat," Valid grunted, wanting to acknowledge Grat's efforts as well, but then the image of the club coming down into the face of the warrior on the ground stopped him. Valid did not know what to say to Grat.

"I am afraid Urs may be fatally wounded," Grat replied after a moment.

They all looked to their leader, who lay writhing on the ground, clutching his rib cage.

The impasse with the Wolfen was, Mal reflected, as when two men met on a narrow path and neither would yield way to the other. He could not very well turn his back on the three men who had come to kill him, nor would it be prudent to allow the one lying at his feet to get up. The other two were still standing in the stream and still had their clubs. Yet they had no viable course of action, either.

Mal gave the one on the ground a look, raising his eyebrows. His question still hung in the air as if returned in an echo. *Why do you do this?*

The Wolfen, sprawled in the dirt and utterly helpless, looked away from Dog's snarl and up into Mal's implacable face and swallowed hard. "We come because you have enslaved the wolf," he ventured, his tremulous voice not at all matching Mal's composed demeanor.

"And you are Wolfen." Mal nodded, putting it together. "So you feel you must set the wolf free."

The two men in the water looked wordlessly at each other.

"What are your names?"

"I am Silex," said the older one. "My son Cragg is before you, and this is my son Tok."

"Well, Silex, this is Dog. If I let her free now, she might kill all of you," Mal observed. *Especially if I spear one of you.* "But otherwise, she can leave at any time. I often untie her and let her run. She returns to me because I saved her and her mother from a lion, and so we are bonded. We share our meals and hunt together. Do you, the People of the Wolf, not give food to the wolf? Do you not follow the wolf on the hunt? That is what everyone says."

"We do," Silex conceded.

"How is what I do any different?"

"The rope," Tok offered from the water.

"The rope." Mal looked at Dog, who still sat, obeying the command to remain. Mal dropped the rope, smiling slightly as Cragg's eyes bulged. "There. You see? The rope helps restrain her from her impulses—such as wanting to kill the three of you. But I do not use it to keep her prisoner. Dog," Mal said. Dog looked around at him. "To me."

Dog obediently moved closer to Mal's side and sat, but she was panting, tense. He put a hand down and gave her a reassuring pat on the head.

Mal looked back at the men who had come to murder him. "Now what?" he asked finally, addressing Tok and Silex as they stood in the water. "If I let this one up, will you two in the river come at me with your clubs? One of you will be speared in the gut and all of you will feel my wolf's fangs rip the flesh from your bones and tear your organs to pieces. Is that what happens next?"

"I think perhaps we did not fully understand the situation," Silex responded slowly.

Mal nodded. "I agree. Still, I do not see how we can prevent you three dying here today."

"We could leave," Tok volunteered shakily.

Mal shook his head. "No, if I allow you to run away you will just return with a better plan. You might bring spears for my wolf and do with your clubs what you originally intended."

"No," Cragg said, staring at Dog as if worried she might take offense. "We are Wolfen. We could never hurt a wolf."

"Oh." Mal nodded. It made sense. "So you would stalk us and spear me, instead. And then you would run. I have heard it said the Wolfen are faster than any other creed, so you would probably get several steps away before my wolf took each of you in revenge for my death. I imagine she would bring you down by seizing your legs in her jaws and crushing your bones, then she would go after the next man. Not until she had felled all three of you would she return to finish you one by one, the way we Kindred pursue reindeer we have speared and then kill them when we find them bleeding in the dirt."

Silex nodded at the sense of Mal's words. "What if we do not try to harm you in any way?"

The two younger Wolfen were nodding furiously.

"Why would you abandon your plans?" Mal challenged.

"It is as we said before," Silex replied. "We thought you were enslaving the wolf. Our only thought was to free her from that slavery."

"Please, Kindred," the youngest Wolfen begged from where he stood in the water.

Mal believed them. "So: if I do not kill you, you will not

attempt to kill me," he summarized. "When my wolf sees that we are not hostile, she will not kill you, either. Are we agreeing?"

Silex gave a tentative smile. "We are agreeing."

"Good." Mal sized up the would-be assassins. The Wolfen's garments were crude—basically hides with head holes and short fox-fur skirts. But otherwise they were men, just like him.

"The way you speak is somewhat odd to my ear," Cragg observed. "The words are the same but your pronunciation differs." He struggled to a sitting position but froze as Dog visibly reacted to the movement.

"All is good, Dog," Mal said. "Yes, I believe it is true for all creeds, that our words sound different as they come from different mouths. You can stand up, Cragg. Dog, remain."

Cragg cautiously rose to his feet. Mal stroked Dog's head reassuringly, while Silex and Tok waded back to the bank and climbed onto dry land. Once the three Wolfen were standing together, they seemed at a loss as to what to do next. How does one converse with someone who was supposed to be murdered?

"Would you like to touch my wolf?" Mal inquired politely.

Silex's hand shook as he extended it. "All is good, Dog," Mal repeated softly as the wolf raised her head to sniff the outstretched palm.

Tears blurred Silex's vision. "I am touching a wolf," he gasped reverently. "I never imagined such a thing could ever occur." He stroked Dog's back, sinking his fingers into the luxurious pelage. "You have the handprint marking, Dog."

"I did not understand you," Mal said apologetically.

"This wolf . . . we have paid tribute to one pack for

generations, and of late in particular to the largest females, many of whom share this same white mark above their muzzles. I believe this is the direct descendant of a great wolf who has eaten from my hand."

"The mother of this wolf was attacked by a lion and killed."

"Ah," Silex replied sadly.

All three men were touching Dog, who was relaxed now. They kept glancing at each other and grinning in delight.

"How long has the Kindred provided care for a wolf? She is still young," Cragg asked.

"I must correct your misconception," Mal replied. "Though I am from that creed, I no longer live with the Kindred, and they certainly do not have wolves of their own."

They gaped at him. "You mean you live by yourself?" Tok blurted.

"Well. Not by myself. I live with Dog. We have a cave upstream from here."

Silex shook his head slightly. "I cannot imagine surviving the winter alone." For the first time, he looked openly at Mal's leg. "How do you hunt?"

"My hunting has not gone well thus far," Mal admitted. "But a day's walk from here I found a place of ice, and buried in it are some young animals I was able to chip out and eat." He shrugged. "We have also done well with worms—it was very wet, this summer."

Silex regarded him solemnly. "That does not sound good."

"It is a challenge."

"Well then." Silex looked at his sons, then back at Mal. "Would you and your wolf like to come live with us?"

FIFTY-NINE

Fifteen Kindred hunters against four savages from the Cohort Valley in a surprise attack, and yet in numbers, the Kindred had suffered far worse from the battle. The Cohort had proved the better fighters. Pex, Bellu's father, was dead, as were four others. Five Kindred dead! It seemed impossible.

Urs could walk, but barely, and after a time Mors, his mouth a flowing wound, went over to support him as they limped along. Grat and Palloc had to help Valid, who could put no weight at all on his man's side leg and who bellowed with pain as they made their way over rough ground.

There was no time to bury their fallen. They left them there in the grass near the Cohort, knowing that scavengers would come and shred the flesh and gnaw the bones. Urs decreed they needed to abandon their kinsmen in case there were other Cohort in the area. They needed to get to winter quarters, where the Cohort had never been seen.

They fled, bleeding and hobbled. Mors kept touching his shattered jaw, probing for the teeth he believed would somehow be there, finding only the soft, torn tissue where the Cohort club had hit him. Mors, so named because he bit other children. He would be able to bite nothing now, nothing ever again.

"I killed two," Palloc announced one day as they marched. "The one I impaled, and the other one with a club."

Valid squinted sideways at him. "I truly remember nothing," he admitted.

Grat was on the other side of Valid. "I do not recall it that way," he argued. "Perhaps you wounded two; I cannot speak to that. But I delivered the death blow to all four of the savages from the Cohort Valley."

Palloc narrowed his eyes at Grat. "You do not earn admiration for hitting a Cohort who is already dead."

"Stop!" Urs hissed, grimacing with the pain in his side. "We would not be in this state if Grat had not urged us to attack. And Palloc, you, too, were eager to rush into danger. I listened to both of you and now we are of such a reduced number we cannot successfully hunt!"

Grat and Palloc stared at him in shock. "That is unfair," Palloc whined.

Valid was walking with his arm around Palloc's shoulder and thus was well positioned to smack the other man on the back of the head with a contemptuous hand. "Do not argue with the hunt master!" he barked.

Grat stayed silent, but he kept glaring resentfully at the hunt master, who had exhausted himself with this slander and was now back to shuffling along, bent over, holding his ribs. Grat thought of the Cohort, the satisfying impact of his club as it crushed their skulls, and how sweetly rewarding it would be to do the same thing to Urs.

Everyone in the Kindred did what they could for the wounded men, but the fight with the Cohort had been devastating. Urs could barely roll over without help, the crushing pain in his ribs keeping him breathless and in constant agony. Valid could not walk; something was broken in his leg, not a bone, but something that made him wince whenever he tried to put weight on it.

And they were the lucky ones. Mors died first, the dreadful mess in his mouth turning black—he could not eat, but he could scream, and his cries lasted two days. Eventually two other men who had been wounded in the attack on the Cohort went on to die from their injuries. The only uninjured members of the hunt were Vinco, Palloc, Grat, and Brum, who was Bellu's last surviving brother.

Upon arrival at winter quarters, Brum was named stalk master to succeed his brother Mors, and Urs seemed to take an odd satisfaction at how much this seemed to offend Grat, who felt the honor should fall to him.

Bellu was so distraught over the tragedy she could not bring herself to administer aid to her husband, but instead lay weeping on her sleeping mat, clutching her pregnant belly as if in deep pain.

Albi swooped in. With an odd apathy, Calli watched the old woman speaking forcefully to Bellu, knowing full well what was occurring. When Albi immediately summoned a council meeting, Calli did not object, and was silent when Albi seized control.

"We are in crisis," Albi informed them. "We need experience. We need strength. I must be made council mother until the crisis has passed."

No one else spoke. It felt as if the Kindred were *dying*. Everyone just wanted to get past their grief.

Because of Bellu's collapse, it was up to Calli to bathe Urs, and to take him food so that he did not have to try to stand up.

Calli was there when Urs summoned Valid. "How is your leg, Spear Master?" Urs asked from a prone position.

With a gasp, Valid collapsed awkwardly onto the ground next to Urs. "I do not know if I will ever walk properly again." He glanced up at Calli and she silently communicated her sympathy with her expression, and he gave her a grateful smile.

The three of them sat silently for a long moment. "I was wrong, not to let you go after your daughter," Urs finally confessed in a rush. Calli's eyes widened in surprise, but Valid was shaking his head.

"No, you were right," Valid replied. "By the time I caught up to her, a great distance would have separated us from the Kindred. Had we encountered Cohort, we would not have survived it."

"That is true. But what I have to tell you now may cause you to despise me."

"Nothing you could say could do that, Urs."

Urs sighed. "Why do we migrate north in the summer?"

"It is as we have always done," Valid replied simply.

"Yes, but *why*? There is hunting here in winter. Perhaps it is abundant all summer long. We have no way of knowing. But what we do know is that the migration is an arduous journey. Why undertake such a thing? Why not live here, follow the herds, hunt, harvest, and remain safe from the Cohort? Why risk crossing their lands, twice every year, when another encounter may well wind up killing all of us?"

Calli could scarcely breathe. If they did not return to summer quarters, she might never see Mal again, would never learn of his fate. But if the Kindred did return, he was slated to die when Valid and Grat went in search of Lyra. Valid might be persuaded that Lyra running away was not Mal's fault, but Grat, she knew, would show no mercy or restraint.

"You are saying that we will not migrate this summer," Valid concluded.

"We will not," Urs confirmed. "We will return to the

ancient ways, following the herds, and will not attempt a summer encampment."

Calli turned her face, weeping quietly.

"You are the first to know," Urs said softly. "I wanted to tell you, because of your daughter."

"My daughter?" Valid gave Urs a sad, candid look. "Oh Urs, I think we both know my daughter is already dead."

Denix spotted the Cohort first—three of them. They were far enough away, and running at such an angle, that she knew she was in no danger, but even so, the sight chilled her skin, raising the hairs on her arm.

And then she saw the girl. She was younger than Denix, perhaps sixteen, and the way she ran, heedless and fearful, clearly moving as quickly as she could, told Denix all she needed to know.

Her eyes drew a connection between the hunters and their human prey. Denix could clearly see the point where they would catch her, though the girl was moving well. She had some time left to live.

"Do not give up. Do not stop," Denix urged in a quiet whisper.

Something occurred to her. She reached down to stroke her belly, where the swell from her child was just barely palpable. She had a responsibility now; she was going to be a mother. This was not her concern; she could not endanger her unborn.

Even still, Denix started to trot. She saw a place where she could cut in front of the Cohort. She had done this sort of thing before, with the Kindred. She would startle the hunters, who would then change their direction to give chase to her, because she would be so much closer and would appear, at first, to be much slower.

Once she had drawn them off, she would gradually increase her speed, leading them on until they were far, far from this girl.

Because no one could run as fast as a Wolfen.

When Lyra saw the trees she ran toward them, intending to hide. She could flee no more; she was exhausted. She turned to see how much more ground her pursuers had gained, and was shocked to see they had vanished. Why? Where had they gone?

The woods were at first unfamiliar to her, but then she came to the Kindred Stream and recognized where she was. Somehow, she had wound up far downstream from summer quarters. She went weak with relief: home.

Darkness was closing in when she came to her cave. The familiar drawings danced in her torchlight, and she found herself sobbing at the sight. She did not build a fire, though she left the torch smoldering at the entrance. She slept before the sun died in the sky, slept deeply and dreamlessly.

The next morning she made her way to the Kindred settlement. It was staggeringly strange to see her family's abandoned fire site, to peer at the empty communal area. Her mind told her there should be people, conversations, laughter. Cooking. There should be cooking as well.

Lyra built a fire and poked at it listlessly, too exhausted to think of what to do next. She could not remember ever being this fatigued. Her plan was to find Mal, who was upstream somewhere. She needed to tell him the Cohort had come north. He was in danger and she had to warn him.

Though in the end, all she managed to do was fall back asleep.

* * *

Mal grinned at his wolf. Dog loved doing this, loved prancing out in the morning to look for food.

Mal carried both of his spears. *Would you like to live with us?* The Wolfen leader, Silex, had asked him. His own tribe had banished him, naming him a curse, and now this stranger was offering him sanctuary. Mal found it a struggle to control his emotions. When he could speak, Mal had replied that he had heard that the Wolfen roamed, following wolf tracks, and ran everywhere they went. They admitted this was true, so he pointed ruefully to his leg, and said, "Then I cannot live with you."

Mal picked up the odor of smoke as he moved downstream. It was so oddly normal—he was wandering south along the stream and it would be around this area where the smell of the Kindred's fires would usually be drifting on the wind—that he did not register, at first, what it might mean.

Somebody was at the Kindred summer quarters.

Could the Kindred have returned? No, that was ridiculous. Some Frighteneds? A hostile creed? Cohort? Mal unconsciously tightened his grip on the spear in his woman's hand, his throwing hand.

When they were very close, Mal slowed. He whispered for Dog to sit, and then made the hand signal: *remain*. Dog tensed, unsure, but this was a game they had played often. Sometimes, her man would leave her for a long, long time, his scent growing so faint she whimpered, but she did what she was told.

Mal crept forward, moving over familiar ground. His whole childhood he had played in these woods; he knew how to sneak up on camp unseen.

The communal fire was burning. He caught his breath when he saw the woman sleeping next to it.

She awoke as he approached, blinking and then smiling at him. "Mal," she greeted, her voice a croak. "I knew you would come."

Valid had fashioned himself a walking stick much like Albi's and used it to support his weight, but even still his face twitched with pain whenever he advanced his wounded leg. Calli watched him limping determinedly out of camp one morning and felt compelled to follow him. His gait was, of course, reminiscent of Mal's, but that was not what made her heart feel as if it were moving strangely in her chest—it was his bravery, his steadfast refusal to allow his injury to become his new legend.

He unknowingly led her into an area of thin growth, sticking to a well-trod path through head-high shrubs that had lost their leaves and long grasses lying flat. She was about to call out when she heard voices to her woman's side. She stopped and, moments later, Renne and Palloc walked into view.

There was no mistaking the intimacy between them, the affection in Renne's light hand on his shoulder. They halted when they spotted Calli, staring at her in shock and alarm.

For a moment they simply gazed at each other like frightened reindeer. Renne was struggling for something to say, her expression pained. Palloc stood mute. It was so quiet they could hear the soft thumps of Valid's crutch landing on the dirt, way up the path.

Calli found herself thinking of a faraway, long-ago time. She knew all too well that a man and a woman might fall in love regardless of impossible circumstances and tribal rules. She was no wife to Palloc. Renne was a widow and perhaps her best friend in the Kindred. Tentatively, Calli raised her hands, palms out in open, peaceful greeting. "All is good, Renne," she called gently. Then she turned and hurried after Valid.

SIXTY

Mal watched Lyra eat. She was wild and dirty, with none of the flowers in her hair or colorful decorative vines adorning her body, but to him there had never been a sight more lovely. It seemed impossible that she was here.

"So you ran," he stated, summing up her story, "because otherwise, you would be wed to Grat this winter."

She nodded, chewing.

"And you evaded the Cohort. That is astounding, Lyra."

"I thought they had me. They must have just grown tired of the pursuit."

"But you came here." He gestured to the oddly empty settlement. "Upon summer, your family will return."

She gazed at him levelly. "I came here because I wanted to find you, Mal. Did you not hear me say that? After I ran *away,* I started running *to.* Running to you."

His mouth went dry. He dropped his eyes, picking a piece of meat out of his pouch. He could feel his heart, strong and hard in his chest. "There is something I have wanted to tell you for some years, Lyra." He looked up at her and had the sense she knew what was coming. "For all of my life, there has been one girl who has been at the center of my affections. As I grew older, as she became a woman, nothing changed for me except that my feelings grew stronger. She is the woman I love. You, Lyra. You are that woman. I love you."

She brushed her hair from her face, eyes bright. "I love you, too, Mal."

He felt the urge to grab her, to kiss her, but he lacked experience in such things and was not sure how to go about it. They were sitting on large stones, two arm's lengths apart. How was he supposed to get over there?

"I am banished, and was never named a man," Mal surprised himself by saying. "I live in a cave beyond Kindred territory."

"You are a man to me."

"What I want for you, for us—there is no women's council to approve."

Lyra grinned at him. "Are you trying to dissuade me from my chosen course of action?"

"Of course not."

She spread her arms open. "Come here, Mal."

For a long time, they said nothing, they just kissed, on that rock. Finally, gasping a little, Mal pulled back from her.

"What is it? Why do you look at me like that?" Lyra asked curiously.

"There is something else I need to tell you," Mal replied.

Denix found Silex and his sons Tok and Cragg by the river, less than a day from the Wolfen gathering site. They had stopped to rest, but stood up as they heard her approach. Her pace was an easy run; when she arrived she panted only lightly.

Silex embraced her, taking in his sons' startled reactions. This would be, he reflected, as opportune a time to tell them as any other. It might be an unpleasant conversation. "You must have reason you have sought us out, Denix. Let us all sit down, the four of us, there is much to discuss," Silex suggested.

They arranged themselves cross-legged in the dirt. Denix had given a lot of thought on how to reveal her news, but the preparation did not make it easy. She saw the rising alarm in the men's eyes as she struggled to speak, and realized that with every second of pained silence, their imaginations were serving up worse horrors.

"Denix?" Silex asked fearfully.

"It is about Ovi. Your sister." Denix went through it as quickly as she could, the three men's faces contorting in grief. When she was finished, she sat helplessly, wanting to go to Silex and comfort him, but unable to do so with his children sitting right there. "Her clothes were folded. I think she just accidentally . . . ," Denix finally murmured. "I am so sorry."

"No," Cragg corrected sadly, wiping his eyes. "You do not know my mother as I do, Denix. This was not an accident."

"You cannot know that," Tok objected harshly.

Cragg fixed his father with a steady stare. "And I do not blame you, Father."

Silex meant to blurt something like, *Blame me? Why would you blame me?* But the words never made it to his lips. Cragg knew, obviously.

Tok stood. "Well I *do*," he spat. "I *do* blame you." He turned and walked down to the river. Tok knew about Silex and Denix, too, then.

Denix also was weeping. "I am so sorry, Cragg."

"You should not be sorry, Denix. You love my father and everyone has always known this. My father, who has always told us that the Wolfen, like the wolf, mate for life."

"And yet Ovi and your father did *not* mate—" Denix started to object, but Silex held up a hand.

"No, he is right, Denix, and Tok has every reason to feel his fury toward me."

Cragg's mouth settled into a sad smile. "We have seen

older wolves leave the pack, to go off by themselves, where they will surely die. They do it for the good of the pack, we say. And we say they welcome death, all for the good of the pack. But what causes them to leave when they do? Often there is a fight in the pack, but other times, they simply *go*." Cragg gazed at Denix. "Perhaps learning you have taken to my father's bed simply gave her the excuse she has always sought."

"You have given this much thought and your conclusions seem wise, Cragg," Silex murmured.

Cragg shrugged. "I have studied my mother my whole life," he replied somewhat bitterly. "Seeking understanding. Trying to find ways to make her happy. But there was a pain in her, a pain that always blocked her happiness. And I believe, when she stepped into that river, that was it. The pain was finally gone, and she was finally happy."

Calli found Valid sitting on a fallen log at the edge of a marshy area. He was sweating, wan and tired from his trek. "Valid," Calli called.

He snapped his head around, then relaxed. "Calli."

She made her way over and sat next to him on the log. "Why did you come all this way?"

Valid grunted. "Each day, I try to make it a little farther. For me to hunt, I must be able to move."

"You still have something broken in you," Calli objected. "Why not sit and allow mending?"

"No bone has been snapped," Valid replied. "This is something else."

Calli reached out and put her hand on the injured leg, feeling the taut muscles under the sun-darkened skin. "Even so, perhaps rest is better. The object is to get well, not to . . . punish the wound."

Valid grinned at this. "You see right into me, Calli. I am angry, yes, at the debilitation, and perversely enjoy making it hurt."

"And perhaps," Calli noted after a moment, "the pain helps you to forget something else that is broken." She pressed a hand to her chest, briefly allowing her pain over Mal to flood through her.

Valid nodded sadly. "What you say is true. I think about my Lyra every day."

"We have a similar loss, you and I."

"Yes."

Calli removed her hand and gazed at him gravely. "And, if we were to return to summer quarters some day, would you really seek out my son and murder him in vengeance?"

Valid grimaced unhappily. "It is Sidee's fervent wish," he answered after a moment.

"Is it your wish, Valid? If Lyra truly left to go to Mal, it is because she loves him. And if they survive, it is because they love each other, and will help each other face the winter."

"I do not see how they can survive."

"Well, I prefer to imagine them together. That they are happy and have found a source of food. That they will survive, and that someday they might come here, return to the Kindred."

Valid studied her. "It must be a happy thing to have such imaginings."

Calli nodded. "And memories—I spend a lot of time with my memories. I know you remember our children playing together when they were young. You remember my only other son, Dog, how our three little ones were inseparable."

A faint smile drifted onto Valid's face.

"Dog," Calli continued, "who was killed at the hand of

men. I do not believe you would really force me to go through that again. You would not really murder my son. Sidee might, but not you."

"No, Calli. What you say is true. I could not do that to you."

She looked fully into his eyes. "What a wonderful thing Lyra did, to declare her love so bravely, to take such a risk to be with the man she loves."

"You are sure of this, then. I am remembering that she loved your other son first."

"Yes, she did. But time changes everything, does it not? And now she loves someone else, and she is with him."

"Time does change things," Valid agreed. "But some things remain the same. I remember when we were young, just named adults. The men all talked about who would be picked for their wives. So many men wanted Bellu, but never me."

"Who did you want, Valid?"

He lifted his eyes until they were staring at each other. "You were only interested in Urs," Valid finally replied.

"Time," Calli responded slowly, "has changed that."

"You . . . are taking that risk."

"Yes, I am."

"I have seen you looking at me at the communal fires," Valid whispered. "And I longed to believe you were trying to tell me something with your gaze."

"I have been. For a long time."

"And when I looked back at you, I wanted you to know, that even though it is not allowed, what I am feeling—"

"Valid," Calli interrupted. "Let us not speak of what is not allowed. My whole *life* has not been allowed, not as I would have it. Let us instead consider what could *be*."

She began trembling when he reached for her, scarcely

daring to believe this was happening. Her thoughts untangled themselves from mists and shadows and became simple and focused, and she gasped when they came together.

Dog sat up when she sensed her man approaching, but she was wary. She smelled another human and she was not wagging her tail when her man came into view and there was a person with him. This was new, this meeting other humans, and Dog did not like it. She preferred to be with just her man, and she could nearly taste the fear coming from this new person, a female.

Her man, though, was not afraid. "Dog, you are good. Remain." The man tossed her a morsel, which the wolf snagged out of the air with practiced ease. "All is good, then. To me."

Dog did as she was told. Her urge to obey him was stronger than any other instinct. It gave her purpose.

This was not like introducing Dog to the Wolfen, who were thrilled to touch a living wolf. Lyra gripped Mal's arm as if she intended to break it, inhaling sharply as the enormous predator trotted over. She was not at all calmed when Dog obediently sat.

"You said . . . Dog?" Lyra whispered.

"Formally, 'She Who Is as Happy and Carefree as My Brother Dog.' And her short name is Brotherly Dog—*Dog Fraternus*. She is my best friend, just as Dog was my best friend."

Dog watched Mal alertly, reacting to her name being repeated.

"Mal, I have never heard of this. A man with a wolf, a wolf *friend*. I do not know what to think."

"Well, now Dog will be your friend, as well," he replied. He pulled a piece of meat from his pouch and handed it to her, Dog watching the exchange with intensity. "I want you to give her this."

I have a wolf friend," Lyra marveled.

Dog was sprawled at their feet, bored now that all the tension had bled out of the situation. The female had put her hands on Dog and finger-fed her some food, but now her man and the female just stood making sounds.

When Mal tied the leash to her neck, Dog got to her feet and shook herself. Soon they were walking the familiar path, headed upstream.

"Is that the rope I gave you?" Lyra asked.

"Yes."

"And look, around her neck! You have put rouge in the leather."

"I thought of you when I did that," Mal admitted.

Lyra looked down at her torn, dirty clothing. "I would like to take a bath."

"I will scoop out a place for you and heat water," Mal declared.

They decided to hold hands, which meant Lyra had to carry one of his spears. "You hold that like a hunter," he complimented her.

"Thank you. Your brother tried to teach me how to throw a spear. I am not very good."

They met each other's eyes, sharing a new truth—they could speak of Mal's brother now, without jealousy or regrets.

"What is it, Dog?" Mal asked softly after a time. Dog had stiffened, and was lifting her nose to the air as if there were a scent on the wind. She turned and looked Mal in the eye, then began pulling on the leash toward some fields to his woman's side.

"What is she doing?" Lyra wanted to know.

Mal regarded his wolf, considering. Should he trust that she might be able to find game, as the Wolfen believed? He wondered if she could have a better sense of smell—her snout, after all, extended farther than his. But smell was smell, what difference would a bigger nose make?

They emerged from the trees into a grassy area and that was when Mal saw it: a large herd of reindeer lazily feeding, paying no attention to their would-be predators. Dog's mouth was tight, her eyes wide open, and a slight whimper of excitement escaped her lips.

"Dog," Mal whispered softly. Dog glanced at him, then went back to staring at the prey. "Dog," Mal insisted more firmly. "If you dash at them they will just run away."

"She understands what you are saying?" Lyra asked incredulously.

"She has learned a few words. I do not know how much she understands," Mal replied, freeing her from the leash. "Dog, you have to do what I say, now."

"I will do what you say as well," Lyra proclaimed.

Mal gave her an appraising glance. Two spears might equate to twice the chance of bringing down prey. "What I want Dog to do is chase the reindeer to us. She loves that part, but I can never get her to follow my instruction once they begin to flee. If they do come toward us, let us try to spear the same animal, whichever one is closest. Dog, sit down."

Dog looked at Mal in disbelief, but did as she was told. *Do you not see the reindeer?* her eyes seemed to be saying.

"We have to do this," Mal said grimly. "We have to be able to hunt, to put away food, or we will not survive the winter."

Lyra put a hand on his arm. "We can do it, Mal."

SIXTY-ONE

For Calli, passions once awakened were not easily put back to sleep, and she and Valid mated twice that afternoon, abandoning subterfuge and lying naked in the grass where anyone might come upon them. "I want to do this again," she whispered into his ear as they lay lazily entwined.

"I am certainly willing but not sure I will be able to manage it," he replied tentatively.

Calli laughed. "Not now. Again in the days to come. I will follow you on your punishing walks, and convince you to lie still instead."

"Not entirely still," Valid noted.

It was only as they approached camp, entering the area where Calli had spied Palloc and Renne, that their insouciance faded. They could not stroll into camp together, not with the secret they shared. Calli went on ahead while Valid, with one last furtive kiss, waited behind to put distance between them.

Nothing could cast shadow on her day, not even when Calli heard someone moving ahead of her and moments later came upon Albi slowly thumping her way up the path. Albi's eyes were sly when they took in Calli.

"So, the girl of mists and shadows," Albi murmured. "Where have you been?"

Calli reminded herself that Albi could not know anything. "I have been looking for edible roots," she said.

"Council Mother," Albi corrected. "I have been looking for roots, *Council Mother*."

With a sigh Calli made to push past, but Albi's stick came up, blocking the path. "You did everything you could, Calli Umbra, but you were not my equal and now I am council mother and the cripple was sent off into the woods to die. I have everything I wanted and you have nothing, all because you dared fight me."

Calli looked into those cruel, pale eyes. "Until the next meeting, then," she spat, losing control.

Albi's eyes narrowed. "What—" she started to ask.

"The curse is lifted, as you say. There is no excuse for you to be council mother anymore. Everyone despises you and now all feel sorry for me, for my loss. I will challenge you at the next meeting and not a single woman will stand with you." Calli jutted her chin at the older woman.

Albi's movement was so swift Calli barely had time to move before the stout walking stick caught her in the side. With a cry she fell to the ground, eyes tearing at the flash of pain. She looked up and the old woman was raising her stick like a club. Calli gasped and rolled and the stick hit the ground next to her face.

"Stop!"

Calli raised her head. Valid was striding forward, his eyes murderous.

He, too, carried a walking stick.

When Albi turned to face him Valid brought his stick down with savage force on Albi's hand. Screaming, she dropped her stick and stared in disbelief at her broken, bloody fingers.

"Calli, are you well?"

"All is good, Spear Master," Calli replied after a moment. She shakily stood, gazing at Albi, who had gone completely white.

"No man—" Albi began, her face contorted in fury as she bent to reach for her staff with her uninjured hand.

"If you touch that stick you will not live to pick it up," Valid warned.

Albi froze, the anger draining from her face, replaced with fear.

"I am recalling a story my dear old friend Nix told me, long ago," Valid said coldly. "About a promise he made to you one time. About what would happen if you ever struck another with that stick of yours. He is not here now to fulfill his vow to you, but perhaps I may serve in his stead. Perhaps I can do you the favor he promised you." Valid grinned fiercely. "So, Albi. Would you like to pick the rock?"

Mal opened his fist, pointing off to his woman's side with all of his fingers, the gesture for *ready to run left*. Dog tensed. Mal took a deep breath, then chopped the air with his hand and pointed. *Away.*

Dog streaked off, momentarily seeming to forget the reindeer. "Good," Mal breathed. She was doing what she had been taught, running where he had gestured, at an angle taking her to the left of the herd instead of straight at it.

When Dog turned back to look, Mal's hand was open. *Remain.* Dog stopped, sitting, facing him. Mal nearly broke silence, wanting to laugh with pleasure. This was working!

Some of the reindeer had seen the wolf and were staring intently, but when Dog halted they went back to grazing, though now the larger ones were stopping every few seconds to raise their heads and watch the predator. This is what they did, conserving energy, not reacting until a true threat emerged.

Mal chopped the air and Dog ran, still at an oblique angle. It was as they had practiced, but she had never kept the discipline with prey so near. "Just a little bit farther," Mal urged in barely audible tones.

Something off to the right alerted the herd and they raised their heads as one, and the coordinated movement caught Dog's eye. She slowed, hesitating, her training at war with her instincts, and then with obvious elation she veered off path and ran straight toward the herd, avoiding antlers and trying without success to jump up on their haunches.

"Oh no," Mal said sadly.

"What is it?" Lyra asked.

"They are going to flee . . . Wait!"

When the ungulates bolted they turned and thundered right at Mal and Lyra. He stood, raising his spear, conscious of Lyra next to him doing the same. The herd swerved away but one clumsy juvenile, full grown but still running a bit awkwardly, was very close. Mal threw his spear and, a moment later, Lyra did the same.

Dog was running next to a small female, jumping up and worrying its haunches, smelling her man and enjoying this wonderful time the two of them were having together, when the scent of fresh blood hit her nose. She hesitated only a moment before turning and running after a young female reindeer who was bleeding from her neck and somehow carrying two of her man's sticks. The blood tantalized and thrilled Dog, who did not even look around when her man called her name.

"Dog! To me!" Mal yelled again. He watched in defeat as the herd stampeded off, Dog alongside the one Mal had wounded, worrying the reindeer, lunging at the bloody gash in its neck. One of the spears fell to the dirt.

"That was the most exciting moment of my life!" Lyra exulted.

Mal did not explain to her that they had accomplished very little—in fact, they had lost one of their spears, and there was no way of knowing where Dog was now.

"All is good," Mal said. He bent and picked up the fallen spear and the two of them followed in the direction of the herd.

When the speared reindeer weakened it fell behind. When it tried to stop Dog instinctively would not let it, lunging and snarling and snapping, keeping it running, keeping its blood pumping. When finally it stumbled, its neck wound came within reach and Dog sank her teeth into the mouthwatering flesh, holding on while the reindeer tried to fling her off. And then it was over, the reindeer down.

Dog fed with savage delight, her whole body intoxicated by the delicious sensation of a new meal on an empty stomach, and then she stopped.

She considered her man. Guiltily, his voice came back to her, the command to return to him echoing in her ears. She had been called and she had ignored that call.

Reluctantly, Dog abandoned her reindeer and turned back the way she had come.

Dog was now back on the restraint. When she and Mal and Lyra came upon the fallen reindeer, a male hyena had claimed it and was plundering the kill. Mal froze, instinctively pulling the rope taut and looking to the trees to see if other members of the hyena clan were emerging. A lone hyena was unheard of, and to be caught out in the open by a pack of hyenas would be fatal.

Dog's reaction was also instinctive, but entirely indifferent to caution and filled with fury. This was their kill, their food. Dog snarled, straining at the end of her leash.

"What is it?" Lyra gasped.

"A hyena. I have never seen one but it is exactly as I have heard them described."

"It is hideous. What should we do?" Lyra asked.

Dog lunged and the strength of the wolf nearly pulled Mal to the ground. He hung on, feeling filled with Dog's power, his own caution evaporating with the heat of Dog's wrath. He let the rage flow from his wolf to his own heart. "Hyena!" Mal shouted. "Go away!"

He stepped forward, leaning back against Dog's lunges. "Away!" Lyra shouted, waving her arms. "Go!"

The hyena stopped feeding and regarded their slow approach with cold eyes, lips pulled back from its fangs, head lowered, its ugly mouth open and repulsive. There was something wrong with it, Mal saw. Its man's side leg, in front, curled off the ground, so that the hyena's limp was even worse than Mal's. That was why it hunted alone—the hyena, like the Kindred, drove its cripples out to die.

Mal smiled grimly. There might be comparisons, but there was no kinship between him and this scavenger.

Dog was in a frenzy. Mal kept a firm grip and raised his spear. Dog was already larger than most wolves out on the plains. Her enraged growls and lunges at the end of the leash meant that she was standing on two legs as she bared her teeth—something the hyena had never seen—and the scavenger's high-pitched warning snarls betrayed its fear. What were these fierce-looking creatures advancing so aggressively?

Mal let fly with the spear and when it struck the hyena it glanced off, but the shock of the impact drew a cry from the canid, and it darted away on three legs, sniveling and crying. Dog wanted to pursue, but Mal sternly pulled her back. They proceeded to the carcass, Mal keeping his eyes on the retreating scavenger in case it decided to circle back. "All is good, Dog," he reassured her. "Please calm yourself." He looked up at Lyra, and her eyes were glowing.

"It is as you said, Mal. Dog makes you a great hunter," Lyra breathed.

"Well . . . it did not go as I had intended. And having you there, Lyra, that was a help I have not had before."

She shook her head at him in wonder. "You are so unlike all the others, who would brag about this kill and steal credit from one another. Dog is your weapon, the way the spear is my father's. And just as he is the spear master, you are the dog master, Mal."

"Dog master," Mal repeated, delighted.

They smiled into each other's eyes, until a whine from Dog reminded them they had a carcass to butcher.

L yra caught Mal staring at her as she ate cooked reindeer by the fire at the base of the natural chimney in the cave. She gave him a shy smile. "What is it? Why do you look at me like that?"

Mal shook his head. "There were just so many times I imagined this exact thing, you sitting by the fire with me. And now you are here."

"And what else did you imagine?" she teased. She loved the way he blushed and then looked away—they were both thinking the same thing.

"This is a wonderful cave," she said after a moment. She hugged herself. "Mal, there were times, when I was alone, when I saw the Cohort, I imagined the worst, and my only thought was that if I could find you, I would be safe."

"My first night here, I was very lonely for my mother, and for the fires of the Kindred," he admitted.

She nodded. "I cried for my father every night. But he is gone and I am here, with you." She gestured around the den.

"Perhaps we should have some animals drawn upon the walls," Mal suggested.

Lyra smiled. "Yes! And the first thing I will paint is you and Dog."

Dog lifted her head at her name, then lay back down on the wolf pelt with a sigh.

"This is my family now. You, and Dog," Lyra declared.

"But what do we do," Mal asked slowly, "next summer, when the Kindred returns? I imagine your father will be very angry with me."

"With *us*," Lyra corrected gently. Then she shook her head. "I do not wish to think anymore about my father, or the Kindred. I do not know what we do then. I only know that if we are family, it is as if we are husband and wife. I only know what I want to do *now*." Smiling knowingly, Lyra lay back on the lion skin, her arms open to Mal, who crawled across the cave floor to join her.

They kissed and it was so much nicer than sitting awkwardly on the rocks. She longed to feel him pressed against her and he responded to the way she was pulling him, climbing gently on top. The feel of his body stirred a heat inside her. He was panting and moving his hips and she responded with small thrusts of her own, swooning.

"Mal," she whispered. "I want us to."

He moved his lips to her ear and she shivered. "I am sorry to say I have no experience in this."

"We will learn together."

Lyra pulled off her tunic and unwrapped her skirt. Shadows from the fire leaped across Mal's face as he stared at her. Lyra reached for him, untying his own skirt. He shivered when she gripped him, and groaned aloud when she guided him into her. A quick, sharp pain made her gasp, but after a moment he began rocking, slowly and carefully, and she felt a glorious sensation build within her.

"You are my husband," she murmured into his ear.

The next morning Mal led Lyra and Dog to the base of a tall rock wall, pointing toward a flock of grey owls circling just off the face, dizzyingly high. "See? There are nests there. I imagine now the birds are hatched; I will climb up and see if I can hunt them."

"You plan to climb up there?" Lyra replied in disbelief.

"All is good. I have done it before," Mal replied with bravado. He wanted Lyra to watch him scale the cliff, to have her see how brave he was. Up there, his leg did not matter.

"I do not want you to do this," Lyra stated gravely. But Mal was already hauling himself up by the first handhold. "Mal! *Please*."

"Tell Dog all is good!" he replied.

And for a time, all *was* good. He felt fully a man, now, a man who had held a woman as a wife in his bed—Lyra, the woman he had always loved. Twice this morning she had called him "Dog Master," and it was as if he had been named to the hunt by Urs.

Looking up, he felt as if he were soaring with the birds overhead. But looking down to assure himself Lyra was still watching served to remind him just how high he was. The last time he had made this ascent, starvation was the motivator—he had felt without choice. Now, though, they had a fresh reindeer kill. What was he doing?

The owls were circling closer, their wings fluttering near his cheeks—soon their talons would claw at his eyes. Mal rested against the wall, feeling certain he was at the point where any further progress would be murderously punished by the birds. *I do not want you to do this,* Lyra's voice said in his head. And truthfully, he no longer wanted to do this, either.

He was high enough to see into a single nest, and it was empty. He decided that was evidence that all the owls were adults and that this quest was without merit. Time to descend.

"All is good," Mal muttered, probing for a foothold. He risked a glance down at Lyra and gulped. Then he looked into the distance—he could see the thin tendril of smoke from their chimney, he could see the thick trees, and to the south, he could see the yellow grasses.

Three men were walking in his direction. They carried clubs and spears.

Clearly, they, too, could see the smoke, and were intent on investigating its origin.

The Cohort had found them.

SIXTY-TWO

Cragg went to get his brother, leaving Silex with Denix. Alone together, there was no awkwardness in their embrace, and she held her man and did her best to comfort him in his grief.

By the time the two younger men had returned, darkness was falling and Silex had built a fire. Tok would not meet his father's eyes when they sat down. Denix sat a discreet distance away from Silex, who gave Cragg a questioning look. Cragg grimly shook his head—Tok was not ready to forgive.

"I have things to say," Silex announced, his voice formal. He nodded at Denix. "I told Denix about our misconceptions. About Mal. How we touched a live wolf." Silex's eyes briefly glowed at the memory. "And then she told me there are Cohort nearby."

His sons stiffened.

"Three of them," Denix affirmed.

"How nearby?" Cragg demanded. "Close?"

Denix shook her head. "I led them far downriver before I came here. They are at least a day away. They are slow."

"Here is what I want to say, and I want these words taken back to the gathering site."

Tok and Cragg frowned in noncomprehension.

"The young wolf is clearly descended from the pack to which we have always paid tribute. The marking on her head proves this to be true—her mother is most likely the one that Denix and I have fed by hand."

"Dog. The wolf's name is Dog," Tok interjected.

"Yes, of course. Dog. So now the Wolfen must pay tribute to this wolf, Dog, but also to the man she has chosen to live with. He is a cripple and cannot hunt. He will surely starve this winter if we do not assist. When we take prey, we must make the journey, no matter how far, to give tribute to Mal and Dog. Everything we have ever done as a tribe leads me to believe we must celebrate and protect both the wolf and the man she has chosen as a companion."

"This seems a wise thing, but why do you pronounce it as a message we are to give to the others?" Cragg asked.

"Yes, why not assemble the Wolfen on our return and tell them yourself?" Tok agreed.

"Because some of us are going back to the cave where the cripple lives with his wolf, to warn him of the Cohort's presence and to defend him from any threat."

"And you think you might not survive this, Father?" Cragg demanded. Denix stared at Silex, her eyes round.

"Well, when man hunts man, the outcome is never certain until the spears have been thrown," Silex replied.

His sons exchanged grim looks. "When you return, Denix, there is a message I would like you to give my wife," Cragg whispered.

"Oh no. It will be Tok who returns to the Wolfen," Silex corrected.

Tok gasped.

"Denix is the swiftest among us, and the best with the spear." *And she would never allow me to go without her,* Silex did not add.

"I do not want to go back," Tok objected.

"This is my decision, my resolve as leader of the Wolfen."

"Father, are you telling me that I am now to lose both of my parents?" Tok asked, anguished.

Denix put her hand on Tok's arm. "No, Tok. All is good. There are three of them, and three of us. And we are Wolfen."

Denix was smiling reassuringly, but when her dark eyes met Silex's, they were both remembering the same thing.

Duro had confronted the Cohort with every male of their tribe, and no one returned from that battle. And they, too, were Wolfen.

I do not understand why we do not just run away!" Lyra wailed as Mal cleared the ground-level entrance to their cave. "Mal!"

"I do not run well, Lyra. Please climb inside."

Dog responded to the routine of having the rocks moved by crawling forward into the familiar den.

"But you said there are three of them!"

"Yes. But you will be safe inside with the wolf."

Lyra shook her head wildly. "No, Mal."

Mal set two spears and a club on the ground and frowned at them thoughtfully. Then he turned and put his hands on her shoulders. "It is the same as with the lion, Lyra. Once they know where we live, they will not leave until they have taken you. But as with the lion, I will set a trap."

"I want to be with you."

"They do not know you are here. When they see me, they will be emboldened because of my leg, and give chase. We must have them think it is just me, a lone man, like a Frightened. Even if . . . If I am unsuccessful, I know Dog will warn them if they try to get into the cave. They will not willingly climb into a wolf den."

"We have been together but a day, Mal. It cannot end like this," Lyra pleaded.

"Yes, it cannot end like this. It will not. But . . ." Mal's lips trembled for just a moment. "Last night was all I have ever wanted and dreamed of, Lyra. Remember that always."

Lyra was weeping, clutching him. "No, Mal."

"Keep Dog with you. Protect her, and if I do not return, hunt with her as we hunted, get her to run the prey at you and then pull it down. It is how you will survive the winter."

Lyra just stared at him. He gently pulled her hands away from him. "Get inside," he whispered, kissing her wet cheeks. "We are out of time."

Mal positioned himself behind some trees, gauging his moment. The three men were ferocious looking, garbed in simple furs haphazardly held together with small lengths of leather thong. Their faces were coal black, and all three carried clubs and two had spears as well. They were close, fifty paces. Their stride was unhurried.

That changed when Mal stepped out into the open. The men instantly halted, staring. Mal was deliberately weaponless, and when he turned to flee, he exaggerated his limp so they would see his leg.

He expected a shout, but heard nothing, so after a moment Mal glanced behind him to see if he had drawn their pursuit. Yes, and they were running fast, so fast that Mal abandoned any attempt at a ruse and increased his own speed, covering ground as quickly as he could. When he arrived at the base of the rocky wall, he could hear their footsteps: he had allowed them to get too close!

Frantically he clawed his way up the familiar handholds. To the Cohort, it must have appeared childishly easy to ascend, but Mal had had much practice, so that when he came to the ledge he thrust himself into the air and over the lip in one smooth motion.

Mal lay where he had hidden the day he had fought the lion, breathing as silently as he could manage. He could hear the Cohort continuing their chase, arriving at the base and awkwardly scrabbling at the steep rocks, sending stones bouncing down to the ground.

Mal closed his hand on his spear. He knew from experience that a club might not complete the task.

The nearest of them was panting loudly, and Mal pictured his progress, knew where he was, could hear him when he stopped just below the ledge, puzzling it out.

Mal rolled to his feet, lifting the spear. The Cohort was looking up at him when Mal threw his weapon and hit him in the throat.

This time they did shout.

Mal did not wait to confirm the kill. He leaped up the last distance to the top of the rocky bluff and ran to the smoke hole entrance, quickly descending and landing lightly near the fire.

Lyra was holding Dog on the leash and stared at Mal with wide, terrified eyes. He held a hand over his mouth: *silence*. Then he crawled quickly to the ground-level entrance and slid back out into the sun.

His spear lay where he left it, next to the club. He picked up both weapons and peered around the rocks.

The Cohort he had killed lay faceup, the spear still pointing skyward. Another was climbing cautiously upward, holding a club, while the third stood with spear ready, watching for Mal to appear again.

Mal stepped out, taking his time, drawing his spear back. When he let fly it was with all of his strength, and the Cohort fighter screamed when the stone point pierced his back. He stumbled forward, dropping his spear, falling to his hands and knees.

Mal switched his club to his woman's side hand. Now there was just one of them.

The Cohort on the wall reacted instantly, leaping away from the rocks and landing heavily on the ground. He rolled and came up clutching his club, crouching and looking in all directions.

When he realized Mal was alone, he smiled.

D og seemed to sense Lyra's terror. The wolf was whimpering and struggling against her embrace, while Lyra put her face in the soft fur, wetting it with her tears.

"Please remain, Dog, remain," Lyra whispered, using the command Mal taught her.

When she heard a man scream, Lyra put a hand to her mouth. Was it Mal? Dog was almost frantic, now, pulling against her rope. Lyra regarded the wolf with wide eyes, nodding decisively. "You are right, Dog," she said.

M al mimicked the Cohort's crouched stance, his club ready. What was needed, he decided, was a feint, get the Cohort to flinch, then swing the club hard and down. Even if the Cohort dodged, the club would hit his shoulder, with force enough to break bones.

For that to work, Mal needed to work his way forward, and a quick lunge was out of the question. He took a tentative step. The Cohort, seeing his withered leg, smiled again, a malevolent baring of fangs in the blackened face.

The man Mal had speared from behind was still on his hands and knees, breathing harshly and struggling to stand back up.

The man with the club came forward. Mal feinted and then raised his club and his blow was blocked! Gasping, Mal threw himself to the side, taking a solid hit in the ribs. His breath left him in a yell and he fell to the dirt. The Cohort stepped forward.

A streak of black and grey flashed past Mal's vision and Dog was there, her massive jaws closing on the Cohort's arm, breaking the bone and shaking the club free. With a harsh scream, the Cohort punched at Dog with his free hand.

Mal groped for a weapon, for the spear the Cohort had dropped, and saw Lyra with it. She ran past him, spear pointing out, and put all her weight behind the thrust to the Cohort's gut.

Clutching his ribs, Mal staggered to his feet. Dog was still savagely tearing at the now lifeless Cohort. "Dog. To me! To me, Dog!"

Dog stopped her assault. Panting, drooling, she trotted to Mal and sat, her eyes wild. He put a trembling hand down on her head to calm her.

The other Cohort had stopped trying to rise and had fallen back to the dirt, his breathing raspy and labored. With a gurgle, he became motionless. Lyra turned to Mal, shock in her eyes. He went to her, Dog at his heels.

When he held her in his arms, she was shaking. Dog whimpered and pressed against them both, and they stood like that for a long time.

"Mal!"

Mal and Lyra whipped their heads up. The Wolfen men were returning, a woman with them—running, of course. Mal again put a hand on Dog's head. "All is good, Dog. These are friends. Remain. Remain."

The three Wolfen slowed when they crossed the stream and approached the flat area with the three dead Cohort. They appeared astounded.

"We came to warn you of Cohort in the area. You did this, Mal? Fought these three by yourself?"

Mal shook his head. "This is Lyra. She is . . . she is my wife. She fought as well."

The Wolfen stood looking at the dead as if unable to believe what they were seeing. Dog yawned anxiously, still panting.

"In our tribe, our best hunter is also a woman," Cragg said. "This is Denix."

"And Dog," Lyra said. "She helped, too. Together we are a Kindred hunt, and Mal is the master. The Dog master."

Silex looked at Dog's mouth, the blood there. Then he glanced up at Lyra with a smile. "Dog master," he repeated. "Just so. An apt term. Dog master."

After they buried the dead, the five people, different creeds, Kindred and Wolfen, ate reindeer meat together by the fire.

Dog was tense and restless until night fell and her man and the woman took her to the cave. She could smell the other humans out by their fire, but now it was as it should be, with her man lying on the mother-wolf thing, the woman next to him. Dog did not fear any harm from the woman.

The events of the day were deeply disturbing to Dog, so she climbed over to the man and put her head on his chest, the way she had slept when she was a puppy. His hand came down to rest on her head.

"All is good, Dog."

She understood that her name was Dog and knew the sound "good" as praise. She had pleased her man.

The woman, too, made sounds, though nothing Dog could recognize.

"I love you, Mal."

"I love you, too, Lyra."

Sighing, Dog felt the tension leave her. They were in the den, safe and together, the way they were meant to be. She closed her eyes and soon fell fast asleep.

PRESENT DAY

Professor James K. Morby met his friend and long-time collaborator Bernard Beauchamp in the small coffee shop just down the street from Morby's hotel. The two men drank strong coffee from delicate china cups, watching idly as people strode briskly past on the sidewalk. Each man kept drifting from the conversation, wandering among his own thoughts. Jean Claude, the graduate student thirty years younger than either of the two PhDs, sat at the table respectfully. Both professors had uneaten pastries on the small plates in front of them, making Jean Claude tense. He did not know if it would be impolite to ask the men if they were going to eat the sweet rolls, but he yearned to snatch them up and bolt them down as quickly as he had finished his own.

"You are all packed, then, Jim?" Beauchamp asked nonchalantly.

"What? Oh yes, yes. All ready to go. Sorry. I'm feeling oddly . . . deflated."

"Deflated? *Je ne comprends pas très bien ce que ca veut dire.*"

"I just mean to say that I always believed we would find her. The wolf, the first dog. I knew it. And now that we have . . . I have completed a quest, a purpose, and I am not sure what I will do to replace it."

"So your work is finished?" young Jean Claude asked. He

found a sliver of almond he had neglected to eat and put it in his mouth.

The other two men smiled at him. "Not finished, no," Morby replied. "I will never be finished. But there is only so much we can guess from the fossil record. All of my work, in the end, comes down to nothing more than an educated guess. Would you like my roll, Jean Claude?"

"Well, perhaps . . . if you are not going to eat it."

"You have been staring at it the way my dog watches me carve meat," Beauchamp observed wryly.

Morby's eyes crinkled as he passed over the pastry. "For just a moment, let's picture it, Jean Claude. The climate is changing, vast sheets of ice preparing to storm the continent. The human race clings to a fragile existence, not even enough of us in all of Eurasia to fill a football stadium. The Neanderthals are, for reasons we still do not understand, slowly dying out. And then one tribe, one group of people, one *person,* manages to tame a wolf. Think how it must have changed everything!"

Jean Claude frowned as he chewed, swallowing before he confessed his doubt. "I am not sure why, Monsieur Professor, a dog would change everything."

Morby nodded. "That is because you are thinking of it as a pet. Try, instead, to regard the wolf as a technology. From hunting—did the wolves kill rabbits and bring them back to their masters? To defense—what predator would take on a man being escorted by a couple of wolves? And finally to war—I do not buy it that early humans lived in Utopia, never fighting other tribes. No, the wolves were a *disruptive* technology." Morby grinned over the term. "It is as Dr. Temple Grandin says, animals make us human."

Jean Claude nodded thoughtfully, cutting his eyes to Beauchamp's uneaten pastry.

"You should know, Jean Claude, that not everyone agrees with this conclusion," Beauchamp observed, passing his *pains suédois à la cannelle* to the younger man without comment. "Our friend here has been rather derisively refuted by our peers."

Morby took a sip of coffee, something like resignation in his eyes. "Current thinking in our field is that we rose to the top of the food chain ahead of the Neanderthals because we were more collaborative. Naturally, we are so narcissistic we believe the collaboration was with our own kind, and not with another species. Not with *Canis lupus*."

"What I would give to be there, to see the game change, with these wolves," Beauchamp remarked almost wistfully.

"You are right, it was a game changer." Morby nodded. "The dogs didn't just help us, they *saved* us! From that point on, as we evolved, advanced, we did it with the dogs by our side. That's why we love them, and they love us—our fates became inextricably bound together, dogs and humans, each *needing* the other. Humans who didn't bond to the dogs were less likely to survive. They were evolving *us*! And meanwhile we bred them—the wolves who did not like us or care for our discipline were not allowed to reproduce. We eventually took over all aspects of natural selection, so that today we have boxers and bulldogs, dachshunds and Dobermans, lapdogs and Labradors. But what we didn't realize was at the same time, they altered our species' destiny. Up until the dogs, we lived our brutish lives as just another species of animal, subject to the whims of the environment, scrabbling for survival in the dirt. But then, with domesticated wolves, we began to see things differently. We began to look at other creatures and wonder if we might tame them, too. And if we could manage animals, what about plants? We began to see ourselves not as subjects of nature, but *masters* of it!"

Morby's face was alive now, his melancholy completely gone.

"But then what happened?" Jean Claude wanted to know. "I know eventually the Neanderthals vanished, though some of them mated with humans. And I know that after a time we domesticated other animals as well. But when the first dog came . . . what happened next, *right then,* when they were completely new? When the game was changing, as Professor Beauchamp said?"

Professor Morby finished his coffee and set the delicate cup down on its saucer. "You always ask the right questions; I wish I had you in my class, Jean Claude. Yes, that is precisely what I, too, would like to know. For the first time, wolves were our companions, so treasured and loved we buried them next to us in our graves. This had never happened before, but suddenly, there they are, man and wolf together. Everything was different. Yet titanic changes do not happen easily. There must have been conflict, doubt, setbacks. There were no dogs, and then there were dogs. So," Morby smiled, "as you ask. *What happened next?*"

AFTERWORD

I was scanning the newspaper for some good news one day (as in, "Author Cameron Wins Everybody's Favorite Person Award") when I came across a simple statement that had such profound implications I could barely comprehend them all. Around 30,000 years ago something extraordinary happened: a wolf became a human's companion. In other words, it was the birth of the first dog.

The article seemed to imply that it was all pretty easy and routine—one day, a wolf, the next day, a dog. But I believed it was such an astounding development in the history of both species, I just had to find out more.

This all happened a little before I was born, so I spent hours and hours doing research on this time period, talking to paleontologists, reading books and articles, even checking out Wikipedia. The era is called the Upper Paleolithic, and it's striking just how brutal life was for those early humans. As primates, we'd been happiest in the northern forests, but now glaciers were advancing like an invading army, shoving us out onto the plains, where we could be easily hunted as meat by animals of tooth and claw and speed. We had no agricultural sciences, no ranching, but lived opportunistically, chasing food and hoping to catch it before some other predator, or starvation, brought us down. We were competing for many of the same resources not just with lions and other killers, but with Neanderthals, who were stronger and faster and maybe even smarter.

But while I could picture all that, I simply could not come up with a scenario that explained how a wolf became a *pet*.

I spent a lot of my research time looking into the canine-side of the equation as well. Wolves back then were far more likely to see us as a food source than they do in the current era—the ones who hunted us have historically been killed off. Over time, our actions influenced the evolution of *Canis lupus* away from aggression and toward elusiveness, so that today, attacks on humans by wolves are rare (and met with lethal retaliation). But 30,000 years ago, we were *dinner* to these animals. Would we really invite a pack of wolves to come join us by the fire and sing campfire songs? That would be like inviting cannibals to lunch and asking them who they would like to eat.

And our own food supply was scarce enough to suggest we would hardly have wasted it feeding another species. Wolves were, after all, competing for the same prey, hunting the same herds. When I was a child, I didn't even want to share food with my sister. If people were starving, would we really have tossed meat scraps to our competitors?

So how did we natural enemies become such good friends that I allow one of their descendants to sleep in my bed, nearly shoving me off the mattress each night?

Evolution is a long process. I promise you no wolf pack gave birth to a Labrador who ran over to the Cro-Magnon camp to retrieve tennis balls. Yet what human tribe would have the patience to lure a wolf pack closer and closer to an intimate relationship? No, for this to occur the evolutionary path took an extraordinary shortcut. One person must have had the time and the will to domesticate one wolf.

The Dog Master is a work of fiction based on an indisputable fact: dogs are our companions, their fates inextricably bound to ours. To write it I had to envision a unique human, an extraordinary circumstance, and a wolf whose ancestors had an unusual affinity for *Homo sapiens*.

That was just the first challenge. The domestication of wolves took place in the most dramatic and dangerous time in human history—the dawn of the last Ice Age. Yet humans almost certainly had no comprehension of the scope of devastation coming their way—they knew local weather, not global climate. The speed of the ice's advance was, well, glacial. They were involved in the sweep of history, a resurfacing of continents, an extinguishing of many species, a cascade of life-threatening challenges, and yet all they would have been aware of was their own situation. The days might be colder, the hunting more scarce, the fruits slower to ripen, but to them it would portend only further and immediate hardship in a world already designed to be cruel. As an author, the best I could do to set the story's stage was allow the characters to react to their individual situations and let the reader draw more grand conclusions.

And here's what we can say for certain about any specific individual human being in this extraordinary time in our history: nothing.

There's no written record. Cave paintings provide some insight, and the sciences of archaeology and geography contribute much, but in the end we don't *know*. Were the people of the time warlike, or peaceful? What was family life like? How did the tribes function? Who were these people? Were any of them kleptomaniacs? Did they have stand-up comedy?

With no manuscripts to study, I could only speculate on what a conversation might be like between two members of the Kindred. I wanted to give the reader a flavor of how their language might have worked, but I was writing in modern English, so all I could do was suggest, through formal sentence construction and an incorporation of vaguely foreign-looking names, that these humans of the Upper Paleolithic were capable of complex statements and had a sophisticated vocabulary, but that it was different from the way we speak today. My choices hopefully convey my artistic choices, but I was aiming for mood and nuance, and in no way presuming to reconstruct how humans would have communicated. For all I know they would say "LOL" to each other.

I am not alone in having to guess: as I read what experts had to say about this particular era, I was struck by how current theories attract consensus and controversy, and how some dogma, accepted in the past, has fallen into disfavor. If you asked me to examine a skull from thousands of years ago and come to a scientific conclusion, the best I could do would be to say, "I think this dude is dead." But through a lot of hard work by dedicated men and women, we have very complex explanations for a lot of the fossil puzzles from long ago. Explanations which are, of course, impossible to *prove*.

If you are one of these scientists, I hope you'll understand that I took artistic license in pursuit of the story I was writing. We cannot for sure identify the diet of every tribe that was wandering Eurasia at that time—in my telling, the Northern Tribes have not yet managed to successfully hunt horses, as an example, though other humans were certainly living on horse flesh. I took a lot of today's generally accepted theories about early humans in general and adapted them to a story about a very small number of people in particular. I will cheerfully admit I am far more likely to have committed errors in this regard than might have been the case if I had first pursued a doctorate in paleontology. Of course, I'm not bright enough to get a PhD, so the story of

The Dog Master would have been put on indefinite hold while I kept flunking my dissertation.

But, as anyone who has ever read *A Dog's Purpose* knows, I am rather fond of our four-legged friends, and I'm pretty enamored with the idea that if it hadn't been for them, we might have entered the Ice Age and not come out the other side.

(I know that technically we are still in an Ice Age, but I went to Hawaii on my honeymoon and can state rather confidently that some areas of the planet have fully recovered.)

Finally, my attention is very much grabbed by the question posed by Professor Morby in the epilogue. The stage has been set, the players are in position, and the most dramatic and challenging time in the entire history of our species is about to commence.

What *did* happen next?

W. BRUCE CAMERON

ACKNOWLEDGMENTS

None of the characters in this book are based on real people, I promise. I don't personally know anyone from the Upper Paleolithic, though I did have a coach in junior high that we were all convinced was a Neanderthal.

At the end of this section I'm going to list some of the books I used in my research, but I need to especially thank John F. Hoffecker, author of many publications on the archaeology of people in cold environments, including *Desolate Landscapes: Ice-Age Settlement in Eastern Europe*. Mr. Hoffecker very patiently answered my questions about what life was like for humans and other animals back 30,000 years ago, steering me away from some of my misconceptions—an early draft of *The Dog Master*, as an example, had packs of hyenas running around everywhere, instead of being the nearly extinct creatures they would have been. I was also persuaded that people didn't have iPods—those would come later.

To learn about wolves I studied my dog Tucker, from whom I concluded that wolves prefer to sleep in the sun all day and bark at the UPS man. Thank you, Tucker, your fierce attacks on your squeaky toy gave me real insight as to the savagery of your lupine ancestors. I also spoke to some people who own wolves as pets to learn what it is like to live with them. The people requested their names not be included here, but I appreciated them sharing their experiences. My opinion: wolves are wild animals and should only be domesticated if injury or other circumstance makes such an arrangement unavoidable. It's better to just get a schnauzer. And it's amazing how much one can learn about wolf puppies just by watching videos on the internet, though usually after an hour I'm wasting time laughing at cat videos.

Some key people assisted me with writing this novel. Connection House, which administers my Web page, also provided research into such things as "what kind of birds were living in cliffs back then? Where did people go to get a latte?" My son Chase Cameron helped me track changes when I did a massive rewrite on the fifth draft. And Cathryn Michon, who I tricked into marrying me a few years ago, suspended work on the most recent movie she directed (*Muffin Top: A Love Story*, still out on VOD if you're interested) to read draft after draft, providing her notes and ideas and insights. She probably married me just for the experience of doing all the extra free work.

Thank you Kassandra Brenot for providing translation so my characters spoke French and not Google.

Tackling such a huge issue as one of the most pivotal events in human history not only requires a lot of stamina in the writing, but the editing process is Herculean as well. Kristin Sevick did a great job staying on top of the details through each rewrite.

Thanks to the people at Forge who are all lined up behind my novels. It's a huge team, but I want to specifically thank Tom, Karen, Kathleen, Patty, and Linda for everything they've done to support my work and my career.

Thanks, Scott Miller at Trident, for fighting the forces of evil and for being my literary agent.

Steve Younger, Steve Fisher, Steve Iwanyk. Thanks for making it so easy to remember your first names. Oh, and also for seeing to it that my works get sold to Hollywood, where they are very, very slowly being made into movies. Very slowly.

Gavin Palone, thank you for bringing sanity to an insane process.

Monica Perkins, thank you for all the coffee and for keeping so many things on track. I get that people have to grow, to move on, to try new things, I just never wanted that to happen with you.

Elliott Crowe does most of the work I am supposed to be doing as producer of independent movies like the aforementioned *Muffin Top* and the soon-to-be-released *Cook Off*. It gives me more time to write and also means things get done correctly, which I so appreciate. If you try to quit, I will hunt you down like an animal.

Thanks Fly HC and Hillary Carlip for wbrucecameron .com and adogspurpose.com, both beautiful sites.

The coolest part about being an author is that I get to meet other writers. No, seriously, to me, writers have always been like rock stars. Claire LaZebnik and Samantha Dunn and Jillian Lauren and Andrew Gross are not only cool people, but they like me, they really like me! Nelson DeMille told me many, many years ago that he would help me with my career, and he's still at it—he blurbed my novel *The Midnight Plan of the Repo Man*. So did Lee Child, known in the literary world as one of the nicest writers alive. I'm really grateful.

My award-winning teacher sister Amy Cameron wrote the study guides for *Emory's Gift*, *A Dog's Purpose*, and *A Dog's Journey*. I'm going to see if I can talk to her about doing one for *The Dog Master*. They are excellent, took a ton of work, are written to Common Core standards, and are available free on my website.

Thanks to Tom Rooker. What, exactly, are we doing?

Thank you, Carolina and Annie. You can stop growing up now.

When I started writing *The Dog Master,* my father, William J. Cameron, MD, was still alive and gave me insight into the sorts of dumb questions writers ask doctors, such as, "what does it feel like to give birth?" (Even though he was a gynecologist, he told me to ask my mother.) Sadly, my father passed away before ever reading even a draft of *The Dog Master*, which I consider the most ambitious work of my career. I am grateful to him for many things, of course, but one of them is being my official advisor for medical topics. That duty has passed on to my sister Julie Cameron, MD, who puts up with my queries even though she's a bit busy saving lives. I am so grateful to have this resource in the family, as asking hypothetical questions about fictional situations usually isn't covered by my health insurance.

My whole family supports everything I do, even though Eloise and Gordon are too young to know or care much about it. Thanks to Chelsea, James, Georgia, and Chase, and especially thanks to my Mom, Monsie Cameron, who forces everyone she knows to buy two or three copies of each of my books and will boycott any store that doesn't sell my novels, even the gas station.

If you've slogged your way through all of this, you probably read the book as well, and I want to thank you for that. Without you I wouldn't have a career, and all of my stories would remain trapped in my head. I feel so lucky to have your support.

W. BRUCE CAMERON
Tuesday, February 10, 2015

BIBLIOGRAPHY

Bahn, Paul. *Journey Through the Ice Age*. Berkeley: University of California Press, 1997.

Barry, Scott. *Wolf Empire: An Intimate Portrait of a Species*. Guilford, CT: Lyons Press, 2007.

Bickerton, Derek. *Adam's Tongue: How Humans Made Language, How Language Made Humans*. New York: Hill & Wang, 2009.

Brantingham, Jeffrey; Steven Kuhn; Kristopher Kerry. *The Early Upper Paleolithic Beyond Western Europe*. Berkeley: University of California Press, 2004.

Busch, Robert. *The Wolf Almanac: A Celebration of Wolves and Their World*. Guilford, CT: Lyons Press, 2007.

Cooper, Margaret. *Exploring the Ice Age*. New York: Atheneum Books for Young Readers, 2001.

Cunliffe, Barry. *The Oxford Illustrated Prehistory of Europe*. Oxford: Oxford University Press, 1994.

Daniels, Edwin. *Wolf Walking*. New York: Stewart, Tabori & Chang, 1997.

Fagan, Brian. *Cro-Magnon: How the Ice Age Gave Birth to the First Modern Humans*. New York: Bloomsbury Press, 2010.

Finlayson, Clive. *The Humans Who Went Extinct: Why Neanderthals Died Out and We Survived*. Oxford: Oxford University Press, 2009.

Hoffecker, John. *Desolate Landscapes: Ice-Age Settlement*

in Eastern Europe. New Brunswick: Rutgers University Press, 2002.

Klein, Richard and Edgar, Blake. *The Dawn of Human Culture: A Bold New Theory on What Sparked the "Big Bang" of Human Consciousness.* New York: John Wiley & Sons, 2002.

Lamberg-Karlovsky, C. C. (ed.). *Hunters, Farmers and Civilizations—Old World Archaeology: Readings from Scientific American.* San Francisco: W. H. Freeman and Company, 1979.

Leroi-Gourhan, Andre. *The Hunters of Prehistory.* New York: Macmillan, 1989.

Lopez, Barry. *Of Wolves and Men.* New York: Touchstone, 1995.

Mellars, Paul. *The Neanderthal Legacy: An Archaeological Perspective from Western Europe.* Princeton, NJ: Princeton University Press, 1996.

Morey, Darcy. *Dogs: Domestication and the Development of a Social Bond.* New York: Cambridge University Press, 2010.

Roberts, J. M. *A History of Europe.* New York: Allen Lane the Penguin Press, 1996.

Sharp, Robert. *Living Ice: Understanding Glaciers and Glaciation.* Cambridge: Cambridge University Press, 1988.

Stringer, Chris. *Lone Survivors: How We Came to Be the Only Humans on Earth.* New York: St. Martin's Griffin, 2013.

Upper Paleolithic. Memphis, TN: Books LLC, Wiki Series, 2011.

Wade, Nicholas. *Before the Dawn: Recovering the Lost History of Our Ancestors.* New York: Penguin, 2006.

Read on for a preview of

A DOG'S WAY HOME

W. BRUCE CAMERON

Available
from Tom Doherty Associates

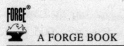

A FORGE BOOK

ONE

From the beginning, I was aware of cats.

Cats everywhere.

I couldn't really see them—my eyes were open, but when the cats were nearby I registered nothing except shifting forms in the darkness. I could smell them though, as clearly as I could smell my mother as I took nourishment, or my siblings stirring next to me as I worked my way to find life-giving milk.

I didn't know they were cats, of course—I just knew they were creatures not like me, present in our den but not attempting to nurse alongside me. Later, when I came to see that they were small and fast and lithe, I realized they were not only "not dogs," but were their own distinct kind of animal.

We lived together in a cool, dark home. Dry dirt underneath my nose gave up exotic, old smells. I delighted in inhaling them, filling my nose with rich, flavorful aromas. Above, a ceiling of parched wood dropped dust into the air, the roof pressing down so low that whenever my mother stood up from the packed depression in the earth that served as our bed to leave my siblings and me—squeaking in protest and huddling against each other for reassurance—her upright tail was halfway to the beams. I did not know where my mother went when she departed, I only knew how anxious we were until she returned.

The sole source of light in the den came from a single

square hole at the far end. Through this window to the world poured astounding scents of cold and alive and wet, of places and things even more intoxicating than what I could smell in the den. But even though I saw an occasional cat flicker through the hole out into the world or returning from some unknown place, my mother pushed me back whenever I tried to crawl toward the outdoors.

As my legs strengthened and my eyesight sharpened I played with the kittens as I would with my siblings. Often I singled out the same family of cats toward the back recesses of our communal home, where a pair of young kitties were particularly friendly and their mother occasionally licked me. I thought of her as Mother Cat.

After some time spent romping joyfully with the little felines, my own mother would come over and retrieve me, pulling me out of the pile of kittens by the back of my neck. My siblings all sniffed me suspiciously when my mother dropped me next to them. Their responses suggested they did not care for the residual whiff of cat.

This was my fun, wonderful life, and I had no reason to suspect it would ever change.

I was nursing drowsily, hearing the peeping sounds of my brothers and sisters as they did the same, when suddenly my mother lunged to her feet, her movements so unexpected that my legs were lifted off the ground before I dropped from the teat.

I knew instantly something bad was happening.

A panic spread through the den, rippling from cat to cat like a breeze. They stampeded toward the back of the den, the mothers carrying their mewing offspring by the backs of their necks. My siblings and I surged toward our mother, crying for her, frightened because she was frightened.

Strong beams of light swept over us, stinging my eyes. They came from the hole, as did the sounds: "Jesus! There's a million cats in the crawl space!"

I had no sense of what was making these noises, nor why the den was filled with flashing lights. The scent of an entirely new sort of creature wafted toward me from the hole. We were in danger and it was these unseen creatures that were the threat. My mother panted, ducking her head, backing away, and we all did our best to stumble after her, beseeching her with our tiny voices not to leave us.

"Let me see. Oh Christ, look at all of them!"

"Is this going to be a problem?"

"Hell yes it's a problem."

"What do you want to do?"

"We'll have to call the exterminator."

I was able to distinguish a difference between the first set of sounds and the second, a variation of pitch and tone, though I wasn't sure what it meant.

"Can't we just poison them ourselves?"

"You got something on the truck?"

"No, but I can get some."

My mother continued to deny us the comfort of her teats. Her muscles were tense, her ears back, her attention focused on the source of the sounds. I wanted to nurse, to know we were safe.

"Well, but if we do that, we're going to have all these dead cats all over the neighborhood. There's too many. If we were just talking one or two, fine, but this is a whole cat colony."

"You wanted to finish the demo by the end of June. That don't give us a lot of time to get rid of them."

"I know."

"Look, see the bowls? Somebody's actually been feeding the damn things."

The lights dipped, joining together in a burning spot of brightness on the floor just inside the hole.

"Well that's just great. What the hell is wrong with people?"

"You want me to try to find out who it is?"

"Nah. The problem goes away when the cats do. I'll call somebody."

The probing lights flickered around one last time, and then winked out. I heard dirt moving and distinct, heavy footfalls, so much louder than the quiet steps of the cats. Slowly, the presence of the new creatures faded from the hole, and gradually the kittens resumed their play, happy again. I nursed alongside my siblings, then went to see Mother Cat's kitties. As usual, when the daylight coming through the square hole dimmed, the adult cats streamed out, and during the night I would hear them return and sometimes smell the blood of the small kill they were bringing back to their respective broods.

When Mother hunted, she went no farther than the big bowls of dry food that were set just inside the square hole. I could smell the meal on her breath and it was fish and plants and meats, and I began to wonder what it would taste like.

Whatever had happened to cause the panic was over.

I was playing with Mother Cat's relentless kittens when our world shattered. This time the light wasn't a single shaft, it was a blazing explosion, turning everything bright.

The cats scattered in terror. I froze, unsure what I should do.

"Get the nets ready; when they run they're going to do it all at once!"

A sound from outside of the hole. "We're ready!"

Three large beings wriggled in behind the light. They were the first humans I had ever seen, but I had smelled others, I now realized—I just had not been able to visualize what they looked like. Something deep inside of me sparked a recognition—I felt strangely drawn to them, wanting to run to them as they crawled forward into the den. Yet the alarm crackling in the frenzied cats froze me in place.

"Got one!"

A male cat hissed and screamed.

"Jesus!"

"Watch it, a couple just escaped!"

"Well, hell!" came the response from outside.

I was separated from my mother and tried to sort out her scent from among the cats, and then went limp when I felt the sharp teeth on the nape of my neck. Mother Cat dragged me back, deep into the shadows, to a place where a large crack split the stone wall. She squeezed me through the crack into a small, tight space and set me down with her kittens, curling up with us. The cats were utterly silent, following Mother Cat's lead. I lay with them in the darkness and listened to the humans call to each other.

"There's also a litter of puppies here!"

"Are you kidding me? Hey, get that one!"

"Jesus, they're fast."

"Come on, kitty-kitty, we won't hurt you."

"There's the mother dog."

"Thing is terrified. Watch it don't bite you."

"It's okay. You'll be okay, girl. Come on."

"Gunter didn't say anything about dogs."

"He didn't say there would be so many frigging cats, either."

"Hey, you guys catching them in the nets out there?"

"This is hard as hell to do!" someone shouted from outside.

"Come on, doggie. Damn! Watch it! Here comes the mother dog!"

"Jesus! Okay, we got the dog!" called the outside voice.

"Here puppy, here puppy. They're so little!"

"And easier than the damn cats, that's for sure."

We heard these noises without comprehension as to what they might mean. Some light made its way into our space behind the wall, leaking in through the crack, but the human smells did not come any closer to our hiding place. The mingle of fear and feline on the air gradually faded, as did the sounds.

Eventually, I slept.

When I awoke, my mother was gone. My brothers and sisters were gone. The depression in the earth where we had been born and had laid nursing still smelled of our family, but the empty, vacant sense that overcame me when I sniffed for Mother brought a whimper from me, a sob in my throat I couldn't quiet.

I did not understand what had happened, but the only cats left in the space were Mother Cat and her kittens. Frantic, seeking answers and assurance, I went back to her, crying out my fear. She had brought her kittens out from behind the wall and they were gathered back on the small square of cloth I thought of as their home. Mother Cat examined me carefully with her black nose. Then she curled around me, lying down, and I followed the scent and began to nurse. The sensation on my tongue was new and strange, but the warmth and nurture were what I craved, and I fed gratefully. After a few moments, her kittens joined me.

* * *

The next morning, a few of the male cats returned. They approached Mother Cat, who hissed out a warning, and then went to their own area to sleep.

Later, when the light from the hole had been its brightest and had started to dim, I picked up a whiff of another human, a different one. Now that I understood the difference, I realized I had had this scent in my nose before.

"Kitty? Kitty?"

Mother Cat unexpectedly left us on our square of cloth. The odd flash of cold that came with her departure shocked all of us, and we turned to each other for comfort, squirming ourselves into a pile of kittens and dog. I could see her as she approached the hole, but she did not advance all the way out—just stood, faintly illuminated. The male cats were on alert, but they did not follow her to the human.

"Are you the only one left? I don't know what happened, I wasn't around to see, but there are tracks in the dirt, so I know there were trucks. Did they take all the other cats?" The human crawled in through the hole, momentarily blotting out the light. He was male—I could smell this, though I would not learn until later the distinction between man and woman. He seemed slightly larger than the first humans I'd seen.

Again, I was drawn to this special creature, an inexplicable yearning rising up inside me. But the memory of the terror of the day before kept me with my kitten siblings.

"Okay, I see you guys. Hi, how did you get away? And they took your bowls. Nice."

There was a rustling sound and the delicious smell of food wafted onto the air. "Here's a little bit for you. I'll go and get a bowl. Some water, too."

The man backed out, wriggling in the dirt. As soon as

he was gone the cats surged forward, feeding ravenously on whatever was spilled on the dirt.

I alerted to the approach of the same person sooner than the cats, as if they were unable to identify his scent as it grew stronger. The males all reacted, though, when he reappeared at the hole, fleeing back to their corner. Only Mother Cat stood fast. A new bowl was shoved forward and there was a meal in it, but Mother Cat made no approach, just stood watching. I could sense her tension and knew she was ready to bolt and run if he tried to capture us like the other humans had.

"Here is some water, too. Do you have kittens? You look like you're nursing. Did they take your babies? Oh, kitty, I am so sorry. They're going to tear down these houses and put up an apartment complex. You and your family can't stay here, okay?"

Eventually the man left, and the adult cats cautiously resumed eating. I sniffed Mother Cat's mouth when she returned, but when I licked her face she turned abruptly away.

Time was marked by the shifting light pouring in from the square hole. More cats came; a few who had been living with us before, and a new female, whose arrival triggered a fight among the males that I watched with intense interest. One pair of combatants lay locked together for so long that the only way I knew they were not asleep was the way their tails flickered, not wagging in happiness but communicating a real distress. When they broke their clinch they stretched out on the ground, noses nearly touching, and made uncatlike sounds at each other. Another fight consisted of one male lying on his side and smacking another one, who was on all four feet. The standing one would tap the sprawling one on the top of the head and the one lying down would respond with a series of rapid clawings.

Why didn't they all get up on their back two legs and attack each other? This behavior, while stressful for all the animals in the den, seemed utterly pointless.

Other than Mother Cat I had no interaction with the adults, who acted as if I did not exist. I tangled with the kittens, wrestling and climbing and chasing all day. Sometimes I would growl at them, irritated with their style of play, which just seemed wrong, somehow. I wanted to climb on their backs and chew on their necks, but they couldn't seem to get the hang of this, going limp when I knocked them over or jumped on top of their tiny frames. Sometimes they wrapped their entire bodies around my snout, or batted at my face with teeny, sharp claws, pouncing on me from all angles.

At night I missed my siblings. I missed my mother. I had made a family, but I understood that the cats were different from me. I had a pack, but it was a pack of kitties, which did not seem right. I felt restless and unhappy and at times I would whimper out my anguish and Mother Cat would lick me and I would feel somewhat better, but things were just not the way they should have been.

Nearly every day, the man came and brought food. Mother Cat punished me with a swift slap on my nose when I tried to approach him, and I learned the rules of the den: we were not to be seen by humans. None of the other felines seemed at all inclined to feel the touch of a person, but for me a growing desire to be held by him made it increasingly difficult to obey the laws of the den.

When Mother Cat stopped nursing us, we had to adjust to eating the meals the man supplied, which consisted of tasty, dried morsels and then sometimes exotic, wet flesh. Once I grew accustomed to the change it was far better for me—I had been so hungry for so long it seemed a natural condition, but now I could eat my fill and lap up as much water as I could hold. I consumed more than my sibling kitties combined, and was now noticeably larger than any of them, though they all were unimpressed by my size and resolutely refused to play properly, continuing to mostly claw at my nose.

We mimicked Mother Cat and shied away from the hole when the human presence filled it, but otherwise dared to flirt with the very edge, drinking in the rich aromas from outside. Mother Cat sometimes went out at night, and I could sense that the kittens all wanted to join her. For me, it was more the daylight that lured, but I was mindful of Mother Cat and knew she would swiftly punish any attempt to stray beyond the boundary.

One day the man, whose fragrances were as familiar to me now as Mother Cat's, appeared just outside the hole, making sounds. I could sense other humans with him.

"They're usually way toward the back. The mother comes closer when I bring food, but she won't let me touch her."

"Is there another way out of the crawl space besides this window?" It was a different voice, accompanied by different smells—a woman. I unconsciously wagged my tail.

"I don't think so. How will this work?"

"We've got these big gloves to protect us, and if you'll stay here with the net, you can catch any cats that make it past us. How many are there?"

"I don't know, now. Until recently the female was obviously nursing, but if there are any kittens they don't come out in the day. A couple others, I don't know what sex. There used to be so many, but I guess the developer must have gotten them. He's going to tear down this whole row of houses and put up an apartment complex."

"He'll never get a demolition permit with feral cats living here."

"That's probably why he did it. Do you think he hurt the ones he caught?"

"Um, okay, so, there's no law against trapping and destroying cats living on your own property. I mean, he could have taken them to one of the other shelters, I guess."

"There were a lot of them. The whole property was crawling with cats."

"Thing is, I didn't hear anything about a big bunch of cats showing up anywhere. Animal rescue is a pretty tight community; we all talk to each other. If twenty cats hit the system, I would have heard about it. You okay? Hey, sorry, maybe I shouldn't have said anything."

"I'm fine. I just wish I had known it was going to happen."

"You did the right thing by calling us, though, Lucas. We'll find good homes for any cats we find. Ready?"

I had grown completely bored with the monotonous noises and was busily wrestling with the kittens when I felt Mother Cat stiffen, alarm jolting through her. Her unwinking eyes were on the hole, and her tail twitched. Her ears were flat back against her head. I regarded her curiously, ignoring the little male kitty who ran up, swatted my mouth, and darted away.

Then a light blazed and I understood her fear. Mother Cat fled toward the back wall, abandoning her young. I saw her slip soundlessly into the hidden crack just as two humans came in through the hole. The kittens milled in confusion, the male cats fled to the back of the den, and I shied away, afraid.

The light danced along the walls, then found me, blazing brightly in my face.

"Hey! There's a puppy in here!"